# The Curious Misadventures of Feltus Ovalton

*For Jasmine, Thomas, Taane and Milo*
– Jo Treggiari

The Curious Misadventures Of Feltus Ovalton
Text © 2006 Jo Treggiari

Published by Lobster Press™
1620 Sherbrooke Street West, Suites C & D
Montréal, Québec  H3H 1C9
Tel. (514) 904-1100 • Fax (514) 904-1101 • www.lobsterpress.com

Publisher: Alison Fripp
Editors: Alison Fripp & Meghan Nolan
Editorial Assistant: Morgan Dambergs, Molly Armstrong & Katie Scott
Cover Illustration: Alisa Baldwin
Graphic Design & Production: Tammy Desnoyers

We acknowledge the financial support of the Government of Canada
through the Book Publishing Industry Development Program (BPIDP)
for our publishing activities.

We acknowledge the support of the Canada
Council for the Arts for our publishing program.

The Canada Council | Le Conseil des Arts
for the Arts | du Canada

Library and Archives Canada Cataloguing in Publication

Treggiari, Jo, 1965-
    The curious misadventures of Feltus Ovalton / Jo Treggiari,
author; Alisa Baldwin, illustrator.

ISBN-13: 978-1-897073-43-8
ISBN-10: 1-897073-43-7

    I. Baldwin, Alisa, 1980-  II. Title.

PS8639.R433C87 2006          jC813'.6          C2006-900618-0

Printed and bound in Canada.

Thank you: Marcus Parris; exceptional authors and great friends – Abigail Thomas, Alison Gaylin, and Jennifer May, the Wednesday Nighters; my astute and relentless editor Meghan Nolan; Stephanie Hindley and everyone at Lobster Press; Susan and Arnaldo Treggiari; the Rajagopalans; my nonna Giovanna and my great-grandmother Jane; Charise Isis; Alexia Paul; Amanda and Danny Patton; Delilah Harding; Sacha McVean's fourth grade class for reading it first; and the original PoodleRats – Loki, Pepino, and Lulu.

# The Curious Misadventures of Feltus Ovalton

written by
## Jo Treggiari

Lobster Press ™

# PART 1

## FELTUS OVALTON IN THE GRAND GEWGLAB FOREST

# CHAPTER 1

## An Unexpected Visitor

FELTUS OVALTON LEROI was not a nice boy. In fact, he liked to think he was odious, or OH-Dee-Usssss, as he had overheard his neighbor Mrs. Fontana say after he'd slipped a large, carefully wrapped stink beetle through her mailbox. *Note to self: if you're the only kid on your floor, be a little more discreet when you revenge yourself on a snitch.*

Perhaps it was because his parents were not affectionate, interested, or home most of the time. Perhaps it was because they hadn't even asked him if he wanted to move to a shiny new apartment, leaving behind his best friend, Chris "Fuzzy" Baer, and the old brick house he'd grown up in. Perhaps it was because he now lived in a big, busy city and he had learned quickly not to make eye contact with people who walked past him on the street. Perhaps it was because his pet hamster had curled up its little toes and died after two short weeks with him at the new apartment.

Whatever the reason, it was clear that he didn't seem to care about anyone but himself. When the doorman, Peter, greeted him in the morning, Feltus merely wrinkled his nose and walked on by. He rarely said anything nice to Rose, their housekeeper, who cooked his family delicious and low-fat meals at least twice a day. When a man in a sharply tailored, pin-striped suit dropped a crumpled twenty-dollar bill right in front of him before walking away, Feltus only thought briefly about picking it up and handing it back before shoving it into his own pocket. And he had purposely scuffed his brand-new pair of glossy dress shoes by kicking the sidewalk when he had been told not to. He always wiped his runny nose on his coat sleeve instead of using a handkerchief, climbed chain-link fences, and tried to rip the starched white shirts his mother always bought for him, which never fit well and buttoned too tightly under his chin. And he teased a smaller kid named Percy at school solely because of his name.

Feltus didn't know why he was sometimes so mean. All he knew was that making someone else more miserable than he was made him feel better. It felt as if he had stepped outside his body and was watching some other boy do the things he did. He was so confused he couldn't talk to anyone about how he felt, least of all his parents who barely spoke to each other these days. Whenever his father returned from a lengthy business trip, Feltus would hope that his parents would have plenty to discuss, but instead, everything was always muffled as if someone had died, as if a deep freeze had descended on the apartment. Meanwhile, outside the sun was shining and other people were going on with their lives. *We never talk about anything*, Feltus thought angrily. We just pretend it's all fine.

He bet Fuzzy had new friends to climb trees and catch tadpoles with. All Feltus had was his room where he sat for hours staring at the gray, bustling street and that sickly tree near the convenience store. After six months, it still didn't feel like home. He hated it here.

What he really wanted was for something – anything – to happen. He had tried everything: getting into trouble at school – mainly talking back to teachers. And although he had enjoyed a short career as an undercover graffiti artist, it occurred to him that if no one knew he was the "masked avenger" – his signature – there was no point to it at all. His favorite way to stir up trouble was by starting arguments with his mother at the table. The usual conversation went something like this:

Feltus: What if the sky weren't blue, but just an upside-down lake suspended in the air?

Mother: Did I not give you a complete set of encyclopedias for a past birthday, Feltus?

Feltus: What if I discovered that chocolate had as much vitamin A as an entire rutabaga?

Mother: We will not be having this discussion.

Feltus: What if I divorced you?

Mother: Eat your rutabaga.

Lately he couldn't get a reaction out of her, no matter how much effort he put in.

He tried acting up in public. His specialty was loud, inappropriate questions such as, "Mom, what is a shotgun wedding?" asked at a slightly hurried marriage celebration, or remarking on the ugliness of Mrs. Fontana's new grand-daughter (she really did resemble a sock puppet that had gone through the wash a few too many times), or accusing his mother of torture in front of an interested crowd – like when she refused to buy him the triple layer, cream-infused, double chocolate cake he had his eye on.

And finally, a month ago, when he'd turned 11 3/4 and still believed in stuff like magic, he had dressed up in an old bathrobe with stars and moons all over it and read from a tattered loose-leaf binder he'd found in a cardboard box in his closet. A box that had evidently made the trip from the old house to the new apartment, though neither one of his parents had claimed it. Besides the notebook, there'd been nothing in the box but a few dead flies, some baggy stockings, and a spangled hairnet. He'd pored over the book excitedly at first and then with growing confusion. The leather binding was mangled, as if something had gnawed at it. He could still trace the faint outline of a coat of arms embossed on the cover. It appeared to be of a large amphibian consuming a worm. The letters *v* and *m* were barely visible.

Inside, the pages were yellowed at the edges and gave off a faint odor of mold and something indefinable, but infinitely nastier. The handwriting was old-fashioned and strange with curlicued *f* shapes standing in for *s*'s and lots of ornate squiggles. The bulk of the text seemed to be a mix of recipes, herbal remedies, and chemical equations. The one page that had made his heart race was the clearly marked "Fpells," and it was from this moth-eaten sheet that he'd eventually read aloud, after lighting four white candles he'd stolen from the pantry.

Feltus still remembered the first line, "Saritah Pernisox Ottarim," but even though he'd followed the instructions closely, walking the perimeter of his room counterclockwise ("widdershins," the witches in one of his spooky comic books called it), holding his wish in his mind unwaveringly, chanting the spell three times each to the four corners of the earth, and not ingesting wheat or milk for twenty-four hours afterward, nothing had happened. He'd thought that when the lights suddenly went off and then on again, and when the wall around his bedroom window had glowed, giving him an unpleasant feeling of vertigo, that he'd actually done something. But afterward, besides an overpowering smell of burnt toast, which he still couldn't get out of his blankets, nothing was any different. He still started each day with a combination of boredom and dread, his parents still ignored him, and nothing interesting ever happened. He convinced himself it must have been an optical and olfactory illusion. And since then, he'd packed the binder away at the back of his closet with all the other toys he'd grown out of.

He made his room his sanctuary, and he would usually hide out there, reading comic books and daydreaming about ways in which his father could save his mother from a burning building or a rabid dog, and she would suddenly look at him with that soft expression. But it never happened. Or he would dream of his dad asking him out of the blue to throw a ball around or go to a movie. But he never did.

His parents stayed the same and so did the apartment with its stark white walls, which were so much different from the bright, flocked wallpaper and thumbtack holes of the rickety old three-story house he'd grown up in. This place had slippery, polished wood floors that squeaked and scuffed if he walked on them with shoes. He yearned for the rag rugs he'd raced his toy cars on, and the heating vents, which bellowed like dragons when they came on, and the bat, which lived behind the tall bookshelf in the cozy sitting room of their old house. But he tried to find comfort by telling himself that he just didn't care about anything anymore.

At breakfast, the only meal of the day during which he was usually guaranteed the presence of one or both of his parents, he would keep his head down and try to finish eating as quickly as possible. "Chew your food, Feltus," his mother would reprimand, that is, if she noticed him at all. Usually she didn't, being absorbed in gardening magazines or the society pages of the daily journal. Feltus would squirm in his seat and cough and just try to get through the meal. His father, if he were there, would shake his newspaper periodically in response to Feltus's fidgets, but he never raised his head to look up.

This particular morning, before breakfast, Feltus was kicking his school satchel around the floor and grumbling to himself. He and his mother were having a difference of opinion about a weekend math tutorial she wanted him to take, and he was planning to respond to the idea with either a hunger strike or a series of glares over the breakfast table for a week or two. He'd perfected a monstrous expression in front of the bathroom mirror that was certain to turn her stomach. Or maybe he would just use the more tried-and-true method of putting a juicy spider in her bed.

When the doorbell rang, it was a welcome interruption. He gave his school books one more good kick, slouched over to the door, opened it, and stood stock-still in amazement. He had no idea who the decrepit, wild-eyed woman who stood stooped before him was. She was leaning heavily on a cane and she looked like a real crazy. He was about to slam the door in her face when she announced in a croaking voice that she was his "Great-Aunt Eunida" (yoo-nye-da). He almost slammed the door anyway.

She was dressed in tattered layers of dusty, musty cloth. Her hair stuck out from her head like grizzled black and gray wires, and her eyes were protruding from their sockets. She spoke out of the side of her mouth, as if her jaw were broken. Then she closed her mouth with an audible crack. He could hear a kind of grinding noise coming from her teeth, as if she were exerting a huge amount of pressure on her jaw muscles. Her face was screwed up in a painful grimace, but she didn't say another word.

Piled in the hallway behind her were a well-worn steamer trunk, a hatbox, and a cloth-covered birdcage. When Feltus reached over to peek into the cage, she grabbed his wrist in a surprisingly strong hold. Her hand was claw-like, and her nails were as shiny and discolored as old bone. It felt as if she were pinching a nerve, and suddenly his head was buzzing. He pulled himself free from her grasp, and after she pointed to her bags with a snarl and a flourish of her walking stick, he dragged the luggage in through the door and left it there. It took a minute before the blood rushed back into his right arm, and he wondered if she was some kind of undercover assassin. He hoped she would show him that death grip sometime.

As she preceded him down the hall to the sitting room, he heard her say under her breath, "Peanut weevil infestation looms snark snark splurt poodles and rats, splork." The babbling was interrupted by a choking sound, and when he looked at her, she was wearing that tight stare again.

Fortunately his mother was close by, alphabetizing the books farther down the hallway. She was kneeling, holding a volume bound in tooled burgundy leather, and was muttering, "Where shall I put it?" with lines frowning across her forehead. Feltus passed the old woman, trying his best to avoid her rank clothing, and sprinted toward his mother.

"Someone to see you," he announced, out of breath. He was thankful to be giving up the responsibility of tending to this unpleasant visitor … who, he realized with a grimace, smelled like deep-fried gym socks.

"Oh no!" his mother gasped, looking past him. "No!" More angry lines appeared between her eyebrows. "Take her to the sitting room, will you?" She stood up quickly and wiped her hands on the trousers she wore whenever she did chores. She clasped her fingers together, the knuckles whitening. "I'll just go and tell Rose." She turned and left the hallway quickly.

"Breakfast!" croaked the crone beside him as his mother hurried by, followed by, "Wex Lethoo Radok!" He would have left his strange relative to her own devices, but there was something about her that intrigued him – besides the odor, of course. He wanted to hear what she had to say. She seemed to have some hold on his mother, and he hoped that her arrival would make today's breakfast something other than the usual toast and cereal.

He led the way to the long room that was used as a combination dining and sitting room and was lined with windows that stretched the entire length of the apartment. At one end was a large oak table with heavily carved legs, and at the other, through a wide archway, an ornate marble fireplace that usually housed a splendid display of orchids. Feltus didn't feel particularly comfortable in either room.

Great-Aunt Eunida peered around the large, light-filled sitting area, a faint sneer on her face. She prodded a velvet pillow with her cane, thumped the overstuffed sofa, and said, with another snarl, that a fern in a brass pot offended her. Feltus moved it into a corner so it would be out of sight. She hovered near a chair, but did not sit down. Instead she indicated with wild gestures and a few guttural adjectives that the view from the windows was disappointing, and that she would like tea and a little snack before retiring to her bed.

Feltus stood bemused as his mother walked into the adjoining dining room, brandishing a teapot and an armful of freshly laundered napkins. She was followed closely by Rose, who staggered under the weight of a large tray. Great-Aunt Eunida's head lifted as she scented the air like a dog. Feltus almost tripped over her as she bolted past him to the table.

"Sit down, Feltus," his mother hissed, before turning to his great-aunt with a stiff smile and motioning toward the seating with a wave of her hand. Eunida flopped into the cushioned recliner normally reserved for Feltus's father and kicked off her shoes. Her big toes stuck out of gaping holes in her striped tights. It was not until she had reached out a grimy hand for the nearest plate that his mother sank into her chair with a small sigh.

Breakfast included hot crumpets with melted butter and marmalade, Rose's homemade scones with clotted cream and strawberry jam, granola, and some toast and sardines. Not the usual fare on a school day – or any other day, for that matter.

Feltus quickly realized that Great-Aunt Eunida had a voracious appetite. She matched Feltus scone for scone, and whenever possible, heaped even more cream and jam on hers than he could fit on the small circle of sweet dough. A smudge of jam anointed her nose, and he noticed that his mother's face was grim and closed – more so than usual. *Who is this old lady and why does she deserve such wonderful feeding?* Feltus thought. Maybe she was blackmailing his parents. He tried to imagine his neat and well-organized mother committing some heinous – a word he had just learned, which sounded as nasty as its meaning – act that necessitated a visit from an elderly relative who just happened to belong to a secret criminal network.

"So, who is Great-Aunt Eunida?" he whispered to his mother. His great-aunt had her nose buried in yet another scone and could not have heard anything over the grunting and snorting noises coming from her mouth. His mother took a small sip of tea, and patted her lips carefully with a nicely ironed linen napkin. She folded it back into its precise, flat rectangle and placed it next to her plate. He figured she hadn't heard him, so he opened his mouth to repeat the question, but his attention was diverted by the old woman sitting at the other end of the table. Great-Aunt Eunida had paused to swallow and was staring at the large family portrait that hung over the fireplace in the sitting room. Her jaw hung slack and as he watched, her hand jerked spasmodically and she flicked a spoonful of thick cream and jam at the painting. It spattered across the bottom section of the painting, transforming it into some wild mix of classical and abstract art. Above the mess, the portrait was delicately rendered in watercolors, a field of flowers barely visible in the background, and he and his father standing in plastic poses in the foreground, hovering over Feltus's mother and her fat dog, Lafayette. Feltus looked like a stuffed fish; the artist had captured him in mid-yawn. It had been a long, uncomfortable session that was meant to commemorate the family's move up in the world. The placard – now sprayed liberally with food – on the bottom of the portrait included their present address: 1401C Orson Wells Way. "Oww" perfectly described how living there made him feel.

"She is your great-aunt," his mother, who apparently had totally missed the jam and cream volley, said in a stern voice, which prevented any further discussion. "Tea or coffee, Great-Aunt Eunida?"

The old lady was again preoccupied with scooping up the contents of her plate in her fingers and took some time before lifting her head from her plate. She gulped down the mouthful of bread, cream, and fish that had pouched her cheeks out, belched loudly, and thrust her cup forward. Her bright eyes drifted over Feltus, betraying no particular interest. He felt a shiver between his shoulder blades. A pungent aroma hung in the air, as if Rose had burned the toast. He could tell that the odor, combined with the riper smell emanating from his great-aunt, had wafted in his mother's direction. Her delicate nostrils flared. She slopped a little of the tea into the saucer as she poured.

"Have you been traveling long, Great-Aunt Eunida?" she asked.

Eunida grunted and applied herself again to the cream, lifting a soft, pillowy mound onto her plate.

"You'll find the guest bedroom very comfortable. Everything you could want. Just down the hall. And your own bathroom. Let me know if you need anything. Dressing gown, toothbrush, change of clothing?" said his mother desperately.

Clotted cream was speckled across the old woman's face and shirt. She raised a messy hand to tuck a greasy tendril of hair behind her ear and wiped yet more of the food into the mats and clumps that adorned her head. Feltus's mother suppressed a shudder. Without a word, Great-Aunt Eunida rose quickly, stuffed the remaining contents of her plate into one of her pockets, grabbed the sardines, and left the room.

His mother cradled her head in her hands for a moment. Feltus could hear her take a few deep breaths, and when she looked up again her forehead was creased, her eyes shiny. Her voice was low and steady.

"Keep an eye on her," she told him.

The curiosity was itching at him. "You never mentioned any great-aunt before."

She smiled wanly. "No."

"What's Dad going to think?"

She seemed to collect herself. "Your father! Yes." She tapped one long finger against her chin. "Just watch her and don't let her do anything ... dangerous."

"How could she be dangerous?" he asked. "She's just an old lady."

His mother answered him impatiently. "You don't know how people are. Anything could happen."

"I want things to happen!" he shouted.

She wasn't listening. Her eyes raked him from head to toe. "Straighten your collar. And for goodness sakes, wipe the smudges off those shoes!" At least she hadn't mentioned his hair – he was trying a new tousled look, which he hoped made him look older and slightly menacing. He walked to the door. When he looked back, his mother was staring off into space again, one hand fidgeting with the brooch she wore pinned to her collar, and the other clenched around a silver teaspoon. *How can one old lady upset her so much?*

On the way to pick up his school books, which he had kicked to the other end of the hall earlier, Feltus pressed his ear up to the guest room door, but he didn't hear anything beyond some heavy breathing. He kneeled down and squinted through the crack above the hallway rug, but the room appeared to be in darkness. After halfheartedly smearing the dirt from the front to the back of his shoes with a wet finger and the corner of his shirt, he stood up and went back to the sitting room to see if he could get some answers.

"What's she doing in there? She doesn't answer when I knock. Do you think maybe she died?" he asked his mother, who was now sitting straight-backed in her armchair by the window. *That would liven things up a bit*, he thought.

His mother didn't reply. She just grabbed her needle-point from the basket next to her chair, her mouth a tight line. She added a tiny brown square to the symmetrical series of white and black triangles. Feltus cleared his throat. She frowned and started unpicking the fine brown silk, winding the thread around the fountain pen she always kept tucked behind her ear or slipped into her hair when she wore it up in a tight bun. Feltus thought she looked happier when her hair was loose, but she hardly ever wore it like that anymore. Even this morning it was restrained in a sleek ponytail and wrapped in shiny black ribbon.

"Rose has your lunch ready," she said.

"It's not baked brie again is it?"

"Most children would be pleased to eat gourmet food, Feltus. But no, this week it's Chinese greens and tofu. Very nutritious."

He thought longingly of the chocolate bar hidden in his room. If his mother kept feeding him like this, he would starve! Before they had moved, she'd been more relaxed, sometimes stuffing potato chips or donuts into his lunch box and not deliberating all day over which brand of whole wheat bread and low-sodium crackers to buy, or obsessing over the nutritional value of each food item. Some days he thought he would kill for something sweet and overly processed.

He went into the kitchen and Rose gave him a sympathetic look as she handed him his lunch box.

"I snuck a couple cookies in there for you," she said in a low voice. "From your dad's secret stash."

His father sat at the kitchen table now, black coffee and two slices of dry toast in front of him. He was bent over the early morning financial report, pen in hand, nothing visible but the top of his sleek bald head. Feltus usually wouldn't have disturbed him, but he couldn't help himself.

"Great-Aunt Eunida's come to stay," he said.

His father crackled his newspaper.

"She's a little weird, isn't she?" Feltus added. No answer. "Eccentric. Do you know what's wrong with her?"

His father looked up momentarily. His eyes focused on Feltus, and after a minute he seemed to recognize him.

"What? Eunida? Here?"

Feltus nodded.

"Tell your mother. I'll be at the office," he said as he rose to leave.

"I think Mom knows. We just had breakfast in the dining room with the old bat."

His father grunted, crammed his papers into his brief-case, and quickly rushed out of the kitchen.

All these non-answers only served to pique Feltus's curiosity further. Something was finally happening. He could feel it in the air, a prickling on his skin. He walked out of the apartment and rode the elevator down to the street in a kind of daze. All of a sudden, the day – and his life – felt full of possibility. He was more content than usual during the walk to school, but soon enough he looked up and realized with a heavy heart that he was standing in front of the spiked wrought-iron fence that enclosed the school property. Somewhere in the near distance he could hear tiny yelps and moans of pain. Someone was getting his butt kicked.

All the excitement he'd been feeling drained instantly. He took a couple deep breaths, fixed his face into a stiff scowl and pushed the gate open.

# CHAPTER 2

## Two Bullies and a Preponderance of Mysteries

MISS MONTMORENCY'S SCHOOL for Boys, founded in the 1970s by the illustrious child psychologist Allegra Montmorency, was an immense gray stone building. It had been a prison in a former life, and as Feltus walked along the linoleum-tiled hallway, his steps echoing off the walls and his lungs filling with the acrid smell of cleaning ammonia, he imagined he could hear the wails of long-dead prisoners. He was overcome with a sense of despair. He hated the thought of having to spend five days a week in this place, and although he had been attending classes here for the last six months, the dread associated with going to this school never lessened for him – partly because he was still one of the new boys, an outsider, and partly because of the humiliating incident with the white ferret in his first week that still haunted him.

And partly because of Miss Montmorency, of course. She was a tall, bony woman who favored severely cut suits and a monocle. She had definite ideas about how to educate and discipline children. Her curriculum was almost solely based on memorization and repetition, which Feltus found very boring, and her punishments for wayward behavior were swift and fierce. Feltus still got a cramp in his writing hand just thinking about all those blackboard detention sessions.

Lately, with his mind so occupied with the parental situation at home, he had even more trouble concentrating on his work. He still didn't have any friends, and it looked as if lunch was going to be horrible this week. At noontime he dumped the tofu and vegetables in the garbage and ate his cookies, savoring the sweet, rich chocolate.

Afterward he still had forty-five minutes before French class and he had to find something to do. Bugging Percy Flannery had become less entertaining lately; the blond boy was wrapped up in extra credit courses and didn't respond the right way anymore. What was the point of harassing someone who just looked off into the distance and wasn't made uncomfortable by searching questions about his home life (everyone knew that his father spent more time with his model train sets than with his own son), or his appearance ("How long does it take you to curl your hair in the morning?"). There was never any emotional response what-soever from Percy anymore. So there was nothing to do but go to the empty French classroom, sit at his desk, and wish he were somewhere else.

Feltus had become an expert in avoiding attention in school, which was a switch from actively seeking to be noticed at home. He was hardly ever called upon to answer a question in class. It was almost as if he weren't there. If he could only use this talent elsewhere – like with the school bullies – he could get through life all right. But unfortunately, it only worked on jaded, cynical older people who had devoted their lives to teaching a bunch of ungrateful kids.

When French class finally started that day, Feltus successfully avoided any direct questions from Monsieur (moo-soo) Brondex, the French teacher, by keeping his head down and looking busy. He raised his hand to answer a simple question about a cow and a pea and spent most of the class doodling pictures of Great-Aunt Eunida as hired killer, as ruthless spy, as escaped lunatic.

For the rest of the class, he worried about running into Jimmy Matthews and his main henchman, Rusty Jackson, between classes. Rusty Jackson probably hadn't put much thought into becoming a bully. He was just built for it: large hands, sinewy arms, a broad, compact frame, and muscular legs. Feltus was sure that pushing or kicking him would feel just like hitting a brick wall. But as scary as Rusty was, he was a regular, everyday kind of bully – not too much up top, but superior physical power. You knew that if it came down to a fight, you'd be dragging your bruised and bloody self off of the floor. And that was comforting in a weird sort of way. With Rusty, you knew what you were getting into.

Jimmy was an entirely different matter. Rusty followed orders; Jimmy thought up unique and tailor-made tortures for his prey. He seemed to enjoy this even more than the lunch or bus money he got from Percy and clumsy Harold Jenkins, and that kid with the lisp – and Feltus himself, although Feltus didn't like to dwell on it. Jimmy even seemed to have a kind of hold on Miss Montmorency and some of the other teachers. They hardly ever hassled him – all the bullies got away with doing a minimal amount of schoolwork. Good thing, or Rusty would still be languishing in first grade.

Feltus chuckled a little at the idea of a lummox the size of Rusty Jackson trying to squeeze into a kindergarten chair. Casting a quick look around the empty hallway, Feltus stopped for a drink at the water fountain. Normally he wouldn't have risked letting his guard down for a second, but he was thirsty and Brondex had let them out a few minutes early. The sound of hoarse breathing interrupted his thoughts. He straightened up slowly and turned around. The laugh caught in his throat, and water dribbled down his chin as he realized that he had stupidly walked into a very unpleasant situation.

"Feltus Ovalton LeRoi," Jimmy hissed. A group of students who had suddenly drifted over from the surrounding classrooms stopped to watch. Feltus cringed and felt heat suffuse his face.

"Smeltus Orangutan ... Malloy," Rusty chipped in, displaying his usual withering intellect. Jimmy glared at Rusty, and Rusty's mouth shut with a snap.

"Is it true that you went to an all-girls school before this one?" Jimmy asked in his soft voice. "And that they kicked you out for being too wimpy?"

Rusty brayed with laughter. "Girly," he said.

Jimmy didn't smile. The pupils of his eyes were like pinpricks. Feltus was frozen, like a bird before a snake.

"No. Wait," Jimmy continued. "It was in the country, wasn't it? With the cows, pigs, and chickens. I heard that your mother was Miss Manure 1992. How does it feel to have a mother who stinks of the barnyard? Who's so full of – "

Maybe Feltus had made an unconscious move toward Jimmy. All he knew was that Rusty's arm swung like a battering ram and Feltus was knocked flat onto the hard floor, his books flying everywhere. From his horizontal position, he had a worm's eye view of Rusty's size twelve feet that were sporting a pair of immaculate new sneakers and tapping an ominous beat inches from his nose. His chin felt bruised and mashed, and his hand came away bloody after he touched it. A few snickers rose from the crowd. No one moved to help him. He would have given anything to exchange places with any one of the onlookers. Then he heard the sound of snapping fingers and Rusty backed off. Feltus pulled himself up to his feet slowly, tensed against another blow.

He clutched the dismal pile of coins in his pocket, then held his penny-filled hand out to Jimmy before he'd even thought about it. He tried to laugh, but it sounded as if he were choking.

"Not much money today," Feltus said. He could feel a

trickle of blood ooze down his neck. Rusty loomed over him, resting a meaty paw on his shoulder. Feltus fought to remain standing under the weight of it.

Jimmy had ice blue eyes. It was hard to guess his thoughts when he looked at you in that considering way, as if he were cataloguing your weaknesses. He didn't speak often – he didn't need to.

"I don't want your pennies, pig boy," Jimmy said, his voice barely above a whisper. "You can pay me tomorrow." His hand flew up in a graceful arc and hit Feltus's arm. The coins flew into the air. Most of them rained down on Feltus's head.

"*Wheeeee!*" Rusty yelled, followed by some snuffling snorts. His hand closed around Feltus's arm, and squeezed until Feltus thought the bone might break. When he finally managed to twist free of Rusty's grasp, he felt the burn of raw skin. The bully guffawed as Feltus slunk off to class, rubbing the painful limb. Jimmy never laughed and hardly ever smiled.

Later in Art class, drawing shaded oranges and symmetrical vases didn't help Feltus take his mind off of things. He wished he could draw what was really in his heart: the small, hard kernel of fear and worry that was devouring him. If he could, he would paint wild, slashing strokes in black and red acrylic. He thought about how great it would be if he could confide in his parents, if he were still a little kid and they could save him from all the bad things in the world. He pressed the point of his pencil into the paper and imagined it going into Jimmy's face.

Thin and dapper Mr. Ringley draped himself over a chair nearby and gazed owlishly at the mess of black lines adorning Feltus's sketch pad. Today Mr. Ringley, or "maestro" as he sometimes insisted the students call him, was wearing a vivid orange corduroy suit with a blue cravat.

*How did he ever survive school?* Feltus wondered. The teacher leaned in closer, caressing the dead-caterpillar mustache above his lip.

"Hmm," he said. "Not precisely what we're doing today, Mr. LeRoi, but interesting just the same." He turned and clapped his hands. "Class. Feel free to be abstract artists! Let anarchy reign!"

Feltus did feel a little better after jabbing his pencil through the page. Thankfully, his final class of the day was Library Study with Mr. Chirono – no bullies allowed. Jimmy and Rusty had Sports History and if Feltus were lucky, he'd be able to avoid the duo completely until tomorrow. Tomorrow, when he had to hand over some serious cash.

In Library Study, he found a secluded nook in the corner, away from the rest of the class, and consulted his book list. He'd already picked out a collection of haiku. Chirono would be able to advise him on the rest. He liked the short librarian, who seemed as leathery and dusty as his books. He'd found that he could ask Mr. Chirono anything, and after a period of quiet reflection, usually involving the combing of his fingers through his glossy beard, the librarian would come up with the answer along with some other recommendations. It was Chirono who had pointed Feltus in the direction of Greek mythology, which almost rivaled his comic books for sheer excitement. Today, Feltus immersed himself in Hercules and found that despite his throbbing chin, the hour passed quickly.

Sometimes he wished that the fantasies he read were true. He wished that his life were not just about bullying and homework and healthy food that tasted horrible. He wished he didn't have to worry that his parents had forgotten that he was alive. He wished everything could just boil down to the eternal fight between good and evil. It would make things so much simpler. Rusty and Jimmy were definitely evil and would perish eventually in some ghastly way, and Feltus, even though he was flawed, would meet the challenge head-on and emerge triumphant at the end of it.

He wondered where his great-aunt fit into all of this. She could be the all-seeing hag; she could be a forked-tongued witch or perhaps a princess under a spell, although he didn't think that a princess could ever smell like Great-Aunt Eunida.

When class ended, he ran out the door and into Percy, who was daydreaming next to the bulletin board that advertised open auditions for this year's student play: *Rancor – A definitive work in six acts.* Feltus pushed Percy aside and dashed into the toilet to check the status of his wounds. A little splash of cold water, and the cuts and bruising from earlier in the day were hardly evident, as long as he kept his head lowered.

He escaped the school without making a trip to his locker, and once he'd sprinted a couple blocks and crossed the busy main road, he felt as if he could finally relax.

* * *

The apartment was dark when he got home. The board by the front door held a curt message from his mother: *Very important Garden Association phone conference! Do not disturb! Dinner on table. No junk food!* She often left written instructions for him, and the sad thing was that, for some reason, he often found himself obeying them to the letter. Maybe it was the throb of pain in his chin, or maybe some of Hercules' heroism had rubbed off on him, but today he felt a small flame of rebellion in his heart. Feltus noticed that a thin sliver of light came from under his mother's bedroom door, and he could hear the faint murmur of her voice. Lately she seemed to spend hours on the phone, and he knew from past experience that he could be standing in front of her singing a rock opera with underwear on his head and she wouldn't notice or even remove her telephone earpiece.

Feltus walked to his room, threw his bag onto the bed, kicked his shoes off, and loosened his shirt collar. After peeking his head out to make sure his father wasn't around, he made his way to the kitchen. Rose left early on Wednesdays, but she'd prepared two tall glasses of milk and a plate with some brownies still warm from the oven. A shred of paper in her looping writing said, *For you and your great-aunt.* Beads of water jeweled the outside of the glasses, and the milk was ice cold when he took a sip. A casserole of chicken and vegetables was on the table with explicit directions about how to microwave it for dinner.

He stuffed two brownies in his mouth, wrapped the rest in a paper towel, put them in his pocket, and crept down the hall to the guest bedroom. It was completely silent – not a groan, not a whisper. He put his eye to the crack between the door and the molding. The room was dark except for a faint glow over the birdcage. He could smell burnt toast again. *What if she's cooking in there?*

"Great-Aunt Eunida? Are you okay? Is that a gas stove? I have food for you!"

No answer. He felt a twinge of disappointment. He'd been looking forward to finding out more about her. However, he did have brownies and relative freedom until his mother emerged from her room. He waited a few more minutes outside his great-aunt's door, but there was no sign that she was even there. He went into the sitting room, turned on the tiny TV his mother concealed behind some oak veneer in the china cabinet, channel surfed for a while, slung his legs over the sofa arm without taking his shoes off, and scattered crumbs everywhere.

And at first it was fun, having the run of the apartment, but after he'd eaten all eight of the brownies, finished the milk, and dumped almost all of the casserole in the dog's dish, his stomach felt funny and he began to feel nervous.

He went back to the guest room door repeatedly all evening, in between trips to the kitchen for more sweets and ice for his chin. He took great delight in pantry-pilfering for roasted almonds, cocktail crackers, and swigs from the bottle of ginger ale that his father kept for his after-dinner drink. Throughout the night, his great-aunt's bedroom was as hushed as the grave. He knew she was there. He'd surreptitiously tried the doorknob and it was obviously locked from the inside. *Who knows what she's up to?*

It was too quiet. His mother's door remained firmly closed, and he sat by it for some time, waiting for a break in the murmur of her voice, but it never came. He went to his room, and moved his bedside table in front of the door so that if someone old and possibly dangerous tried to force her way in, he would be warned. He curled up at the very end of the bed with some comic books for company. When his mother, looking pale and tired, finally pushed the door open against the barrier, she found him slumped against the headboard, barely able to keep his eyes open.

"Your father must be working late again," she said, picking up Feltus's magazines and putting them on the bedside table, which she had put back in its customary position. He'd have to figure out some other way to keep Eunida out of his room.

"I think I got some positive responses," his mother continued. "It might have been better if I'd called an emergency meeting at the Floribunda Conference Center, but I will not leave you alone with that woman."

"She didn't come out of her room all night," Feltus said. "Except to eat the entire casserole. By herself," he added, in case it was unclear.

His mother fidgeted with the band of her gold watch,

then pushed it above her wrist bone, turned the face upwards, and gave the winding knob three good turns.

"Have you brushed your teeth?" she asked.

He shook his head.

"That's all right."

She pulled the covers up around Feltus's shoulders and stood there watching him. Everything seemed to shift out of focus and blended together. Then the lights went out.

\* \* \*

The next morning, a furry moss seemed to have grown over Feltus's mouth, but other than that, the nervousness of the previous night had vanished with the morning sun. His stomach felt ready to take on the world and only the thought of Jimmy was unsettling to him. After dressing hurriedly in the same clothes he'd worn the day before and smoothing his hair down with wet fingers, he went in search of breakfast and his parents.

He found his mother sitting at the dining room table, her desk calendar next to a thin slice of low-carbohydrate bread and a cup of weak tea. She barely looked up when he entered, other than to motion him toward his plate. She had her arsenal of pens out – red, green, and blue. The upcoming week was already filled with meetings and social events.

His father sat folded over the paper as was customary. Feltus hadn't seen his father's face in the morning for years – it was always buried in newspapers and stock reports. Ever since they had moved, there had been more papers, more meetings, and more urgent phone calls during mealtimes. He felt the distance between him and his father solidify until it was a wall that nothing could breach.

Feltus was used to quiet, solitary meals, he and his parents each inhabiting their own little worlds. He would have been overwhelmed now by any family discussion or observation. If his father had ever asked him about his day, he would have been speechless. Sometimes he could smuggle a comic book to breakfast and read it under the table, but today he'd decided not to run the risk. His curiosity about their strange guest was immense and he wanted to try to get some answers.

"So, is Great-Aunt Eunida still here?" he asked his mother.

"Ask your father," she snapped, without looking up from her calendar.

"Dad?" He kept his voice low.

"Of course she is."

"And she's all right?"

"Listen, Feltus," his father said, putting down the paper, which was a first. "She's an old lady with strange habits and dietary issues. She may act irrationally. She may say some weird things. It's best to let her be and go on with your life. End of discussion."

"We can't just ignore her," his mother declared, finally looking up. "You don't know. You haven't been here. She's a danger!"

"Surely you're being theatrical. She's just an old lady with no other family. Try to be kind," his father said.

"She smells and her table manners are atrocious. I have meetings set up. Business matters to attend to. It's not just you, you know. I have responsibilities, commitments!" His mother's voice ended on a high-pitched note.

They appeared to have forgotten Feltus's presence, as usual. He watched, half horrified, half exhilarated. He hadn't witnessed his parents having a conversation for many months.

"Of course, you have your groups and book clubs. But surely you have time to look in on her once in a while and make sure she has enough to eat. She won't stay long. A week or two," his father said, trying to sound rational.

"You know that she'll stay forever if given half the chance. She'll ... she'll eat all our food, ruin the bedsheets!"

"Come now. You're exaggerating."

"I try to be hospitable, and she just ignores me or says things in garbled sentences. I can't understand her. She hid an opened can of sardines under the cushions in the living room. Fish oil over everything! She roams while we're asleep! You told me she'd never find us again!"

"*Raowrrr*," said his great-aunt suddenly, though it may have been "Good morning." Feltus managed to turn the scream she'd surprised out of him into a coughing fit. He hadn't seen her come in; she just popped up like a nightmarish jack-in-the-box.

Today she wore a dressing gown cinched at her waist that looked as if it were stuffed with pillows, and a turban she'd made by winding flannel pajama bottoms around her head. His parents stopped their conversation immediately. His father went back to his newspaper. His shoulders hunched as he buried his nose in it. His mother sat playing with the clasp of her ponytail and gazing over Eunida's left shoulder.

The old lady was now sitting at the table and picking her teeth with a silver fork.

"Fardage offal," Eunida croaked suddenly.

"What?" his mother responded. "We have an impressionable young boy here, so I'd rather you keep that sort of language to yourself."

Feltus repeated the words silently to himself. They were unfamiliar – nothing like the phrases he'd overheard on the street and occasionally practiced saying in a low and threatening voice.

"I believe she said 'garbage disposal,'" his father clarified mildly. Eunida now had her whole face almost hidden in the jam pot.

"Why on earth would she say such a thing?" his mother said. "What does that have to do with anything?" She spoke slowly and with a clipped, clear enunciation as if she were speaking to an idiot.

"Doorways," Eunida said thickly. "Illicit comings and goings." She fluttered one shriveled, liver-spotted hand in a curiously graceful fashion. "Farffluffle. Blueberry muffins."

"Toast? Cereal?" his mother asked in a strained voice.

Eunida leaned forward across the table and pulled the butter dish toward her. She took a large spoonful and shoved it into her mouth. Then she helped herself to the marmalade, eating directly from the jar. She inverted the teapot above her mouth, but only a thin stream came out. She tapped on it with the spoon in an irritable manner, then hauled herself up and went out the door and into the kitchen.

"Did you see that?" his mother said, a glint of fear in her eye.

"What?" his father replied in a bored tone, not bothering to put his paper down.

His mother straightened her back and grasped the edge of the table with her thin hands.

"She's a lunatic. She is impossible."

"She has moments of lucidity."

"You can't call her normal. What was all that about? Do you want to wake up one morning and find the dog stuffed halfway down the drain?"

Feltus's father snorted impatiently. "You'll just have to try harder. She probably doesn't understand our customs." He stood up suddenly, tossed his napkin on the table, and tucked his newspaper under his arm. "I'm late for a meeting. I'll be back tonight."

His mother jumped up too and followed him over to the doorway. Feltus turned to watch.

"Wait. You don't understand. I'm trying," explained his mother.

His father placed a hand on her shoulder. "It's not that hard," he said. "Just muster up some sympathy."

"But she's insane!" his mother blurted out before noticing that Feltus was watching from the dining room. She lowered her voice. Because he could only hear the rumble of their short talk, he lost interest.

Feltus was working on swallowing the last piece of toast when he felt a nudge against his leg. He almost choked. A second push followed, insistent and demanding. Feltus thought it was his mother's obese pug, but no, Lafayette was snoring as usual on his pillow. And Great-Aunt Eunida, who could conceivably be crawling on the floor, was, Feltus imagined, still in the kitchen. The old lady couldn't have sneaked back in without his parents noticing. They still blocked the door to the hallway. He couldn't hear what they were saying, but his mother's voice had reached the high pitch that signaled extreme irritation, and her cheeks were marked with two defined circles of color. His father just looked irritated.

Feltus's stomach roiled. Whatever had just pushed against him had felt warm and possibly hairy. There was yet another nudge followed by the sensation of someone or something yanking on the leg of his pajamas. *Can't be a giant spider.* Feltus decided that the not-knowing was worse than the knowing. He dropped his fork dramatically, making a big show of it, but because neither of his parents looked in his direction, he slipped himself out of his chair and under the table to see what was touching him. The damask table-cloth draped voluminously and it was dark underneath, but after his eyes adjusted, he realized with a shock that he was looking at six or seven animals that were standing upright. They were about the size of well-fed cats and had glistening black eyes and thick, abundant fur. Their faces were long and pointy, and their mouths, which curved into what could have been either smiles or grimaces of faint warning, were lined with rows of sharp teeth.

"Who are you?" Feltus whispered, his heart knocking against his chest, the fork now held stiffly in front of him.

"We are the Giant PoodleRats of the Grand Gewglab (gool-yob) Forest," they whispered back in unison. "And we are hunnnngggrrryyy!" Feltus noticed that one of them, who was the pink color of salmon and came up to about shoulder-level as he squatted under the table, was drooling on his foot.

Feltus let out a little whimper. Overhead, just a couple feet away, he heard his parents leaving the hallway. He lifted a corner of the tablecloth in time to see his mother's pink, fluffy slippers and his father's pinstriped trouser legs walking away. Feltus reached his arm up and snatched his father's plate from the table. He held it in front of him like a shield. Two pieces of buttered toast and half a grapefruit fell off of it and onto the carpet. He forced his eyes all the way open. So far not one of the animals had attempted to tear his throat out. The pink, drooling PoodleRat lunged at the food immediately and was now dividing it into equal portions. But none of them seemed to be eyeing him as the next course.

The biggest PoodleRat, the one Feltus assumed was the leader because of his size and general air of magnificence, daintily accepted a piece of toast and brushed it off. He had very pink, delicate paws with dexterous fingers, and Feltus could see by the faint light streaming in under the table that his lustrous white fur was clipped in an ornate series of peaks and looked like whipped cream. Pompoms adorned his wrists and ankles, his torso was enveloped by a hand-some velvet and brocade waistcoat, and a small pair of golden scissors hung at his waist. His feet were disproportionately large and tipped with curving black claws. *Sure his teeth are big, but he looks like a meringue,* Feltus thought, gaining confidence with every second he remained alive.

"I am Saldemere Og," the PoodleRat proclaimed grandly. "And these are the PoodleRats of my High Court: Theremus, Fosden, Bostwick, RinMal, Maurph, and Mellewyn."

One by one the PoodleRats stepped forward on massive furry feet and made elegant bows.

"What are you doing under my table?" Feltus asked. "What do you want?"

"We have come to your world," said Saldemere Og, "because we are in need of sustenance. We are experiencing an awful famine. We have been forced to eat nothing but sand, and soup made from pebbles and rainwater. I am but half the PoodleRat I once was." There was a collective sigh from the rest of the group, and the grapefruit was passed hurriedly from paw to paw.

"For hundreds of years," Saldemere continued, "we have watched your civilization evolve and prosper as we have prospered in our world. We enjoy a symbiotic relationship with your kind."

"Huh?" Feltus couldn't hide his confusion.

"Over the eons, the destinies of our two species have become linked. We depend on you for our continued survival, and recently this has become of the utmost importance." He polished his claws against his waistcoat. "And, although I hope I will not sound boastful, humans have benefited from our survival."

"Why haven't I ever heard of you?"

"We have kept our existence a secret."

"So why can I see you then?" asked Feltus.

"Because we will it so, dear boy. Normally we choose to appear to humankind as clumps of fine particles; you humans call them 'dust bunnies,' which is a dire misnomer, obviously."

The PoodleRat drew himself up and proudly wiggled his tiny, nearly transparent ears, which were anything but bunny-like. "We are here, Feltus, because our species is threatened. Now more than ever we need to ensure that all the port holes remain open. Specifically that the one here under this table remains viable; also ..." He consulted with a small black and beige PoodleRat who had removed a notebook from somewhere about his person. "Ah yes, there's a secondary one under the kitchen sink. These port holes, which are scattered along the Veil, allow for the distribution of food to our people during this terrible time."

Feltus looked at the reddish PoodleRat who was eating the remnants of the grapefruit rind with much relish. "Why are you starving? Did your crops fail or something?"

Saldemere Og looked a little uncomfortable. "There are certain extenuating circumstances." Before he could go on, he was interrupted by a taupe PoodleRat with a feathery topknot of clipped curls. "Ahem, Sir, are you going to tell him about the ..." Here the taupe fellow made a sound deep in his belly – much like that of a consumptive chicken. "... Kehezzzalubbapipipi (ka-hezza-lubba-pee-pee-pee)?"

Saldemere Og stepped on the taupe PoodleRat's foot, not very discreetly, before addressing himself to Feltus. "*Harumphhh.* As I was about to mention ... a small matter, my boy, a small matter. This famine has come about because our land has been invaded by a dreadful enemy. Not everyone is anxious to ensure that our kind prospers. There are some who are more predatory than peace-loving, who thrive on everything, especially detritus. Rodents, vermin who threaten the very foundation of our existence."

Feltus hesitated. "I mean no insult. But if they are rodents and you are PoodleRats, then aren't you related in some way?"

A hush descended on them and all eyes turned to Saldemere Og. Feltus had the sudden, awful feeling that he had said something very, very wrong.

Saldemere removed his spectacles and cleaned them slowly and with great care. After a few minutes, he said very quietly, without looking up, "'PoodleRat' is actually vernacular for 'clever bipeds with opposable thumbs and luxurious coats.' We are not now, nor have we ever been, related to the genus Rattus."

"So you're some type of dog ... like a poodle?"

Saldemere heaved a rumbling sigh. "We are a breed unto ourselves, one thousand times more intelligent than the common canine, but possessing certain physical similarities." He smoothed the furry pad above his waistcoat. His tail twitched violently a few times. "In the golden days, we were called the JharraddlFaahghGlie (har-rat dell fay-lee) and given much honor."

Feltus let out his breath in a great *whoosh*. This was unreal. "And the keheza-whatsits?"

"As far as we can tell, they are true rodents with all of that family's cunning. They appeared in our world without warning, cutting through all our defenses. It seems as if something has catapulted them into our reality; as if the Veil that separates all worlds has been breeched in some way. They consumed all the good and growing things in our Forest, and turned it into a desert. And they outnumber us ten thousand to one. But with your help, we can rebuild our strength and drive them into the Great Barren Wastes."

"The prophecy! The prophecy!" murmured the other PoodleRats in hushed voices.

Saldemere Og ran his fingers through his fur.

"Oh yes, the prophecy. More riddle than rhyme, I'm afraid. Composed two hundred years past by an elder named Horrofallalice (horro-fal-alice) and imprinted on a biscuit. I have it here somewhere, I think." He patted both of his pockets, coming up empty. "RinMal!"

The reddish-brown PoodleRat stood up straighter. "Sir," he said and handed over a small grayish object. Many words were incised into one smooth side.

"My youngest charge and ward," Saldemere explained to Feltus. RinMal bowed his head and looked at Feltus with dancing black eyes. Saldemere continued, "For what it's worth, the lines of the prophecy are:

> *When summer's bounty*
> *Is turned to dust, and*
> *The ravenous flood runs wild*
> *On sharpened claws*
>
> *And all hope is lost,*
> *Then shall wintergreen come again,*
> *And the cat that lurks amongst the pepper pots,*
> *When at last in the red dawn of the very last day,*
> *Like a spear in the hands of a king*
> *Will rise again the Folk of Gewglab Forest*

"What does it mean?" asked Feltus. He'd never been good at poetry.

Saldemere pointed to a series of letters scratched into the opposite side of the disc. They read: *Countdown CIV0VI00.*

"Sivovieoo?" said Feltus, sounding it out.

"Not letters. Numbers – 104 and 0600 – indicating how much time we have to solve the prophecy after the first sighting of the Kehezzzalubbapipipi."

"And?"

"The initial confrontation was seven days ago, which leaves us exactly ninety-seven days to figure out what Horrofallalice was trying to tell us. On the ninety-seventh day we shall perish at sunrise unless we solve the prophecy."

He handed Feltus the small, dirty disc, and heaved a huge sigh. "Unless we learn the meaning of the prophecy and rid our land of the Kehezzzalubbapipipi, we are destined for extinction."

"Extinction!" echoed his companions. Feltus's mind clicked over. Was there a way he could turn this to his own advantage? Saldemere looked pretty hefty, his teeth razor sharp. One never knew when an intelligent, talking animal could come in useful.

"Look, that's loads of time," Feltus said. "Eat the rest of the toast and I'll try to think of something while I'm at school today."

Saldemere clasped Feltus's hand warmly and gave him a good thump on the back. "We shall await your return with eagerness, Feltus Ovalton LeRoi!"

Feltus backed out from under the table, and the moist and hopeful eyes of the PoodleRats followed him. It was only after he'd straightened out his cramped back and stretched the kinks in his neck that he thought to wonder how Saldemere Og had known his name.

He walked to the front door in shock, one hand deep in his front trouser pocket feeling the smooth circle of the prophecy. He was concentrating so hard by the coat rack that he didn't hear his mother's question until her hand was right under his nose. He recoiled. She held something that seemed to be full of mud and shredded coconut. A vaguely familiar smell emanated from it. His mother jerked it back and forth. Flakes and lumps of unidentified matter hit the floor.

"Do you know anything about this, Feltus?"

He shook his head. "I don't even know what it is."

"It is my second-best hat," she said tightly. "Filled with mashed potatoes and chocolate syrup, and possibly a veneer of hairspray. Any ideas?"

Long ago, he'd borrowed a pair of her stockings and a wire hanger to make a fishing net, and he remembered her face when she'd discovered him messily transferring frog spawn from the net to the bathtub. But that had been in his old life, before they'd moved to this clean, white place. He'd since been banned from experiments with nature, not that there was anything but pigeons and sparrows around. He shook his head again. She fixed him with the direct, hard gaze that never failed to make him confess. His conscience was clear for once. She compressed her lips – and then a single word exploded from her.

"Eunida!"

He scurried along behind her as she marched down the long hallway to the guest room. A polite knock became a series of hard pounds, but his great-aunt did not answer and the door appeared to be locked.

He would have loved to hang around, but he was already in danger of being very late for school. With regrets, he left his mother to stew. He headed out the door, and on the way down the busy main road, he paused for a minute at the corner by the newsagent to ponder the massive change in his life.

One second he was preoccupied with his parents and the general misery of home, and the next, strange relatives and magical creatures were popping up out of nowhere. He thought about the kindness in Saldemere Og's eyes and the worry in RinMal's as he'd clutched the powder puff at the end of his tail. If someone had asked him his thoughts on talking animals the day before, he would have expressed disbelief, but now having met them, he decided he wanted to help in any way he could. They had understandable goals – food and comfort, the avoidance of unpleasantness, a desire to keep their homes safe – things Feltus understood and wished for too. Maybe by helping them, he could help himself.

As far as Great-Aunt Eunida was concerned, he was less sure. She seemed dangerous and unpredictable, and he was half-inclined to avoid her as much as possible.

He found that the prospect of a beating from Rusty didn't even concern him anymore. For the first time ever, Feltus was happy thinking about all the things that were happening outside of school. All he had to do was make it through the day in as good a shape as he could manage, and then at the end of the six and a half hours he spent behind those thick gray slabs of rock, he'd be able to go home to his apartment building, where PoodleRats and a crazy great-aunt roamed free.

# CHAPTER 3

## PoodleRats, Pain, Port Holes and Prophecy

AT SCHOOL THAT long day, Feltus could concentrate on nothing but a solution to the plight of the PoodleRats. He knew there must be some clue to their mystery within the phrases of the prophecy. The words danced before his eyes as he pretended to listen to his various teachers. Since he was usually a dour, silent student, no one noticed any difference.

One thing did occur to him, but he felt silly even bringing it up. It was this: the prophecy mentioned something about "a king." In French, his family name, LeRoi, translated into "The King" and maybe, just maybe, that was important in some way. Maybe there was something he could do for his new friends.

Nobody had ever asked Feltus for help before or even insinuated that he was capable of being helpful. He knew he must be a disappointment to his parents, and although he would have liked to have friends in this new place, he felt so shy and awkward that he had retreated behind a wall of indifference. The guidance counselor had advised him to open up, told him that his prickly demeanor made it impossible for anyone to approach him. But Feltus dismissed his words, since anyone who thought it was that easy had obviously never been a kid.

That had been during his first week at the school when he was filled with rage and resentment, but as time went by he found it no easier. Sometimes he went for two days at a time without speaking to anyone. But now, when he thought of the PoodleRats, he felt a warm glow somewhere in the middle of his chest. Heartburn, probably.

During a break between classes, he found an out-of-the-way corner and took the prophecy from his pocket. He looked at it more closely. The words were clear, but their meaning was not. Was it a poem? He tried to find some symbolism in it, but came up with nothing better than Elvis Presley and creeping felines, and you couldn't fight an enemy with those. The only part that made sense was the last line – *Will rise again the Folk of Gewglab Forest.* Obviously this referred to the PoodleRats. He turned the disc over in his hand, hoping to find some kind of clue etched into the other side. But, except for the numerals, it was disappointingly blank and smooth.

He soon discovered that daydreaming at school was extremely hazardous to his health. A rabbit punch knocked the breath from his body and doubled him up until his lungs started working again. Rusty danced around him, fists bunched like fleshy cabbages.

"Oho, piggy!" he chortled. "Thinking about mud baths?"

Feltus tried to look up, but the pain had spread through his back and radiated to his knees. He struggled to keep his breakfast down. Where was a teacher when you needed one? Rusty aimed a kick at his knee and Feltus's legs collapsed, spilling him onto the ground. The floor was wet and muddy with the tracks of hundreds of feet. He thought maybe he'd just stay down there forever.

"Snort, snort, piggy!" Rusty said as he planted a boat-like foot on Feltus's back. He increased the pressure and it felt as if his vertebrae were snapping like dry twigs.

"Enough. If it's broken, it won't play or pay," Jimmy said. He squatted down, wiping the mud from his shoes with the tail of Feltus's shirt. "You know, you're taking advantage of my patience, and that's not friendly behavior. Don't push it too far." Rusty bounced up and down as if to emphasize the last five words. Feltus groaned and shut his eyes.

When he opened them again, the hallway was empty, and the final bell for fourth period rang. His white shirt was a mess of muddy streaks and rivulets of dirty water. He scrubbed at his face with his sleeve, combed his fingers through his hair, and zipped up his dark blue jacket, which concealed most of the stains. He shoved the prophecy deep into his pants' pocket. At least he'd managed to hold onto it.

It turned out that he was not alone. Percy was watching wide-eyed from the water fountain. Feltus made a threatening motion toward him, and Percy skittered off like a mouse when he met Feltus's burning gaze.

It would be so easy to take out all his frustration on someone else, and part of Feltus wanted to do just that. He wasn't very big or tall, he didn't know how to throw a punch, but he could still make mincemeat out of the likes of Percy Flannery. The anger now bubbled up inside Feltus's chest. No one ever helped anyone else at school. No one cared. If the bullies had their way, all the weirdos and nerds and new kids would just be wiped out. Erased. Like the PoodleRats.

He was all alone in the hallway for the moment, and he took the opportunity to kick a couple of lockers. The Poodle-Rats seemed like nice creatures, happy to be left alone to get on with their lives. The Kehezzzalubbapipipi were like a black cloud hanging over them, and thinking of them reminded Feltus exactly of the feeling Jimmy and Rusty gave him – that of impending doom and utter helplessness.

By the time he got to French class, he felt like one big bruise – injured, but in control of the pain. Maybe he was just getting used to the beatings. Or maybe he had things at home to finally occupy his thoughts – things bigger than school and bullies and homework. He would figure out the prophecy and save the PoodleRats, and someday he'd stand up to Jimmy too.

He tapped his pencil against his teeth and frowned in concentration. There must be a clue somewhere in the lines! What was that one sentence? Like a spear in the hands of a king. If he, rather than Elvis, was the king, then what did the rest of it mean? He was hardly hero material and he wasn't living in some adventure book. You couldn't just buy a weapon from the corner store. He sighed loudly, earning a frown and a rap across his knuckles from Monsieur Brondex.

It seemed as if Brondex had finally reached the end of his patience. Usually the plump, pear-shaped man was easily distracted. They could usually get him going on memories of his childhood – endless descriptions of Sunday dinners, his country grandparents, and the wonders of Paris in the '50s; before you knew it, time was up and the class could escape into the halls for a few minutes of freedom. But today, there was steel in the teacher's concave spine. Even his mustache stood at attention. The class was studying sentence structure, and Feltus was heartily bored. He shifted uncomfortably in his seat, trying to ease the tenderness in his tailbone.

"What are you doing with that adverb, Monsieur Jenkins?" the teacher fumed, the buttons on his embroidered satin vest straining mightily. "And pick up that participle immediately!"

Harold Jenkins mumbled something in French about taking croissants for a walk and blushed. He was a large, soft boy completely unequipped to survive the rigors of school. And if Feltus hadn't had his own problems, he might have felt sorry for him.

Harold was thoroughly confused, and for a while, Mr. Brondex's attention was occupied with explaining to him the difference between adjectives and adverbs, and why he was destined to remain at the bottom of every endeavor unless he learned this simple grammatical fact. "You will always be last, Arrolde! And that is insupportable! I will drag you from the bottom of the ranks myself!"

Brondex assigned the rest of the class some simple translation exercises from the blackboard and, readjusting his satin vest so that it fit smoothly over his paunch, he returned to Harold.

Somewhere between "La plume de ma tante" (the pen of my aunt) and "Le jardin de mon oncle" (the garden of my uncle) it occurred to Feltus that perhaps the answer existed in the nouns of the prophecy. At first glance it didn't look promising: Summer, Bounty, Dust, Flood, Claws, Hope, Wintergreen, Cat, Pepper, Pots, Dawn, Day, Spear, King, Folk, Gewglab Forest.

He realized with a start that he had been muttering the words under his breath. Percy was staring at him again and Feltus glared back, his upper lip lifted into a snarl. Percy had started at the school about the same time Feltus had, but he and Feltus shared no brotherhood. They had nothing in common besides Jimmy's enmity, and Percy was even lower on the totem pole than Feltus. So Feltus took this opportunity to try to scare him. Perhaps a little pummeling by the water fountain was in order? Feltus mimed punching motions until the blond boy turned away.

At the end of the day, however, Feltus was so anxious to get home that he ran the whole six blocks in a headlong tilt. Arriving breathless and with an acute cramp in his side, he forgot to act reserved with Peter at the door. In fact, he yelled "Thank you!" over his shoulder as he entered the elevator at a run.

Once upstairs and inside the apartment, he ran into his room and hurled his book bag on the bed. It was National Teachers' Day tomorrow – which meant no school – and then the weekend! He'd be fully recovered from Rusty's beating by the time he went back to school on Monday, and maybe he could filch some money from his mother before then. Things were looking up.

He could hear his mother talking on the phone in her bedroom. No doubt his father was still at work. He ran to the kitchen and grabbed a handful of tortilla chips and a mint chocolate chip ice cream sandwich from his father's small refrigerator at the back of the pantry, and then he ran back to his room for some peanut butter cookies from the secret hoard in his wardrobe. Clutching the cookies to his chest, he made his way to the dining room. After ensuring that everyone was out of the way, he lifted the tablecloth with a careful nonchalance and concealed himself under the table.

He cleared his throat.

"Umm, hello?" he called.

There was a faint circular glow on the floor – an opening. When he craned his neck and peered down the hole, he could not make out a bottom. It made him feel dizzy. Saldemere Og quickly popped up like a gopher, gave a low whistle, and was joined by a few of the others. Feltus handed over some chips and cookies. The russet PoodleRat, RinMal, sat down next to him grasping a chip; his black eyes were wide and curious.

"Have there always been port holes?" Feltus asked Saldemere Og, imagining invisible holes under everyone's sinks and dining room tables.

"Yes. As far back as my tenth father's father's time, there have been official openings in the Veil, but we used them mostly as collecting stations. Many are situated next to dumps and there are a few within human residences. Did you never wonder what happened to your kitchen waste, for instance? The peelings, the skins, the rinds, and cores? Lawn clippings, tree stumps, and poison ivy? What about plastic wrappings, lids, and corrugated cardboard?" He stroked his bottle cap bolero. Feltus had never spent much time thinking about garbage collection. He only knew that Rose bagged it up and the building supervisor put it out at the curb once a week. Saldemere looked quite self-satisfied though, so he decided not to get into it.

"The port holes were placed in a few key environments where the elders felt we would gain the maximum knowledge and benefit, and the locations were swathed in secrecy," Saldemere continued. "It was all done of course with full approval of the Patrol, and the passages were keyed to PoodleRat use only. When our troubles began, we were forced to use the port holes to acquire most of our food. Your kitchen sink port hole is now directly connected to the disposal unit that feeds into our communal hall, providing a steady stream of sustenance, although coffee grounds are hardly filling."

The PoodleRats sighed in unison.

"So you're scavengers?" Feltus asked, slightly disgusted. *Like common rats*, he thought.

"Yes," Saldemere Og replied proudly. "Our civilization is based on the simple laws of 'waste not, want not.'"

"And what is the Patrol?" Feltus asked.

"The Patrol is made up of guardians of the Veil, which runs through all the different worlds. Their task is to monitor all byways and crossing points and make sure that no rogue openings occur. It is rare, but it has happened in the past. Once by wild magic, and on more occasions than I care to mention, forced entry by greedy pirates. Punishment by the Patrol, which is sanctioned by the Federation of Worlds, has always been swift and severe."

"Let me get this straight," Feltus said, using his fingers to tick off points. "You come from some world that is attached to ours through these port holes. For some reason I can see the port holes *and* see you. But not everyone can see this, right?"

The stately PoodleRat nodded.

"So then why me?" Feltus asked.

"We've observed you and your family for a while. We thought you would keep our secret. You are not a terribly social person. The older woman who cooks the meals is kind also. I think she sometimes leaves the dirty dishes till the morning, stacked beside the kitchen sink where we can easily get to them."

"And we liked your name," RinMal interrupted. "It sounds like a PoodleRat name."

Feltus's mouth twisted into a grin. No one had ever complimented him on his name. It was a weird feeling. He basked in the strangeness of everything for a moment.

"Everything is changing," said Saldemere Og enigmatically.

Feltus didn't quite understand him, but he nodded anyway as he ripped the wrapper from his ice cream bar. Noses quivered when the ice cream was fully exposed.

"What is that delicious-smelling thing?" Saldemere asked. RinMal inched closer. He was almost sitting in Feltus's lap.

"It is mint chocolate chip ice cream sandwiched between two chocolate biscuits," Feltus replied. "Care for a bite?"

All of them made avid noises and the sandwich was disposed of quickly. Feltus sadly licked a few remaining crumbs from his fingers.

"An amazing invention, my boy. Wonderful! You humans really are masters of creativity. Now, have you had a chance to think about the prophecy?" Saldemere Og asked as he carefully wiped his whiskers with a lacy pocket handkerchief.

Before Feltus could begin speaking, he heard his mother calling him from her bedroom.

"Feltus! Feltus Ovalton! Where is that boy?" Her voice got closer. She seemed to be heading for the kitchen. "Rose, can you make sure that Feltus packs his bag? We're leaving at six o'clock sharp tomorrow morning to spend the long weekend at Uncle Remus's farm and I won't have time to waste. We'll be back late Sunday night. And can you water the kumquats while we're gone? Oh, and remember, the building's superintendent is coming to move the furniture tomorrow."

"Is Madame Eunida going with you?" Rose asked.

"No. Just put some crackers or something nonperishable out for her."

"I'll make her some meatloaf, or maybe a shepherd's pie. That should last the weekend," was Rose's answer from the kitchen. "And there are blueberry muffins, fresh-baked this morning."

"Don't spoil her," his mother spat. "We're on a tight budget."

Everyone under the table relaxed as they heard the sound of a door closing.

Feltus was disappointed. Trust his mother to ruin his plans. She always treated him like a child, incapable of amusing himself. Something drove her to fill every day with character-building activities or extra credit courses. He hardly ever got time off school and for the last few holidays, she'd enrolled him in a program through the local native-grasses museum, which had consisted of all-day seminars and hands-on weeding. A weekend at Uncle Remus's was only marginally less painful, but he'd still have to be useful and pretend that he really was the perfect robot his mother seemed to expect. Three whole days would be wasted chasing rabbits and pheasants out of his uncle's soybean fields when he could be helping the PoodleRats.

Saldemere Og's shoulders bowed and he heaved a sigh. "Oh well. Mustn't fret. Plenty can be done when you return, my boy. But perhaps another ice cream sandwich or two might help pass the time?"

Feltus fetched a few more ice cream bars and a family-size bag of ruffled potato chips from his father's secret stash. For some reason, junk food was necessary for his father's twenty-four hour corporate takeover strategies, but was not allowed for Feltus's nightly homework. Feltus dropped them off under the table and endured the sympathetic glances the PoodleRats gave him. They were being driven out of their home and they felt sorry for him! He then shut himself up in his room and brooded until dinnertime.

His father had phoned to say he was working late, and Great-Aunt Eunida was still locked in her bedroom, so it was a silent and uncomfortable meal with his mother, who seemed distracted herself. Besides telling him to slow down between bites, she was so wrapped up in her own thoughts that she never even noticed when he slipped the rest of the sprouts off his plate and into his napkin to be thrown away as soon as possible and flicked his broiled liver to the dog. He made his escape quickly enough and spent the rest of the evening holed up with his comic books, wishing he were a superhero who didn't have to attend family meals when he was called.

\* \* \*

Feltus did not sleep well that night. He had horrible dreams about a menacing shadow that spread like a pool of sticky black tar. In the midst of the darkness, he thought he could distinguish the red eyes and sharp incisors of hundreds of rats. He awoke the next morning hot and sweaty and completely exhausted. The sun seemed very high in the sky. When he wandered out into the apartment in his pajamas, it was unusually quiet. He knocked softly on his parents' door, then eased it open. Their bed was made up neatly. Lafayette's dog pillow was gone. He went into his parents' bathroom and noticed that their toothbrushes were missing from the gold-plated holder. He couldn't believe it. They had left without him!

For a moment, he panicked. He wandered around the silent apartment before stopping in front of the guest bedroom.

"Great-Aunt Eunida? Are you there?" He tapped on her door once, and then again, this time with force. No answer as usual. He couldn't be sure if she were there or not. Except for a scrawled note that had been pushed under her door requesting marmalade, crème fraiche, and a medium-rare porterhouse steak, there'd been neither sight nor sound of her since breakfast the day before. And other than a perplexed query on the whiteboard from his mother regarding the disappearance of better than seventy-five feet of aluminum foil, his parents didn't seem to care. In fact, his mother was probably grateful that the stinky old lady kept to herself.

Feltus ran to the kitchen to see if his parents had left him a note, but there was nothing. The board was scrubbed clean, erasable markers neatly lined up in rows according to color. He swept them to the floor, flung himself down the hall to his room, and slammed the door not once but four times until flakes of plaster were dislodged from the ceiling.

Feltus indulged in a tantrum (he was only 11 5/6, after all) that left him weary but feeling a little better. Afterward, he gazed at the disaster he'd wrought. Clothes had been pulled from hangers and thrown on the floor, books heaped, papers scattered. It looked as if a typhoon had blown through. He then jumped up and down on the bed, cranked his stereo up to ten, drank three bottles of cherry soda quickly, and yelled "Me! Me! Me!" as he pumped his fist in the air. He soon discovered that he could slide in his socks all the way from one end of the shiny-floored hallway to the other, that he could don his mother's best bird of paradise hat and pretend to be a turkey, and that no one was there to say, "Hey! Put some shoes on! Put some clothes on!"

When he finally collapsed on his bed, surrounded by a smorgasbord of purloined snack food, he began to realize that being abandoned really wasn't so bad. Since he was home virtually alone, he could start helping the PoodleRats right away. He dressed quickly, heaped the mess he'd made into a pile next to the bed, emptied his schoolbooks out of his satchel, and hurried with it to the kitchen.

The pantry shelves were carefully organized. There was canned food, alphabetized according to his mother's instructions, and necessities such as candles, matches, and kitchen string, neatly boxed and labeled. He stuffed the bag with packages of dried soup and noodles; boxes of nuts, raisins, and cereal; and packages of macaroni and cheese; he also took some books of matches, a flashlight, and a spool of string. Remembering how much the PoodleRats enjoyed them, he dithered over the ice cream sandwiches, but grabbed some cookies instead.

He climbed under the table and shone the flashlight down the port hole shaft. He still could not see the bottom. It seemed a long way down, but Feltus closed his eyes, took a deep breath, thought about the PoodleRats, and jumped.

As soon as he did, he sincerely wished he hadn't. He opened his eyes and saw that the tunnel was pitch black; the sides of the hole were very cold, slick, and straight. They felt as if they were made out of glass or marble and were perforated by small holes that snagged his vainly grasping fingertips. It was no use trying to slow down his plummet into the unknown.

He slid helplessly for what seemed to be hours, plenty of time to think about imminent death, until at last he glimpsed a faint light ahead. The tunnel corkscrewed from side to side, and gradually his speed lessened until he was deposited with a thud on the ground at the end of it. He looked around. It was weird. He must be miles underground, but he could feel the sun on his face, warm and bright. Before him was a path made out of shiny, sea-smoothed pebbles, all carefully laid out in intricate patterns and lined with pieces of broken glass in a myriad of colors. And in the near distance was a cluster of curiously-shaped buildings that sparkled in the sunlight.

As Feltus approached the buildings, he saw that they were largely made of copper-colored clay. They had domed roofs like beehives, and were ornamented with silvery pie pans and aluminum foil, punched and pierced into fanciful designs. The windows were fashioned of multi-colored bottles and jam jars cut short and mortared together with clay so that the bottoms faced outward. The glass was green, rust-red, brown, and opaque white, and some of it had squiggly patterns etched into the surface.

Everywhere he looked there were small but perfect details and embellishments. Each house was neatly enclosed in a fence made from tin cans, and each had windmills and scarecrows made out of plastic bottles and detergent containers. It was very pretty, but there was not a green growing thing to be seen. Not one tree in all of the Grand Gewglab Forest was left. Every gust of wind blew up a spray of dust and small pebbles, and Feltus began to feel slightly flayed. The wind carried a smell of burning bread with it – or was it cinnamon?

He was so engrossed in what he was seeing that he failed to notice that a few of the residents had left their homes and were now following him down the street in single file. They were quite as curious about him as he was about their city. By the time he reached the largest and finest house, there were twenty or so of the creatures dogging his heels. He stopped and looked up at the grand clock surmounting the highest tower of the house. The house was lavishly decorated with gold foil and glass flowers and was crowned by a large bell, horn, and a flashing red light. Saldemere Og traipsed down the steps holding his arms out wide. RinMal bounced closely behind him, revealing sharp teeth through a broad grin.

"My dear, dear boy!" Saldemere said. "You are most welcome here. Welcome to our home!" He turned to the gathered PoodleRats, who were all colors of the spectrum, trimmed and clipped and curled, but none as magnificent as Saldemere Og, who wore a cloak of red satin and a pair of jewel-encrusted spectacles. "This is the savior of us all!" he proclaimed to the PoodleRats. Feltus eyed him suspiciously. It sounded like work.

Inside, the house was decorated with all manner of gaudy, gold, glittery objects, but it was plush and comfortable as well. Feltus was a good two feet taller than the PoodleRats, but he was thankful to see that they liked their furniture oversized. Feltus relaxed into the depths of an overstuffed armchair that was capable of seating half a dozen PoodleRats. He held a cup of tea in his hand, and his feet were cozy and warm in a pair of slippers borrowed from RinMal, which were woven from plastic containers and lined with what could have been dryer lint.

He laid his gifts of food on a large, beaten aluminum coffee table. The offerings were examined with much interest, curiosity, and hunger by the multitude of PoodleRats who perched on every available surface and looked at him with something approaching awe. Feltus liked the attention. RinMal, sporting a new paisley design shaved into his foxy red fur, took a spot by Feltus's side. Feeling benevolent, Feltus shared a few nuts from his bag with him. Feltus was completely unprepared for the sudden sound of a bell ringing wildly, followed closely by the bugling of a horn.

"The Kehezzzalubbapipipi!" RinMal gasped.

The PoodleRats leapt to their feet and hurried as one to the door. In a furry tide of bodies, Feltus was carried down the stairs and into the dusty street. He looked up to see a small, white PoodleRat on the roof, swinging the bell rope with his foot and blowing with all his might into the horn.

A red light flashed in intermittent bursts from a tall steeple on the roof. With a free paw the PoodleRat pointed to the south. A little way in the distance, Feltus could see a darkness, as if an insect multitude were rushing in one direction. His skin crawled a little – he didn't like bugs. These bugs seemed to be bigger than termites, bigger than grasshoppers or cockroaches. As they came closer, he could hear a chittering as if thousands of little feet were marching in unison, or as if thousands of little teeth were gnashing together; and what ground they passed over was immediately stripped of any grass and plants that still remained.

The black shadow became distinct, and Feltus realized he was looking at a horde of mouse-like creatures that moved as one. It was just like the awful dream he'd had the night before, but worse. The PoodleRats were grouped behind him in a frozen block of fear. Slowly they retreated, disappearing into their individual homes until Feltus stood alone.

"Go away!" he yelled at the horde that was now mere yards away. It came on nonetheless and at a speed that left him incapable of retreat. He would not turn his back on them for fear of feeling those tiny claws on his neck.

He rummaged in his satchel, which was still slung around his shoulders. His groping fingers encountered string, a box of matches, and the hard, comforting shape of the flashlight. The Kehezzzalubbapipipi had stopped about twenty feet away and were undulating and oozing in a peculiar fashion. He squinted and realized in horror that each creature was entwining its tail with its neighbor's, forming a thick mat of squirming, living animals.

Slowly this mat rose up and up, until Feltus stood facing a writhing, twenty-foot tall thing of darkness. It possessed two thousand eyes and one thousand razor-toothed mouths, and it was fearsome and horrible. Feltus inched away slowly, the blood ice-cold in his veins, and the thing turned its massive head in his direction. One thousand quivering noses sniffed the air and the mass took a step toward him.

"Hey, I need some help!" he yelled to the PoodleRats.

No one came.

Feeling hysterical, Feltus pulled the flashlight out of his bag and threw it at the monster. He threw the kitchen string and the box of matches, but to no avail. He cursed all rodent-canine hybrids using some choice words gleaned from his father, who sometimes forgot himself over the budget reports. The Kehezzzalubbapipipi took step after ponderous step and the ground shook as it got closer.

Feltus rummaged deep in his bag and his fingers came up empty. He cast a quick look behind and to the side. There was nowhere to hide – no bush, no tree he could try to climb, no rock to conceal himself behind. He was utterly exposed. He felt his breath clog his throat. He closed his eyes even though in his thoughts he saw the thick, black shadow ooze its way toward him, enfold him in a furry mantle, and then suck out his vital juices. He could imagine the incredible pain as his organs were ripped out by thousands of teeth, as his skin was torn and shredded. His knees gave way and he sank to the ground, steeling himself against that first nibble. A sweat broke out on his forehead.

Nothing happened. Feltus pried one eye open. The Kehezzzalubbapipipi had halted their progression and turned in the direction of a field of rippling, golden grasses. Under his horrified gaze, they swarmed over the meadow, and in only a few minutes the ground they crossed was reduced to bare soil and stubble.

He rose unsteadily to his feet and backed up until he was far enough away that he could turn and run to Saldemere's front door. RinMal must have been keeping watch behind the thick glass, because he threw the door open as soon as Feltus reached the top of the stairs.

"Why didn't you run?" the PoodleRat gasped, pulling him into the house.

Feltus made a strangled noise in his throat. RinMal gazed at him with something akin to respect, and Feltus forced back the bitter rant that threatened to burst forth.

He allowed himself to be lead back to the comfortable sitting room and he let RinMal remove his slippers and massage his feet. He condescended to eat two helpings of the delicious creamy dessert Saldemere Og had concocted for him. The fire roared, his chair was comfy, RinMal's gaze bordered on adoring, the other PoodleRats sat in quiet respectful rows hanging on his every word, and Feltus found he was feeling pretty calm and proud of himself for not completely wimping out. *Actually, that wasn't bad*, he thought to himself. Maybe the Kehezzzalubbapipipi had been scared of him and that's why they turned away. He sat up a little straighter and squared his shoulders.

After the sun went down, the others, except for RinMal, returned to their respective homes. They seemed to disappear, melting into the walls. Saldemere explained that during the attacks by the Kehezzzalubbapipipi, the PoodleRats followed emergency procedures and traveled by subterranean tunnels. Saldemere lifted a knotted-rag rug in the hallway and showed Feltus the wooden plug beneath it.

"Each of the houses is linked by these underground passages, which also connect with your port holes," he explained. "We are able to live indoors quite comfortably for a time. Two hundred years ago, in the time of the seer

Horrofallalice and following a prophetic vision he had in a mud wallow, the tunnels were extended and reinforced, and rooms and gathering places were hewn out of the earth. We have never been forced to use them for survival, but it is good to know they are there."

The old PoodleRat patted Feltus on the hand, heaved a sigh, and began polishing his monocle vigorously. "To be truly happy, Feltus, we need the scent of green, the wind in our fur, and the happiness that springs from an organic vegetable garden!"

His eyes were moist, and Feltus, embarrassed by Saldemere's display of emotion, feigned interest in the wire-and-pipe-cleaner sculpture by the front door. He didn't have to fake enthusiasm for long. It was truly amazing what ingenious uses the PoodleRats found for almost everything – bubblegum wrappers and the chewed up wads of gum, bicycle inner tubes, beer can tabs, egg cartons, reels of old audio tapes, film canisters, and plastic flower pots. Everything was made into items of everyday usefulness or pieces of beautiful art.

The hours flew by. Feltus was turning a small diorama – constructed out of shards of the blue glass that mentho-lated rub came in, dental floss, and modeling clay – around in his hands when Saldemere Og came in with an armful of pillows and blankets. He was followed closely by RinMal, who carried a large and floppy mattress pad covered in brown and white ticking.

"Should be nice and cozy in here," Saldemere said in a blustering tone. "All the windows are shuttered and the doors are closed tight. There'll be no disturbances, I'm sure." Feltus shot him a quick glance and noticed that the PoodleRat would not meet his gaze.

"If the Kehezzzalubbapipipi eat all the plants and crops before the next ninety-six days are up, will they leave?"

Feltus asked. "You know, go back to where they came from?"

"That is the penultimate question, dear boy. The Kehezzzalubbapipipi will eat anything. They will gnaw through electrical wires and grind up a concrete wall from beginning to end. Gewglab and everything in it is doomed. But we know that you will find a way to help us."

Feltus shivered and moved closer to the cheery peat fire crackling in the grate. He felt exhausted but too keyed up to fall asleep. He still felt the adrenaline pumping through his veins, and the memory of all those furry bodies buzzed around his brain. He was exhilarated, but deep down inside, some small part of him wanted his safe and boring bedroom.

Right before he fell into an uneasy sleep, calmed by Saldemere's rumbling snores and the warmth of RinMal near him, an awful thought occurred to him. *How will I get back up the port hole?* He couldn't remember seeing a rope or a ladder on his plummet downward. It was hardly comforting.

# CHAPTER 4

## Up the Down Port Hole

THE NEXT DAY, after a somewhat bland breakfast of dry cereal and raisins (Feltus did without the reconstituted milkweed juice), and after a check with the posted sentries, Saldemere Og showed Feltus around the town. The central area was dominated by a large gathering arena of yellow limestone dotted with what had been glorious trees and shrubs that were now sadly stripped of leaves and bark. Noble buildings, tiered and decorated like wedding cakes, overlooked the park and housed the offices of the Poodle-Rats of the High Court and other public servants. The most glorious edifice was made entirely of blue and green pottery shards and topped with turrets of copper. Feltus noticed it leaned to one side like that famous tower of pizza he'd heard about in Geography.

"The Bureau of Useful and Beautiful Things," said Saldemere Og with pride. "If one can have both, why not? It breaks my heart that we may have to abandon all of this – centuries of art, design, and engineering, years of innovative salvage. "

"I made a log cabin out of Popsicle sticks once," Feltus admitted shyly.

Saldemere raised his shaggy eyebrows. "Most admirable, my boy!"

Beyond the square, the desert stretched as far as Feltus's eye could see – an expanse of uniform brown, uninterrupted by shrub or tree. The air shimmered, and Feltus was about to dismiss it as merely a trick of the heat, when it rippled again. Beyond it were vague shadowy shapes suspended in nothingness. It gave him a slight feeling of vertigo. Could it be those foul, crawling rodents again?

"Is that ... ?" He mimicked creeping feet with all ten fingers and got ready to run.

"Oh, no," Saldemere replied. "That's the Veil made visible. Sometimes when the light hits just right, the unblessed eye can glimpse it. You may be seeing inhabitants of a world that intersects with our own. "

"Is it a wall then? Why doesn't it keep the Kehezzzalubbapipipi out?"

"That is the mystery, dear boy. The Veil runs through all worlds, and all worlds march side by side, separate but linked in destiny. Somehow our enemy has breached the Veil. I fear it will echo everywhere, perhaps with devastating effect. It is theoretical, but I have heard that a rift in the Veil can cause weaknesses throughout its length and breadth. We have been invaded and it is likely we are not the only ones."

Feltus could not shake the creeping feeling between his shoulder blades. It was as if hundreds of eyes were fixed on him. He turned his back. When he dared to look again, the desert was empty.

"Have you ever seen the Kehezzzalubbapipipi scatter the way they did yesterday?" he asked.

Saldemere sighed. "In the past, when they have come upon us, we have had no other recourse but to run and hide, and they have systematically razed every living thing in their path. For whatever reason, they did not see you. Perhaps it is because you are alien to our world, or perhaps they mistakenly deemed you unimportant."

Feltus tried not to feel insulted that the Kehezzzalubbapipipi had not thought him worth eating.

Saldemere continued. "Whatever the reason, you have

an edge that we lack. It is not that we haven't attempted to fight, you understand. My own dear brother, Koncriticon Lar (con-krite-ick-on-lahr), fell before them in the first battle." Saldemere blew his nose loudly and patted the area above his stomach. "All that was left was the small ring he wore on his littlest finger. I wear the ring on a rope around my neck in remembrance. Our losses have been exceedingly great – whole battalions wiped out."

Saldemere Og cleared his throat and clapped Feltus on the shoulder. "I have every confidence in you, my lad. You have already accomplished far more than any of us."

Feltus found himself reluctant to accept thanks for what had been merely a combination of luck and terror. The PoodleRats looked at him with such hope that he was feeling a little guilty. He had to figure out the prophecy, or he could never come here again. Already he found himself caring about Saldemere and RinMal in a way that he hadn't experienced since he'd been friends with Fuzzy. These were friends he could count on. Friends who accepted him the way he was.

Saldemere's paw was a warm weight on his arm. Feltus was interrupted in his musings by the sudden klaxon of a horn. Instantly, adrenaline surged, the hair stood up on the back of his neck, and every muscle prepared for flight. His mind pictured that wriggling mass of matted fur, and he felt terribly faint.

"Lunchtime, dear boy. Lunchtime!" Saldemere Og boomed. "We eat together as a family."

Feltus's breath rushed out in relief.

Saldemere eyed him with affection. "One horn – lunch; two – a sighting; three – immediate danger; four – utter destruction."

"Oh," said Feltus.

"You're very pale, boy," Saldemere said, offering his

shoulder for support. "You probably need a little feeding up."

Feltus leaned on the PoodleRat as they made their way to the Bureau of Useful and Beautiful Things, which also housed the communal dining hall. To his surprise, Feltus found that he was ravenous. Delicious smells wafted through the air. Feltus took a seat at the head of the table, at Saldemere's right hand, and felt saliva flood his mouth. The PoodleRats sat politely in rows with napkins tucked under their chins. RinMal perched next to him. The entire polished surface of the long, wide table was covered in tureens and platters from which steam rose.

The PoodleRats passed Feltus a plate heaped with large portions of food. The casserole was hearty and hot. Feltus could identify beans, potatoes, and carrots. There were some other round chewy things, something that was vaguely sausage-like, and a small mound of tangy leaves, but it was tasty and he decided not to inquire too closely. Flagons of a sweet, fruity drink that reminded Feltus of lemonade were passed back and forth.

"Sumac berries," RinMal whispered as Feltus took a sip.

"I thought sumac was poisonous," Feltus replied after spitting the sweet liquid into his napkin.

"It's safe. We ferment the berries and age the juice in recycled rubber casks," RinMal assured him.

Feltus swilled his mouth out with water from a small bowl filled with rose petals and decided he'd had enough exotic food for one day. Having finished his meal, he leaned back in his chair and looked around the dining room. Heavily-framed portraits of austere and valiant PoodleRats lined the walls. One of a military individual with wonderful white whiskers and a large saber was labeled "Brigadier General Lar." Feltus could see the family resemblance to Saldemere. Bow-legged cabinets stuffed with treasures and oddments stood next to shelves overflowing with dusty leather-bound books. An umbrella stand filled with frilly parasols, cue sticks, and walking canes stood by the main entranceway. In the corner, by a verdigrised copper urn commemorating the Battle of Nantly Dun, was a tall rectangular box draped in curtains. A faint glow emanated from it.

"What is that?" asked Feltus, pointing.

"The port hole to sector K5," RinMal announced in reverent tones. "Your kitchen sink cupboard."

"My kitchen ... " he repeated in wonder. The new apartment might be dull and overly clean, but it had port holes, PoodleRats, and a suspiciously quiet great-aunt who could be up to who only knows what by now. Feltus threw his napkin down, stood up, and walked over to the port hole.

Once he had drawn the cloth aside, he realized he was looking at what had once been a simple phone booth. The telephone was still in place, though the phone cord hung loosely from the box. A large copper washing tub, empty at present, but smelling of coffee and potato peelings, occupied most of the floor space. He remembered that Saldemere had said that this port hole was now used solely for collecting food scraps. It seemed too beautiful for such a mundane purpose. The outside and inside of the booth were completely covered in bone and glass buttons, sea shells, old golden and silver coins, beads, and cat's eye marbles.

He could see the end of the tunnel meandering its way up above his head and realized that his fears about getting back home were well-founded. The sides were as smooth and polished as a slab of ice, and although there were small holes spaced regularly up the length of the tube, they were made for claws – his fingers were too big to fit in them. Climbing out would be impossible. Feltus started to panic. Home was awful much of the time, but he had to get back. He couldn't stay in the Grand Gewglab forever.

Saldemere Og did not seem overly concerned when

Feltus explained the matter to him. Having finished his meal, he reclined in a well-worn leather armchair, tamping a silvery gray leaf into his mahogany pipe and playing with his enameled matchbox.

"Now, now, dear boy. I understand. Never fear. You must get back today and you are unable to negotiate the port hole. We shall have to consult with Professor Krankle, our problem solver extraordinaire."

Since this Professor Krankle had not been able to solve the PoodleRats' present predicament, Feltus was dubious. He followed Saldemere Og's scarlet cloak out onto the street. They walked a short distance along the colorful, paved road lined with bright red and bronze tulips, and eventually through a darkened doorway that bore no distinguishing feature besides a large question mark scrawled in white paint. RinMal had followed close behind and Feltus gave him a grateful smile. He could not help but be cheered by the young PoodleRat's enthusiasm and positive attitude. Funnily enough, those were two of the qualities he hated most in other people, but things were so alien down here that he welcomed them now.

Upon entering the low-ceilinged, dark place, which looked as if it served as both laboratory and workshop, Feltus was immediately engulfed in a cloud of noxious smoke that came pouring from a hole in the floor. This was followed by a filthy personage wearing goggles, rubber gloves, and a flowery apron. There were missing patches of fur on his elbows, legs, and head. What fur was left was a dingy yellow and resembled a well-worn bath mat. Once the goggles were removed, Feltus could see that he was missing an eye. The left one.

Saldemere Og addressed this mangy creature in all honor and explained the dilemma. The Professor's one eye gleamed with interest. He limped over to Feltus and stood before him, muttering to himself and scratching a raw place on his arm.

"An ascension. Hmmm. What do you weigh, boy?" He pinched the fleshy part on Feltus's thigh. Feltus slapped his hand away. "About ninety-two half-ingots weight, I'd guess. Let me see. A pulley system, maybe," the creature said as he uttered a short bark of laughter. "Hoist you up like a sack of potatoes." He paused and looked at a spot above Feltus's ear. "... potatoes. Fried. Baked. Mashed. How 'bout croquettes? Or rockettes? What about a rocket? Carbide fuel, sulfur base?" His eye rolled wildly in its socket.

"Arrival intact?" The professor cocked an eyebrow at Saldemere Og, who assented rapidly. "Oh well. Rocket's out. Would likely blow you to smithereens. Can't be helped."

Professor Krankle pulled out a tape measure and made a few notes on a scrap of brown paper bag. He licked the stub of his pencil as he wrote down Feltus's measurements.

"Inside foot. Inside leg. Inner arm. Outer cranial circumference ... come back in half an hour," he ordered Feltus.

\* \* \*

Half an hour passed by as slowly as a math class. Feltus tried to count seconds as well as sunburst designs on the building opposite and finally, he attempted to alphabetize superheroes while he, RinMal, and Saldemere Og were waiting in the small square across the street from Krankle's lab. Saldemere Og broke in on his thoughts while he was trying to think of a superhero that began with $g$. The dignified old PoodleRat tried to squash Feltus's fears and doubts – "Krankle is completely sane, I assure you" – by enumerating the wonderful inventions that Professor Krankle had conceived and executed: "The transfiltration water system and underground aqueduct, for instance, and the smog diffuser, and the alembic treatment that turns sewage and waste matter into building materials."

"And he got a wad of chewing gum out of my fur once," RinMal added. "Didn't hurt at all."

"He is also a fine kite maker and a consummate portrait painter," Saldemere Og continued. "You may have noticed a singularly attractive portrait of my brother in the long gallery? But to the matter at hand," he said as he consulted a gold-filigreed pocket watch. "He's had exactly thirty-two minutes."

* * *

RinMal skipped ahead, raising a fine cloud of acrid dust as they reentered the murky building. Feltus blinked in the sudden gloom. A small light shone in the corner, but the workshop was very dark after the bright sunshine of the outdoors. A queer stilted figure moved out of the shadows. It appeared to have a large, completely round head, a short torso, long hands with skeletal fingers that reached almost to the floor, and trunk-like legs. As it approached, Feltus heard a strange muttering, which eventually separated into distinct words.

"Probably have to let it down a little in the length. The wristbands could do with some tightening. Climbing mechanism and tactile response is good. It will have to do!" The figure turned around slowly and spied Feltus and the two PoodleRats. "*Ahhh*, good. You're back. Come here and try this on for size, boy," came the muffled scientist's voice from inside the suit.

Professor Krankle removed the helmet from his head. He had affixed a miner's light to the front of the helmet, and there were holders for bottles of water and straps for attaching packages of food. He wore knee-high boots, which were swathed in garish orange tape, and from the center of each toe, a metal spike protruded. He was struggling to remove a pair of leather gloves. Saldemere Og hastened to his aid.

"As you can plainly see," the professor said, holding the gloves out to Feltus and pointing to four metal hooks attached at the end of the fingers, "these grapples recreate the climbing claws that we have been endowed with naturally. Evolution and all that." He permitted a smug smirk to play across his face.

"Well at least humans don't eat other people's garbage," Feltus pointed out.

The professor glared at him and then retreated in a huff.

"You may have noticed the holes that are spaced at hand and foot length – in PoodleRat measurements, of course – throughout the length of the tunnel." Saldemere Og interrupted hurriedly. "It will be strenuous, but RinMal and I will accompany you. You will be home before you know it." He bent to help Feltus get the boots on. "A trifle unwieldy, but you'll soon get the hang of it."

Once Feltus was properly attired, they made their way to the port hole he had arrived by. "Wouldn't do to come up under the kitchen sink, would it?" RinMal remarked. Feltus laughed. He couldn't help but imagine the horror on his mother's face if he showed up under the sink covered in waste. A procession of PoodleRats had assembled outside the laboratory and cheered him through the streets until they reached the port hole. It seemed much steeper from this end. With the helmet on, he was almost completely restricted to seeing only that which was front and center. He felt Saldemere Og grip his arm encouragingly and direct him toward the mouth of the port hole.

He turned on his helmet light, adjusted the gauntlets so they didn't chafe as much, took a deep breath, and stretched his legs. The congregation of PoodleRats shouted approval and Feltus waved a negligent arm. When he turned his head upward, RinMal was already twenty feet up. He felt jealous at the ease with which the PoodleRat climbed. Feltus then hooked his "claws" into the first set of holes and pulled himself up.

Behind him, he could hear the crowd of PoodleRats break into song. The words were clearly distinguishable and he felt his ears burn red with embarrassment.

> *Feltus, Feltus*
> *King from up above*
> *Take our thanks and love*
> *Feltus, Feltus*
> *King so great*
> *Two desserts is what he ate ...*

The singing continued until he had traveled quite a distance up the port hole and the corkscrew turns had finally muted all sound from below.

RinMal set the climbing pace, keeping it slow and steady, while at the rear, Saldemere Og yelled encouragements. Feltus's wrists soon felt the strain of supporting his weight, and his knees hurt from banging into the slick walls of the tunnel repeatedly. Because he was so much taller than the PoodleRats, he had to climb with his back bent in an awkward curve. On more than one occasion, he lost his footing and ended up dangling from one "claw" until Saldemere or RinMal could come to his aid. He was thankful when they stopped midway up, where a short and narrow ledge protruded, to eat crackers and drink some water.

"Elevators. Do you think your wonderful professor could invent some of those?" Feltus asked bitterly after much too short of a break. The good-natured PoodleRats snickered.

There was nothing to do but to continue, even though every one of Feltus's muscles was screaming in protest. He kept his eyes up, ever hopeful that he would soon see the glow of the port hole under his dining room table, but it remained dark and the flashlight beam bobbing from his helmet picked out only RinMal's small, red body climbing five feet above him.

RinMal stopped suddenly. "I can go no farther," he said. "The port hole is not here!"

Feltus pushed past him, panic rising in his chest. "It couldn't just close by itself, could it?" he gasped.

Feltus saw that it was true. The tunnel ended but something was covering the opening. Something dense. He climbed up past RinMal and pushed at it. He felt it give a little. Relief flooded him. "It's not solid. If we all heave together, I think we can move it."

Saldemere Og and RinMal braced their rear claws on either side of him and on the count of three, they all shoved hard. The blockage shifted slightly, and Feltus could feel a space between it and the floor around the port hole.

"Put your backs into it," Feltus pleaded. "If we can make enough room, I'll crawl out. You two stay here and don't follow me until I tell you it's safe."

Feltus squirmed out of the hole. By lying on his back and inching his way with his feet he was able to move out slowly. Whatever was covering him extended for quite a distance in each direction. His foot and hand gear made turning impossible. His helmet allowed for no peripheral vision. He could only look up into the darkness, feeling increasingly claustrophobic, until at last he emerged from the heavy covering and saw light.

He sat up and removed his headgear. He was in his dining room, but the furniture had been rearranged. The table was against the far wall and in the place where it had stood just two short days before was a thick, lush, and exquisite carpet in hues of crimson, emerald green, and ocean blue. It completely covered the port hole.

He stripped off the climbing gear, tackling the knots binding his wrists with tooth and nail until he was free of its cumbersome weight. He pushed the gear behind a large, bushy potted plant in case he ever needed it again, although he hoped he'd never have to repeat that terrifying climb. Remembering that Saldemere Og and RinMal were waiting patiently for a signal from him, he tapped gently on the rug, working his way over it toward the middle, and was finally rewarded with a hollow knocking from below.

His mother, apparently speechless, walked into the room as he sat there on the middle of the carpet trying to decide what to do next. Her shirt was buttoned up incorrectly, her hair didn't look as if it had been brushed recently, and she was twisting her fingers together. He tried to look innocent and detached. His mother, after all, had a nose for mischief.

"Mom! Mother!" he said loudly enough – he hoped – for the PoodleRats to hear. "You're back early," he added as nonchalantly as possible

"Feltus! Feltus Ovalton. How could you?" she replied, her voice cracking on the last syllable.

# CHAPTER 5

## Great-Aunt Eunida Saves the Day

"WHAT HAVE YOU been doing? Couldn't you leave a note? I had to rush back!" his mother cried, her voice high-pitched and querulous. She didn't wait for him to reply to her questions. She just kept ranting.

"How do you think I felt when I got to the country and realized that you were nowhere to be found? Luckily, Remus was positive you weren't even in the rental car when we arrived. And then I had to find some way to get home quickly. And your father wouldn't hear of me taking the rental and driving all the way back by myself." She leaned forward and shook him. "Do you know how hard it is to get a cab outside the city? It took all night to find one that would make the trip. And then you weren't here either, Feltus!" She knelt down and hugged him once quickly and then again harder. "Thank goodness your great-aunt was home!"

She held him at arm's length, her fingers busy smoothing his hair down. She wouldn't meet his eyes.

"You do realize that I'm overwhelmed with the details of our big gala dinner at the moment, don't you, Feltus?" she said in quite a different tone. "My head was just occupied with place settings, guest lists, and flower arrangements, otherwise ... " her voice trailed off.

"Sure," he said.

"I'm sorry."

He began to realize that she was more relieved than angry and also that he was off the hook somehow. Looking over his mother's shoulder, he saw that Great-Aunt Eunida, her hair even more matted and dirty, and the skin of her neck a dark gray, sat hugging her knees on the ottoman. Her eyes gleamed and she inclined her head. The smell of burnt toast was strong, and he was amazed that his mother didn't seem to notice. She was still holding him, and he could now feel that his neck was moist with her tears.

"If Eunida hadn't written me a note about the extracurricular school activities, I would have been beside myself, Feltus!"

Feltus looked at the old lady and saw her close one eye and give him a thumbs-up.

"Oh, yeah," he said, thinking fast. "We get credit if we volunteer to help clean the library, and I figured there was nothing else for me to do. Here. All alone. It was pretty educational," he managed to add, while grinning at his mother. He noticed she was only wearing one earring, and hugged her back before she pushed him away.

"That's enough of that," she fussed and then stood back up quickly. "You are positively filthy. Go wash up before dinner and make sure you scrub those fingernails well. If it's not one thing, it's another. You've put me in a very embarrassing position. And to top it all off, now I have to hunt down some wild boar and figs for dinner. Great-Aunt Eunida asked for them especially!"

"Where's Dad?" Feltus asked.

"He's coming later in the rental car. Well, we couldn't both disappoint Remus, could we? It's bad enough that I ran off without much of an explanation." She clapped her hands together, dismissed him, turned, and in a dulcet tone asked Great-Aunt Eunida if she would mind sitting on a towel.

Feltus strolled along to the bathroom, whistling a merry tune. He couldn't believe that he'd gotten away with it. And all because his crazy great-aunt had come to his rescue.

Perhaps PoodleRat dirt was more tenacious than the usual variety, but whatever the reason, it took a lot of soaking and a lot of scrubbing before Feltus even came close to being clean. His mother probably wouldn't be pleased with the ring of oily filth he left on the bathtub, but scrubbing at it with his toothbrush hadn't done much good, and he couldn't figure out how to remove it any other way. He left his grimy shirt wadded up on the floor and hoped her good feelings toward him would last a while longer.

He dressed quickly and then decided to cross-examine Great-Aunt Eunida while she was being helpful. He ran into her by the door to her room. She bobbed her head and smirked when he thanked her for covering for him.

"How did you know that I needed help?" he asked. She held her hands out palms up and shrugged her shoulders.

"Can't you talk?" he asked.

She made a face as if she were petrified and shook her head. He knew that she could speak – there was all that nonsensical babble that usually came out of her mouth – but obviously something was seriously wrong with her. She rolled her eyes and patted him on the shoulder before turning back to her room. The burning smell was almost overwhelming, like when he'd singed his eyebrows leaning in too close to a campfire.

"Come and have dinner with us later. Mom's picking up your favorites," he called, but Great-Aunt Eunida had already disappeared into her room. Feltus slouched against the nearest wall and wondered what to do. He was worried about the PoodleRats, and it would have been nice to confide in someone, even if it was a smelly old woman who wouldn't – or couldn't – answer him. At least if she accused him of being crazy, no one would believe her.

He wandered into the sitting room and cast a quick look around. No sign of Saldemere Og or RinMal anywhere – not even a suspicious bump under the carpet. *They must have returned to the Gewglab Forest,* he thought. *What's left of it.*

His mother, now properly groomed and outfitted in pale blue with matching shoes, was busy at her needlepoint. It looked like another cushion cover. The style this season seemed to be art deco, and she'd already completed a series of red and black interlocking circles for the hall settee. Personally, Feltus never felt comfortable in this white painted room with its dark wood furniture, and he hardly thought that new covers would change anything. The room would remain sparse, uncomfortable, and unwelcoming no matter what.

"Did Dad get home?" he asked, sitting down on one of the hard couches. He'd heard the front door, and then the study door with its peculiar groaning squeak, open and shut.

Her fingers pushed the needle through the minute holes and drew the thread through in a precise motion. She pierced the cloth again and again before she answered.

"He has work to do. Don't disturb him."

"I thought he was supposed to be relaxing this weekend," Feltus grumbled.

His mother shot him a look.

"Well, will he have dinner with us? I asked Eunida too."

"Perhaps. And don't go bothering the old lady. She's tired."

\* \* \*

His father did make an appearance at dinner later that night – well, at least physically. But Feltus was disappointed to see that his great-aunt stuck to her hermit crab ways. He thought that if he could hang around her, he'd eventually figure out what her presence in the house was all about and if it was connected to the PoodleRats in any way.

It was a somber and silent meal as usual. He pushed his food around his plate, making mountains and valleys out of the mashed taro root and bitter greens, and he wished they could just have hamburgers or tuna casserole sometimes.

"Should I take some food to Great-Aunt Eunida?" Feltus asked, struck by a good excuse to leave the table.

"I said to leave her alone," said his mother. "Sit up straighter." She then proceeded with a monologue that neither Feltus nor his father paid much attention to. Feltus was immersed in the problem facing the PoodleRats, and his father, as usual, was buried in his newspaper. Every once in a while he rustled the pages in answer to some question or other.

"Bill, what do you think about moving the chandelier a bit to the right so it's centered above the table? And what about some emerald curtains to flatter the new carpet?" Feltus's mother asked.

His father responded with a grunt.

"Hey, now that the table has been moved, we can't see the Von Doolsings at their table anymore," Feltus pointed out helpfully. "And they won't be able to see us."

The Von Doolsings lived in the apartment directly across from the LeRois. Their dining rooms were each graced by floor-to-ceiling windows, and his mother spent an inordinate amount of time looking across the street when she thought no one was watching. She planned dinner parties around the Von Doolsings' schedules and each one was more ambitious and lavish than the last. On the nights they had guests, Feltus's mother threw the curtains open and they dined under a glittering array of light and candles. Feltus hoped his mother would now move the table back so that he could have the chance to sneak down the port hole again. It would be too hard to keep in contact with the PoodleRats if he had to slink under the rug.

His father's newspaper flagged a little. Feltus held his breath. His mother clasped her fingers together tightly. "Perhaps I've been too hasty," she said. "Bill, would you ask

Albert to come here after dinner? I'd like him to move the table back where it was."

After dinner, Feltus hovered near the intercom by the front door while his father buzzed down to the superintendent. "Yes," he heard his father say. "I know you just shifted it, but she wants it moved back. Yes. Great. Thanks."

"He'll be right up," Feltus's dad yelled down the hallway, and then, gathering his briefcase and papers under his arm, he went to his study and firmly closed the door.

Albert, humming a jaunty melody, passed Feltus in the corridor on his way into the dining room. As usual, his pockets bristled with wrenches and screwdrivers and his sleeves were rolled up over his brawny forearms. Feltus hoped he'd grow up to be as muscular as Albert some day. That was what he imagined a hero would look like.

"How's it going, Sport?" Albert asked and ruffled his hair as he went by. Curiously, Feltus didn't mind. He drifted behind the superintendent and watched. After a lot of heaving and careful positioning that mostly consisted of Albert following orders from Feltus's mother and making minute adjustments to the angle and specific location of the table, it was finally back in its original position. The rug was carefully unrolled alongside the big sofa. Feltus heaved a sigh of relief. Now he had full access to the port hole again.

Feltus waited until his parents went to bed and then sneaked into the dining room with a paper bag of food he'd rustled from the pantry. He lifted the tablecloth and was reassured to see the familiar glow of the port hole. But Saldemere Og and RinMal were nowhere to be seen. He left the food under the table, backed out from under the cloth, and leaned against the wall by the windows, crossing his legs comfortably. He needed to consider a few things.

First and foremost, he decided he'd stop getting distracted by his great-aunt who was probably suffering from nothing more than senility. Worrying about her and her body odor and strange mutterings was a waste of time. He'd let her go her crazy way and he'd go his. He'd dedicate his free time to the PoodleRats and the prophecy. Sure, he still had lots of time before doomsday, but he had no idea where to start.

He took the prophecy from his pocket and examined it. Nothing had changed. It made no more sense to him than before. He tossed it into the air and watched it spin in the silvery starlight.

"*Hmmmm,*" remarked Great-Aunt Eunida, who appeared out of nowhere and grabbed the prophecy out from under his nose. She turned it over in her crooked fingers and held it up to one jaundiced eye. "Perhaps I've been wrong about you," she croaked, then snapped her jaw shut.

Feltus stared at her in surprise. She'd barely strung two intelligible words together before now. He grasped futilely at the prophecy, but she easily whisked it away. *Where did she come from?* he wondered desperately.

She must have sensed some of his distress because she eventually took pity on him and tossed the small gray disc back to him. "Here's your cookie," she wheezed.

He fumbled the catch and almost dropped the prophecy before shoving it back into his pocket and sitting against the wall. He'd have to watch himself around her.

She hobbled over to the fireplace and plopped herself down in the white leather armchair. This was a pristine piece of furniture normally reserved for very important guests. Her fright wig of hair was sticking out from under a thick foil beret, and she had picked up a plate from the coffee table that held a congealed slab of boar meat and some disemboweled raw figs.

"Perhaps there's more to you than meets the eye," she continued.

"What do you mean?" he managed to ask in his shock.

"I had you pegged for a nincompoop."

"Well I thought you were a crazy old lady and I'm right," he said triumphantly as he stood up.

She snorted; then her eyes sharpened and he felt as if his feet were glued to the floor.

"Ever mess around with magic, Feltus?" she asked.

"It doesn't exist," he said with false bravado, trying to push all thoughts of the PoodleRats from his mind. The thing was, he didn't believe in magic, really. The PoodleRats were an exception to the rule and not precisely magical, anyway. They were just large talking animals from a different world.

"I've looked in all the cupboards and there's clearly no access from the toilet, but otherwise I've drawn a complete blank," Great-Aunt Eunida said in the same conversational tone, sucking bloody juices from all ten fingers. She insinuated her index finger between the foil and her head and scratched. "*Ahhhh,*" she said. "Temporary relief."

"What are you talking about?" Feltus asked, wondering if she had a split personality. Nothing but insane ravings for days and now they were having some kind of conversation. Not that any of it made sense.

"Places where one can just pop in and out. Haven't you noticed any strange occurrences lately?" she said.

"You're about the strangest thing here," Feltus retorted. No way was he going to tell her about the port holes and PoodleRats unless he was sure she wasn't an enemy.

She peered at him short-sightedly. Her voice was suddenly pitched higher, quite different from the raspy, guttural croaks she usually emitted. "The Veil between worlds unravels, the fabric is torn. There is a smell upon you, youngster. Watch your step!" She reached out a bony claw. Her eyes were wide and blank.

Feltus ran to his room. That night, he made sure the bookshelf *and* his desk firmly blocked the door.

# CHAPTER 6

## Show-and-Tell

SOMETIMES FELTUS THOUGHT that Sundays should be abolished. It wasn't that he'd rather be in school, it was just that time ticked by so slowly when you had no friends and nothing to do and no money anyway for anything fun.

He'd checked under the table a few hundred times for a sign of the PoodleRats, but apart from the disappearance of the food he had left, there was no evidence that they were near. He'd amused himself for a while by writing short, cryptic notes in code to RinMal and turning them into paper airplanes that he shot down the port hole, but after a while, that lost its thrill.

Back in his room, he paced and tried to think of something to do. His comic books were old and he'd read them all a thousand times before. He'd read all of his books too. He knew the Greek myths almost by heart, although he did waste an hour acting out the labors of Hercules, using a vacuum cleaner hose as a stand-in for the Hydra. A moth-eaten old fur coat made an almost perfect Nemean lion, and he took great glee in pretending to hack it to pieces.

He'd glanced at his homework. He'd completed the geography assignment and done some of the math, although he was positive his answers were all wrong. Luckily, old Pidgeon, the math teacher, never expected much from him.

The only thing he'd tried not to think about was the personal expression item he was supposed to bring to English. He'd racked his brain trying to think of something cool, something that would not subject him to the ridicule of his classmates. He had examined and decided to pass on: a pharmacological diploma belonging to his great-great-grandfather, a genuine bird feather ink quill, a seahorse encased in a paperweight, his rendition in pen and ink of the Medusa as a high school girl, and a weird seed pod he'd found at the beach last year. Out of sheer frustration, he'd almost decided to go with the diploma and make up some exciting back story, possibly involving a poisoning, but he knew he was in for another humiliating experience and probably a beating afterward. Rusty and Jimmy, who both took the class, delighted in merciless heckling, and it looked as if he'd be providing them with plenty of material tomorrow. He felt his spirits droop.

There was the unsettling matter of Eunida's strange words the night before too, but apart from her mention of a "veil," he'd forgotten the rest. At least he could ignore her most of the time.

He lay down on his bed. *If I still lived in the old house,* he mused, *I'd be running in the woods, and climbing up to the platform Fuzzy and I rigged in that old oak tree.* He remembered how they'd only had a handful of nails and a few lengths of rope. The whole thing rocked, teetered, and creaked, and it was perfect for pretending that you were on a ship in a squall.

Or he'd be up in the dusty attic, which only he visited, surrounded by old, moldy suitcases covered in labels from strange hotels in exotic lands, and boxes spilling sepia-toned photographs on the floor, which must have belonged to the previous owners. He'd spent hours at the oval glass window watching the bats wheel at dusk or the horned owl sleep in a tree nearby. But now he looked out onto the wide, busy road. Beyond it, there were more roads and row upon row of tall, gray, identical buildings and only a wedge of washed-out sky visible between them.

When he ventured outside his room again, he found the rest of the apartment quiet. Everyone was home, he knew, but no one was around. His mother was in her office – the small area set aside in his parents' bedroom that contained a desk, a phone, a calendar, and a large, red-bound copy of *Who's Who in Society*. His father was in his office. Eunida was in her room with her mysterious birdcage. Rose had the day off.

Feltus went out in the hall of the building and rode the elevator up and down, up and down – ignoring the distinct possibility that his snooping neighbor, Mrs. Fontana, would be calling his mother about it later on – until it was time for dinner. Afterward, he went to bed.

* * *

The next day, Feltus awoke early and in surprisingly good spirits. He lay for a few minutes in bed, relishing the quiet and the sunlight streaming through the window. The weirdness with Eunida seemed distant and blurry. He had probably misunderstood, anyway. She talked as if she had marbles in her mouth – that is, when she talked at all.

He wandered into the kitchen in pajamas and robe, idly rubbing his wrists, which still hurt where the stiff leather bindings of the climbing gloves had chafed. He had taken the opportunity yesterday, while everyone was busy with their own concerns, to shift all the climbing equipment from the hiding place behind the plant to a safer place – under his bed, in a trunk with his camping gear.

Rose was bending over a large pan on the stove. Feltus liked to imagine her at home, surrounded by children and grandchildren, and lots of dogs. Her house would be bright and noisy, full of chatter and laughter. He wished he could live there too.

In this apartment, she was a bright spot of color in the pristine silver and white kitchen, her floral shirts and dresses a riot of yellows, blues, and oranges. She always smelled of good things – strawberries, olive oil, applesauce, and fresh bread. Her hands were large and warm and her eyes kind.

She turned and greeted him as he walked into the kitchen.

"Good morning, Feltus." He liked the way his name sounded when she said it.

"There's fresh orange juice in the fridge and cinnamon waffles in the oven, and I'm just frying up some eggs and bacon. Why don't you wait a few minutes and then help me carry it all into the dining room."

He helped himself to a glass of juice and gestured toward the stove. "Is all this for Great-Aunt Eunida? I never thought I'd see bacon grease again."

Rose smiled. "Just following your mother's orders."

"I don't get it. Why is she doing all this for an old lady she can't stand?" He remembered how his mother had seemed almost scared when Eunida first arrived, as if his great-aunt were capable of doing something terrible.

"Eunida is different," Rose admitted. "But I like her. I bet she's got some interesting stories to tell."

"Yeah, if you could ever understand what's coming out of her mouth."

Rose put the spatula down. "You know, the other day she came in here when I was fixing your lunch, and mumbled something about exploding seaweed. Not three minutes later, the jar I was holding with the kelp wraps for your tofu rolls just shattered in my hand."

"*Wooooo*," he said mockingly.

She shrugged her shoulders and turned back to the frying pan.

He thought about the port holes. "Rose, have you ever noticed food disappearing from the kitchen?"

"You mean in addition to your discreet raiding?" she said. "It's very clever, the way you eat all the cookies from the bottom of the tray first."

"I meant leftovers – crusts and bones – things that get thrown away."

"Well, your mother is certain there are mice, but I've never seen hide or hair of them." She planted her hands on her hips. "I'll tell you something, Feltus. My grandmother used to leave a little plate out for the kitchen fairies." Her eyes twinkled. "Now I'm not saying I do, but I'm not saying I don't either."

Apparently the PoodleRats had been right about Rose's generosity. Maybe that meant that they were right about him too – that he was the one who could save them. Feltus turned around. "I'll just go and set the table."

The dining room seemed empty. He strewed the forks and knives in a fan shape on the tablecloth and piled the plates in the middle. Then he walked slowly around the perimeter of the room. He made sure to look in the deep armchair that faced the window. He didn't want any Eunida surprises – she often showed up out of nowhere, and she seemed intent on poking her nose into his business.

Lafayette was snoring loudly on the sofa, and Feltus used a pillow to dislodge him and herd him toward the door, ignoring the growls. The spoiled pug had nipped him more than once, and Feltus had no regrets about directing a push toward the dog's fat backside now. Then he closed the door to the dining room firmly and crawled under the table. He was happy to see that the bag of provisions from the night before was gone. He hated to think of the PoodleRats going hungry.

The port hole glowed with its soft light. He gave a low whistle, then called RinMal's name. His voice seemed to echo down the shaft. Much to his disappointment, none of the PoodleRats responded. He backed out from under the tablecloth, stood up, and was stretching out the stiffness from between his shoulder blades when he heard a squeak like a rubber sole against polished wood. The smell of burnt toast wafted over to him a bare instant before his great-aunt's voice. He whipped his head around.

"Wanderings," she croaked from the door. "Illicit rendezvous. Capricious goings-on. Mysteries. Increased demand for tangerines." Her foil hat was a little lopsided this morning.

*Darn the old bat! Why is she always around?* Feltus thought angrily.

"Snoop," he said unkindly. "People should keep their noses in their own business."

"What's under the table?" She moved surprisingly fast for an aged woman. She knelt down clumsily, pulling the material of her quilted silk dressing gown out of the way. Feltus threw himself to the floor in a futile attempt to stop her, seconds after she had flicked the corner of the tablecloth up. He caught his breath.

There was nothing under the table now but a few clumps of dust. The port hole wasn't there.

"Drat," said his great-aunt very disappointedly, before she turned and left the room.

Feltus remained on his belly for a moment, running his fingers over the place where he knew the port hole was and feeling nothing but the floor. He turned away, preparing to exit from under the table, when something grabbed him suddenly by the ankle. His mouth was covered just as quickly, before the scream that threatened to burst forth could be released. He choked it back down, feeling as if he were swallowing a chunk of potato, and looked into the dancing black eyes of RinMal.

He swept the PoodleRat into a hug before he really thought about it. Somehow, this creature had become as close a friend as Fuzzy had ever been and he felt very happy to see him. He was not overjoyed, however, by the sharpness of bone he could feel under RinMal's fur, which seemed to be molting and four sizes too big, or by the way RinMal's eyes were so huge on his thin face. When he released the PoodleRat from the hug, RinMal teetered a bit before regaining his balance. *Why aren't I spending every waking moment trying to figure out a way to help the PoodleRats? What is wrong with me?* Feltus looked down, red-faced, and mumbled a quick "Hello." A somewhat awkward silence followed, but luckily, he remembered a chocolate bar in his bathrobe pocket that was only a little squashed. They hunched under the table, sharing it, and by the time they had finished, Feltus was more comfortable.

"Say," he said. "How come my Great-Aunt Eunida couldn't see the port hole? She was looking right at it."

"It is our choice who can see us and who cannot. Remember?" RinMal replied.

"Good. I'm still not sure about her. She helped me out with my mother, but she's just too weird. Sometimes I think I almost like her, and then she'll burst out with some crazy stream of words in a language I've never heard before. At first I thought it was Italian, but there aren't enough vowels. Anyway, what are you doing here? Not," he hastened to add in case the PoodleRat was sensitive, "that I'm not glad to see you."

"The Kehezzzalubbapipipi have attacked yet again. Remember the tulip promenade?"

Feltus nodded. Amidst the browns and golds of stripped earth and sand, the vivid red and orange flowers had looked like flames of fire.

"Gone," the PoodleRat said sadly. "Saldemere fears

they will turn their sights on us as food soon. He told you of his brother?"

Feltus nodded.

"Utterly consumed. It was awful," RinMal whispered. "But," he continued in rallying tones, "Saldemere sent me here. To you."

Feltus was uncomfortable again. "I know you think I'm named in your prophecy, but I'm really just a ... nobody. I'm failing all my classes. I have no friends." He said this last bit in a whisper.

"It is you. I know it. And the prophecy means something – something that will help us. We just have to figure out what."

"Okay," Feltus said. He became curiously heartened. It was weird how RinMal's unconditional faith in him could actually make him think he could achieve what seemed impossible. He clenched and unclenched his fists. "Let's go get started then," Feltus said and promptly bashed his head against the heavy walnut ribs of the table as he tried to stand. RinMal didn't even smirk.

Feltus crawled out from underneath the table and, after making sure that no one was lurking in the hallway, he gave the go-ahead. After that, they both tiptoed to Feltus's room. Feltus was strangely reminded of spy games he'd played with friends, and he felt that familiar and pleasant tingle down his spine. He was concealing an animal of sorts in his room without his mother's knowledge. *What can be better than this?*

Once they were in his room, Feltus gave RinMal a hurried tour, pointing out the comic books, his secret stash of candy, the complete set of encyclopedias his mother had bought him for his eighth birthday, and the telescope he had trained on the ballet studio across the road.

But real life suddenly hit him with a *whumphhh*.

"I have to go eat breakfast with my parents. And then it'll be time for school. Will you be okay in here by yourself?" Feltus wondered if he could fake a sudden illness. But he figured that his mother was onto all of his tricks. She'd been very suspicious ever since the twenty-four-hour mumps.

"I can do some research while you're gone," RinMal said, folding himself onto a pillow and dragging a heavy encyclopedia volume into his lap. "Then when you get back, we can attack the prophecy systematically. I'm here to help you in any way I can."

Feltus closed the bedroom door behind him and wedged a thick wad of toilet paper between the jamb and the wall – a simple trick that made the door stick and that had so far foiled his mother. Feltus wondered how the PoodleRat might be able to help him.

He was still pondering this when he entered the dining room. His mother, sitting stiffly upright, and Great-Aunt Eunida, messily hunched over, were now both at the table, and his father was in his customary position, buried under reams of newspaper and computer printouts.

The old lady fixed her beady eyes on Feltus and sniffed loudly before returning to her eggs – sunny side up and served on fried whole wheat bread that was plastered with raspberry jam. Her mouth was smeared with grease and she consumed another rasher of bacon noisily as she stared at him. It was enough to put him off food forever.

"How are you?" he asked his mother as he poured syrup on his waffles. She had her chair turned away from Eunida, and only a cup of black coffee sat before her. Her fingers were restless, tapping on the table, and she reached for her embroidery. Feltus noticed that she was onto a new design that was quite unlike her usual basic geometric patterns. This was a gentle undulation of blues and purples and the lightest pinks. It made him think of a sunset and the ocean.

She glanced at him, failing for the first time since the move to notice that he was wearing the same creased and dingy shirt as he had worn the day before. He ran his fingers through his hair until it stood straight up, and then he peered more closely at her craft project.

"That's nice," he said. "Different."

"It's all part of my repetitive therapeutic relaxation."

"Is it working?"

"I'm still at the 'letting go' stage, but I feel somewhat numbed, thank you."

"You know," he said boldly, thinking that one crazy old lady could hardly impede his PoodleRat investigations, "I think you and Dad need to get out more. Do something fun. Great-Aunt Eunida can look after me."

Eunida snorted into her cup. His mother was speechless and returned to her needlepoint.

His father had raised his head from the paper, its pages concealing the disgusting sight of Eunida slurping heavily sugared coffee, and he directed a quick look at his wife's newest project. Feltus could see surprise in his father's eyes, and he thought, as his father put his paper away and applied himself to his breakfast – a muffin rather than the usual dry toast – that maybe some small thing had changed after all. Feltus was quite happy as he excused himself from the table after snagging the last waffle out from under Eunida's whiskery nose. He concealed it in one of his handkerchiefs (nice to know they were good for something) and went back to his room to gather his school books and ask RinMal for his first favor.

\* \* \*

For whatever reason, this particular day felt different. Feltus hoped that it would turn out to be the one day when he actually succeeded in making it to the end of school unscathed. That for once he would be seen as something more than a wimp or a geek. It was with this hope that Feltus crept into English, evaded the foot Rusty Jackson obligingly placed in his way, and took his seat as far back in the room as possible. He kept his head down. He could feel a pair of eyes boring into his back. The eyes belonged to Jimmy Matthews.

"Greg. Harold. Feltus," Miss Hanking called. "Do you three have your personal expression items ready?" She sat down on the edge of her desk and looked encouragingly at her students. She was young and new to teaching. Sometimes her enthusiasm and gentle air were enough to make things bearable, but only sometimes.

"Smeltus. Smeltus. Smeltus," a low, whispering mumble rippled through the room. Feltus's ears burned and a large spit wad hit him on the back of the neck. He hunched lower in his seat.

Greg Williams swaggered up to the front of the class, a big smirk across his face. He reached into his capacious pockets, pulled out some limp, brown material, and held it up. Carefully, he pulled the stretchy cloth over his face.

"My sister's panty hose," he announced thickly. The room fell apart with laughter as he walked back to his seat, twirling the stockings above his head.

Harold Jenkins had brought a rock, which he announced was a fossilized oyster. It looked just like a plain, ordinary rock. The class suppressed yawns of boredom. He presented a long report on Neolithic geology to support his claim, and Feltus began to be hopeful that time would run out before it was his turn.

Harold started on a long, stream of consciousness poem that supposedly drew similarities between his father and the rock, but it was hopelessly free-form and most of the students turned their attention to other things – more spit balls, for instance. Feltus could feel a row of them stuck to the back of his shirt in patches of wetness, and one had slipped down his neck like a snail. Unfortunately Harold's report, though exhaustive, ran just short of forty minutes, which gave Feltus a good ten minutes to make his offering. He had never brought anything from home to school before and he was nervous.

He pulled the cloth-draped cardboard box out from under his desk and went to the front of the room. The class leaned forward in their seats. He knew that this looked better than panty hose and rocks. With a flourish, Feltus removed the cloth.

There, appearing spectacularly feral, lurked what Feltus told the class was a genuine "Andalusian Marmot," teeth bared menacingly, brilliant red fur clipped in whorls and peaks.

The boys gathered around the box excitedly, and for once in his short life, Feltus was the center of attention and an object of grudging admiration.

"Online," he responded to someone who asked where he got it.

Percy pushed his way to the front of the group. "Andalusian Marmots have black pelts. It's a biological trait," he declared in a superior tone.

"Oh, put a sock in it, Priscilla," Feltus said. "What do you know?" Greg gave Feltus a high five. The class closed in around the box, and Percy was shoved roughly to the rear.

"I think I saw one of those in the back of a comic book," announced Greg. "Twenty-five bucks!" There were loud exclamations at this apparent proof of Feltus's largesse.

"Is it a carnivore?" Jimmy asked, his eyes shining with a weird light. "Does it eat baby mice and chicks?"

"Yeah, make it move. Make it do something," Rusty added, poking it with his pencil and shaking the box from side to side.

Feltus caught RinMal's eye and winked. RinMal obliged by yawning widely, grunting loudly, and biting Rusty, whose hand dangled just a little too close.

At 11:52 on Monday morning, at Miss Montmorency's School for Boys, it would have been observed, if anyone had cared, that Feltus Ovalton LeRoi smiled at school for the first time.

* * *

Back at home after the first school day in which he was not physically assaulted, Feltus's smile was quickly wiped off his face. He barely had time to conceal RinMal in the chest of drawers in his room before he was summoned to the sitting room. His mother was on a rampage. Perhaps after spending time with Eunida, she had reached her breaking point. Perhaps the breathing exercises and repetition therapy she'd learned in yoga had ceased to work. Perhaps his grace period after the Uncle Remus trip disaster had worn off. Whatever it was, she'd lost her temper as soon as he'd come home from school, before he'd had a chance to grab a snack and relax.

"What do you mean you lost it, Feltus?" she said, her face screwed up in a frown. "It" was the name tag she'd insisted he wear pinned to the lapel of his coat ever since they'd moved to the city from the suburbs. As if he were a six-year-old! She waved a long, thin finger in front of his nose. He felt like chewing it off.

She was still going on and on, and he looked at a spot just past her right shoulder and made his eyes go blurry like they do when you try really hard not to look directly at anything. He hoped it might look eerie to her, as if he had a sudden brain tumor, but she never even paused for breath.

Then he imagined he was concealed in the trees, like a monkey – No! Like a vampire bat! – and his mother and father were walking underneath, their clumsy feet snapping twigs and rustling the leaves. He stretched his black wings, and the poison dripped from his fangs in anticipation ... and then he was interrupted by more rants from his mother.

"I don't know why you should feel any embarrassment," his mother continued. "Perhaps your friends have conducted themselves with greater maturity, have shown that they can be trusted. Try to ignore them. I'm sure everyone gets teased a little. Please don't smirk like that, Feltus Ovalton. This is serious."

Feltus made a noise like an angry squirrel. "Friends!" he managed to choke out.

"Yes. Friends." She eyed him with curiosity. "Associates. Acquaintances. What?"

"I don't have any." It was the hardest admission he had ever made.

"Don't have any? How is that possible after six months?"

"You don't have any either," he reminded her.

"I have my work," she said as she looked away and then back at him.

For sixty seconds, she didn't say anything at all, her gaze fixed on him. Feltus knew his expression had hardened. He refused to break eye contact. He waited to hear how she would reply – what advice she would offer. Her eyes wavered.

"Feltus! Your hair needs brushing! It looks like you've been backwards through a haystack," she yelled.

These were the things that made Feltus Ovalton crazy. These were the times that made him feel invisible and wonder briefly, before the anger and hurt drowned other feelings, exactly what had happened to his family.

After he'd gotten up, returned to his room, and slammed his door, he noticed a scrap of paper on his pillow.

It was a short note from RinMal that stated simply that he had to return to Gewglab suddenly and that he would have to help himself to a few supplies from the pantry before he left. Feltus was conscious of a deep disappointment. It didn't matter that the PoodleRat assured him he'd return as soon as he could; he needed RinMal now! He lay on his bed and drummed his heels against the mattress then turned over and punched his pillow until his arms were tired.

If he squinted his eyes, he could see shapes in the water stains on his wall. Picking out a shade for a new coat of paint that would complement the rich hues in the hallway ("Pineapple Delight" and "Cheddar Biscuit") was on his mother's "to do" list, but Feltus sort of liked the patchiness of the paint on the wall now. He pulled on his eyelids until everything looked kind of smeary. *There's a pirate galleon.* And if he looked sideways, he could make out the coils of a sea serpent. *And over there in the corner are the toothy jaws of a dragon in mid-flight, and there, maybe that could be a warhorse, but really it looks like a blot.*

He sighed. He could only play stupid games for so long. Especially by himself. The truth was, he was lonely and bored again. He swung his legs over the side of the bed and sat up. He looked around his room and it seemed so empty. He could see a clump of red fur under his desk. He hopped off his bed, picked it up, and slipped it into a drawer with his pencils and markers.

*When RinMal gets back, I'll teach him about scooters and jam-filled donuts.* The PoodleRat had already promised to show him how to make catapults, build tunnels, and grow algae forests on a bath sponge. But RinMal would be gone for who knew how long. Feltus didn't know how he would stand it.

He sat back down on his bed and shifted his hip on the mattress. Something in his pocket was jabbing him. It was the prophecy, which he'd carried with him ever since the PoodleRats gave it to him. He took the biscuit out of his pocket, ran a thumb over the worn surface, then tossed it up in the air and caught it. The thing was weighted nicely; he was able to get at least three full rotations before it fell back into his palm. It fit perfectly in his hand too.

He curled his fingers around it. What does it mean? He puzzled over the words again. "And the cat that lurks amongst the pepper pots." *Cats kill mice. Could that be it? Where would I get enough cats to take on the Kehezzzalu-bbapipipi though?*

The thought of trying to push a bunch of cats down the port hole nearly made him laugh. And his mother was allergic on top of everything else.

*Okay, how about the pepper? Pepper spray, maybe, like the police use.*

He had no idea where to get that either.

*I could go ask at the station, but I doubt they just hand it out to eleven-year-olds.*

The first two lines seemed pretty obvious and must refer to the present situation. He sighed and shoved the prophecy back into his pocket. *Some hero I'm turning out to be.*

Out of the corner of his eye, he caught a sudden flash of light as if a bulb had blown, and when the loud popping sound came, the first thing he thought of was the six-pack of cherry soda he had concealed in his closet. But the noise originated by the window and was followed by the buzzing drone of an angry and possibly very large insect. Feltus was not fond of any bugs, never mind winged bugs, and he threw his shoe at it without taking a closer look.

It seemed for an instant, though it was almost certainly a trick of the light, that the humongous beetle or fly was of some exotic variety – purple, sparkly, and boasting a pair of brilliant violet eyes. He also thought that just before the shoe hit it squarely, leaving nothing but a large smear of glittery goop on the wall, that he heard a high-pitched, "Help! No!"

But of course that was impossible. He was turning as crazy as Eunida. He threw a pile of dirty laundry over the remains, and went back to beating up his pillow.

\* \* \*

Later that day, Feltus sat at the table and stared at his great-aunt. She had come out of her room for good now, it seemed, and he hadn't yet decided whether to be glad or sorry about that.

There she was, perched on the edge of her chair, odd turban listing to one side, the long sleeves of her voluminous dingy clothes dragging through her food. Sure she had helped him out once, but he still thought she should clean herself up before coming to the table. Now she appeared to have piled on all the dirty clothes in the wash basket, and he couldn't help but look at her with ill-concealed disgust. There was a brown smear of something on her cheek, which he hoped was anchovy paste from the small de-crusted squares of toast she was eating with afternoon tea.

His mother, in full hostess mode, sat at his left and talked animatedly at them about the large garden show she was organizing, "With all the best people, you know." Her mood had once again swung in another direction, and she was determined to be cheerful. Neither Feltus nor the wizened crone really listened to her.

Eunida had her head down and was shoveling as much bread and cake into her mouth as she could, washing it all down with huge gulps of heavily-sweetened tea. Her thin lips were tightly compressed when she wasn't eating, and her eyes darted about like butterflies, never fixing on any one thing for long. And Feltus couldn't stop staring. He found her slightly disorientating and very disgusting. The fabulous stories he had invented in his head about her life – secret agent, assassin, bungee jumper – paled before the reality of her face. What could he have been thinking? She was just some weird old lady.

His mother didn't seem pleased with Eunida's table manners. She cast a worried eye out the window at the Von Doolsings' apartment and demanded that Rose close the curtains. But she had asked for two kinds of cake and the nice bread and shrimps to be served, so that was pleasant and out of the ordinary.

She switched topics suddenly.

"Enjoying your tea, Great-Aunt Eunida? I was hoping you could occupy yourself in your room this evening. I was planning a family dinner, something intimate with just Feltus and his father. We could rent some videos and supply you with a variety of food."

She smiled widely and waited for the old lady to agree. But there was silence, except for some guttural noises and lip smacking.

Finally, Feltus understood the royal treatment. His mother was trying to soften Eunida for reasons of her own. His eyes were drawn back to his great-aunt. Really, it was impossible to look anywhere but at her. Her nose snaked its way down her face. It made at least two acute turns before it came to a hook just above her mouth. Her teeth were long and yellow and so were her eyes, which were also narrow, squinty, and lemon colored like a cat's.

"Hey, she's family isn't she?" he said unhelpfully to his mother, just to watch her squirm.

His mother's smile slipped a bit. She was still waiting for an answer from the old woman. She twisted her napkin nervously before saying brightly, "So it's settled. How nice. And will you be staying much longer, Great-Aunt Eunida?" Her voice was beginning to sound strained, and a little tic jumped at the corner of her eye.

Feltus had never seen his controlled mother in such a nervous state. Great-Aunt Eunida lifted her face from her plate.

"Few days more. Week," she rapped out. Her eyes bulged and she forced her hands into her mouth. There was an odd sort of groaning sound. "West Nile virus on the rise. Iff noffle bean," she said around clenched teeth. She shoved her napkin into her mouth as well; her cheeks swelled like a wrinkled chipmunk's.

"Is she your aunt?" Feltus asked his mother. "Or Dad's?"

"The relationship is distant, but she's always been around. Dropping in and out without any warning," replied his mother, not really answering the question. He could detect no resemblance between them, but he knew that families often varied greatly. His own nose, for instance, didn't appear on anyone else's face, although he had scoured the dusty photo books on the hallway bookshelf for traces of resemblance.

"I don't remember ever seeing her at our old house," Feltus remarked.

"She came once. Just after you were born," his mother continued in a lower voice. "She vanished without a word in the middle of the night, and the guest room was left in shambles – bedding thrown everywhere, stacks of books and papers, dirty linen in piles. Your father wouldn't let me throw anything away, and I had to spend days boxing it all up and carrying it to the attic. It was a horrid nightmare." She cast a look of loathing at the old woman.

"Eunida Van Melderel is welcomed everywhere!" his great-aunt said magnificently with a flourish. She had spit out the napkin to speak and it lay in a sodden mass on the tablecloth.

His mother left soon thereafter.

Feltus sat staring. *What on earth is wrong with this old*

*lady?* To his horror, she followed him when he got up to leave the table. He impolitely and unsuccessfully tried to wave her off, but she stuck to him like a leech.

"I have homework to do. A lab experiment involving explosives. There's a corn on my big toe I have to trim. Nose hair removal! Can't you bother someone else? The fat dog?" he pleaded.

But she followed him anyway. Outside his room, she squatted on the floor. Swathes of material billowed about her plump body, and her elbows and knees stuck out sharply like the legs of a grasshopper. Her eyes followed him about the room, but she didn't make a sound. He watched her watching him, and he felt frozen in one spot until at last, she broke her gaze. Her mouth pursed and she looked down at the floor.

Trapped between the faux oak trim was another small tuft of fur. Even from across the room, Feltus could see the fur's bright color. She leaned down, picked up the tuft, and held the vivid red hairs between thumb and forefinger.

Feltus decided to ask her point-blank.

"Do you know what those are? Do you know where I've been? What I've been doing?"

She remained mute and Feltus had a sudden impulse to shake her. Violently.

"Are you sick? Demented?" he asked, getting straight to the point. He was standing near the door and figured he could close it quickly and then lean against it until she went away.

She shook her head "No." Her mouth turned down at the edges. He thought there was something plaintive about her now. When she got up she looked like a battered old doll, all fluff and wire. She left, her scarves dragging along the floor behind her, and Feltus closed his door thankfully. After considering things, he shoved a chair under the doorknob.

Feltus hated to admit it, but he felt sorry for his old relation. It had suddenly occurred to him that she might not be insane, but rather possessed or under some curse. Rose, for instance, believed that Eunida was relatively normal and worth listening to. Besides the exploding seaweed scenario, Rose had also told him that Eunida always seemed to know what was for dinner while Rose was still figuring it out in her head. Circumstantial, perhaps, but interesting all the same. Feltus decided that it might be worth looking into, especially since he could make no progress on the prophecy until RinMal's return.

Upon further consideration, he removed the chair from under his doorknob. Another surprise encounter with his great-aunt would at least liven things up a bit, and maybe he'd get an angle on exactly what it was that the old lady was up to.

# Part 2

## Feltus Ovalton
## & the
## Magical Ewe

# CHAPTER 7

## The Plot Thickens

"DID YOU HAVE a nice day, Karen?" Feltus's father asked at dinner, serving spoon poised above the green beans. Feltus would have suspected him of humor if he didn't already know that his father rarely made jokes. This was the first time in a while that his parents had exchanged words in front of him at the table, and Feltus was beginning to give up hope of getting any more hints about what Eunida was doing here. If anything, his parents seemed even more clueless about their visitor than he was.

"Bill, I think we need to make some decisions." His mother looked meaningfully at the old lady who sat to her right, happily stuffing her mouth with sprouts, mushroom gravy, and a dollop of butterscotch pudding. The remains of half a roast chicken lay scattered all over her plate and the surrounding white tablecloth.

Feltus observed his mother with interest. Maybe he'd find out some stuff about his great-aunt from this conversation. Under the table, his hand – pen at the ready – was poised over the notebook he'd decided to record Eunida observations in. "What kind of decisions?" his father demanded irritably, lowering his paper and turning to her. "I thought we had decided on the paint. The purple and green, wasn't it?"

"'Damson Plum' and 'Sea Foam,'" she corrected. "But I was talking about the other thing. The topic of last night's conversation."

"And I thought I had made it clear that that was your decision. If you don't like it, then ask it to leave."

"That would be very rude. I was hoping that you would do it."

"It doesn't impact me. I don't care if we have half a dozen relatives living with us, as long as I can get my work done." He shot Great-Aunt Eunida a glance. She grinned sunnily back at him. There were green flecks between her teeth.

"How is a man supposed to eat with all this rigma-role?" he asked.

"What about the impact on your son?" Feltus's mother said desperately. "He could be corrupted – all of this eating in bed, raiding the refrigerator after we've all retired for the night, consuming the entire chocolate cream cake that Rose prepared specially for the Association."

Feltus had discovered the cake in the pantry earlier that afternoon and had not lost the opportunity to stick his finger in and scoop out a portion. Apparently his great-aunt hadn't been able to resist it either. He was glad that his small crime was erased by this larger violation, and he couldn't help but feel some respect for his great-aunt's appetite. Right now, for instance, she had licked her plate clean and was still looking around for more.

"Nonsense," his father stated. He shook his head and applied his attention to his dinner. His mother stifled a half-hysterical sob, and Feltus took advantage of the opportunity to wolf down a second helping of potatoes.

"Toiletries. Buy low. Sell high," Great-Aunt Eunida murmured and then motioned with her steak knife toward the rest of the chicken.

Feltus's father's eyes gleamed speculatively. "Inside tip?" he asked, putting down the *Financial Times*.

"Ya ya ickkkkk," Great-Aunt Eunida answered. "Floop, slippery steps, whoopsie daisy," she continued, wielding her fork with emphasis and jabbing it toward Feltus's nose before attending to the new round of food heaped on her plate. Feltus wrote down her words phonetically. Perhaps some sense would become apparent later.

After dinner, in his room, he did try to work out a meaning, but mostly the combined letters just sounded like someone throwing up – except for "slippery steps." That part almost made sense. By the time he turned the light out, his brain was frazzled.

\* \* \*

The next day Feltus overslept. He figured it was the amount he'd eaten at dinner trying to make up for all the evenings he went hungry rather than sucking down kidneys and tofu and curried parsnips – all those mashed potatoes and slices of roast chicken had sent him into a catatonic state. He got to school halfway through morning assembly. He earned a scowl from Mrs. Pidgeon, but thankfully no more than that, and was able to slide past her and out of the auditorium with the stream of other students. A pretty good start to a school day that was only going to get worse – he was sure of it.

On his way to Art from an uneventful French lesson, which they'd spent going over the conjugation of *être* once again for Harold's benefit, he rounded the corner to his locker – then skidded to a halt. Jimmy and Rusty were leaning against the lockers in an intimidating manner. Fortunately, neither of them were looking in his direction, but he had to backpedal quickly to avoid Jimmy's pale gaze.

*Where to go?* he thought, zigzagging his way down the hall. There was only one place he could think of.

Feltus ran into the bathroom, hurried into a stall, and sat on the closed seat of the toilet, tucking his feet up and sliding the bolt shut. The bathroom door opened a moment later, and to his dismay, he realized the voices he was hearing belonged to Rusty and Jimmy. He desperately wished they would go away. He knew they would love to find him. There was that matter of his lunch money that was way past due. He would have handed it over, no problem, but yesterday, distracted no doubt by Eunida, his mother had forgotten to give him his weekly allowance – money she intended for his mid-morning snack and a carton of milk, but which he used almost entirely for comic books and sometimes a candy bar from the newsagent on the way home. He didn't mind going hungry, especially since his stomach was in knots all the time at school anyway.

He clasped his arms around his belly and tried to ignore the fluttering of fear. Right now, he figured, they were hoping to catch him or some other poor sucker on his way to class. It was only a matter of time before they thought to check the stalls.

He tried not to breathe. So far, this day was shaping up to be one of the worst ever. He'd been in such a hurry to get to school that he'd been halfway there before he'd even remembered that this was supposed to be a special day. Unsurprisingly, his parents had forgotten it too. When he said goodbye, his father had been long gone and his mother had barely looked up from her desk.

*My twelfth birthday and I'm spending it stuck in a toilet! My life is so pathetic.*

The porcelain was cold against his legs, and his bottom was falling asleep. He rubbed his knee where he had hurt it falling down the slick stairs in his rush that morning. It felt as if the skin was drawn too tight across the bone. His book bag was an increasing weight on his neck and shoulders, and he began to feel that if he could not move, he would scream. He gently eased it off his shoulder and onto his lap, avoiding the gigantic bruise that was blossoming on his leg, and stifled a groan.

He heard the sound of the bathroom door opening. Leaning forward quietly, he put an eye to the crack between the wall and the door. Could they be leaving? A timid voice said, "Sorry." Feltus recognized Percy, that teacher's pet.

Percy, besides having an unfortunate name, was also cursed with a delicate build. He tried to exit quickly, but Rusty was already blocking his way, his arms hanging loosely (*like an ape*, Feltus thought), his large hands slightly clenched. Jimmy leaned over Percy, his arm resting heavily on the smaller boy's shoulders, which bowed under the weight. The fluorescent lighting emphasized Percy's pallor and Jimmy's odd eyes. Jimmy whispered softly in Percy's ear. For a moment, with his thick, blond curls flopping down over his face, Percy reminded Feltus of a large PoodleRat. Feltus winced in sympathy, although there was no way he was going to interfere. He'd been in that same position too many times and was narrowly avoiding it now. He didn't like Percy anyway. The kid was a pain.

What happened next was inevitable, the conclusion predetermined. Percy's book bag went into the sink, and Rusty turned on the taps full blast as he held Percy's wriggling body effortlessly in one arm. He made a quick maneuver, and then Percy was upside down, being shaken methodically. There was a musical tinkling as coins began to hit the floor in a steady stream. Jimmy picked them over. "Shake him again," he said. "There must be some bills in there as well."

Rusty pulled Percy's pockets inside out. They were empty. "I'll check his blazer pockets."

Sure enough, Rusty uncovered a fat wallet stuffed with money. "*Ohhhh*, look what your Daddy gave you!" he taunted.

"Must be guilt money for running your mother off,"

Jimmy added with a venomous smile.

Percy cowered in the corner. He was making a valiant effort not to cry, but Feltus could tell from the trembling of his lower lip that he was close. Jimmy shoved the cash in his own pocket and waltzed out of the bathroom, shaking his finger at Percy in a warning fashion. Feltus sighed silently in relief as Rusty lumbered after him.

Percy pulled his drenched bag out of the sink, swabbed it futilely with paper towels, and picked up the small pile of pennies Jimmy had not bothered with. "My logarithms!" Feltus heard him moan. Behind the metal door, squatting on the toilet seat, Feltus rolled his eyes. That was precisely what was wrong with Percy! He actually cared about math and homework and everything that made school so dull.

When Feltus heard the bathroom door open and close, he climbed down from his perch, flung the stall door open, and ran down the hallway for the last fifteen minutes of his art lesson. Fortunately, Jimmy and Rusty did not take Art, opting for Landscape Gardening instead, which allowed them to sneak off into the woods and try to start fires. Even luckier, Mr. Ringley lived in some perfect world of his own creation and hardly ever bothered to come down to earth. Feltus slipped unnoticed into his seat and tried to look as if he had been working on his sketch for the full hour. The subject, he noticed, was grapes. Again.

After he wrapped up his sketch, he made sure his bag was packed and that he was ready to leave five minutes before the final bell. Jimmy and Rusty never bothered to chase their victims. They knew precisely where they could find them and had all the time in the world to do so during school hours. When the clanging began, Feltus was already out the door, speeding toward the street and safety.

For some reason, fortune was suddenly favoring Feltus today – he'd successfully avoided them. But he knew his luck couldn't last.

The apartment was quiet when he got home. He ran immediately to peek under the dining room table, but felt his heart fall when there was nothing underneath but the grocery bag of food he'd left that morning before he rushed out the door. *When is RinMal going to return?*

He scuffed his way to his room, purposely leaving black rubber tracks on the linoleum, tossed his bag on his bed and then wandered into the kitchen. Rose was trimming radishes. A neat pile of salad fixings was stacked in front of her. Feltus grabbed a bagel and a jar of peanut butter. "Folks out?" he asked thickly around a sticky mouthful.

She nodded assent. "Your great-aunt is here though. I heard some peculiar noises coming from her room a while ago, but she wouldn't let me in. Why don't you bring her a cup of herbal tea and some shortbread?" She indicated a tray on the counter.

He picked it up and turned to go.

"And Feltus," her voice drew him back. "Happy birthday."

He grinned shyly and walked down the hallway with the tray. When he got to the guest room, he pushed through the door, for once not bothering to knock, and peered through the gloom and into the bedroom. He saw that his great-aunt had draped the windows with lengths of gauzy black material. What light came into the room was muted and dappled and made Feltus feel as if he were underwater. He placed the tray on her bedside table and was peering into the birdcage, trying to make out its contents in the darkness, when a grunt behind him made him jump.

His great-aunt was sitting on the corner of the far side of the bed. Her legs, clad in stripy tights, were drawn up under her chin, and there appeared to be something sticking out of her head.

"I brought you some tea," he said. "And cookies."

Moving closer to her, he realized that the protrusion was a TV antenna. She had duct taped it onto her scalp, fastening it under her jaw. She looked at him morosely from under beetling brows, her mouth firmly shut.

Drawing a little closer, he noticed that the antenna was dangerously close to the electrical socket. Surely this couldn't be safe. He made a move toward the plug and instantly she was on her feet, bristling. He left the room hurriedly. *Old loony! There is something seriously wrong with her!* But as odd as she was, and as much as she scared him, he just had to find out what was going on!

* * *

The few days following his birthday seemed to pass in a frenzy of peeping around corners and loitering outside his great-aunt's bedroom, straining to make sense of the noises she occasionally uttered. His notebook was almost full of strange words, but only a handful of them made any sense. He wasn't even sure that she was speaking a known language. What could she mean by "sprocklite" for instance, or "squashed pixie," not to mention "catapult," "fusion," "salt cod," and something that sounded like "derryel loochi"? He found himself no closer to solving the puzzle. And he'd heard nothing from the PoodleRats, although he faithfully left bags of food under the table that were usually gone within a day. He tried not to worry too much, but he couldn't help feeling anxious when the last food bag had stayed under the table for almost two-and-a-half days before it was collected. He was further concerned that the slightly moldy odor given off by a loaf of bread might alert his parents, and he decided that from then on he would only pack non-perishables.

He didn't understand why RinMal couldn't pop in for

a few minutes, just to say hi. He admitted reluctantly to himself that things must be truly horrible down there and that all the PoodleRats must be preoccupied with basic survival and have no time for social calls. *They must be living under siege*, he thought. And that was the fear that kept him from going back down the port hole. He was sure he couldn't face the Kehezzzalubbapipipi again.

Feltus kept the prophecy with him always, but he'd begun to almost hate the words. *Why on earth hadn't that old PoodleRat just written what he meant instead of hiding his meaning in a jumble of words that made no sense?* The other day in math class, while seated far away from Mrs. Pidgeon's eagle eye, he read the biscuit, which he held under cover of his desk, and he'd almost burst into tears. The words "All hope is lost" had conjured the image of RinMal's quivery nose and fluffy tail.

To keep his mind off the PoodleRats and the gnawing suspicion that he was a coward, Feltus applied himself ever more strongly to the enigma that was his great-aunt. Yesterday, before school, he had brought her another cup of tea and tried to hang around afterward. She'd kept her head turned to the wall and refused to look at him. It had sounded as if she were chewing on her tongue. And she appeared to be wearing a hairnet filled with mashed potatoes.

He rushed home that afternoon to check in on her and found that the hairnet had been replaced by the familiar teetering aluminum foil bonnet. Eunida never said a word these days, but he fancied that her eyes were a little softer when they lit upon him.

He took the opportunity to dawdle about the room a little, stalling for time. She'd never let him stay for so long before. Usually she threw a slipper at his head, although once it had been the potted African violet from the guest bathroom. She was a good shot and that one had hurt.

He glanced over at her and saw she was watching him.

Her beady eyes glowed sulfur yellow in the half-light, and reflections bounced off her headgear, but she still hadn't raised her throwing arm. He brazenly walked over to the birdcage and threw the cover aside. In it, looking like a deflated basketball, was the biggest toad he had ever seen.

"Winston," Eunida said. "He likes marshmallows."

"I don't think we have any," Feltus replied, dying to see the monstrous toad eat. He racked his brain for something else to offer. "We do have French yogurt – with cream on top. Would he like that?" He offered it even though he knew it was his mother's favorite treat and was strictly out of bounds. She had a special shelf in the refrigerator marked clearly with typed labels.

A curious shriek rose from the toad's jaws and Eunida nodded abruptly. Feltus ran with great excitement to the kitchen, grabbed the yogurt, and ran back to the guest room.

Winston made an awful mess of the yogurt. His mouth was easily as big as an anglerfish's, but his thumbs were just too clumsy. Feltus held the pot for him, averting his eyes. Eunida was sitting on the floor with the foil wrapped around her head, and her posture seemed almost relaxed.

"Poor Winston," she said. "He was so hungry." She smiled, and dozens of wrinkles appeared around her eyes.

Feltus decided that this was the time for answers. All of a sudden, his great-aunt was practically garrulous.

"Are you a witch?" Feltus asked, eyeing her long, black cobwebby dress and narrow-toed shoes.

She cackled long and hard and, wiping the tears away, answered pointedly, "No."

Feltus stood waiting for more, and after a long moment she relented, patting the floor beside her.

"I never could abide your family – nasty, grasping folk – but you smell different. There's something about you, although you were a pestilent brat of a baby the last time I saw you. Witch! I'm no witch, but perhaps I've run afoul of one. My sensors are out of balance, just plain fizzled out and I can't control *it* anymore. The foil gives temporary relief. Potatoes did nothing and I got a horrible shock from the antenna."

"What is *'it'* exactly?" Feltus asked. He sat down, grimacing as he bent his bruised knee, and swiveled to face her. Winston sat happily in his cage, busily licking the yogurt off of his back. His head could rotate almost 180 degrees, Feltus noticed with horror.

"My gift. Of prophecy, of course. I'm a soothsayer and my sooth has gone south. Absolutely no anticipating it. No warning. I'm apt to say anything. It's a danger. To myself and to you as well."

"How could it be dangerous? People will just think you're odd. I did," Feltus admitted.

She looked at him under hooded brows. She had a slight mustache, he realized. "Normally, I'm able to extend my sensors peripherally and exclude unwanted signals from worlds beyond the Veil, but the way things are right now, I'm like a giant sponge sucking up everything around me for miles and miles. On my way here, I was followed by a large group of businessmen because of an ill-considered remark about the stock market that I made outside a bank. They became hostile when I refused to say anything more about surplus Styrofoam supplies. I think I may know some people who can help me, but I'm afraid to go by myself. Anything could happen!"

She sniffed loudly and blew her nose on her sleeve.

"There are people who can help you? Are they nearby?" he asked.

"Just a hop, skip, and a jump away, dearie," she replied with some vigor. "At least, so I've been told," she added. "I do have very specific directions, in any case." And she pulled a crumpled, torn piece of paper out of her pocket and waved it under his eyes.

It appeared to be a map of some kind, though there were no street names and all the directions were in some foreign language that looked like hieroglyphs. The only two things he could make out were the picture of a dog in the middle of a crossroads and a signature in gold ink that said "Dare Al Luce."

"What does it say?" Feltus asked.

"They are 'Instructions for Those Who Have Lost Their Way.' I am to meet a certain individual in order to receive aid," she said.

The script shimmered before Feltus's eyes and he felt as if the air had warmed somewhat. "Who is this dare al loose person?" he asked.

"Dare Al Luce (da-ray-al-loochay)," Eunida corrected, "is one of the Patrol and is inclined at present to give aid."

It occurred to Feltus that he owed her a favor for covering for him with his mother, plus it would distract him from the PoodleRats and the prophecy. The other day he'd felt so frustrated that he almost tossed the prophecy into a Dumpster at a construction site.

For these reasons, he decided to be brave. "I'll take you then. Tomorrow after school," he said with much more confidence than he felt. Her bushy eyebrows lifted in surprise and her hands trembled slightly. Feltus left the room before she tried to hug him or anything equally ghastly.

* * *

At school the following day, the minutes ticked by so slowly that it seemed as if the school clocks must be running backward. As Mrs. Pidgeon droned on and on about algebraic equations, Feltus looked around the class. Harold had fallen asleep with his mouth open. From the looks of things,

Greg Williams was about to wake him in an unpleasant way – possibly involving a lot of spit and a rubber beetle. Percy was sitting up front taking copious notes and listening avidly. He looked paler than usual.

Percy was the only student who enjoyed math and the only one who seemed to understand it. Feltus couldn't see the point of math as a class when all he needed to be able to do was produce the correct change at the store. *Maybe it comes in handy for that electronics club Percy is involved in*, he thought idly. Every sign-up sheet posted around school had Percy's meticulous signature on it. Feltus figured that Percy had put his name down for lots of clubs so that he could stay late after class. It was another black mark against him as far as Feltus was concerned. Most normal students, including the bully contingent, left school behind as soon as they could each day.

To his right, he could just make out the bulky shapes of Jimmy and Rusty. He looked at them under his eyelashes – it wouldn't do to make eye contact with either of them. He sensed that his brief reprieve was almost over and pretty soon, they'd come looking for him again.

The two bullies were making slingshots out of rubber bands, paper clips, and thumbtacks. Rudimentary, but effective. Feltus rubbed the sore place on the side of his neck where a tack had hit him in History. He'd yelped so loudly that Mr. Gruber had given him detention. Feltus hated the sour teacher, and he'd compounded his punishment by sassing him and calling him "potato tuber," a nickname he'd thought was especially witty. It wasn't so funny now that he was scheduled to spend Wednesday after school cleaning blackboards for hours and hours.

At least he wasn't going to be hauled up before Miss Montmorency. The last time she'd sent a note home, he'd had to suffer a nightly lecture from his mother about his behavior and was forced to study Dr. Evelyn Proctor's *Guidelines for the New Millennium: Ground Rules for Raising Good Citizens from a Pool of Disenfranchised and Disaffected Teens and Pre-Teens* before bed. It had given him nightmares for weeks. Dr. Proctor was an avid supporter of the "Big Three" – the belt, the cane, and the cellar (or closet, for those who lived in apartment buildings). Feltus had an intense dread of Miss Montmorency – she was the one who had supplied his parents with the book.

The only good thing about having detention was that Jimmy and Rusty would be long gone when he got out. This happy thought was sustaining him when the bell finally rang. He dreamily packed up his bag, joined the mad dash to the door, and walked straight into the open and waiting arms of Rusty.

"Where ya goin' in such a hurry, Smeltus? Ya didn't think we forgot about you?" Rusty drawled, taking the opportunity to pinch Feltus's arm until the neurons screamed in outrage. Jimmy was lounging against the wall; his face was an unreadable mask. Usually Jimmy spoke with a coldness that sent shivers up Feltus's spine. This time, however, his tone was almost mild. "You owe me for two weeks. I want it all by tomorrow morning," Jimmy said.

Rusty gave Feltus's arm a final, vicious tweak and pushed him away.

Feltus, wondering how he was ever going to amass that kind of money, was about to walk out the school doors when he noticed that the two of them now had Percy backed up against his locker. Jimmy had his mouth right next to the blond boy's ear, and Rusty was methodically crumpling a sheaf of papers with his boat-like boots. As Feltus inched his way past them, he heard Jimmy say to Percy, "You will do this for me. I know that brain of yours is good for something."

"Yeah," Rusty chimed in. "Or I'll smash you." He

pounded his fist against the metal locker door next to Percy's head. A stack of books fell inside with a loud thud.

"What if I get caught?" Percy asked. "Some of the teachers are going to be pretty suspicious."

"You won't," Jimmy replied. "But if you do, you're on your own. Just get me all the assignments before they're due and remember that you'll need to cause some kind of disturbance so that the science exam is cancelled."

"I'm already working on it," Percy muttered.

Rusty thumped the lockers again for emphasis.

Feltus had heard enough. He didn't want to know what evil Jimmy was up to, especially if it involved cheating. He couldn't believe that Percy was letting himself be strong-armed into helping them pass.

Feltus now had more than enough to worry about, and he was deeply regretting his stupid offer to accompany Great-Aunt Eunida on her outing. Who knew where he'd end up? It could be a séance, a drum circle, a new-age potluck, or something even worse.

# CHAPTER 8

## Weak Tea and Stewed Chitterlings

WHEN HE GOT home, Great-Aunt Eunida was waiting for him in the downstairs lobby of the apartment building. She was bundled up in a coat that appeared to be made of brown paper bags. An oversize woolen cap was pulled down over her greasy-looking hair, and Feltus caught a glimpse of shiny foil underneath. She held a spindly umbrella under her arm, and a leather bag was slung over her shoulder. Feltus eyed it suspiciously. She put a finger to her lips.

"Winston. Mini-hibernation. He's much more than a regular toad, but he's still subject to nature's rhythms. I just hate to go anywhere without him."

"*Mmm.* Are you sure you're dressed, *ahhh*, warmly enough?" Feltus could not believe he was going out in public with someone who looked like an animated heap of rags and trash.

"Absolutely," she exclaimed, flashing him a wide smile. "I have my umbrella, and look," she reached her hand into a large pocket and pulled out something shiny. "My emergency supply of aluminum." She returned the roll of foil to her pocket. Feltus tried to push his worries to the back of his mind and concentrate on the journey ahead.

They exited the building and made a right turn. Feltus attempted to walk slightly behind his great-aunt as if they weren't together.

Eunida seemed to navigate purely by luck. At first they

just made a big circle around the block, and she seemed surprised when they ended up in front of the building again. She looked up and tracked the flight of a flock of pigeons. "Rain," she said under her breath and then headed across the road. Feltus had to trot to keep up.

Every once in a while, she stopped and examined a leaf on the road or the twisted branch of a sycamore tree silhouetted against the bleak sky. An array of broken glass that spread across their path occupied her attention for a full five minutes. She took no guidance from street signs, indeed didn't even glance at them. Instead she operated by inner compass, or by voices only she could hear.

For what seemed like an eternity, she stood motionless in the middle of the street. A taxi careened past her, the driver angrily gesticulating out the window, but she didn't move until she saw a Jack Russell terrier going about its business a little farther down. "Dog," she murmured with satisfaction.

They turned down a dark and dirty street that Feltus had never noticed before. It was lined with buildings with boarded-up windows and doors hung with "Condemned" signs. And it was littered with garbage. It felt colder than it had been on the main road they turned off of, and none of the streetlights appeared to be working. He pulled his thin jacket tighter around him and turned the collar up.

Great-Aunt Eunida continued on in front of him, moving from one side of the street to the other. Her head was down and she seemed to be looking for something on the ground. At last she stopped, kneeled, and brushed some dead leaves aside. Feltus, coming to stand behind her, could see nothing on the ground but some faint chalk lines.

"This is it!" Eunida proclaimed triumphantly.

She hitched her skirts up, baring bony legs and the usual stripy-stockinged knees. Feltus looked around, embarrassed, but the sidewalk was deserted. Inching closer, he could make out the ghost of an old hopscotch game. His great-aunt was standing on the first square.

"Well, come on then. Don't dillydally!" she said crossly.

He stepped into the box, trying to avoid contact with her coat. A moldy, fungal smell rose in wafts from her body, and there were bits of fluff and matter caught in her hair. *Is that a piece of apple?* He stood rigidly, arms crossed in front of his chest, as she prepared herself.

"Follow directly behind me and mimic my movements exactly. We're going through the Veil, so you may feel a bit strange, as if you're falling. All right?"

She gave him a whack on the chest with her umbrella. "Let's go. Pay attention – you don't want to get caught halfway between this place and the other. First a hop." She suited action to word, looking like a bulbous brown frog. "Then a skip. And finally a jump." On the word "jump" there was a flare of golden light, and she disappeared in wisps.

Feltus hurriedly copied her and was momentarily blinded by another flash of light. When his eyes cleared, he saw his great-aunt directly below him, only a few feet away, in a kind of zero-gravity free fall. Around him was nothingness. He was falling through the air, but he felt no sensation of movement, no air current, no change in temperature.

He paddled his arms frantically to catch up with Eunida and barely kept himself from grasping at her filthy sleeve like a little kid. She gave him a thumbs-up, and suddenly, shockingly, he felt firm ground beneath his feet again. He staggered and almost fell. Eunida patted his hand absent-mindedly and adjusted her hat around her ears.

Directly in front of him, an island in the midst of rubble and mildewed newspapers, he saw a derelict storefront. A rickety sign, depicting a woebegone sheep with wings, read *The Magical Ewe.*

Behind the smeared glass of the window, Feltus

glimpsed a display consisting of a few limp toilet paper roll sheep, some clumpy cotton-batting snow, an angel made of toothpicks hanging from a piece of wool, and a worm-eaten plastic jack-o'-lantern. This despite the fact that it was already the end of May.

"Where are we?" he mumbled, pulling his thin coat more tightly around his chest. A bitter wind howled down the street and he could feel it deep in his bones.

"We're here, of course," Eunida replied. She was looking in her bag at Winston, a small smile curving her lips. "Sleeping like a baby," she said.

Her smile vanished as quickly as it had appeared, and she eyed Feltus with disapproval. "Well, what are you waiting for?" She jerked her head toward the shop's grimy glass-fronted door.

He was starting to feel just a little bit annoyed. He pushed open the door with more force than necessary and walked headfirst into a curtain of wind chimes, setting off a cacophony of discordant bells. It certainly made a racket, allowing Great-Aunt Eunida to enter somewhat surreptitiously. She stood at a distance from him as if they weren't together, worrying her umbrella between bony fingers.

Inside were tall, rickety bookshelves crammed with a collection of cast resin figurines – mostly angelic children and animals, all wearing a thick coat of dust. The books were falling out of their bindings, pages torn and crumpled. A series of placards were nailed haphazardly to the walls – "Fear not the falling leaf" said one, and "Rancid butter will not a waffle make" another.

A casual grouping of café tables and small wrought-iron chairs provided seating for a motley assembly of people. Feltus supposed it must be a restaurant of some kind; the smell of burnt toast hung in the air. He stared unabashedly at a woman as stick-like and multi-jointed as a praying mantis, who sat hunched over a plate on which small black things crawled and twisted.

Two other women, one dark-haired, one fair, stood behind a counter. They were in the middle of a heated argument when Feltus and his great-aunt entered, but they stopped yelling to glare rudely at the new arrivals, mouths half open. One mirrored the other, Feltus noticed, and as they moved toward the center of the room, he realized that they were joined together, possessing four arms, two waists, and one pair of muscular legs clad in black bicycling shorts.

"What is this place?" he whispered. "Bookshop, coffee shop, or freak show?"

"It is a place outside of place," Eunida answered "Extra-ordinary as opposed to intra-ordinary."

"Strangers!" the brunette announced.

"No. They've been here before. I served them. Remember it clearly. Brownies and tea," said the blond forcefully.

"You're crazy. Your brain is like a sieve. I don't know why I bother with you. We haven't had brownies for years. Ever since the cocoa fiasco."

"*Ahh*. Too true, too true. Bad beans," the other admitted, nodding sagely. In accord for the moment, they extended their arms to the newcomers.

"Come, sit," they said in unison, motioning to a table in the middle of the room.

Feltus and Eunida sat somewhat tentatively, and Feltus resolved not to eat anything. On one side of them, perched on a stool much too small for it, was a gigantic rabbit, and across from it sat a tall, theatrical man wearing a cape and top hat. The rabbit was looking unhappily into a large bowl that appeared to be full of tapioca pudding. The man noisily slurped tomato soup from a cup, his white-blond mustache stained red. With his free hand, he shuffled and reshuffled a pack of cards. They fell in a steady torrent of faces and suits, and each time, the Queen of Spades turned up on top.

He turned his eyes toward Feltus – they were such a light blue that they appeared to be silver, and his eyebrows and lashes were frosted and almost invisible. Such glacial chill emanated from him that Feltus would not have been surprised to see ice rimming the table. The man in the top hat turned his attention back to the deck of cards that was fanned out in front of him.

"Five card stud, one-eyed Jacks wild," the magician proclaimed in stentorian tones. The rabbit nodded and tossed a red leather bag onto the table. It jingled faintly.

"Rabbits are very poor card players," Eunida said in a low mumble. "And worse gamblers. I made billions off of them in my day."

"Isn't that, like, cruelty to animals or something?" Feltus said.

Eunida snorted and rapped him over the knuckles with her umbrella.

The twins stood waiting.

"You'll have tea," the blond said.

"You'll have coffee," the brunette said at the same time.

"I'll have my usual," Eunida said and dismissed them with a wave of her umbrella. They walked back to the kitchen bickering acrimoniously.

His great-aunt had fallen into a glum silence and Feltus took the opportunity to look around. The mantis lady was eating, shoveling her food into her mouth with hooked fingers. He averted his gaze.

Behind him, he could sense someone or something. He turned. From out of a shadowed corner, a long leg encased in plaster gleamed. The person attached to the leg was difficult to see.

Feltus rubbed his eyes. It was like looking at a blanket of fresh snow in full sun, as if – he? she? it? – drew the light and then reflected it back one thousand times the strength. He could make out long ropes of platinum hair and flowing robes that rose high over its shoulders in graceful arcs.

She – Feltus decided that something so beautiful must be feminine – stood in one fluid motion, barely favoring her hurt leg. Her hands were made of snowy marble, and her eyes were as blue as the midday sky in summer.

"Bobbie, Sue," she sighed in a voice that was like a warm breeze. "Sugar water, please."

The sisters rummaged under the counter, clanking pots and pans, and reappeared with a tray, on which was arranged a sugar bowl, a flagon, and a kettle, all of polished silver. They set it down in front of the shimmering apparition, who decanted the water into the kettle in a silken cascade. Steam rose from the mouth of the kettle instantly, and she poured the boiling water into the cup with the sugar. She stirred it languorously. Every motion she made was precise and perfect. He could have watched her forever.

*Dare Al Luce*, a voice breathed in his head. He sat up straight. *The writer of the directions – it must be!*

She looked right at him and he found it impossible to tear his eyes away. Feltus made an odd little bow, remaining seated and bending from the waist. A melody like the caterwauling of junkyard cats interrupted Feltus's reverie. With a start, he remembered his great-aunt. She was hunched over, head lowered, crooning a discordant lullaby into the satchel that held Winston. The sound was ear-piercing. While he'd been engrossed in Dare Al Luce, the old woman's food had arrived – a pungent concoction that brought a sea of bile to his mouth.

"Are they here?" he asked, mostly to get her to stop singing. "The ones who can help you?"

Great-Aunt Eunida shrugged. "Maybe. Maybe not. Bobbie and Sue used to arrange things, or so I hear. They've received the plea. Now it's just a matter of time."

She poked at her food. Feltus thought, though he couldn't be sure, that it was a root beer float made with oatmeal and whipped cream and came with a side of sardines.

"The person over there," he said, pointing in the golden creature's direction. "She's the one who gave you the map?"

"Yes," Eunida said and gave him an amused look. "*He* does penance in this place so he can one day return to his rightful environment. Once he has been judged to have completed his task, he will be able to return home. He has helped me with mundane affairs in the past."

She raised her cup briefly to Dare Al Luce in acknowledgement. "Close your mouth, Feltus. Have your ideals of feminine beauty been shattered?"

Feltus sensed that his ears were burning red with embarrassment.

She relented. "In their world, questions of gender are deemed unimportant. Try to think of him as you would a snail."

Feltus tried to digest this for a minute.

"What could *he* have done," Feltus asked with difficulty, "to deserve such a punishment?"

"The Patrol has its own code of honor and its members must follow the rules," she remarked, and then resumed her contemplation of the tabletop.

Noting his curiosity, she unbent a little. "In Dare Al Luce's case, perhaps it was rebellion, or perhaps a simple fall from grace. He does not always like to do what is expected of him, or so I hear."

Feltus looked again at this entity and couldn't imagine anything further from a snail – he looked like an angel. Feltus resolved not to look over in his direction again, if he could help it.

"Is he a guardian angel?" Feltus asked, thinking he'd

quite like to have one as tall and powerful looking as Dare Al Luce.

"Absolutely not," Eunida replied. "The Patrol has no jurisdiction over, or indeed any great interest in, the inhabitants of different worlds. Dare Al Luce *is* different though." She looked around and lowered her voice. "The story is that his injury came about because he fell out of a tree while trying to help a stuck cat. He probably thought it was a cute little furry thing." She frowned. "Cats are insidious creatures. He would do well to stick to what he knows. "

Feltus remembered what Saldemere Og had said about the Patrol. "The Patrol kind of watches over the Veil, right? They make the rules."

"How do you know that?" she asked.

"Lucky guess."

Eunida shrugged. "The Patrol deals with anything and everything that pertains to the Veil." She was stirring sardines into her float and bits of shiny skin had floated to the surface.

Feltus scrambled for something to distract himself from his great-aunt's foul beverage. "Can you explain the Veil to me?" he asked. Perhaps if he could understand how it worked, he'd be able to apply the information to the prophecy and the PoodleRats' situation.

"Nothing to explain, really. It's always been there."

"But is it a wall of some kind, a barrier, a force field, or," he thought desperately of what he could remember from his geography classes, "the outer crust of another planet?" His head had started to throb.

"The old onion theory? Worlds within worlds?" Eunida said. She upturned the sugar bowl onto the scratched Formica tabletop and drew a finger through the crystals. She roughly etched out a large circle, then added smaller circles that intersected through it and each other. She added more and more until the patterns were obliterated. Feltus started to get the same confused feeling he often got in Math.

"Yes, there are other worlds, other realities, but they exist inside their own dimensions, only occasionally occupying the same space as other worlds. The Magical Ewe is such a place. Here," she tapped the messy pile of sugar. "Here is where the folds of the Veil overlap. And there are other approved crossing places for travelers like myself.

"Normally," and she shot him a hard stare, "everyone stays inside their own worlds and things proceed in an orderly fashion. It's like having a gigantic window between two rooms that's securely fastened on both sides. Only a fortunate few can even see it, much less see through it."

"But I can see it," he said.

"Yes, but it seems impossible," she proclaimed, removing her straw from her float and using it to noisily suck up the sugar.

"You can't say it's impossible if it's been happening!" Feltus said, feeling the stirrings of anger.

She coughed. "Transmigration *is* possible, I suppose, if the Veil is no longer holding true." She scratched her forehead, leaving it shiny and sugary. "I remember reading something somewhere about a breach, but that was centuries ago, so why would it be happening again now?"

"What's transmigration?" Feltus whispered, thinking of the huge flocks of Canada geese that descend on the tiny neighborhood park in the spring. He'd already guessed the answer – it must have been how the Kehezzzalubbapipipi had entered the Grand Gewglab Forest, but he had to hear it said out loud.

"Travel between worlds of course. There's a delicate balance that cannot be disrupted. Ever. The Veil is like gravity. It keeps things up and it keeps things down, or rather inside and outside. There are laws that govern it. I'm a trifle hazy on the details.

"I sense a rupture and I've been looking, but so far I've found nothing. With my sensors so overloaded, I find it difficult to narrow my search."

"Do you think he is here looking for the breach?" Feltus jerked his head in Dare Al Luce's direction.

"Without a doubt," Eunida agreed. "The Patrol monitors all aspects of the Veil. Even though he's here working off some kind of penance, the integrity of the Veil must be his first concern."

Talking to Eunida made Feltus rethink his attitude toward her. Maybe she was off-kilter, but who better than a crazy person to figure out the craziness that had suddenly become his life? He decided he could trust her.

"You do know about the port holes under the dining room table and kitchen sink," he said nonchalantly.

She fastened her gaze upon him.

"PoodleRat port holes?"

He nodded.

"I *knew* the Veil ran through your apartment!" She thumped the tabletop, sending sugar flying. "Have the PoodleRats been concealing themselves from me?"

He nodded again. "I wasn't sure you were completely trustworthy, so I didn't want to tell you."

"And yet they confide in you? Interesting. The port holes are approved doorways though. They wouldn't register with the Patrol. Have you noticed any other places in the apartment where entities have entered?"

"No. It's just been them and you. Did you come to make sure the Veil was okay or something? Maybe that's what brought you to our home."

"I came because your parents' apartment was the safest place for me while my gift was out of whack. I thought it would be uneventful and safe and I'd be protected from this bombardment of prophecies. Instead there's been an almost unbearable barrage." She sipped from her cup. Feltus could smell the sweet fishy odor and it made his stomach churn in a truly unpleasant way.

"There was also a vestige of something," she continued, "buried in the middle of all the other shouts I've been receiving and seemed like it could have been a cry for help. And I finally pinpointed that it came from the environs of your home." She fixed her gaze on him. "Do you need help, Feltus?"

"I don't think so," he muttered. Too much was happening all at once and he found it baffling.

She raised her bristling eyebrows at him, and after a moment continued. "Once I arrived and felt the weaknesses in the Veil, it occurred to me that that was the reason for all the messages I've been receiving – the Veil is not keeping anything out, and the volume is so great that I am unable to block it." She drained her glass and wiped the froth from her upper lip with the hem of one of her numerous petticoats. Afterward she lapsed back into silence and it appeared that their conversation was at an end.

Feltus was beginning to feel antsy. The chairs were uncomfortable and for some reason, the thermostat seemed to be turned to greenhouse humidity. He felt hot and sticky. His little *tête-à-tête* with the old lady had raised more questions than answers – above all, *why oh why* was this all happening to him? It made him feel extremely disoriented. He decided to hurry things along if he could. He got to his feet, peeling the back of his thighs from the vinyl seat cushion, and carefully avoided the more peculiar customers as he made his way over to the counter. Bobbie and Sue were whispering in the corner, apparently having a difference of opinion regarding a startling centerpiece constructed of cacti, gold-painted Styrofoam balls, and a collection of very sharp kitchen knives.

"My great-aunt. She's ill. I'm afraid for her," he said to the women as he leaned against the glass countertop with what he hoped was an ingratiating smile. They stared at him.

"The message has been sent. Just sit and be quiet," Bobbie snapped as Sue looked at him with pity.

Sue beckoned him close and whispered in his ear. "Don't mind her. She never knew her mother. I'll send over some nice stewed chitterlings and fried banana bread in a moment. Just the thing for a growing boy!"

"Nonsense. Pressed duck liver confit and raspberry syllabub. Good for the bones," countered Bobbie, giving him a boisterous shove toward Eunida.

Feltus sat down again and went back to shifting in the uncomfortable iron chair. His great-aunt had her greasy head resting on her clasped hands. He thought he could hear a gentle snoring emanating from her, but it could have been the usual incoherent muttering. The rabbit at the next table had perked up a little, and there was a small pile of coins in front of him now.

Dare Al Luce was sipping his drink with a clever device that attached to his mouth and mimicked a hummingbird's beak. Feltus stared with interest; it really was quite ingenious how it adhered without visible means.

Bobbie and Sue had delivered the promised food and it reached far higher on his nausea scale than expected. He had no idea what pressed duck liver was supposed to look like, but he'd imagined something brown and meaty. What he received was cleverly molded into the shape of a watchful rabbit, had the consistency of jellied putrefied mud and sat in a pool of reddish brown liquid. It smelled like Lafayette's dog blanket. The chitterlings were small, burnt, fatty lumps, and gave off a pungent aroma that made his eyes water. He used his fork and spoon to move the piles around his plate, wiped his mouth occasionally with his napkin, and hoped that Bobbie and Sue were less observant than his mother.

A pop and a whirring sound by the back door heralded a new arrival. It was a compact gentleman, clad in a green metallic waistcoat and a shiny black overcoat, and carrying a small attaché case. After adjusting the monocle he wore screwed into an eye, he clicked his way over to their table. Eunida straightened up from her slump and ran her hands over her hair.

"Are you my five o'clock?" he asked, peering at them. "I'm Doctor Shafer."

He had startling eyes, Feltus noted, like his mother's jet earrings. And there were four of them, squinting simultaneously. He had three pairs of arms as well, although two of them were neatly tucked into a wide sash that tied around his waist. He removed some papers from his bag and thrust them at Eunida.

"Sign here. Here. And here." He indicated each place with a flourish of all six arms and handed her a fountain pen.

"And now. Let's have a look at you." He held Eunida's head gently in a pincer grip and turned it back and forth. "Open your mouth and say *ahhh*," he instructed. "Follow this light with your left eye exclusively. Interesting." He turned the small flashlight off and scratched an orbital ridge over the uppermost eye reflectively.

"Complete absence of dampeners. And you say this happened weeks ago? How have you maintained your sanity?"

"She hasn't," mumbled Feltus under his breath.

Dr. Shafer packed up his bag. "I'd like to conduct some further tests. Were you going home soon?"

Feltus stood up quickly. He could feel the imprint of the hard metal seat etched into his bottom, and his shirt was stuck to his back with sweat. He was ready to leave. The praying mantis lady had ordered another plate of wriggling things, and he didn't think his stomach could bear to watch her eat again.

Feltus left his confit on his plate without much dismay. Eunida nodded, grunted, and heaved herself to her feet. "I would like to go home. My float has not agreed with me. I think I am too worn down with care to enjoy it properly." She leaned heavily on Feltus's arm.

Bobbie and Sue kissed him goodbye, stroking his hair and pressing small pink cupcakes into his hands. Feltus rubbed the moist kiss spots from his face with the back of his sleeve and tried to keep the distaste from his expression.

Dr. Shafer tapped his toes and glanced at his watch every few seconds while the farewells were being said, and eventually called in a loud and impatient voice, "This way. Come, come," and indicated a door behind the front counter.

They went through the door and made their way slowly to the back of the coffee shop, where behind some empty cardboard boxes, packages of paper towels, and dozens of immense jars of "Mayo-naze – Just Like the Real Thing!" was a small turnstile. Feltus followed Eunida's crooked back through it, and Dr. Shafer brought up the rear.

As the turnstile clicked around, he felt as if he were pushing his way through molasses – his legs seemed unattached to his body and he had to concentrate on putting one foot in front of the other. There was an awful moment when he couldn't tell if he were right-side up anymore. Once the dizzy spell had passed, he found himself on a familiar street a mere block from home.

The doctor had somehow become taller. His extra arms were camouflaged by a lurid waistcoat striped in black and scarlet that stretched over his round belly, and his two visible hands were encased in pristine white gloves. He wore a pair of wire-rimmed spectacles, a bowler hat, and a short-haired graying wig that concealed two of his eyes. He still made a whirring noise when he walked, as if encapsulated wings were beating away, but his shoes were lovingly polished to a high sheen, and Feltus hoped that no one would notice the sound effects.

They passed no one on the street, which was fortunate, as the doctor stopped every few steps to examine things he found curious. Since his interests spanned everything from a mailbox to a telephone directory to a discarded, broken video cassette recorder, their progress was slow.

"And you say that written communication is conducted by way of this box?" the doctor asked Feltus, his voice echoing eerily as he stuck his head close to the open letter slot of the mailbox. "It seems archaic even for humankind."

Feltus was trying to explain e-mail and telephones to him when he was interrupted by Eunida's hollow groan. She had dropped her umbrella and was clasping her head in apparent pain.

The doctor scanned the skies as if they contained an answer. His tone became brusque and businesslike.

"We should get her inside immediately," he said, snapping his fingers at Feltus. "I do not like to get wet."

Great-Aunt Eunida had fastened one hand around Feltus's forearm with some force, so it was through clenched teeth that he said to Dr. Shafer, "It's that way." He indicated the stairway and front door to the apartment building, which was only a few yards ahead.

"1401-C," he yelled at Dr. Shafer as the doctor rushed ahead. Feltus hurried to catch up with him as he hauled his great-aunt's mostly inert weight along the sidewalk. He felt the first droplets of rain hit his head as he tried to heave Eunida up the marble steps.

Once inside, he found the doctor paused in contemplation of the elevator buttons. He reached past him and pressed the upward-pointing arrow.

"Listen," he said quickly as they exited on the third floor. "My mother doesn't like strangers. And she doesn't like Eunida either, for that matter, so try to keep the talking to a minimum and be polite. Maybe you can pretend you're a visiting professor from the school."

"Pretend?" Dr. Shafer said, lifting a few eyebrows.

"She doesn't like things out of the ordinary either," Feltus added desperately, trying to find his keys and retain his grip on Eunida, who had lapsed into lethargy.

It appeared that he had left his keys on the desk in his room, and he dreaded having to explain this all to his mother. When they first moved, she had insisted that he wear them on a string around his neck. He had eventually stopped because the jangling he made when he walked alerted every bully within a two-mile radius that he was near. Now he'd have to put up with that "I told you so" expression of hers that he loathed so much.

He gently pressed the doorbell. When his mother opened the door to his knocking, the look on her face was stern and skeptical. Her gaze swept over the three of them, lingered with distaste on Eunida's slack face, and examined the doctor from the top of his hat to the polish of his shoes.

Dr. Shafer clicked his heels together, removed his hat with one smooth motion, managing to straighten his toupee at the same time, and extended a gloved hand to her. "*Enchanté, madame*," he said smartly.

She held out her hand with a dazed expression on her face. He kissed the top of her hand with a loud smacking sound. Feltus looked upon all this with disgust. The doctor was nothing more than an educated, supernatural bug, but his mother seemed entranced.

She ushered them into the hallway and then into the sitting room without even asking Feltus to remove his shoes. She carried the doctor's hat and neatly folded gloves as if they were treasures, and laid them carefully on the coffee table.

Feltus pushed Eunida into the nearest chair. She collapsed without a murmur.

"The doc's an old friend of Great-Aunt Eunida's – from Paris," he said. "We ran into him, *uhh*, downtown, and he thought they could come here to catch up."

"Fine, fine," his mother replied. "We'll have tea, shall we?"

"He's probably hungry too," Feltus said, sensing an opportunity.

His mother soon returned with the teapot and a serving platter cluttered with teacakes, sugar, and cream. She surrendered it all with a grateful smile when the doctor jumped to his feet and relieved her of it. "Such perfect old-world manners. And such a lovely accent. I always wanted to learn another language," she admitted with a shy smile. "One of the Romance languages, preferably."

"Oh, yes. *Les langues romantiques*," the doctor said, rolling his eyes and making smoochy sounds.

Dr. Shafer sat knee to knee on the small sofa with Feltus's mother, with his teacup carefully balanced, discoursing on hematomas, roses, and common garden pests. From time to time, he sprayed her with a small shower of toast crumbs.

"Oh, Doctor Shafer," she breathed. "You're so knowledgeable! I must get you involved in our garden show. Perhaps you could chair a panel?"

"Yeah, maybe a talk on the dung beetle," Feltus suggested, glaring at the doctor.

Eunida sat eating crumpets soaked in butter and honey and grumbling to herself. "All the time in the world! Ixsterioscoposirisis. I'm perfectly comfortable, thank you." She poked a long finger under the foil cap and scratched her scalp furiously. Her tight shoes were pushed off, and she brought her right foot up to eye level where she could examine a bunion that was forming.

Feltus's mother turned away from the horrifying sight and addressed herself to the doctor.

"You'll stay for supper, I trust? I'll send out."

The doctor had already put away a loaf of bread, a substantial quantity of cream and crumpets, and about a vat of tea, from what Feltus could tell. His waistcoat was beginning to gape, and from time to time, he stifled a belch. Feltus's mother appeared not to notice, although normally she had preternatural radar for that kind of thing. All during tea, she had eyes for no one else, not even for Rose, who ran around setting places and organizing warming pans, and folding napkins into exotic shapes.

When his mother and the doctor finally raised their heads from the fascinating discussion they were having about the gardens at the Louvre, the dining room had been transformed. His mother, escorted by Dr. Shafer, led the way to the table, and Feltus and his great-aunt brought up the rear. Feltus's mother had ordered all the candles to be lit, including the massive candelabra that hung above the table. The curtains were thrown open to reveal the stormy indigo sky, and small tea lights floated in brass bowls with hibiscus and magnolia blossoms. A gold tablecloth dazzled the eye.

Dishes were filled with all manner of delicacies: roasted, flambéed, and braised meats running in juices; vegetables julienned; shrimps butterflied and swimming in lemon-scented sauces; custards and aspics; jellies and creams; and for dessert, fine puff pastries, and heavy fruit-studded cakes. All the best courses from the delicatessen down the street.

"*Ahhh*, vegetable matter and animal matter served at one sitting. How glorious!" the doctor exclaimed, rubbing his hands together as they all sat down at the table. The doctor shot his cuffs, arranged his coat tails behind him, and took the seat at the head of the table.

For Feltus, it was a very tedious meal. His mother monopolized Dr. Shafer, filling the doctor's ears with society names and gala events, and interpreting his monosyllabic grunts as compatibility. Dr. Shafer was engaged in heaping his plate with as much food as it could hold – puddings mixed with greens and pork, brandy sauce with sweet almond paste, and salad dressing. He paused every once in a while to swallow huge glasses of wine and seltzer water.

Eunida withdrew to her bedroom after she had piled her plate with cream-filled vol-au-vents and thick, dripping slices of rare roast beef. Feltus's father, who arrived halfway through dinner, was involved in the hostile takeover of a small hospital called Our Lady of the Beneficence, so his cell phone rang intermittently throughout dinner.

"Go for the jugular! Bury them!" he yelled, mortifying Feltus's mother, who quickly turned to Dr. Shafer and said, "He's very committed to charity. We attended six balls only last month."

The doctor patted her on the arm and applied himself to the peanut butter custard tart. His eyes twinkled greedily behind their thick spectacles, and he readjusted the napkin tied around his stubby neck.

Feltus, as usual, was ignored. He belched loudly – no response – and slipped from his chair. He went to the guest room and, getting no answer from his knock, pushed through the door.

Eunida was sitting on the bed, sadly spooning whipped cream into Winston's gaping maw. The empty pastry shells lay scattered on the carpet next to a crumple of foil. The toad looked as if he had some kind of illness – his rubbery skin was patchy and peeling in places. And Feltus noticed that he was eating without his usual gluttonous enthusiasm.

Feltus pointed this out to Eunida. "He's sloughing. Every three years or so he sheds his skin," she explained.

His great-aunt wasn't looking healthy herself. Her hair was plastered to her head, her face was long and forlorn, and her eyes were swimming in tears.

"Eastern seaboard deluged by storm," she sobbed. "Presidential impeachment a certainty. Blork! Blork!" A tear rolled slowly down the length of her nose and hung there, glistening. Feltus could see his face and the room behind him reflected in it.

Winston finished the last of the dessert and moved toward the steak piled on the floor of his cage. Feltus turned his head – he had no wish to watch a giant toad consume oozing meat. The windows were open, and a fresh breeze stirred the flimsy drapes and brought the smell of the rain to his nostrils.

Eunida had pulled a hundred feet of foil off a new roll and was occupied with winding it around her head. The metallic turban teetered like the Eiffel Tower.

"Are you going to be all right?" Feltus asked.

Eunida shook her head dumbly.

"Do you think it's this bad because the rift in the Veil thing is somewhere around here?"

She made a sound that was clearly an affirmative.

"And the foil doesn't keep all the voices out?"

She gazed at him with wet eyes.

"How can we find out where the breach in the Veil is?" he asked abruptly, helping her wrap the foil more tightly. She was swathed in six or seven layers from her eyebrows to the crown of her head. He molded the hat around her ears so it would hold firm. She accepted his help docilely. The aluminum barrier seemed to be working again.

"I mean, we can't go door to door. And wouldn't it be on the news or something?" he asked.

"This is not something that concerns normal people," Eunida said with as much dignity as was possible to muster while wearing a metallic pyramid. "It is far above the notice of most downward gazers. In fact, there must be more of my blood in you than I had originally thought, otherwise you wouldn't have noticed anything either." She looked at him with approval.

"It hardly seems possible after all these weeks," she continued, "but I've had no luck finding a clue to the Veil's whereabouts. And I've looked everywhere and have done everything – including a little creative forced entry where required. Did you know that this insipid apartment building sits on a crossing of six or seven folds of the Veil? Very rare.

"Did you also know that, besides being a very nasty and suspicious person, your neighbor Mrs. Fontana kidnaps cats off the street and forces them to submit to bubble baths before releasing them? However, her apartment, which I checked while she was at the store stocking up on antacids and kibble, contained nothing more than a very old and very spiteful ghost who may be responsible for her terminal bad humor."

Feltus had thought that Mrs. Fontana got all her enjoyment in life from being unpleasant.

"You haven't been snooping in my room, have you?" Feltus said suddenly.

Eunida's eyes gleamed. "I can't cross a threshold I haven't been invited over first. Mrs. Fontana had me over for milky lukewarm tea when I had just arrived. Turned out she just wanted to complain about your mother."

Feltus decided that Fontana was due for another nasty, multi-legged special delivery through her mailbox.

Although he quite enjoyed being mean to his mother, he had an almost territorial attitude about it, and Fontana had definitely trespassed onto his turf.

"I know the rupture is somewhere in this vicinity, but I

can't poke around with this almost incessant volley of information filling my head," Eunida continued.

"Did Dr. Shafer ever tell you his plan?" he asked.

"Between courses, he said he would conduct a further assessment after dinner," Eunida replied dully.

"How do you know he'll be able to help? Did Dare Al Luce send for him?"

She nodded. "Dare Al Luce made no promises, but Shafer is well-regarded in the community."

There was a sudden tremendous clap of thunder. The windows were blown shut with a clatter, the lights flickered off and on, and lightning illuminated the room briefly. A knock on the door followed immediately and it swung open.

Dr. Shafer stood in the doorway, a dark shadow outlined by the brilliant flashes rocketing across the sky. He approached Eunida, who looked at him unfavorably. His gloved hands were sticky, and he needed to wipe his mouth. Oily crumbs and leafy bits dotted his chin.

"Well, well, well. Let's get to business, then." He took a seat, waistcoat creaking as it bulged over his rotund stomach. "I've been giving this some thought, and the only solution I can think of is trepanning."

Feltus, Eunida, and Winston looked at him without comprehension.

"I will bore into your skull and relieve the pressure that is obviously responsible for your discomfort."

He seemed to wait for the light of understanding to shine in Eunida's eyes. She stared steadily back at him. He removed his gloves and unfurled a long, barbed digit on each hand. "I will use these to drill through the cranium. It is a relatively simple procedure, quick and painless."

Eunida got to her feet and scuttled backward like a horseshoe crab.

"I prefer the malady to the cure!" she shouted. "Come

stand behind me, Feltus. Away from that ... that ... butcher!"

"You silly woman, you are overreacting! Once I penetrate your skull, I will merely stir the contents lightly, and *voila*! You will be as good as new."

"Out! Out!" Eunida screamed. "Before I set Winston on you!" Indeed, the toad was sitting up on its haunches and an ear-piercing bugling was coming from its mouth.

Dr. Shafer left the room in a hurry and Feltus slammed the door behind him. "Perhaps I could come back tomorrow and discuss it over dinner?" Shafer yelled beseechingly.

Feltus helped his great-aunt into bed, propped her up with pillows, and fetched her a soothing cup of tea and some digestive biscuits. Winston settled down to the remnants of his beef, and after waiting until Eunida's posture had relaxed and she seemed calm enough for sleep, Feltus went to his room.

His brain was buzzing. He felt as if he'd never used it as much as he had been lately. First the PoodleRat problem had occupied his every waking moment, and now there was Great-Aunt Eunida's trouble to worry about too. He promised himself that he would dedicate a serious number of hours to finally getting a grasp on the prophecy, but he admitted guiltily that without RinMal or Saldemere's faces in front of him, it was easy to let the time pass.

The good thing was that he hardly ever found himself worrying about his parents anymore. He didn't hang on his father's every word or try to decipher his mother's mood. He didn't feel as if he were holding his breath all the time and walking on eggshells.

But he couldn't help feeling dismayed because the second time he'd tried to help someone with their problems, he'd failed yet again. Eunida was still messed up. And he'd been so sure that Dare Al Luce and the doctor could help her! It had been a complete waste of time – *Time*, he thought with a little guilt, *that would have been better spent figuring out the prophecy*. Instead he was no closer to solving it, and as long as Eunida was suffering from her ailment, he'd be stuck with her and her weird moods, strange smells, and insatiable appetite.

In the immediate future he still had the little matter of the money he owed to Jimmy to worry about and still no idea of how to get it. Tomorrow was likely going to be another one of those painful days.

He grabbed a well-worn comic book from his stack and curled up under the covers with it, escaping into a world that was comfortingly familiar.

# CHAPTER 9

## Percy Disposes

THE STORM RAGED all night. In the morning, Feltus looked out his window and onto a world that was clean and washed. The streets, scoured of stains, steamed under a butter-yellow sun and each leaf shone as if it had been waxed. He felt his heart lift. What was the message in all his comic books? *Persevere and triumph.*

When he brought his great-aunt her morning tea, she too had brightened visibly. She patted the bed beside her and he sat down on the edge. Splashing sounds came from Winston's birdcage. "Semi-annual bath," she said, dumping a package of saltines into her tea and stirring it with a finger. She had tied a pink scarf loosely around her scrawny neck, and her hair and foil were mostly concealed under a wide-brimmed floppy hat.

"Any day that does not involve a trepanning procedure by an oversized insect is a good day," she said. "Oh, and by the way. Thought you might be needing this." She handed over an extremely dirty handkerchief.

"Oh, I don't think so. Thanks anyway."

"Take it. Take it," she beseeched, thrusting it into his hands. Inside was a wad of money and an old hairpin.

"That's right, isn't it?"

He counted the money and nodded.

"I thought so." She seemed very satisfied. "Some of us are aware of your problems, you know."

Feltus was pleased, but embarrassed. "What are you

going to do today while I'm at school?" He remembered he had his Gruber detention after class. "I'll be late getting home."

"I might check the basement for gaps again. Wouldn't mind running into that doorman, Peter, either," she murmured. "I like them good-natured and not too bright. Like cows, you know. Nothing more eager to please than a cow.

"And," she sat up straight, "Winston needs his loofahing, salt rub, and honey wrap. That could take all day."

"Well, enjoy yourself," Feltus said, folding up the money carefully and sticking it into his pocket. He felt armed. If Jimmy and Rusty muscled him for the cash, he could hand it over right away. He almost hoped they would, just so he could enjoy the look on Jimmy's face. He'd always paid with coins in the past – loose change he'd found between the couch cushions or at the bottom of his mother's purse. Paying with bills meant he was moving up in the world.

He whistled a little tune as he went to the kitchen to get his lunch, smiled at Rose, and kept the grin in place even when he discovered that his lunch this week was some kind of eggplant, carrot, and textured-protein stew.

Outside, the air smelled clean, and the sun warmed his face. Sure there were problems at home, but in his pocket, he now had a solution to his school troubles. It was as if a third of the battles were won. It was the teeniest battle of the three, but something nonetheless.

It was amazing how much relief he felt from not having to worry about Jimmy and Rusty anymore, even if it only lasted for a week before the next payment was due. He'd discovered that a lot could happen in a week.

When he arrived at school, he noticed there were small puddles of standing water in some of the school hallways where rain had seeped under doors. As Feltus made his way to his locker, someone slammed into him from behind, and he almost fell to the slippery floor. He turned and looked into Rusty's smirking face. Rusty prodded him in the side, but kept going, moving down the hallway like an armored vehicle. Rusty then ran smack into Percy, who had his head in a book as he mouthed French conjugations.

Feltus watched everything unfold in slow motion. Percy went one way, his bag went the other. The bag flew open and papers and books spilled everywhere. Rusty just continued on his way, as unfazed as if a mosquito had just landed on his arm. Feltus touched the skin around his ribs and winced. He decided he would hand the money over only if it were demanded of him.

By some rule of unfairness, most of Percy's papers fell into the wet patches on the floor and instantly sucked up moisture. Ink spread and fanned out, and reams of carefully researched and presented work were ruined. Feltus got up off the floor, walked over to the puddle, and picked up a few pages that had floated to the ground by his feet. They were diagrams of what looked like electronic gizmos.

Feltus recognized some of what he was looking at because of the shop class he had taken last year at his old school. He understood at least enough to realize that the devices were similar to CB radios or walkie-talkies. One diagram had elaborate wiring charts and sketches of proto-types for electrical conduits. Heavily underlined in the margin were the words "Human brain waves???"

"Excuse me!" Percy said as he snatched the pages out Feltus's hands.

"Hey, lighten up," Feltus responded. The guy was wound too tight. It did occur to Feltus that maybe if he'd been friendlier with Percy, he could have asked Percy's opinion about the Eunida situation. Unfortunately, Feltus despised the guy, and besides, he could never trust Percy to keep his mouth shut about it. If the school ever found out about Feltus's weird great-aunt, it would be all over for him.

Then it would be the end of any chance he had to blend in.

As Feltus turned toward the stairs that led to the second floor where his geography class was located, he noticed that a soggy piece of paper had stuck to his shoe. He picked it off, standing awkwardly on one leg, and turned it over. It was a different diagram. This one showed the wiring of what looked like an electronic door opener attached to an alarm clock. In another picture below, Percy had drawn a wire mesh cage complete with white mice, like the ones they kept in the science labs, and a detailed sketch of the cage-locking system.

Feltus wasn't sure what Percy was up to, but he thought it would be worthwhile to hang onto this small piece of incriminating evidence. He folded it carefully and put it in his back pocket.

The rest of his day was uneventful and, miraculously, he didn't see Jimmy. He saw Rusty once more at the end of the hallway during a break between classes, but the bully was too busy shaking down poor Ashton Aushinclosser, the kid with the lisp, and was oblivious to anyone else. Perhaps he was going alphabetically, in which case Feltus was safe for a while.

By the time Feltus got out of Art, the school was quiet and practically deserted. He'd spent a little extra time working on the ink drawing he was doing of Winston. After about half an hour of concentration, he'd thought that he'd managed to get the warts on the toad's back exactly right. All that practice shading grapes had really come in handy.

He wandered down to the history classroom where Mr. Gruber was packing up his papers. The remains of his lunch were on his desk: a small container of canned baked beans, some apple juice, and a stalk of wilted celery. It was pretty apparent that old Tuber lived by himself.

"You can start here, LeRoi," Gruber barked, pointing

to the dusty blackboard behind him, "and work your way around. And no skimping. A good teacher, err, needs a clean slate."

Feltus stood silently while the teacher closed the clasp of his scuffed leather satchel with a *snap* and eased his long, skinny arms into a plaid jacket with torn seams across the shoulders. Mr. Gruber always had on at least one item of clothing that needed sewing. Feltus found himself feeling just a twinge of sympathy, but that faded when Tuber shot him a look of irritation and growled, "Well get to it, LeRoi. They're not going to clean themselves."

When Feltus was finished wiping down the last of the blackboards, he found the school in near darkness, except for the greenish light coming from the science lab. He peered through the door and saw Percy bent over a desk. He held a welding torch and a pair of wire clippers.

"What are you doing?" Feltus asked, perhaps a little too loudly. Percy jumped.

"I'm *allowed* to be here," Percy said a trifle irritated, throwing an oily rag over a bundle of red and white wires and a collection of parts salvaged from an alarm clock. "What about you? Scrubbing the bathroom floor? Working on your ABC's?" He hadn't known that Percy could be so sarcastic.

"Detention. Blackboards," he said suavely.

Percy didn't look happy to see him, but he didn't tell Feltus to leave either.

"These are receivers. I'm trying something new with natural magnetizers. Wiping the memory chips clean, then reloading them with information – " Percy paused. "If you can grasp that." He bent over his work again.

None of this meant anything to Feltus, but he was suitably impressed.

"Looks complicated," he offered.

Percy was obviously up on all the new gadgetry.

Feltus's hands-on knowledge of communication systems began and ended with two plastic cups attached to a long piece of string. He wondered again if Percy could help find the answer to his great-aunt's predicament. Could he risk it?

He figured that if Percy turned into a snitch, he could blackmail him with the piece of paper in his back pocket. Or, of course, he could bribe him with the money Eunida had given him. Or he could jump Percy after school some day and hit him a few times.

"Listen. I have this homework, and you're in advanced physics, so maybe you know the answer," Feltus said.

Percy grunted.

"Say you had a receiver and it was, umm, getting messages from all over. Like, a ton of them. Is there a way that you could decrease the number of, *ummm*, hits? Block some of them out?"

Percy was fusing a tiny piece of wire to a receptor cap, but when he spoke he sounded mildly interested. "You could dismantle the electrical device and then reset it so that it could only decipher signals that were at a certain frequency – like a radio. Set the dial to the frequency you wanted to hear. Now that's an intriguing scenario. In fact, it's in line with what I'm working on now – receivers and radio signals."

"Could you do it?" Feltus asked. There was a little bubble of excitement rising in his stomach.

"Yup."

Feltus's mind was racing. How could he get his great-aunt to the school? He could phone her, but his mother was sure to answer. Could he get Percy to come home with him? But then he'd have the same problem of avoiding his mother. She liked to have visitors to the apartment front and center where she could keep her eye on them, and he was still on probation after yesterday's escapade with Eunida.

His mother may have been smitten by Dr. Shafer, but that didn't mean she was happy with Feltus. As usual he'd had to endure a lecture about forgetting his keys and leaving the apartment without her permission. Also, he wasn't sure that Percy would agree to come. It wasn't as if Feltus had ever been friendly to the guy, and he'd recently watched with everyone else as Rusty gave Percy a beating.

Feltus tried to paste a smile on his face. "So, you know what college you're going to?"

Silence.

"Those half-year exams were a killer, huh?"

Cold stare.

"You like hanging out at school, I guess. Nice and quiet." His voice trailed off.

Oh, how he wished he could get a message to Eunida!

There was a static drone rising from the box on the desk in front of Percy. He twiddled a couple of knobs, adjusted a wire, and suddenly music filled the room. Percy seemed pleased with himself.

"The first one of these I built got its juice from a potato. Same basic principle, but that music you're hearing now is being broadcast from outer space."

Feltus tapped his fingers to the erratic beat. He was impressed – it was pretty catchy. But all he could think about was his great-aunt. If he could only get Eunida and Percy together, maybe science would prevail where magic had failed.

Feltus's blood was beating in his ears, and his palms were sweaty. He was wondering if the potato chips he'd gotten from the snack dispenser at the end of the school day had been tainted with some strain of bacteria, when he felt a kind of a flare behind his eyes and the room turned upside down. Just before the world went dark, he had the sensation of flying with a host of winged beings.

Far below him, the Veil shimmered and twisted. He saw it meander through places of light and dark, until his eye could no longer perceive it. Then he felt a feathery touch on his arm, his wings failed and he fell into the dark, blue depths of Dare Al Luce's eyes.

He came to and found himself flat on his back in the dark classroom.

"Whoa," Percy exclaimed. "That was really cool. You fainted."

"I didn't faint," Feltus said groggily. "I just passed out for a moment."

"Semantics."

"Hey, I didn't faint!" Feltus replied, suddenly aware that if Percy spread it around school that he, Feltus, had collapsed like a girl, then he might as well run away to the circus now.

"Don't worry about it. I won't air your little secret." Percy bent back over his work again, a small smile on his face.

Then there was a loud sound as if a cork had popped, and Eunida appeared abruptly by the door, clutching a half-eaten muffin in one hand. She was wearing a housecoat, washing-up gloves, and fuzzy slippers. Her foil hat was on lopsided, and her mouth was half open, as if she had been plucked away between one bite and the next.

"Harakkkkk! Plague of locusts hits the Midwest. President ousted in landslide defeat," she said thickly. "Why did you call me here?"

Percy glanced up, raised one eyebrow and then went back to the wires and dials he was tinkering with on the lab desk. Feltus hurried over to his great-aunt. "I was just thinking about you and your problem ... and you came!"

"And then he fell over," Percy supplied, with a smirk.

Eunida made a sound like screeching brakes.

Percy finally looked at her with some interest and rolled his eyes. Then with a shrug of his thin shoulders, he fired up a small blowtorch and bent down to his work. He acted as if odd occurrences were just par for the course. For the first time, Feltus considered Percy's home life and wondered if it was as lonely as his own. He took Great-Aunt Eunida by the arm and led her forward.

"Percy," he began.

"Yes." Percy replied, not bothering to lift his head. "I'm at a crucial stage. Maybe I can meet your girlfriend later."

"Ha!"

"Mother?"

"Ha ha!"

"Lepidopterist moves into cocoon. Walla walla whoops it up. Hooley booley rarara," Great-Aunt Eunida mumbled.

Percy finally looked up again.

"That scenario I outlined to you – the hyperactive receiver?" Feltus explained hurriedly. "This is it. I mean, it's my great-aunt who has the problem. She's picking up unwanted predictions and signals."

"Well, that's a little different, isn't it? We're talking about a person, not a machine. Is she a psychic?" Percy asked, sounding a bit more interested.

"No, she's a soothsayer. But does that mean you can't help us – I mean, her?"

"Why should I help you? Camaraderie? Basic human kindness?"

"In the interest of science?" Feltus replied hopefully.

"Hmmm." Percy tapped his pencil against his mouth.

"Please, can you fix my aunt? And can you not say anything to anybody at school about this?" Feltus begged.

"Well, I guess fixing her will be a challenge. It'll look good on my college applications. As far as keeping my mouth shut ..." He shrugged. "Who am I going to tell?" He gestured at Eunida's head with a pencil. "She'll have to take her hat off."

Feltus removed the foil cone, and almost instantly Eunida drooped. She stood in some kind of catatonic state, one corner of her mouth trembling.

Feltus hoped it was not too painful for her, but at least she was biddable. Percy indicated a chair, and Feltus pushed her into it.

"You do understand that this is somewhat experimental?" Percy said as he connected some wires to her temples and forehead. He took four highly-polished black stones from his pocket and taped one to the back of her neck, one on each arm, and the last at the base of her throat.

"These are lodestones, which are naturally magnetic. You know how you're supposed to keep credit cards and computers away from magnets? Well this is the same principle. If this works, we're going to remove all the clutter from the portion of her mind that is overloaded, and then I'll reset her to a different frequency."

"If you're wrong," Feltus asked hesitantly, "will she be the same, or will she be a mindless vegetable?" She was crazy already, but he knew somewhere deep inside that it would be wrong to mess around with her too much. Plus, she apparently knew where to find him at all times.

"We'll know in a moment, won't we?" Percy giggled maniacally, and Feltus began to be very, very afraid. Perhaps Dr. Shafer's technique would have been better than this.

His great-aunt had fallen forward in her chair and her feet, which barely touched the ground, twitched uncontrollably. After a long, terrifying moment, during which Feltus racked his brain for a way out if things got really bad, she roused like someone waking from a long sleep, stretched, took a bite of muffin, and looked around the room.

"Who are you?" she asked, looking at Percy. "And

where am I? Feltus, you miserable boy, where have you brought me? And in the middle of the night, too. I was about to go to bed. I was just having a little snack when *boom, whoosh,* and I was dumped here. "

Feltus heaved a sigh of relief. She was her usual grumpy self and somewhat rational too.

"I don't think it was me," Feltus said. "I mean, I was thinking really hard about how to get you and Percy together, and then Dare Al Luce kind of appeared in my head."

"Dare Al Luce? He must have decided you were worth helping in some way," Eunida said. "Taken you under his wing, as it were. Fratcha fratch."

"How are you feeling, Great-Aunt Eunida?" Feltus asked.

An explosive sound burst from her lips. "Yahkoov alt likstat!"

"I don't think all the clutter is gone," Feltus remarked to Percy. "She's still speaking nonsense. But she seems alert and is able to speak some words of sense without her foil cap."

"I haven't finished yet," Percy said with a touch of impatience.

Eunida twisted in her seat, picked up a battery charger, and dropped it with a thump. "So why am I here? It's hardly a seat of higher learning, is it?"

"I thought you could get some help," Feltus said.

"Phase one completed successfully. And now for phase two," Percy said smugly. He hooked the wires that trailed from Eunida to a black box bristling with strands of copper, and turned a dial on one side. "A little left of center, I think." There was a small spark, and twists of smoke appeared above Eunida's eyebrows. A faint smell of burning hair reached Feltus's nostrils.

Eunida scratched her chin thoughtfully. Her eyes gleamed.

"Nothing!" she exclaimed. "It's as if I'm wrapped in

cotton wool! Oh glorious, oh blessed silence!" And she slid off the chair and sat down heavily on the floor.

"Great-Aunt Eunida! Are you all right?" Feltus asked.

"Fine, dear boy. All that weight is gone. The awful burden I have been carrying has vanished."

"Is your gift gone too?"

"No, no, it's just slumbering, curled up like a sleepy cat. Give me a moment to collect myself, and I'll show you." She ripped the wires from her head, picked the muffin up from the floor, dusted it off, and proceeded to eat it slowly, looking around the room with interest.

"So this is your school. What a horrid place. And who is this little worm?"

"Oh, this is Percy. He's the one who reprogrammed you."

"Really? How precocious. I owe you a debt, young man," she said gruffly to Percy. "See me about it next week."

Percy looked surprised and then shyly pleased.

She held an arm out and Feltus hurried to help her to her feet. There was an awful creaking as she got up, but she seemed to be all right. Noticing Feltus's worried expression, she muttered, "Corsets," blushed faintly, and then ordered them to, "Stand clear. Stand clear." Feltus and Percy stood against the wall and watched.

First she licked her forefinger and held it up in the air as if she were testing the wind. She slowly rotated 360 degrees, her finger held up like a beacon. "My sensors! Reception loud and clear!" she exclaimed, and Feltus noticed that little tufts of hair right above her ears were standing up in bristly clumps like quivering antennae. After a long moment, she lowered her finger.

"All I have to say is 'scritchy scratchy little mouse, never leave your safe, warm house.'" She seemed to look with an especially penetrating gaze at Percy as she said this, and Feltus was astonished to see that the blond boy's face had reddened. Feltus thought Great-Aunt Eunida must still be a little bit off. He couldn't imagine what Percy had to do with mice.

"Mark my words," she said as she waggled a finger in front of their noses. "Homework, shmomework." She still didn't make any sense, but Feltus took comfort in the fact that at least she was speaking comprehensible English. He put his aunt's "soothsaying" out of his head. Then, before he and Percy could avoid it, she'd pulled them both into a bear hug. It was bearable, although she still exuded a peculiar aroma – grilled cabbage, perhaps, or fried kidneys. Feltus did not quite know how to thank Percy, so once Eunida had let them go, he settled for a quick handshake and a thud on the back. Then they stood and glanced at each other hesitantly, while their feet scuffed the floor.

"I'll see you," Percy said, picking up his briefcase and packing away his papers. His hair flopped into his eyes and he wouldn't look at Feltus.

Feltus chewed on a fingernail as he watched Percy awkwardly stuffing his things into his bag. He took a deep breath, steeled himself ... and made the monumental decision to be friends with Percy.

"Yeah, see you," Feltus replied.

The blond boy left.

"What an odd duck," Eunida observed. "Seems just like your cup of tea."

"What did you mean about the mouse?" Feltus asked suddenly. It was curiously similar to Percy's diagram. He pulled the crumpled piece of paper out of his back pocket and looked again at the cage, the automatic lock, the timer, and the small white rodents Percy had carefully drawn. "Hey, this isn't just a coincidence!" he yelled. "He's going to release the mice, isn't he? The school installed special cages after the last time someone forgot to lock up." He shuddered at the memory of the small animals hanging from the curtains and swarming the tables in the cafeteria.

"Hundreds of them were running around all over the place. They had to close for a few days." His voice trailed off and he looked at his great-aunt.

"I read 'em as I see 'em," she replied. "Let's go."

She turned and he was about to follow her, when she stopped suddenly and held one hand up to halt him. When she swiveled around to face him, her skin had taken on a ghostly pallor and her eyes were wide.

"I see ... I see ... desolation and despair. A destiny unfolding." She gripped his arm. "And you in the middle of a wasteland strewn with rubble and the bones of PoodleRats."

He unclenched her fingers and watched as the color slowly returned to her face. His heart was racing. "Just because you see it, doesn't mean it has to happen ... right?" he gasped. His breath caught in his throat and he had the same feeling he had when crossing the Veil – lightheaded-ness combined with vertigo, as if the ground had shifted under his feet. "It can be changed still? Right?"

"Of course," she replied, the frozen look replaced with one of kindliness. "Absolutely. The future is not writ in stone. Now come along. I'm hungry and there are things we need to talk about."

* * *

Back at home, they entered a dark and empty apart-ment. Feltus was relieved. He was too tired to think up lies, and Eunida was a mess, even more disreputable-looking than usual. The thought of all the questions his mother was sure to fire at him made him quiver, and Eunida's last prediction had really startled him. Feltus and Eunida parted ways to get washed up, and then they reconvened in his bedroom. He had slipped his pajamas on, as well as the soft terry cloth robe his mother had given him at Christmas after finding out that all the young European royals were wearing them. A coat of arms adorned the chest pocket – crossed hockey sticks and an alert ground squirrel.

Eunida had merely removed a few layers and had scrubbed most of the dirt from her face, although there was still a smear of grime under her ears and around her neck. It looked like the tide line on the beach. She held Winston's birdcage in one hand and a pastry box in the other.

"Well?" she snapped, raising an eyebrow, probably hoping he'd clear a place for her to sit. The only chair held his stack of encyclopedias. Looking at them now reminded him of RinMal.

His bed was piled with clothes, both clean and dirty, and he swept them off onto the ground. Eunida deposited the cage on top of his pillow and made herself comfortable. With a flourish, she then pulled a platter of assorted donuts out of the box. Feltus chose to sit on the floor.

"When you showed up at the school, you said I had called you. Did you hear my voice?" he asked.

"Remember the cry for help I told you I picked up before? It was the same as that. Are you admitting now that it was you all along who was calling? Way back when I first arrived?"

"It may have been," he said grudgingly. "It still sounds crazy to me, but I did do a spell a few months ago, and I wished that everything would change. I might have thrown in some extra stuff about not having any friends and hating it here too."

"How did you make this spell? Found it in the back of a comic book?" she snickered.

"I found it in this weird book that just turned up among all my boxes after we moved." He clambered to his feet, went to his closet, and pulled the binder off the top shelf. As he passed the pastry box on the way back, he grabbed a powdered donut and shoved it into his mouth.

"Give that to me," Eunida said in a serious voice, and got up off the bed. A trail of cinnamon crumbs was scattered down the front of her dressing gown.

"My exercise book," she said wonderingly, drawing a gnarled finger over the embossed letters on the front cover.

"It's yours?"

"Of course, my initials, V.M., are right here – for Eunida Van Melderel. Who else would it belong to? It's from when I was at school – Basic Charms 101. I actually failed the class, but I still maintain it was because I intimidated the professor. He was a horrible old gnome, very nervous around young girls."

Feltus coughed and tried to imagine a youthful Eunida. He failed. She had the kind of face that must have always been ancient. But the school sounded really cool and he imagined how different everything would be if he were memorizing incantations rather than mathematical formulas.

"You don't mean you did one of these?" she said, flipping through the pages.

"Yeah, a simple one. Here, let me show you."

She seemed reluctant to let the book go, but finally relented. He thumbed through the loose sheaf of papers until he came to the one headed "Fpells." "It was this one. I did everything it said and nothing happened."

"Nothing?" she asked, reading as she spoke. She mouthed the words of the spell silently, then she looked up and said, "Feltus, this is an unlocking spell – straightforward, yes, but potent. Could you have left a couple of words out? Mispronounced something?"

"No, it was easy. I still remember it. 'Saritah Pernisox Ottarim.'"

She clapped her hand over his mouth. It was unpleasantly sticky.

Slowly she removed her hand and went to sit back down heavily on the bed. Her face had turned a pastier color than usual. "An unlocking spell. I wonder. Could *that* have caused the rift? Could it have unlocked the mediocre amount of power that you have? If the Veil runs through this very apartment ... an ancient magic ... was there enough pure, selfish will to give it potency? I need time to think." She shut the book with excessive force and tightened her fingers around the binding.

Feltus looked at her with concern. He'd thought she was cured, but once again she was babbling nonsense, although at least now it was in a language he recognized.

"Are you saying that I have magic powers? I mean, you're saying that I'm the reason that you showed up at the apartment in the first place – but I don't remember calling anyone ..."

"Yes, yes, and you definitely got me to the school tonight," she admitted impatiently. "But that might just be because we share blood, and your need was so strong I had to answer it. There are bigger things at stake here," she said with a distant look in her eyes.

"So, I could be a powerful magician!" he persisted.

"No!" she snapped, with a bark of laughter. But noticing his disappointed expression, she relented. "The port holes were always here. The PoodleRats were always here, even though you couldn't see them. You may have a very small amount of arcane blood through your father and me – enough at least to summon me, enough, perhaps, to have caused a rift by casting the spell. But I think it's more likely that it was an inopportune blend of coincidence and magic, and that it has more to do with location than anything else. Right place, wrong person."

She looked at him under shaggy brows. "Oh, what

catastrophe is wrought through ineptitude and plain bad luck," she intoned.

Feltus ignored her. He was overcome with excitement. "But then I *am* magical. I could turn Jimmy into a warthog! I could pass Math! I could have all the chocolate in the world ... and I could save the PoodleRats." He had the grace to blush. "I meant to say the last thing first," he muttered.

"I said small. Negligible. Maybe only enough to add a little extra hair in your ears." She pointed to the crop flourishing in her own trumpet-shaped appendages.

Feltus scowled and punched his pillow. For one golden second, he'd felt in control of his own life.

"It may change. You are not mature yet," Eunida assured him.

"Is that a prediction?" he asked hopefully.

"Take it as you will. I see through the glass darkly." She handed him the half-eaten donut she held, leaned close to the shrouded birdcage, and pressed her lips to the cloth. Feltus heard her say Winston's name but nothing else. After a moment, Feltus left the room, taking a couple more donuts with him. He curled up in the armchair by the window in the sitting room where he could look out at the night sky.

He felt too excited to sleep. For once in his life, he had made something happen. He wasn't really sure what or how, and the ramifications of it were not all pleasant, but he had done it. He himself. Feltus Ovalton.

Hugging this thought to himself, he returned to his room. Eunida had gone, taking Winston and the rest of the donuts with her, except one, which she'd left sitting on his pillow. He lay his head down beside it. He was still lost in thought. Eventually he fell asleep and woke early with raspberry jam and glazed donut smeared all over his face.

\* \* \*

He was thankful the next morning when he found out that somehow all the mouse cages in the science lab had unlocked themselves at precisely two minutes after midnight, and all classes for the day had been canceled. He burst through his great-aunt's door without knocking and threw the breakfast tray down on the nightstand with a clatter. The whole world looked different to him now, and he wanted to know what would happen next.

But Great-Aunt Eunida sat primly next to her packed suitcases. Feltus looked at her in surprise. She was dressed, her usual grubby clothes topped with an overcoat that appeared to be constructed out of PVC vinyl and a burlap bag; she had tied the long, blue satin ribbons of a bonnet in a bow under one ear.

"What's going on?" he asked, staring in surprise.

"I have to go, child. I've dillydallied long enough." Her tone was brusque and she wouldn't meet his eye.

"But you still need to find the rift in the Veil and fix it."

She cleared her throat. "The thing is, Feltus ..." She stopped and cleared her throat again. "The thing is ... I'm not much of a spell caster or a spell un-caster. Winston informs me that I might be a little out of my league. The best thing for me to do is arrange a consultation with the Patrol."

"But can't you do that here? What about Dare Al Luce?"

"I need to go straight to the top," she said, exasperated. "Dare Al Luce has his own problems to deal with and he can't see the whole picture from where he is."

"Oh." Feltus never thought he'd be so sad to see her go. Somehow she had insinuated herself into his life, and he didn't think he could handle the loneliness once she'd left.

First RinMal, now her. He'd be stuck trying to find the meaning of the prophecy by himself.

"Will you come back and let me know what's happening?" he asked. She stopped chewing on a hangnail for a moment to reflect, then said, "Yes." When he asked if it would be soon, she replied, "Sooner than you think."

Feltus nodded and then hauled her bags to the front door. A faint clinking came from one of them, and he wondered if she'd filled it with his mother's silverware.

Once they were in the foyer, Feltus noticed that the sitting room door was open.

"Great-Aunt Eunida is leaving," he announced loudly. His father was hunched over some papers covered in numbers and angry exclamations written in red ink. He grunted a goodbye.

Feltus's mother, who was in the sitting room as well, looked up from her needlepoint. She'd finished the abstract ocean view and was now doing a series of wild animals: zebras on the savannah; jaguars partly concealed in foliage, the dappled light blending with their pelts; a lone lioness. The colors were bright, tawny golds and rusty oranges.

Once she'd finished, the sitting room would be transformed. Feltus wanted to run his fingers over the threads, feel the velvety fur beneath his fingers.

His mother seemed tired as she always did these days, but she gave a little wave.

"Cheerio!" Eunida yelled back at such high volume that Feltus's father dropped his pile of papers, his pen, and his reading glasses.

Feltus followed Eunida's dumpling form to the front door. He glanced at her. "Will everything work out? You know, with them? Me?" He faltered. There weren't enough words to explain what was wrong and how much he wished it could change. His great-aunt's fierce gaze softened.

"It was a pleasure meeting you, Feltus," said a deep, melodious voice from the depths of the covered birdcage.

Feltus backed away, but Great-Aunt Eunida was delighted. "Winston! He must like you. Normally he's a toad of few words."

She pressed an envelope into Feltus's hand and laid her palm against his cheek briefly. "You'll be all right. You have friends already – you just need to know where to look for them. Don't mess around with anymore spell-casting. And remember that it takes a good two years for any place to feel like home." Then she sailed down the hall and into the elevator.

As Feltus closed the door, he could hear her lambasting the elevator operator. "Careful with that cage, you buffoon! I don't care if it's heavy!"

He walked down the hallway, went to his room, and lay down on the bed. When he opened the envelope, he discovered it held a small plastic bag of crushed black flakes. He turned the envelope over. A small label affixed to it said, in his great-aunt's spindly writing: "Skin of Winston: Irritant. Not to exceed 1 teaspoon per 120 lbs weight."

Feltus Ovalton looked up at the ceiling and laughed out loud. He was certain he could find some use for an irritant. Mrs. Fontana was still due for some punishment for the little shots she was always taking at his mother, and he could think of at least two other people who were deserving as well.

He whiled away the hours imagining how different his life would be if he actually were more magical than Eunida seemed to think and had a deeply hidden aptitude for spell-casting. Then he could make sure that everything always went his way. He could make people like him, and he could probably get all his grades switched from Ds and Fs to As without even doing any work.

Every once in a while, Eunida's words about the PoodleRats resonated in his skull, but he pushed them away. Why were the PoodleRats so sure he could help them anyway? Why had they burdened him with all their problems? He was just a kid, and a pretty mediocre one at that.

He couldn't even handle his own life.

He felt a bubble of resentment rising in his chest and went back to imagining himself dressed in silver robes with light shooting out of his fingertips, stalking the school hallways.

It was with some guilt that he sneaked into the dining room later on that day with an assortment of canned food and a few bottles of seltzer water that he'd grabbed from the kitchen. By now he was stealing from the back of the pantry, and it was mostly leftover supplies from his father's office dinner parties. He'd snagged smoked oysters in oil, melba toast, vacuum-sealed roasted peanuts, and maraschino cherries.

When he got under the table, he noticed that the port hole glowed with less light than usual. He put the food down and felt around the edge of the hole. He gave a low whistle, but there was no reply.

His scouting fingers found something smooth and cool. It was a small figure of a PoodleRat, exquisitely carved from a piece of bone and polished until it felt like silk. He sat under the table for a long time, holding the figurine in one hand and the useless prophecy in the other, letting his mind go around in circles. Absolutely nothing became any clearer. He was all the PoodleRats had and he had to admit that he was pathetic.

"Feltus," RinMal said in his ear.

Feltus jumped and banged his head.

His friend was so altered that all Feltus could do was stare. RinMal was emaciated and his face looked different – angular and off-color around the muzzle. His eyes were sunken black pools with none of the lightheartedness they'd had before.

The PoodleRat's fur was dull and matted, as if he'd neglected his grooming. Feltus had had a cat once that had stopped caring for its coat near the end of its life. He couldn't bear to think of it. All of a sudden he was engulfed in a flood of misery. RinMal laid a paw on his shoulder comfortingly, and that made it all worse.

"I guess I'm not living up to being the king you've all waited for," Feltus said sadly.

"You have helped us all the same. If it wasn't for the supplies you leave us regularly, our story would be told already."

"Is it so bad?" Feltus whispered.

"The Kehezzzalubbapipipi continue to rampage. We cannot stop them and have been forced to live under the forest. It is against our nature to live in such a confined manner and without fresh air. Already some of the very young and very old have become sick. We are all weak. I wanted you to have something to remember me by, if ... And I wanted to tell you that our friendship has meant a great deal to me."

Feltus was silent. This could not be how it was all going to end.

"We can study the prophecy together again. I have those encyclopedias – maybe the answer lies in there. I can ask the librarian at school, Mr. Chirono. He knows every-thing. You can't stop fighting. You just can't," Feltus pleaded with the PoodleRat. "I'm sorry that I haven't been studying the prophecy as hard as I should have. There've been distractions." This last admission sounded lame even to his ears, but the PoodleRat just nodded.

"I should return so that I can be with Saldemere Og and the others for these last weeks," RinMal replied. "I heard you calling to me and thought I'd make one last trip up to see you. No one is saying that you have not done your best, Feltus."

But Feltus knew he had not. It wasn't until this very moment, looking RinMal straight in the face, that he could admit to himself that he had not taken the PoodleRats' problems as seriously as he should have.

"Stay. Just for a little while. I know we're close to the answer," Feltus pleaded. "I've found out some stuff about the Veil and about how the Kehezzzalubbapipipi got in. It's happened before – a breach, I mean."

RinMal nodded. "I'll ask Saldemere if I can return briefly. If he consents, I'll see you soon." He patted Feltus on the back and was gone down the port hole.

Feltus sat brooding under the table for a while longer and felt his self-pity turn into a cold rage. A new sense of determination overcame him.

He would do everything in his power to help the PoodleRats vanquish their foe. But while he waited for his friend to return, he would try to settle a few scores with two of his own enemies. Maybe that would make him feel a little better.

# CHAPTER 10

## Revenge: A Dish Best Served Cold

FELTUS WOKE WITH a brilliant plan for revenge already formed in his head. The solution to Jimmy and Rusty had been sitting in front of him for a while – in fact, from the moment of Eunida's arrival.

He dressed quickly, put a few things of importance in his pockets, including the prophecy and the PoodleRat figurine, ate a hurried breakfast of cereal and milk, and was whistling down the street before his mother could open her mouth and criticize his rumpled hair and loosely laced sneakers. He was actually pretty excited about getting to school today. His good mood lasted through assembly, French, and even through gym class, where they played dodgeball and Rusty took the opportunity to hammer him in the face a few times.

Every once in a while between classes he'd catch a glimmer of white speeding along the linoleum floors, and occasionally he'd see the janitor, Mr. Quirot (or "Old Carrot" as most of the students called him), in hot pursuit with a butterfly net. Apparently they still hadn't caught all the mice.

In Math, Feltus took a seat next to Percy. The studious boy was bent over his homework, which consisted of neat lines of numbers and carefully plotted graphs. He'd done the extra credit problem too, Feltus noticed.

Feltus's own work was messy, with multiple cross-outs and badly erased mistakes, and he was pretty sure he'd gotten number four completely wrong. He had done it quickly, after his brief visit with RinMal, and skimmed over the questions without really reading them. *You can't serve one-and-a-half fish to three-and-a-half people, can you?* He didn't care. There was only one thing occupying his mind today.

"I meant to thank you for your help," he whispered to Percy.

Percy looked surprised. "No problem. Everything work out okay?"

"Perfect. I mean, she's still nuts, but she calmed down a lot." He preferred not to mention the magical part of his great-aunt's problems.

"Something you'd like to share with the class, Mr. LeRoi?" asked Mrs. Pidgeon grouchily. She was slightly on edge and jumped at any sudden movement. Some of the other students were throwing crumpled balls of white paper just outside her peripheral vision, and Greg Matthews kept making squeaking noises behind his cupped hands.

"Come up here and give us the answer to this word problem. That should keep you busy."

It took Feltus the rest of the hour to work out the wrong answer on the board. When the bell rang, Percy jumped out of his seat, grabbed the chalk out of Feltus's hand, and quickly jotted down a series of numbers, circling the last one with a flourish.

"The answer is two," he said. "You were almost there."

It was just a lot of squiggles to Feltus, but at least he'd gotten through it and now it was lunchtime. He remembered what he had in his pocket.

"I want to show you something," he said to Percy. "Let's go eat lunch over by the sports field."

Percy gave him an assessing look as if he didn't quite trust him, and then slowly nodded. "Okay," he said.

Technically, the field was off limits to everyone but the football players who trained at all hours, but Feltus knew of a dusty patch of grass surrounded by cedar bushes where you could eat your lunch undisturbed.

His sandwich today was oxtail and watercress – not his favorite, but something his mother insisted Rose prepare for him from time to time. His mother believed that bone marrow was strengthening – food for the mind and body. Sometimes Feltus was able to convince Rose to make him plain old peanut butter and jelly, but lately his mother had been closely supervising the contents of his lunch box.

"Care for some?" he asked Percy, who wrinkled his nose and shook his head.

"Do you want half of mine? It's baloney on white."

"That sounds great. My mother would never allow it. Nitrates," Feltus added in a low voice. He wasn't exactly sure what nitrates were, but knew that they were really bad.

"My dad makes my lunch. He doesn't have a clue," Percy explained.

"Is your mom ...?"

"She left when I was only five. I remember thinking the ceiling was going to fall down when my parents really got going in their arguments."

"Mine don't talk." It was the first time Feltus had said it out loud.

"That's how it starts," Percy explained knowingly. "It'll drive you crazy, trying to fix everything. Don't let it."

Feltus pondered this for a while. It seemed like sound advice. What could he do about it, after all?

"So someday you're going to tell me what that whole thing with your great-aunt was about, right?" Percy asked with a direct stare. "I mean, you couldn't classify that as normal. Paranormal, maybe."

"I promise, but right now, I can't. I still haven't figured

it out. The Great-Aunt Eunida thing is just part of what's been happening to me. Really, really weird stuff."

"The marmot too, huh?" Percy looked at him for an instant longer, and then turned his attention back to his sandwich.

Feltus wondered if he should ask Percy about the Great Mouse Escape. But it didn't seem fair, as he was still reluctant to share his own deepest, darkest secrets with this new friend. He decided he'd wait until they knew each other a bit better.

"This is what I wanted to show you," Feltus said into the awkward silence. He dug the little packet of Winston's skin powder out of his pocket and handed it over.

Percy examined it with interest. "Organic, acidic," he said, intrigued. "Not a spice, I would guess." Feltus stopped him from dipping a finger in. "I wouldn't if I were you," he said.

"So what does it do?" Percy asked.

Feltus explained, and the two spent the rest of the lunch hour chuckling about their revenge plan.

When lunch was over, they returned to their lockers and found Jimmy and Rusty leaning casually against Percy's locker. Feltus kept his face as unemotional as possible, but inside he was gleefully contemplating the discomfort that was soon to come to both the bullies. For once, he was able to stare at Rusty without flinching or instinctively protecting his belly with his forearms.

"Good job," Jimmy said to Percy. "How'd you get all the cages open at the same time?"

"Timer and remote control openers," Percy said in a low voice, ducking his head.

"And you're sure they can't trace this back to me?" Jimmy said in his usual menacing tone.

"I snuck in this morning and removed all the equipment," Percy said. "They're used to seeing me here early."

He handed Rusty a thick folder of papers. "That's all the science and math assignments for the rest of the year."

Rusty did a little dance, and waved the folder around.

Percy looked uncomfortable. "So the deal stands? You'll leave me alone?"

"Sure. We'll get off your back for now," Jimmy said, and then put a finger to his lips. "Remember. *Shhhhh*."

With furious eyes, Feltus followed Jimmy and Rusty down the hall.

"I hate those guys. I hate that I let them intimidate me. One of these days, I'm going to tell them exactly what I think of them," Feltus raged.

"Me too," Percy agreed. "But not today, right? Today is for actions, not words."

Feltus and Percy walked down the hall together, and Feltus stopped at the fountain.

It was as if he'd never been in this position before, Feltus thought glumly. Once his attention had wandered and his guard was down, that was when Rusty would strike. He was like a hyena going for the soft underbelly of an antelope. As he was straightening up from his refreshing drink of water, his arm was suddenly pinned behind his back and he was hustled into the bathroom.

It turned out that it was an easy thing to trickle a little bit of powder down Rusty's shirt when the brawny boy threw Feltus over his shoulder and then hung him upside down over a gleaming white porcelain toilet bowl. Feltus may have been a little overzealous with the quantity, but as he heard the contents of his pockets hit the water with a splatter and felt the pain in his shoulders from having his arms wrenched back, he decided that Rusty deserved whatever he got.

The effect was almost instantaneous, and he was fortunate that the bully put him down, though none too gently, before reaching behind to claw at his back. A strangled whimpering escaped from Rusty's throat as he rubbed his back against the open metal door of the stall and then rolled around on the floor, arching his spine and ripping at his shirt. Feltus, Percy, and a few other kids stood by mesmerized. When Rusty removed his button-down and tried to aim water from the sink to the itching places rubbed raw, he lost whatever intimidation factor he'd had. The bully had broken out in a nasty rash, but instead of the usual spots and bumps, his entire body was ringed in vivid welts that encircled his thick neck, arms, torso, and legs.

Feltus observed Rusty's wobbling belly, the meaty fat of his arms, and the shock of hair that never seemed to submit to a comb, and thought to himself, *This guy's just a clown.*

The same idea seemed to have occurred to the rest of the onlookers in the bathroom. As they slowly filed out, he heard Harold Jenkins say under his breath, "Bozo rides again." At least they retained enough sense to hold their laughter until the heavy door had closed behind them.

Rusty was still a threat, but now Feltus would have the image of the boy wriggling on the wet bathroom floor to sustain him in times of need. Jimmy was due for the same punishment.

Feltus and Percy convened by their lockers.

"That was a present from your great-aunt, I'm guessing," Percy said, once they'd gotten their laughter under control.

"Yup. Although I didn't know it would have such a dramatic effect." Feltus patted the envelope in his pocket. The paper crackled. "One down, one to go," he said to Percy.

"Let me get Jimmy," Percy pleaded. "It's karma. Justice. Especially after what they just made me do. You owe me."

Feltus considered. "Okay. But remember, just one

teaspoon. I may have overdone it with Rusty."

"Nothing he doesn't deserve," Percy replied.

"You're right. Use your own discretion. As far as I'm concerned, you can use the whole packet." He handed it over and Percy slipped it between the pages of his textbook. The blond boy's eyes were shining and he seemed almost giddy with excitement. Feltus understood that feeling – it still felt as if lightning was ricocheting through his own nerve endings.

Barely able to contain themselves, they took the stairs up one floor to the science lab.

The biology room was in darkness. Percy slid into the seat directly behind Jimmy, who was hunched over an anatomical model of a frog. Feltus watched anxiously from across the room. This would require quickness and daring, two qualities he didn't think Percy possessed.

Mr. Leggett, the cadaverous science teacher, flicked on the slide projector.

"Behold the planaria worm," he uttered. "Some of you will be happy to learn that we are finally moving on from the principles of Archimedes and volume displacement."

Feltus suspected that Leggett's gaze was turned in his direction. Try as he might, he just hadn't been able to grasp the concept of volume displacement. They'd spent weeks submerging apples in vats full of liquids, and all he'd comprehended at the end of it all was that displaced fluids made a terrible mess. He had mentioned it to Percy at lunch, and his friend had gotten that vaguely pitying expression that made Feltus feel stupid and then rambled on about equality of matter and how two objects of similar density couldn't occupy the same space at the same time. Feltus had sighed and tuned him out.

The teacher indicated the twin, false eyes that peered unblinkingly from the worm's head. "Used to deter enemies, of which this creature has many. Man, for instance." Feltus poked his pencil into the beaker on the desk that contained his worm. The creatures were minute. He couldn't imagine what they would be doing with them.

"You will notice that you have been equipped with small batteries. The red wire is a positive charge, the black negative. *Do not*, I repeat, *do not* allow the wires to touch. Harold, are you listening?" Mr. Leggett's spectacles caught the light from the hallway. Feltus thought he looked a little like a planaria himself.

"When I give the word," the teacher continued, "you will apply the positive charge to your worms repeatedly."

"Doesn't it hurt them?" Harold asked. He'd been violently sick when they'd studied chicken eggs.

"The pain is minimal," Mr. Leggett answered. "Afterward we will mince the worms in a blender and feed them to other worms, which will, you will be amazed to learn, retain the information learned by their predecessors. If only children were as easy. Harold, if you would, turn the lights back on, please."

Harold's face looked green in the glare of the fluorescent lights.

"Grasp your electrical conduits," the teacher said, raising his arms as if he were about to conduct an orchestra. "And-a-one, and-a-two. Zap the worms now!" His hands tapped out a steady rhythm.

If not for a timely distraction, dozens of worms would have experienced a severe degree of discomfort; but fortunately, at that exact moment, Jimmy let out a piercing squeal. He leapt from his chair, his body shimmying and writhing. Percy casually moved one chair back and two over so that he was directly behind Harold. All eyes were on Jimmy, who was squirming along the edge of his wooden desk, shirt hiked up across his back. A brilliant reddish-purple rash in the shape of dozens of bull's-eyes was visible across his torso.

"Boy! Stop this behavior immediately!" Mr. Leggett shouted.

Jimmy continued to wriggle. "It's so itchy!" he gasped. "Make it stop!"

"Itchy! What is it? Fleas? Poison ivy? Stop moving, boy, and let me look." The teacher leaned over, but Jimmy was unable to stay still. The class gathered around. Now Jimmy was flopping like a fish out of water.

"Aargh!" he screamed. "Get it off! Get it off!"

Harold, displaying a flash of inspiration, dumped his beaker of planaria in water over the bully's head. That halted the frenzied movements for a second, and, following his example, everyone rushed to retrieve their beakers.

Soon Jimmy was soaked with worm water. His black hair was plastered to his scalp and his clothes were sodden. Harold scooped up the wriggling worms and gently deposited them into a spare receptacle, looking pleased with himself.

Mr. Leggett stared down at the dripping boy, who still squirmed and writhed on the ground.

"I think that will be all for today, class. You are dismissed. Mr. Matthews, I'll be sending a note home to your parents. There may be head lice involved, which would necessitate complete hair removal." He stroked his upper lip thoughtfully and repeated the words, "Complete hair removal."

In the hallway, Feltus shook Percy's hand firmly. "Great work," he whispered. "Just the right amount."

"I know. I emptied the whole envelope on him. A little payback for all the months of misery," Percy said.

The boys left school together. Feltus was surprised to learn that Percy lived only a few blocks away from his apartment building, in a short, narrow house with a rickety metal handrail and crumbling cement stairs. The house was squeezed between a Laundromat and a liquor store. Percy didn't invite him up, and there was an uncomfortable moment before Feltus said, "Well, see you," and Percy replied, "Yeah."

Feltus jogged the last couple blocks home. He felt great – happiness wrapped in a huge sense of accomplishment. He had finally gotten the upper hand after months of being made miserable at school, and he hoped it meant that something *had* finally changed. Jimmy had never been humiliated before; now he had been in front of scores of witnesses who would not delay in spreading the news all over the school. Surely the shame would rob him of some of his power?

Feltus decided he was capable of anything if he really put his mind to it. First on his agenda now was the PoodleRat problem.

He entered the empty apartment, kicked his shoes off by the front door and headed to his room to dump his stuff, making his usual detour to the dining room for a quick look under the table. The food bag was still there.

He continued down the hallway, kicked his door open and pulled his sweater up over his head with one hand. His head was shrouded in thin cotton when he heard a strange crackling sound. He uncovered his eyes slowly – someone or something was in his room.

When his eyes focused, he saw that it was a very skinny and haggard RinMal. The PoodleRat sat in a corner by the closet, polishing off the last potato chips in a family-size bag.

"Hey – you came back!" Feltus said.

RinMal must have been very hungry, because he'd made a mess of crumbs all around him and his whiskers were sprinkled with salt. Feltus knew that PoodleRats were very tidy eaters. He was embarrassed to feel a few tears leak from his eyes – he wiped them away hurriedly.

"You look pleased with yourself," RinMal observed.

"It was a pretty good day at school," Feltus replied, thinking how odd those words sounded coming out of his mouth. "And now you're back."

The PoodleRat nodded.

"Let's get to the prophecy then," Feltus said, pulling it from his pocket.

RinMal sat up, brushed the fragments of food from his fur, and squared his shoulders.

"Ready?" Feltus asked.

"Ready."

# PART 3

## FELTUS OVALTON
## & THE
## ANTI-MOM

# CHAPTER 11

## Hot Sun in the Summertime

IT WAS HOT. Horribly humid. Feltus broiled in the confines of his room and brooded on the gross unfairness of it all. Only a few days since school had let out, and he was too busy to do anything fun!

He moved every few seconds, trying to find a cool spot on the chair. Pages of variations on the prophecy were strewn across his lap and on the floor. He'd tried a cut-and-paste method he'd learned in beatnik poetry class, superimposing this word here, that word there, but it still didn't make sense. Cat pots, bounty spear? What did it mean? He needed to take a break.

RinMal was sprawled unhappily on the big floor cushions Great-Aunt Eunida had sent. They were patchwork splotches of brightly colored cotton velvet and they drew the heat; his fur was standing up in damp spikes. Outside, the summer sun beat the sidewalks until the tarmac melted into syrupy puddles.

Feltus's mother had compounded the misery he was feeling by having all the rugs and carpets taken up while she mused over color samples and decided on a new scheme for the apartment. Dust motes hung in the air, trapped in bolts of sunshine that pierced through the curtains in every room. She didn't believe in air conditioning. "It's so drying to my skin," she always said; so every summer, they would swelter and drip and wait for the cool kiss of fall.

The heat put everyone in a bad mood. Feltus had twice

snapped at RinMal – once for leaving the door open and once for disarranging his comic books. Everything was irritating – the sound of his father's jaw as he ate his dinner, the TV announcer's droning voice, the way his shorts brushed against his legs, the way RinMal's fur swooped into peaks like that. He was also angry about Percy skipping town for math camp. How could anyone choose to do logarithms during vacation?

"What I wouldn't do for a pool. Or a lake, for that matter," he grumbled.

"Be careful what you wish for," RinMal cautioned. "Remember what your great-aunt said? You said she told you not to mess around with magic after the fiasco with the unlocking spell. Obviously your wishes carry some weight."

The PoodleRat was turning around in circles, like a dog. Feltus's heat-induced irritability increased.

"Eunida, Eunida," he muttered. "Who cares what that old loon says?"

"She may be a little odd, but her predictions seem to be right on," RinMal said mildly. "Have you heard from her recently?"

"No," Feltus replied in a prickly voice. And that was another thing. Eunida had just taken off, leaving him with a dangerous rift somewhere in the apartment and no clue what to do about it.

He tossed the comic book he'd been trying to read aside. RinMal looked up briefly from Eunida's witchcraft manual that he'd pulled out of the closet.

"You know, this is quite interesting. We have no mystical doctrine in Gewglab at all. I'm a novice, but I'd say there's some potent stuff here. The prophecy is an incantation of sorts after all."

"But what good is it – this magic? There's nothing in that book that can help you and the others," Feltus said crossly. "Maybe the one spell I did had some small effect, but I'm not sure I believe in any of it."

RinMal sat up. "How can you not believe?"

"Eunida suggested it was just a string of coincidences, set in motion by some action she couldn't pinpoint. It's the Veil – the apartment – not me. I'm still nobody."

"Maybe she was trying to protect you," RinMal said. "Not telling you the whole story."

"Rubbish!" Feltus replied, feeling his bad temper surge again.

Feltus then pointed to all the pages on the floor. "And this makes no more sense to me than it did the first time I read it."

"We've made a little progress," RinMal reminded him. "We know who the enemy is and when they'll attack for the final time. And I think your idea about pits and sharpened spears is a good one."

Feltus had adapted the concept from a book on the ancient Romans he'd read last summer.

"Yeah, but where do we get the spears?" Feltus asked angrily. "You said there aren't even any *trees* left in the Grand Gewglab. We can't make them out of Popsicle sticks!" He was yelling at RinMal, but he was really upset with himself.

He got up and went to the kitchen to get something cold to drink. When he walked in, he saw Rose kneeling on the floor, picking up the broken shards of a mayonnaise jar. Feltus took a perverse pleasure in kicking some pieces of glass under the cabinet and in tracking the mayonnaise across the linoleum. He got a glass of ice water, and then, discovering Lafayette in the pantry, callously dripped freezing cold water onto the dog's head. Later he would probably feel bad about it, but just now he wanted everyone to be as miserable as he was.

He despised the dog anyway. It was always yapping, sneaking food, and nipping at his ankles, and when RinMal had first come to stay, Lafayette had staked out Feltus's bedroom door, howling at all hours of the night and refusing to leave the PoodleRat alone. Finally RinMal had bared his teeth, unsheathed his claws, and stood in front of Lafayette at his full height of two-and-a-half feet. The dog didn't come around much after that.

Feltus took his drink back to his room and then stood looking at the photograph he'd taped up of a calm, cool lake. Beneath the picture, there was some kind of nail sticking out of the floorboards. He leaned against the wall, thinking about how great it would be to jump in that lake. As he mused, he idly kicked the nail, worrying it back and forth like a loose tooth. It felt really wobbly. He bent down to pull it out and was surprised to see that it wasn't a nail at all. It was a tube of some sort, covered in dust. He licked a finger and rubbed a clean patch, but it was an inky green color inside as well. It seemed to be made of glass, like the test tubes they used in chemistry class, but heavier.

One end was sealed with a metal cap and bound around with cloth. Feltus shook it and held it up to his ear, but nothing shifted inside.

RinMal sat up, put down the manual, and peered at Feltus's hands.

"What's that?" he asked.

"Nothing," Feltus said meanly and stuck the tube in his pocket.

He glanced outside through the window, hoping to see a breath of air move the wilted leaves of the maple tree. The air shimmered and the cars moving down the street blurred in the intensity of the summer day. His brain felt sluggish. He knew he should be studying the prophecy some more, but he just couldn't face it right now. He wondered if it was as hot as this in the Grand Gewglab Forest. He hoped not. They had enough to deal with, and thick fur besides.

He heard the sound of RinMal flicking the pages of an encyclopedia – they'd gotten to *e* already – and turned around to watch him. The small PoodleRat was almost squashed by the weight of the book and struggled to keep it steady while he read, one pink paw tracing the words.

Feltus took a deep breath. He was truly glad the PoodleRat had come to stay, and he forced the depressing thought of the other PoodleRats out of his mind. He sat on the wood floor and held the glass cylinder out to RinMal, who put the heavy dictionary aside and examined it curiously.

"Look, there's some writing on the outside of the tube, but it's too grimy to read," RinMal said. "I wonder how old it is? And what it's made of? We could have Saldemere or one of the other elders look at it, if you want."

Feltus snatched it back and stuck it in his pocket. It was strange, but for some reason he felt he couldn't let it out of his possession.

Just then, his mother swung the door open. Feltus jumped. He'd been meaning to rig some kind of lock or booby trap. She didn't respect his privacy, and now that RinMal was around, Feltus didn't want his friend to have to remember to act like a dog. It had taken a few nights of study and repetition for Feltus to familiarize the PoodleRat with tail wagging and scratching. All that RinMal could learn from Lafayette was how to beg, root through the trash, and lick his own bottom.

"Don't forget that you promised to put the garbage out, Feltus," Feltus's mother said, sweeping her eyes around the room. Feltus could see that her orderly brain was making a list of chores for him to complete. "What a mess. And look, your dog is shedding everywhere! I told you when you brought it home that you had to keep it clean and quiet.

Otherwise it'll be sent to the pound.

"We have important guests coming for dinner, so I would appreciate it if you would groom your animal, vacuum the floor, and air this room out. It smells like a pet store. I've put your clean clothes for the evening in the bathroom."

She took his silence for assent, directed another displeased look at RinMal, who wagged his tail hesitantly, and closed the door firmly behind her. "And wash behind your ears!" was her parting shot from the hallway.

"It's too hot to clean and too hot to argue with her," Feltus grumbled.

"I can help you straighten up the room," RinMal said as he stood up. "Just block the door so she doesn't see me with the vacuum."

"Or folding my laundry," Feltus replied, feeling better. "Maybe I could tell her you're one of those trick dogs on TV."

The chores went quickly with the PoodleRat's help, although if Feltus was being honest, RinMal did more than his fair share since he proved to be amazingly adept at folding button down, short-sleeved shirts. After thanking the PoodleRat and leaving him with a bottle of lukewarm soda and a very soft, gooey pecan cluster from the back of his newly organized closet, Feltus made his way to the bathroom, looking forward – for once – to a shower.

He took his time, standing under the cold water for a good while and pretending he was a fearless explorer bathing in the glacial waters of a cataract in the middle of a prehistoric forest. He was positively pruney when he finally got out, but he felt as if he'd lowered his body temperature about ten degrees.

His mood dropped a couple notches when he saw the clothes his mother had left for him. She still seemed to think he was five years old.

*Can I challenge her on this?* he wondered. But in the

end, he put them on and made his way to the sitting room. It was simply too hot to fight.

The guests had not arrived yet, but his mother waited, legs crossed elegantly at the ankle, pale blue shirt and white linen skirt pressed and fresh-looking. The only indication she felt the heat were the damp tendrils of hair at the back of her neck below her tight bun. Feltus stood before her and held out his hands. She inspected his fingernails and then turned them over to peer at his palms. He passed muster.

"The Herrings will be here any minute," she said. "Go and sit on the sofa until they arrive, and try to stay clean."

They sat on the sofa in silence; the only sound was the ticking of the large clock on the mantelpiece over the fireplace. When the doorbell sounded, his mother leapt to her feet, indicating with a pointing finger that Feltus should take his place by the door to the dining room. He stood up reluctantly.

As she passed by him on her way to let the guests in, she smoothed his hair down and pulled his shoulders back. "Nice and straight, Feltus, and smile." He made a comical face at her. "Not too much," she snapped.

As soon as she left the room, he slumped against the wall, listening to the bustling of the front door opening, coats being removed, and footsteps coming his way. He pasted a foolish grin on his face and stood aside as a small, fat man and a very large woman entered, followed by his mother, who seemed quite wound up.

"Please sit," she said. With one hand, she motioned the guests to the sofa and with the other, she signaled Feltus toward the trays of appetizers that waited on the coffee table.

"Nuts?" Feltus held the serving tray under Mr. Herring's nose. "Grasshopper?"

Feltus waited a couple of seconds and then returned the tray to the table. He yearned to sit down, but that was contrary to the "eager to be of service" demeanor his mother desired of him, so he ran back and forth between the hors d'oeuvres and the guests.

At the dinner table, he sat and fidgeted with the collar of his shirt. It was much too tight. His mother failed to notice that he was bigger and taller by the day. He could barely breathe in the velvet jacket and shorts ensemble that she considered "Proper attire for evening functions." He promised himself this was the last time he would let her cajole him into wearing these ridiculous clothes. It was too high a price – even if she had bribed him with box seats at the monster movie marathon, an all-day event in a building with air-conditioning!

He glowered at the elderly couple sitting across from him. They were not likely to take his mind off of his discomfort. All he could think about was RinMal and the time he was being forced to waste by sitting here.

Mr. and Mrs. Herring were the co-founders of the Floribunda Garden Society, the organization his mother worked for. They held the top executive positions, which his mother had her eye on ever since they'd moved to the city, and now there were rumors that the Herrings were stepping down and looking for a replacement. This latest dinner was just another in a long line of culinary schemes she had thought up.

Feltus eyed the jellied-mongoose consommé with disfavor. In an attempt to control the mongoose population, the animals were now being shipped in the tens of thousands to America from India, touted as the next gourmet delight. *It tastes just like something that eats snakes*, he thought sourly.

Mr. Herring was a little bald man who breathed loudly through his mouth and uttered short statements as if they were an indisputable fact. Most of his height was in his head, which rose above his neck splendidly like the Easter Island monuments. He sat floppily folded in the middle, his legs sprawled in front of him as if the weight were too much to bear.

His wife, on the other hand, was not fat, but she had heft. She wore a voluminous bright red cape and made big gestures when she talked. Feltus tried to imagine how long it would take the Kehezzzalubbapipipi to eat her. She dominated the conversation, which was punctuated by her husband's fish-out-of water gasps; and she dominated him too, insisting on cutting his meat (ostrich) for him and selecting the proper vegetables. Feltus expected her to chew his food for him as well and then regurgitate it like a mother bird. He shuddered at the thought.

For his part, Feltus decided that ostrich was overrated. It was tough and stringy, as were the foraged greens (flown in from France), and the birch bark and liver soufflés. In fact, all the food was tough and stringy, although the Herrings didn't seem to notice.

Even dessert was a disappointment – a violet-scented jelly in the shape of an orchid, dotted with nasturtium, borage, and rose petals. He thought longingly of the chocolate bars stashed in his sock drawer, but smiled politely as Mrs. Herring asked what his favorite classes were. School was the last thing on his mind, so it took some thought before he could think of an answer. Finally he grunted "Art" and "English."

He tried not to stare at her husband, who had lapsed into a coma after three helpings of everything, a green bean attached to his upper lip and sweat beading his forehead. All the candles Feltus's mother had lit added to the oppressive and humid atmosphere. Feltus undid the top button on his shorts and shifted in his chair. His legs stuck to the leather seat, making a suction-y noise. He chuckled. His mother glared at him.

"We are all so excited about the bonsai exhibition. I've

often wished for a bonsai to grace this dining room. A big one, to fill that large space over there," Feltus's mother gushed desperately. She pointed to an alcove by the farthest window.

Mrs. Herring withdrew her piercing gaze from Feltus and looked at the corner in question. "My dear Mrs. LeRoi, the bonsai is an expensive hobby! Not for everyone, you know," she said squashingly.

After that, there didn't seem to be much to say. Mr. Herring had been rendered speechless by his gorging and seemed to have gone to sleep with his eyes open. It took the combined efforts of Mrs. Herring and Feltus's mother to get him to the sofa. Feltus's mother stood for a while wringing her hands and then announced in a quiet voice that she would just call for the aperitifs – which meant disappearing to the kitchen only to stagger back under the weight of a tray laden with a variety of bottles. Neither guest offered to help unburden her.

"I'll just have a large brandy to settle my stomach," Mrs. Herring said curtly, fingering the curtains before sinking into the sofa. Feltus half expected the couch to tilt like a capsized ship. "And my husband will have a seltzer water," she continued. Mr. Herring let out a small whimper, but closed his mouth when his wife turned her globular eyes on him.

Mrs. Herring filled all the space on the couch. Her little husband was crammed into a tiny corner and propped up with cushions. Thankfully, Feltus was excused as the drinks were served, but before he could get out the door, Mrs. Herring beckoned him over. She looked him up and down and then pressed a quarter into his hand. He escaped gratefully into his room; she reminded him a little too much of a wolf in granny's clothing.

Back in his room, Feltus noticed that RinMal had thrown the curtains open and the air was finally beginning to cool. Feltus went straight to his chest of drawers, and, tossing socks left and right, emerged triumphantly with a chocolate bar. He ate most of it and then offered some of the melted mess to RinMal, who accepted with pleasure – he'd already gained back some of his weight because of his new diet bolstered by lots of sweets and snacks. They sat licking the chocolate off their fingers, content for the moment with the peace and quiet.

"How was dinner?" the PoodleRat asked.

"Miserable," Feltus replied, scrambling out of his uncomfortable velvet shorts and into a pair of light pajama bottoms. "I don't think even PoodleRats could eat that kind of food."

"Our stomachs are quite adaptable."

"Yeah, but this was way worse than orange peels and coffee grounds. I think it almost killed the old guy. Afterwards he didn't say a whole lot."

"Well, at least it's over," RinMal said.

"So how did you do?" Feltus asked, looking at the piles of open books all over the floor.

"I found some references to plagues and scourges. You know – locusts, termites, the Black Death; but nothing specific to the Kehezzzalubbapipipi. It was quite discouraging," the PoodleRat continued, wiping smears of chocolate from his whiskers. "So I thought I'd take another look at that curious tube of yours, but I couldn't find it."

"Oh, it's right here," Feltus said and reached for the discarded shorts without getting up.

He jolted upright. It wasn't there. Where had he left it?

He suddenly remembered shoving it into the back pocket of his denim shorts – which were, he groaned to himself, stuffed behind the toilet in the bathroom. He had kicked them there after his shower.

"I left it in the bathroom," he said. "I'll just sneak out and get it."

He peeked out into the hallway in time to see Mrs. Herring's ample behind on its way to use the facilities. He would have to wait until after the guests left. He didn't want to run the risk of getting cornered by Mrs. Herring – especially in the bathroom. "Well," said RinMal, "in the meantime I can show you the photos I found of locusts stripping a wheat field down. I think they must be even faster than the Kehezzzalubbapipipi."

"How can you be so matter-of-fact about it?" Feltus asked. "I mean, that's what's happening to your own home right now."

"I don't know. I guess I can remove myself a little and look at it from a purely scientific point of view. And I'm still positive that the prophecy will hold true."

"Yeah, but what use is it, if we don't know what it's trying to tell us?"

"It will become clear in time, I'm sure," RinMal said positively.

It was quite late when they finally heard the muffled sounds of the guests' goodbyes and the closing of the front door. Feltus decided he would stay up until his mother had gone to bed and then venture out to find the tube. He didn't want to explain why he was still awake. He was just curling up on the bed to wait, when his door flew open.

"How could you, Feltus? When I wanted everything to be perfect!"

Feltus sat up, his heart pounding. He wished his mother would at least learn to knock on the door before barging in. What if RinMal had been reading or writing – he had exceptionally fine penmanship – or doing some other un-doglike activity?

Feltus's temper rose. "I've asked you to knock before coming in. Can't you listen to what I say for once? Can't you leave me alone?" Sometimes he almost hated her.

"Look what I found wadded up behind the toilet." She shook his denim shorts in exasperation. And as if in slow motion, Feltus watched the glass tube fall out of the back pocket, hit the floor, and break into a thousand pieces.

A murky green vapor swelled and spread. It rose up and enveloped Feltus's mother in a noxious cloud. In only a moment, it had covered her from head to toe.

Feltus rubbed his eyes as the room began to go hazy. The last thing he heard before he passed out was an anguished howl from RinMal and his mother's piercing scream.

\* \* \*

Feltus opened his eyes and immediately shut them again. He was assailed by a horrid feeling of vertigo, and his stomach lurched in response. His head felt as if it were stuffed with wool. Before he'd shut his eyes, he'd seen nothing but white edged with blackness. *Maybe I'm dead.*

There seemed to be a heavy weight across his legs. He tried to move them, but they felt leaden, lifeless. He clenched and unclenched his fingers, trying to find out what hurt and what merely felt unusual. He could tell he was lying on something hard. His nose was bruised, perhaps broken, but if he could feel pain, then surely that meant he was alive.

He squinted one eye open again, but only saw more white. He rotated his eyeball to the left – more white – and then to the right. He was lying right up against the molding of the wall and he didn't think he could move.

There was something to his right that he glimpsed peripherally. A shadowy object. He opened both eyes, feeling the dull thump of a headache around his temples, and his vision cleared and sharpened suddenly. As he shifted his position, the weight fell away with a muffled thump and moan, and his feet were jabbed with thousands of pins and needles. The pain was unbearable, absolutely excruciating, and it got him moving immediately. He sat up, mashing his mouth against the molding in his haste, and started to massage his limbs as the circulation began to flow. He could taste blood at the back of his throat.

It was still dark outside, but by the light of the full moon he noticed that wisps of green smoke hung like tendrils from the ceiling, and there was a strange, sweet smell, as if someone had been burning lawn cuttings.

RinMal lay next to him in a heap. Feltus prodded the PoodleRat carefully, trying to drive images of road-killed squirrels from his mind. Finally RinMal groaned and rolled over. Feltus almost cried with relief. After a few minutes of whispered entreaties and invigorating pats on the back, RinMal was able to get up.

"What happened? All I remember is that vial breaking and your mother screaming," RinMal said groggily.

"Mom," Feltus said, his breath catching. He stood up so quickly that his head spun and his knees buckled. His mother lay on the other side of his bed. He knelt beside her, ignoring the pain in his legs. She was breathing steadily, but her skin was cold and clammy and had a yellowish cast to it.

RinMal pushed his furry face close to hers. "She's just unconscious. She may have hit her head," he announced. "I can sense some confusion. She feels muddy."

"Can you help me get her up onto the bed?" Feltus pleaded.

The PoodleRat nodded. RinMal was small, but wiry and strong.

RinMal lifted her head and shoulders, and Feltus staggered behind holding her ankles and trying to keep her skirt from riding up. They placed her on the bed, propped her up on some pillows, and arranged her arms by her sides. Feltus smoothed her hair away from her face, which was still much too pale, he decided. He tried to remember the last time he had touched her, had hugged her, had even smiled at her. It seemed a long, long time ago. RinMal was now at his side, holding a glass of water.

"Should I try and open the window?" the PoodleRat asked.

Feltus shook his head. "You know that window is jammed. Just open the door. Dad was working late, and even if he's come home he'll be in the study or his bedroom. He can't hear anything from there." Feltus dipped a clean sock in the water and wiped his mother's forehead.

To his relief, her eyelids fluttered and her hand went to her face.

"Oh, Feltus. I have such a headache," she murmured. "My skin is too tight. Get me to my room ... medicine in the night table drawer." Her eyes closed again.

"I'll help you," RinMal whispered.

Feltus looked down at his mother. She was biting her lower lip as if to keep from being sick. She seemed bewildered, still drowsy, and he thought perhaps later on she wouldn't remember much of this.

"Okay, but try not to talk too much," Feltus warned RinMal. "Remember, you're a dog as far as she's concerned."

They managed to get her down the hallway and up onto her bed, although Feltus was afraid they were a bit rough going around the corners. Except for a few groans, she didn't make much noise. He helped her to sit up and take a few small yellow pills with a fresh glass of water. Almost immediately, her shoulders relaxed and her head fell back. The worry lines smoothed from her face.

RinMal stuck his whiskery, pointed nose close to hers.

"She's sleeping deeply. I think the worst of her pain is gone," the PoodleRat assured Feltus.

Feltus motioned RinMal out of the room, then stood in the doorway for a few moments listening to his mother's steady breathing. Then he eased the door closed and rejoined RinMal in his room.

RinMal had raided the pantry for potato chips, sodas, and butter cookies and was now digging into the feast. Feltus looked out onto the quiet street and tried to work through the confusion of his thoughts. He picked up a cookie and was intending to take a bite. But his stomach still felt disturbed, so he crumbled it between his fingers instead.

He didn't want to meet RinMal's eyes; as he looked away, his eye passed over the smear next to the window where he'd crushed the giant flying insect months before. It had dried to a spindly light violet silhouette sprinkled with glittery powder. *Probably a variety of exotic Japanese beetle*, Feltus thought. He knew that some of them were toxic to humans.

"Hey, do you think that vial held some kind of poison?" Feltus asked with alarm.

"There was a trace of something," RinMal said slowly. "But I don't think it was malignant. I don't think she's hurt. The overwhelming sense I got was of confusion and uncertainty."

"How can you tell?" Feltus asked.

"You know how dogs can smell fear? I can sometimes sense feelings. I always know when you're mad, for instance. The air feels hot and there is a glow of red."

"Yeah, right!" Feltus blustered. He noticed that the floorboards where his mother had been standing were now lighter in color than the surrounding wood. "I think it's this apartment," he said. "Maybe there are unhealthy vapors coming from somewhere. I mean, look at Eunida, she was clearly under the influence of something even after Percy cured her," Feltus pointed out, taking a turn around the room.

"Lead paint, perhaps? Leaking gas? But we check all that out pretty thoroughly before we pipe in the port holes."

"I'd forgotten we were under observation," Feltus said bitterly, thinking of mold growing in a petri dish. "Why on earth did I ever wish for a change to my life?"

RinMal pounded him on the arm. "Come on, it's not so bad. She'll be fine in the morning, I'm sure."

RinMal may have felt confident that Feltus's mother would be all right, but Feltus didn't. Too much had happened recently for him not to fear the worst.

He got into bed, but tossed and turned the rest of the night, trying to find a soft and cool place on his pillow. It was still too hot and the anxiety was gnawing at him. He almost dreaded what the next day would bring.

# CHAPTER 12

## Topsy-Turvy

FELTUS WOKE SUDDENLY the next morning, catapulting out of bed and onto his feet before he had fully shaken the sleep from his head. Without bothering with slippers or a bathrobe, he hurried to his mother's bedroom door.

Loud music was blasting from inside the room and he pinched himself, thinking for a moment that he was still dreaming. She didn't respond to his knocking, so he pushed the door open.

Feltus looked at his mother with amazement. Gone was her usual uniform of prim blouse, knee-length skirt, and pearls. Instead, she was wearing layers of clothing in all colors of the rainbow. She sported a few of his father's T-shirts over her own button-down shirts, golf shorts under dresses and over jeans, and a velour dressing gown that hung open over everything. Most surprising of all, she was jumping up and down on the bed while rock and roll blared from the stereo.

Feltus went over and turned the radio off. She kept on bouncing.

"Mom! Are you okay?" he asked in disbelief. Whatever he'd been expecting, it certainly wasn't this. She was so different from the pale mother of last night that he almost started giggling hysterically. Her cheeks were flushed, her hair was tousled, and a grin split her face from ear to ear.

She stopped mid-bounce and sank ungracefully to the bed. He looked at her lying in a spread eagle, hands behind her head, feet on the fancy pillowcases she always sent out to be dry-cleaned, blowing bubbles from a huge wad of pink gum. She was staring at him with a confused expression, as if she had never seen him before. And then her eyes cleared.

"Feltus, right? There are peanut butter and jelly sand-wiches in the kitchen, if you're hungry. Also some strawberry shortcakes." Then she flounced over to the mirror, sat down, leaned in close, and began pulling at the skin around her mouth.

Feltus left the room, his head spinning. He closed the door with suddenly nerveless fingers and stumbled down the hallway to the kitchen. He wondered if this were some kind of elaborate practical joke, but when he got to the kitchen, the food she'd promised was there. He grabbed some without even looking at it, piled it on a plate, and went back to his room, still feeling as if he must be in some waking dream.

"Something is seriously wrong," he announced to RinMal.

RinMal looked around from his seat at the desk, where he was now building a tiny solar-powered rocket from some copper wire, a mirror, and a few Popsicle sticks. Feltus had noticed that the PoodleRat always had to be busy with something when they weren't poring over the prophecy. The concept of idleness seemed completely alien to him. The rocket was just the latest in a series of RinMal's hobbies.

"What?" RinMal asked. "Is your stomach still upset from last night?"

That was the worst thing about sharing a room – no privacy. And the PoodleRat was matter-of-fact about most things that Feltus found embarrassing.

"No," Feltus said coldly. "My mother has lost her mind!" He set the plate laden with food down on the chair and helped himself to a cake piled high with strawberries and whipped cream. His stomach grumbled in protest.

"Look," he said, pointing to the food. "Never in a million years would she ever let me eat this for breakfast. And she was dressed weirdly, and ..." his voice dropped to a hush, "... she was jumping on the bed."

"Maybe she's just happy."

"She's not happy," Feltus said, putting his food down. "That doesn't just happen all of a sudden. It takes years of being miserable before you're allowed to be happy."

"You seem content to me, and you were very morose when I first met you," RinMal countered.

"That's different. Besides, she's completely different – she's not just cheerful. She would never put on all of those clothes, or listen to bad rock and roll. I think something happened last night. To her. Because this apartment is so peculiar."

He looked around the patchy walls, half expecting to see something horrifying lunge from a corner. His gaze caught on the purple stain. "Check that out," he said. "Tell me that that is just bug juice."

The PoodleRat gave him a look that bordered on patronizing amusement and made Feltus's palms itch to slap him. Not that he ever would have. RinMal was totally capable of throwing and pinning him even now when he was undernourished.

RinMal walked over to the spot and put his snout just inches away from the purple blob. He stayed there for a few minutes, before scratching gently at the wall with his pronged fore-claw. He then walked toward Feltus with something pinched between his fingers. The PoodleRat's face had lost all trace of glee. He looked extraordinarily thoughtful.

He waved his paw in front of Feltus, and Feltus inched away slowly until the backs of his legs hit the edge of the bed. What the PoodleRat held was a spindly, striped limb ending in a brown whipstitched shoe. It reminded Feltus of Great-Aunt Eunida and suddenly he felt ill again.

"What is it?"

"Brownie. Pixie. Fairy. I'm not sure, but definitely one of the little people. There was a bit about them in Eunida's spell book."

"Well, what was it doing in my room? What was it pretending to be a bug for?" Feltus vaguely recalled the shrill "help" he'd heard just before his shoe nailed the insect, but he reminded himself that that was crazy and had only been the result of stress and lack of sleep.

RinMal had turned back to the window. He closed his eyes and took a deep breath.

"What?" Feltus said impatiently. "What it is?"

The PoodleRat's forehead bunched in thought. "Now I smell hot and cold, and wet and dry. Leaves and earth and air and fire and water. All juxtaposed here, at this exact place."

"Well, aren't you helpful all of a sudden," Feltus muttered and threw himself onto the bed. "I told you that window is jammed – has been ever since we moved here – so I don't know how you could be smelling any nature."

"I didn't say it came from outside," the PoodleRat replied. "I'm just wondering if there's more to this window than is apparent. For instance," and he waved the fairy leg so that the little shoe flopped up and down, "how did this get into your room?"

"I don't know," Feltus said, watching the leg jerk. "Great, now I can add 'Fairy killer' to my resume."

He didn't think he could handle any more weirdness unless he had to, so he avoided his mother and spent the day bent over the lines of the prophecy. What if he read them backwards? Reflected in the mirror? Standing on his head? It was the second bit that didn't make sense. He'd had no trouble figuring out who the "ravenous floods" "on sharpened claws" were – he'd seen them with his own horrified eyes. But what did "wintergreen" have to do with anything? Winter was months away and time would run out for the PoodleRats long before December rolled around.

When he did finally drag himself to his feet, he felt grouchy and a little nauseated from too much rich food and a lack of any fresh air. With sympathetic eyes, RinMal watched him leave the room.

\* \* \*

Feltus went into the dining room later that day and saw that it was transformed. Against the wall where the china cabinet had once stood was the biggest television set Feltus had ever seen. It was far bigger than the old-fashioned set his mother tolerated because of his father's frequent need to watch the up-to-the-minute stock reports. And the oak table where they normally sat down to elegant and fastidiously presented meals of exotic and generally inedible foods was stripped of tablecloth, napkins, and candlesticks. Three plain trays graced the polished wood surface, each holding a regular plate piled high with french fries, fish sticks, fried chicken, and potato croquettes.

"Nice, huh?" trilled his mother from the depths of the sofa. "Why don't you bring two of those trays over here and get comfortable? There are fudge sundaes with extra everything for dessert. Rose is just whipping them up." She patted the distressed leather chair beside her.

"Come on, the movie's just about to start. Crank up the air conditioning a few notches on your way over."

He wasn't sure what to say. He'd been expecting the usual uncomfortable silences as well as the nutritious food that required a full five minutes of chewing to get down. Instead he was getting a veritable banquet of fried food and, glancing at the TV screen, *Madcap Fraternity*

*Adventures* 2. Not to mention she already had the air conditioner going full blast and it was positively glacial in the room.

"Is Dad home?" he asked, aware that his voice had cracked on the second word. Bearing witness to a huge fight was not his favorite way to spend the evening and he hated to see his mom cry.

"That fuddy-duddy – always working," she said, springing up from her seat. "Here, have a hush puppy. Where are the corn dogs? Rose?"

Rose came in wearing a bemused expression and she met Feltus's gaze with a shrug and a questioning look of her own.

"Surely there are corn dogs? I can't wait to try one of those. Feltus," his mother said, waving a french fry in his face, "did you know that they can take a hot dog, put it on a stick, and give it a little overcoat made of batter? It's absolutely amazing. Will you have one with me?"

"No thanks," Feltus said, forcing a smile. "This is plenty."

He took a seat next to her. Surprisingly, he felt sad. He'd spent hours wishing he could eat junk food, and now when it was handed to him, all he could think about was that his mother was insane and that maybe it was all his fault. Just like everything else that was happening.

\* \* \*

The next morning brought nothing but another pain in his stomach and a worry that nagged at him like a toothache. It was another brutally hot day, and before Feltus even finished pulling on his shorts and a loose T-shirt, he was sweating.

He left his room, skirted the kitchen doorway, and ducked into the pantry. He was searching for prune juice when his father hurried past him into the kitchen, angrily knotting his tie. "Hey! How ya doing?" he heard his mother say from the kitchen in an abnormally cheerful voice.

Feltus poked his head around the corner.

"Is it too much to ask that you wake me at 6:30 as you've been doing for the last twelve years, and that my coffee, the paper, and a plain piece of toast be waiting on the kitchen counter? Time is money – " his father broke off, aghast. Feltus followed the direction of his gaze.

Instead of his father's breakfast, his mother was on the counter, sitting cross-legged and eating chocolate spread out of the jar with a large silver serving spoon. In addition, she was wearing a pair of his father's pajamas and her hair, normally sculpted into a modest bun or ponytail, was standing on end.

She looked at his father blithely, and Feltus tightened his shoulders in anticipation of the explosion he knew was coming. The sun streaming in the window had turned her eyes a brilliant green. The thought passed momentarily through his head that her eyes had always been blue.

His father slowly fastened the top button of his crisp, white shirt. He was breathing hard through his nose, always a sure sign that he was about to lose his temper.

"Look who crept in," Feltus's mother quipped, ignoring everything his father had just said.

A frowzy-haired figure emerged from behind the opened refrigerator door, holding a baguette, cream cheese, and a bottle of maple syrup in her arms. "You're out of sardines, Karen, dear. Pity!"

"Eunida!" Feltus gasped quietly from the pantry. Then he ducked down out of sight. His father stood frozen in place and Feltus, the ache in his guts forgotten, waited for the fireworks to begin.

The last time Great-Aunt Eunida had popped in, she'd driven his mother to the verge of a nervous breakdown. But now he watched as his mother jumped off the counter and went to help Eunida find a worthy substitute for sardines.

"Tuna?" his mother asked brightly. "Or mackerel fillets? They're delicious with powdered sugar or syrup."

Eunida mulled it over. "I suppose the mackerel would be all right. Does it have the little bones? I love to crunch on them."

"Will you be staying long, Great-Aunt Eunida?" his father asked in a quavering voice, looking even more distraught than when he'd first walked in.

Eunida bunched her preposterous eyebrows together and looked at Feltus's father as if he were a variety of mold. "There are forces at work here that must be dealt with. Persons who spend all their time at the office might be unaware, but we know. This is the center of some strange magic. It clogs the ether. Where is Feltus?"

"In his room, I imagine," his father answered without interest. He appeared to be having trouble with his tie. "What's clogged? If the toilet is blocked up, call the plumber," he told Feltus's mother.

"It is the very air that is obstructed," Feltus's mother said, waving her arms about and knocking his briefcase off the counter.

"You're as crazy as she is," Feltus's father replied, pointing at Great-Aunt Eunida. "The home inspector checked everything before we signed the lease, and I am positive he would have mentioned anything strange in the asbestos and lead reports he gave us. What was that waiver in the contract? And keep Feltus out of it. A nine-year-old boy has other things to think about."

"He's twelve. He just turned twelve, and Rose told me that we forgot his birthday! I think we should buy him a pony," his mother said.

His father finished knotting his tie and Feltus could hear the bones of his jaw crack as he bore down on his teeth.

"I will be back at seven o'clock sharp tonight. Perhaps

you will be so good as to have my black suit pressed and ready. I'll accompany you and Feltus to the Floribunda dinner conference, as agreed, although I don't believe you deserve my support. You have become intolerable. I would really appreciate some help and understanding."

Feltus's mother looked at his father unfazed. His father grabbed some crackers and a bottle of water from the shelf, shot one more look at her and the decrepit, dusty figure opening the tin of fish and spilling oil all over the floor, and left. Feltus's mother waved sunnily and reapplied herself to her impromptu breakfast.

"Peanut butter!" Feltus heard her say. "Now that would be perfect. And let's turn on the air conditioning!"

Feltus listened to his father's footsteps stomping down the hall, followed by a mighty slam of the front door. He found that he was actually glad that Great-Aunt Eunida was back. He couldn't wait to hear what she had learned from the Patrol. And maybe she would know what was going on with his mother. He could only hope.

He felt as if he'd been holding his breath since she'd gone, and now he could finally find out what was causing all the turmoil in the apartment and how the Patrol could fix it. He imagined the Patrol coming in like a flock of angels and turning the apartment into a wonderful place and his parents into happy, normal people. And maybe once things at home were okay, the situation in the Grand Gewglab would magically right itself too.

Feltus peeked his head out from the pantry, but Eunida was gone. He trundled along the hallway to the guest room and found her already making everything comfortable for herself and Winston. This involved throwing all the pillows on the floor and hanging bedsheets from the windows to block the glare. She also appeared to have moved most of the refrigerator stock into her bedroom.

Feltus shook his head and thought, *I only hope that she knows what to do about Mom.*

* * *

"What to do?" Eunida repeated back at him. Feltus had just finished explaining the situation and had asked for her help. "In what way, dear?"

"What will we do about my mother? You must have noticed that she's ... different."

"Only a change for the better as far as I'm concerned. Surely you must be enjoying it. No more tofu, no more flaxseed oil."

Feltus was assailed with a suspicion. "You didn't zap her or anything, did you? Put a potion in her herbal tea before you left to see the Patrol?"

The old lady inspected a jar of marinated artichokes and stirred the contents into her granola. "Ha! You know I'm only a simple soothsayer. Spells are the territory of witches and wizards. And Winston, of course."

"Did Winston come with you?" he asked.

"Of course, dear. I never travel without him. While peering into his scrying bowl the other night, he had an inkling that we might be needed here sooner than I had planned."

"An inkling?"

"Nothing serious, I'm sure. Perhaps there has been a visitor of some kind?"

Feltus shook his head impatiently.

"I'm sick of everybody telling me that it's nothing serious when obviously it is! Am I the only sane person here?"

Eunida added some thick clover honey to her bowl. "Oh, I wouldn't think so, dear."

"Did you come back with answers to *anything*?" he yelled. "It's only getting worse and nothing is getting fixed and I don't know how to do it by myself!"

Eunida nodded with approval. "That's right, Dear, let it out. No good bottling up all those emotions, they'll only give you gas pains."

Feltus knew that his face had turned bright red with rage. He shook his finger at her but did not trust himself to speak. "Wait here," he whispered through clenched teeth. "And release the toad, please. We need *some* intellect in this room."

He stormed back down the hallway to his bedroom. *Old bat!* he thought to himself.

RinMal looked up from his encyclopedia and, noticing Feltus's expression, asked, "What is it? Not your mother?"

"No, no, she's no different, but Eunida is back and she doesn't seem to understand how serious everything has gotten. I want you to come talk to her."

Much to his dismay, Feltus heard a tremble in his voice. He hadn't cried since he was little (or at least not very often in the last six months), but anger always made him lose it.

"I ask her about the Patrol and she tells me nothing. I ask her about my mother and she just jokes about it, saying I should be happy that Mom is acting like a teenager. "But *I'm* the one who'll be thirteen next year and *I* want to be the irresponsible one. She needs to act like a mother – concerned and affectionate and patient, and *there* for me." He felt the tightness in his chest ease and brushed a hot tear from his cheek.

RinMal was looking at him with sympathy. "Let's go," the PoodleRat said.

Since he had to act like a dog whenever he left Feltus's room, RinMal trotted ahead on four paws, his long claws making little clicking sounds on the wood floor. Once they'd entered Eunida's room and closed the door, he stood up again.

Feltus was feeling a little calmer, but he still had a hard time looking at his great-aunt who was on her third breakfast now, judging by the empty containers strewn around the room. He spied Winston sitting on a fluffy pillow and made his way over to him.

"It's good to see you," he said.

Winston nodded and his large mouth spread into a fleshy grin.

"I brought RinMal to meet you so you can see how bad it is," Feltus continued.

"Goodness, child," Eunida exclaimed. Feltus glanced up but she was not looking at him. She was gazing at the PoodleRat with a peculiar expression on her wrinkled old face.

She waddled over to RinMal and took his paw. "You're fur and bones. I thought the boy would be feeding you."

She pulled him back to the bed and offered him a sandwich. From the bits and pieces hanging out around the edges it looked to be concocted of sliced beets, eel, and blue cheese. She hovered over him until he'd taken a bite and then began to walk around the room, trailing her scarves behind her.

"The situation here is indeed worse than I expected." Now she looked at Feltus. "I suppose I should thank you for pointing that out to me, however rudely you may have done so. But I have been very concerned with the Veil. Since speaking to the Patrol, it has become clear that there is not only a breach, but many ruptures caused by the initial tearing. It has made the entire length of the Veil weak. There have been some horrible incidents, and I know that yours, RinMal, must rank up there with the worst. The Patrol has assured me that finding the breach is high on their list."

"But fixing the breach won't help the PoodleRats now," Feltus pointed out. "The Kehezzzalubbapipipi are already on the wrong side of the Veil. They have to be destroyed."

Winston had raised himself up on his haunches. His eyes gleamed with interest. "Did you say the Kehezzzalubbapipipi?" he asked in his rich, velvety voice.

Feltus nodded shortly, his attention wholly on his great-aunt.

"Astounding," the toad muttered to himself.

Eunida was pacing around the room, fiddling with the tasseled ends of her scarves.

"I'm sorry, Feltus, but that's the best I could do," she said. "The Patrol answers to no one, and they have their own way of handling matters concerning the Veil. They will be in touch at their discretion."

"*Well that just stinks!*" Feltus roared. RinMal tried to shush him, but Feltus was feeling helpless and angry. "There's a deadline to all of this! The prophecy only gave us a certain amount of days to figure it all out, and we've already wasted ... how many days are left, RinMal?"

"Four."

"Four?" Feltus squeaked. "That's not possible!"

He rounded on Winston. "Can you help the Poodle-Rats?" he demanded.

The toad clasped his long digits thoughtfully. "Coincidentally, following a rather strong impression I had during my last meditative retreat, I *have* recently done some research into the Kehezzzalubbapipipi, but there are only one or two entries in my books and they mostly have to do with their native world, which sounds like a dusty, desolate place. And their diet seems to encompass the full spectrum of organic and nonorganic matter. But there was no information about how to stop them."

"It sounds pretty hopeless then," Feltus said in a small voice and slumped against the wall. He felt worn out.

"There is still the prophecy," RinMal reminded him.

Feltus uttered a short, bitter laugh.

Eunida surveyed him. "Well, while we are here, we can look into this little matter of your mother," she said briskly.

"And perhaps some of the other knotty problems will

work themselves out."

"Can we start now?" Feltus asked. "Because in about six hours I have to accompany Mom and Dad to a fancy dinner party, and I'm guessing she's not going to be able to keep it together."

"First you can tell us exactly what happened the other night," Eunida said, settling down on the bed with Winston on her lap and a large pot of cold cream close at hand. "And then you can fill us in on all her behavioral changes. It might be helpful if you noted any extreme actions tonight as well."

"Will you start working on her immediately?" Feltus asked.

"We'll gather all the information and then move on from there," Eunida said in a nonchalant way that seriously annoyed Feltus. He wanted results now.

She began to smooth cream into the toad's pimpled skin, and Feltus, trying unsuccessfully to ignore this vaguely repellent sight, brought her up to date with RinMal's help.

# CHAPTER 13

## Herrings and Horticulture

**AFTER TWO EXHAUSTIVE** hours filling Eunida and Winston in on all Feltus's mother's new personality quirks, some of which Eunida had witnessed that morning, Feltus and RinMal left her room. Eunida and Winston were hunched over a large pile of dusty books "Searching for clues," as Eunida put it. Feltus was grateful that at least in this one problem area he was finally getting some help, even if he'd had to yell for it.

"Maybe you need to lose your temper more often," RinMal said in that uncannily intuitive way he had. "Remind people that you're here, you know."

"Well, it's great that they're helping, but I'm pretty worried about the situation tonight. The Herrings will be there, and they weren't even nice to Mom when she was her old self. What are they going to think if she starts dancing on the table or something? It could be the most embarrassing night of my life, and Dad won't make it any easier. He'll just lose his temper, or say something mean, and she'll cry."

"I'm sure once she's in a formal setting, she'll calm down a bit," the PoodleRat said soothingly. "Try to relax. We'll have some chocolate and do absolutely nothing until it's time for you to get dressed."

Feltus tried to ignore the pangs of guilt he felt. Four days left and he was griping to RinMal about mundane stuff like being publicly humiliated. He accepted the chocolate, but for the first time ever it didn't taste very good.

* * *

Feltus stood in the hallway a few minutes after 6:30 and tried to loosen his bowtie. His father had fastened it, seeming to take great pleasure in cutting off Feltus's circulation.

He felt like a penguin in a suit; he was the twin of his dad, wearing a tuxedo jacket, satin-piped trousers, and a starched light blue dress shirt. Feltus was moving like a squat, flightless bird too, since no one had noticed once again that these clothes were two years old and much too small.

His father hadn't said much to him since he'd arrived back from the office in his usual flurry of papers, briefcase, and financial documents. He'd just nodded curtly, told Feltus to get dressed, and, after throwing a pot of hair gel at him, ordered Feltus to "Get that mop tamed."

Feltus had spiked his hair and let the front part flop over one eye – his hair was the only cool thing about his attire as far as he was concerned. Luckily, his father hadn't noticed. And his mom – or anti-Mom, as he had started to think of her – had just given him a high five and called him "dude."

"Is Eunida coming too?" Feltus asked while they tried to hail a taxi. His father liked to be driven everywhere in the city, even when they were only going a couple blocks uptown.

"Absolutely not," his father retorted. "This evening will be painful enough without her."

"He bribed her with a deli platter and a video collection about anteaters," Feltus's mother elaborated. "And Rose made her a cinnamon nut roll garnished with garlic-stuffed olives." She smiled mischievously and punched Feltus's upper arm. "We should be so lucky, huh?"

"You look really pretty," Feltus ventured. "Don't you think, Dad?"

His mother pirouetted, then sank into a deep curtsy. The skirts of her long, sky blue evening dress flared and fell back into minute pleats around her legs. The sleeves were puffed, the bodice embroidered with flowers. Feltus thought she looked like a princess.

"I like the dress," his father said. "Mrs. Von Doolsing owns one, doesn't she? It looks expensive." He stood back and appraised his wife. "You were a little heavy-handed with the eye shadow and lipstick, but you look good," he said finally.

"Eunida helped me with my make-up," his mother said, blinking glittering green eyes accentuated with a broad sweep of blue eye shadow.

"Contact lenses?" Feltus wondered out loud, but his mother didn't answer. He'd wanted a pair of blood-red ones for Halloween and she hadn't let him get them.

His father raised a hand and flagged down a cab. As he followed his mother into the car, Feltus couldn't help noticing that she was wearing long polka dot socks and a pair of pink high-top sneakers. It smacked a little of Great-Aunt Eunida's fashion style and he wondered if the old lady had lent them to her.

The cab ride was cramped and short and was endured in silence, save for the sound of his mother snapping her bubblegum, and the almost perceptible echo of his father's displeasure. They disembarked outside a vast white marble building and ascended a long stairway to twin bronze doors.

Feltus had to grab his mother's arm to stop her from sliding down the long wrought-iron banister, although he would have given all his Ragat-Har comic books to have seen it. That is, if she wasn't his mother.

Mrs. Herring, clad in voluminous lawn-green crepe, came forward to greet them. She wore a nodding lily in an elaborate headdress that was stiff with pearls and Astroturf; a massive, egg-shaped tourmaline nestled in her bosom.

"Ahhh, my dear Karen and Bill!" she gushed, aiming

kisses in the air near their ears. "And the ... child," she continued with a saccharine intonation. Feltus managed a smile while a chorus of "Pickled Herrings" sang through his brain. Her small, egg-shaped husband fidgeted behind her, half-concealed by the immense bustle of her dress. Feltus glowered and pulled his hair farther down in front of his eyes.

He noticed that the conference auditorium was hung with garlands of orchids and fuchsia, entangled with lengths of cloth commemorating the various flower shows and awards. The cream of society assembled around a long table that was decorated with the blossoms of many rare and protected plants and was groaning under the weight of a thousand dishes.

Mrs. Herring led the way to a group of five chairs at the head of the table, passing through a horde of people dressed as colorfully as a flock of parrots. She tapped a golden fork against the slender trumpet of a champagne flute, and instantly all conversation ceased and all eyes turned toward them.

"Be still. Be silent," Feltus's father said to him, "and sit down." Feltus collapsed into the chair next to his father.

He looked at his mother who was beaming and swaying in time to some music that only she heard. "Mom," he said, but the word was lost in the feedback whine from a table microphone that suddenly switched on. He snagged her by her sleeve and pulled her into her chair, keeping his hand on her arm as if that would control her in some way.

Mr. Herring cleared his throat nervously and the sound reverberated around the room. His wife stood behind him like some massive shrubbery. His normally purple complexion darkened a couple shades until he resembled an aubergine. He ran his finger under his collar, donned a pair of wire-rimmed spectacles, and adjusted the waistband of his trousers. When he spoke, it was in short sentences interspersed with panting breaths.

"Welcome to the twenty-third annual meeting of the Magnus Floribunda. Please join me in welcoming our illustrious chairwoman – " Mrs. Herring stepped forward, beaming widely, " – and secretary."

He paused. Feltus nudged his mother who was deep in the pursuit of a stealthy hangnail. She stood up and surveyed the crowd amassed before her, blinked once or twice and started giggling. Feltus heard a small explosion of irritation burst forth from his father's throat as he dragged her back into her seat.

"Well, let us get down to business," Mr. Herring continued, taking a deep breath. "We are here to decide the fate of the big lawn. The entire design of the gardens hangs on this two-acre square in the middle of the city. There have been several motions for an Italianate model complete with fountains, statuary, and topiary. Other votes have been for an English knot garden, beech hedge, and maze.

"A third choice is a '*n-o-t*' garden (ha ha) which would follow the tenets of the school of anti-European design: six tons of pure, white sand; twelve boulders; a willow tree; and a genuine monk to create superbly swept designs twice a week.

"We will ignore the plan for a dry garden. There is no place in this city for desert cacti! I am sure of that!"

Feltus squirmed and suppressed a yawn. This was even more boring than he'd feared, although Herring's mention of cacti reminded him of the arid wasteland that had been the Grand Gewglab Forest. Too bad these people hadn't voted for a desert. He could just import some Kehezzzalu-bbapipipi and let them loose. *That's not so funny, actually.* He hoped the Veil around his world was hole free, and then he wondered how RinMal was doing at that moment.

Herring pushed his glasses back up his nose, inhaled, exhaled, and continued.

"Madame Secretary." This time, Feltus's mother jumped from her chair and bounced to her spot by Herring's side.

"I will now hand over the floor to our young and, ah, energetic secretary who has studied all the proposals. I'm sure that her announcement of the new garden design will please and gratify us all."

Feltus's father buried his face in his hands as Feltus's mother hitched her skirts up, tapped a fingernail on the microphone, causing a shrill whine of feedback to echo around the room, and sat down on the edge of the table.

"I'm completely unprepared," she said conversationally. There was a murmur of concern.

"Unprepared, that is, for the generosity of our hosts." She motioned toward Mr. and Mrs. Herring. There was general applause. Then she cracked her knuckles and got comfortable.

"Seriously, folks, I put a lot of thought into this plan and upon re-reading my notes," she pulled a wad of paper from her delicate evening purse and commenced to shred it, "I don't know what I was thinking!" She tossed the pieces of paper into the air. Feltus gazed out over an expanse of stunned faces and had to bite his lip to keep from laughing.

"We don't need some ornate park where everyone is afraid to walk on the grass because it's so full of flowers that no one even recognizes. Flowers that have no scent and need mountains of manure" – there was a collective gasp from the audience – "and excessive care. We need a place with friendly, happy plants – a place for children.

"Look at this child. This specimen," she said as she pointed to Feltus. "Pale, unhealthy, and prone to depression, he is a typical city kid. He's afraid of the outdoors, and he is addicted to comic books. Ladies and gentlemen, take a look at *that*!"

Feltus sank down deeper into his chair. His worst nightmare realized – he was being publicly shamed before hundreds of people.

"I propose we build a playground. I have a plan here for a play area with a nice redwood structure, a jungle gym, bungee jumps, etcetera; and we can plant rows and rows of sunflowers.

"Then, for the big green space in the middle, I was thinking dandelions." Her eyes were dreamy. "Such a pretty flower, and so misunderstood. And dirt cheap. Why, someone would probably pay us to haul them away! Anyway, that's it. Simple but effective."

She jumped to her feet, vigorously rubbing her hands together. The room was silent, jaws agape. Mrs. Herring dropped her pince-nez. Someone dropped his champagne flute. There was a tinkle of broken glass, and that was all.

Feltus's mother stood rocking back and forth with her skirts held out and then sank into a curtsy and flounced back to her chair.

After an interminable silence that seemed to last an hour, the hushed crowd began to whisper. The mutterings steadily rose in volume, although no words were discernible besides "young" and "crazy." Feltus's mother waved airily to the crowd and stifled a giggle.

Feltus slouched with his face in his hand, and prayed that they were all looking at her. His father pulled Feltus's mother upright, snapped his fingers at Feltus, and turned to Mr. Herring, whose mouth hung open slackly. Feltus's father shook his hand firmly, said "She's on cold medicine," then turned on his heels, steering Feltus's mother toward the door with one hand firmly clenching her elbow.

Feltus followed closely behind with his head hung low. Luckily, they did not have to wait long for a cab.

In the taxi, his mother kicked off her sneakers and wiggled her toes. "I think that went well, don't you?"

Feltus cleared his throat nervously. She punched his

father playfully on the arm. "Where to now? How 'bout a dance club?" she asked.

Feltus slumped. His father had begun the steady inhalation and exhalation from his nostrils that always signaled anger. Feltus could feel the tension in the air. He studied the smiling photograph on the driver's ID card. "I bet Iowa's nice," he said to the driver. "It's nice there, isn't it? How long would it take to drive there?" The driver shrugged.

"Are you insane?" Feltus's father asked his mother in a low voice.

"Maybe," Feltus's mother answered. "But in a good way."

"If you intend to waste my time in the future, I'll thank you to warn me in advance. I thought the Association was important to you. You begged me to come, and then you reduced it to a farce. Perhaps you should see a doctor," he said, turning to look out the window.

Feltus waited for his mother's face to crumple and the tears to start. But her smile never waned, and she even stuck her tongue out at his father.

As soon as they got home, their paths diverged in three directions. Feltus's mother headed for her bedroom, and Feltus heard the radio turned on full blast before he'd even reached his own room. Feltus's father headed straight for the kitchen pantry, where he kept the fixings for his weekend aperitif. The material of his suit jacket was stretched tightly across his back and Feltus could see the muscles jumping in his jaw.

Feltus's bedroom door was closed, and when he tried to turn the doorknob it was stiff and immobile. He kicked at the wooden panelling. There was a curious odor wafting through the room, like mud mixed with onions and melted chocolate.

"RinMal," he said – and then, "here, boy," in case his father was listening. There was no answer. He kicked at the door again, jamming his toes painfully. Then he put his shoulder into it and shoved. It swung open suddenly, as if the hinges had been greased, and he was thrown off balance.

Inside, Eunida squatted above a small smokeless fire and a brass pot, one of Rose's prized cooking utensils, Feltus noted. RinMal crouched next to her, holding a pen poised over a notebook. The foul smell originated from the pot and as Feltus watched, it gushed forth a torrent of dirty yellow smoke.

Eunida clapped her hands. "Bravo, Winston!" she said.

Winston sat at the head of the bed on one of Feltus's pillows. A plate containing the remnants of a can of dog food and a mound of lime gelatin balanced precariously next to him. Feltus wouldn't have minded, except that the toad was exceedingly large and quite moist, and the pillow had been his favorite from the age of four on, as it had the perfect ratio of firmness and softness.

"Feltus!" RinMal said, "Magic! We're doing magic!" The PoodleRat's voice tended to rise a few octaves when he was excited.

"Great." He was tired. He hated it when his parents were fighting. And he couldn't erase the image from his mind of his mother sticking out her tongue. He felt as if he didn't even know her anymore, and at this point her old stickler personality would have been preferable. At least he knew where he stood with her then.

He threw himself down on the bed, avoiding Winston. He felt the PoodleRat's eyes on him.

"What?" Feltus said.

"*Tut tut*," said Great-Aunt Eunida. She had a smear of burnt wood ash across her upper lip. It gave her a rakish air, as if she were a dissolute pirate. "Perhaps we can help with that bad temper, Feltus."

"We're going to find out what happened to your mother," RinMal said excitedly.

"It's true," Winston interjected in his deep bassoon voice.

Feltus looked up from the farthest corner of the bed.

"Right now?" he asked, trying but unable to keep the whiny tone out of the words. "You didn't seem to think it was that urgent earlier."

"It's not a matter of urgency," Eunida said briskly. "It's only a matter of acting on indisputable facts."

"Eunida," said Winston. "Tell the boy the truth."

His great-aunt blushed. "Your mother hugged me today. She made my two favorite desserts – dried-clam chocolate roulade, and pickled herring and peanut butter parfait – and brought them to me on a silver tray. And she smiled at me lovingly. It was terribly unsettling."

"So what are we going to do?" Feltus asked, interested despite himself.

"First, we'll cast a net in this room and see if it picks up any markers," Winston said.

"Markers?" Feltus asked.

"Magical indicators. If anything paranormal has entered within these four walls we'll be able to track its entry point and path," the toad elaborated.

Feltus got off the bed and peered into the pot.

"And the sludge?" Feltus asked.

"Sludge," Winston repeated and looked at the mess Eunida was brewing. "You've let it go too long. Did I not say it should be the consistency of thick cream? This is more like chocolate pudding. Take it off the heat."

"My herbal skills are rusty," Eunida fretted. "I was always so much better at alchemy."

As soon as she had removed the pan from the flame, the contents lightened to a golden brown that was rather like wet sand. Eunida rolled her sleeves up and gathered a small quantity.

"To the east first," Winston instructed, "then widdershins."

She tossed the first handful in the air, followed by the second, third, and fourth. The sand glistened, but did not fall to the ground; rather, it hung in the air for a moment, before falling like a dry rain. Then it began to glow with a blue fire.

Initially only the window was outlined in sapphire licks of flame, but then a weaving pathway appeared on the floor. Feltus could almost see the feet that had trodden that way. The steps stopped at the place where the floorboards had been bleached by the shattering of the glass vial. Then there was a blaze and for an instant, just a few seconds, he thought he saw the outline of a body, then two forms – one a strangely familiar silhouette – and finally, in the last flare-up, just one again.

"Was that a melding – a fusion of two separate beings?" Winston asked, rhetorically, it seemed, because before Feltus could ask, "A what?" and before Eunida could get more than half a grunt out, he'd continued.

"Clearly there was an entity. And," he added, "It entered from over there." He pointed one prehensile digit at the window. They all turned and looked at the jammed window, and then back at the floor where the tracks of two feet still glowed with a faint blue fire.

"At least 'it' has feet," Eunida pointed out. "Just think if it had tentacles!"

"Or thousands of little feet, like a giant millipede," Winston added with a smirk.

RinMal giggled.

"Yeah, well maybe if it was your bedroom or your mother, you wouldn't think it was so funny," Feltus said coldly.

Winston coughed apologetically. "We're just excited by the success of the spell. It's never a sure thing when your great-aunt is doing the mixing."

"And we have discovered that there *was* a presence. You were right, Feltus. Something happened to your mother in this room," RinMal pointed out.

"But there were two entities?" Feltus asked. His tired eyes felt hot and scratchy, as if the sand had fallen into them; but he knew that he'd seen two figures, one of which looked exactly like his mother would look if she'd been outlined in blue fire. "One was my mother. What was the other one and where did it come from?"

"I think, at least, we know the answer to the whereabouts of its entrance," Winston said. "Yes. The answer is plain."

"Feltus," RinMal said in his ear, "you need to face facts. Somehow that window over there allows entry through the Veil, and something managed to come through."

Feltus shook his head.

"Yes," said RinMal. "You can deny it no longer. The squashed pixie and this entity, whatever it was, both came here specifically. You have a portal."

"I don't care about that. All I care about is that something alien has fused with my mother and is making her act wacky. Who knows if it'll harm her? It could be a parasite or something," Feltus said desperately. "Eunida, can you get it out?"

"No. I'm no witch. I told you I failed basic spell-craft. The only art I ever excelled in was prophecy. Winston, what do you recall of the ancient magic? Perhaps that could be helpful to us."

"There are many laws to the ancient magic. Autonomy. Geography. The tenets of flight, practice, and outward responsibility. Pronunciation. Arguable response. Initiative. I've made the study of the laws my lifelong concern," the toad replied.

"What's the autonomy one?" RinMal asked.

"That each entity belongs solely to itself and retains the right to be true to its deepest self no matter what, why, or wherefore. There have to be constants in magic, otherwise it goes wild," the toad explained.

"What if this other being ... swallows my mom up or something," Feltus asked, remembering a film he'd seen in science class of an anemone consuming a crab.

"The law states that your mother and this other entity are separate even if they are temporarily occupying the same space. They are in juxtaposition but no 'one' has eaten the other ... yet," Winston replied in what he probably thought was a comforting tone.

"*Yet?*" Feltus croaked. RinMal thumped him reassuringly on the back.

"We're sure that Feltus's mother still exists inside her body?" RinMal asked.

"Indubitably. In fact, young PoodleRat, she is most definitely still here," Winston said.

"And how long can they stay in a juxta – whatever you called it?" Feltus interrupted. He was feeling increasingly drained.

"I don't know," Winston admitted. "Both entities seem to be getting along well together at the moment, but I think it would be best if they were separated soon."

Feltus picked up on the underlying current of concern in the toad's voice. He hated all this talking. He needed action.

"Since we've identified the problem, do you think we could figure out the solution?" Feltus demanded. "RinMal and the PoodleRats have only a few more days before they face extinction. I need to be working on that. But I can't concentrate if I'm worrying about my mother never coming back."

Both Winston and Eunida flapped their arms at him, which was as good as telling him to be quiet. Even RinMal, who should have been thinking about his own skin, seemed more interested in Feltus's mother at the moment.

"Autonomy," the PoodleRat repeated, writing it down

in his notebook. "But that means that whatever is in her is still its own self too, right?" he asked.

Winston nodded, "According to the ancient law, yes."

"So how do we separate them?" Feltus said, trying to get straight to the point without all the scholarly burblings. He had started feeling as if he were in class with one of his dull teachers.

Winston wrinkled his brow. "Aye, there's the rub," he said.

Thinking of school, Feltus was suddenly reminded of apples stuffed into a water-filled beaker too small to hold all of them. "So ... it's like that guy Aristotle. You can keep adding apples, but you'll lose water in equal amounts."

RinMal and Winston looked confused. Eunida was peeling some silver paper off of a lump of sticky and lint-covered nougat and paying no attention at all to the conversation.

"It's something we learned in science class," Feltus continued, thinking it through. "At some point, there's not enough room for all the apples." His face paled as an awful thought struck him. "She's not going to burst, is she?"

"Explosion?" Winston said slowly. "Oh, surely not. But implosion?"

The question hung in the air, and Feltus sat down heavily on the bed. RinMal handed him a bar of milk chocolate with almonds and Feltus unwrapped it with shaking fingers.

"I hate science," he said.

Eunida heaved herself to her feet. "It's been a long day, and Winston and I need our beauty sleep," she said. "We can pick this up in the morning."

Before she left, she placed a hand on Feltus's shoulder. "Don't take it so much to heart. Things have a tendency to work themselves out."

"Is that a premonition?" Feltus asked.

"No, but I read it on a cereal box."

Feltus cast her a look of loathing. As she scooped up Winston and exited the room, he forced himself to swallow a bite of chocolate, but he barely tasted it. Exhausted, he lay down and faced the wall, more than ready for sleep to come and quiet his tumultuous thoughts.

# CHAPTER 14

## Mica on a Mission

MUCH LATER THAT night, Feltus tried to find a comfortable place on his pillow. It smelled faintly of moss and mold and essence of Winston. He pummeled it, turned it over looking for a dry spot, and finally threw it on the ground.

RinMal whimpered in his sleep. He had nightmares every night now, Feltus noticed. Feltus tried not to dwell on his own memories of the Kehezzzalubbapipipi, but when RinMal was crying and growling and grinding his jaw in his sleep, Feltus could not help but remember that towering mass of teeth and claws, and think about how he had failed the PoodleRats miserably. The reminder of it slept at the foot of his bed every night, and even though he was glad that he had saved one PoodleRat, and even gladder that it was RinMal, he knew that all the negative feelings he'd ever had about himself were all warranted.

*Why can't I be the person everyone wants me to be?* The number of people who were disappointed in him seemed to grow ever larger no matter how hard he tried, and now RinMal and all the PoodleRats could be added to the list.

There was a full moon that night, and silvery light cascaded over the windowsill. If his thoughts had not been so turbulent, Feltus would have climbed out the sitting room window and onto the fire escape to watch the twinkle of distant lights over the barely visible river and the creepy shadows that the twisted maple tree below made on the sidewalk. But instead he turned his face toward the wall and brooded on the prophecy, his mother, and all the questions Eunida's spell-casting had raised.

He thought he finally understood what Mr. Leggett had been going on about in science class, but he wasn't sure if the ideas applied to his mother. Can magic and science follow the same principles? He jammed his tense fingers in his ears to block out RinMal's moans, and tried to clear his mind.

Suddenly, there was a loud popping sound that reverberated through his skull and unplugged his nose. He had the oddest sensation that the air had been pushed aside, the same feeling, he recalled, he'd had right before the giant bug-fairy had appeared.

He sat up and blinked into the shadows by the door but saw nothing, heard nothing – until a fork-shaped object suddenly appeared about a millimeter in front of his chin. Its points were sharp and pronged like the ends of a fish hook. He inched his way backward, but the giant fork followed him. He coughed loudly, but RinMal didn't stir. *How can he be sleeping through this?*

Feltus's left hand groped under the mattress until he found his flashlight. He brought his arm out and switched on the light in as quick and smooth a motion as he could manage.

The trident was at his throat in an instant, and he saw eyes in front of his – brilliant green eyes that belonged to a girl. Her lips were drawn back over pointy teeth, and her pupils were dilated so the iris was just a thin band around the blackness of her pupil. Feltus closed his eyes and waited for the pain of metal spikes puncturing his throat.

"Where is she?" the trident-wielding girl said.

"Who?" Feltus croaked, holding his hands over his face and peeking at her through his fingers.

"My sister!"

The edge of the weapon nicked the skin along his jaw. He was sure it had drawn blood and it made him angry.

"Your sister isn't here," he spat at her. "You can't just come busting into someone's bedroom, with a ... a ... fork, and make insane accusations ..." His voice trailed off. "How did you get in here, anyway?"

"Through there," she said, gesturing toward the window.

In the brief moment that her attention was distracted, he pushed her arm away roughly, reached over and flicked on the light. As she stood blinking, he scrambled over the bed and put it between them.

"That window doesn't open," he sputtered.

"So? That's where I came in," she replied in an insolent tone that made him feel stupid.

They stood four feet apart, glaring at each other. She was about his own age, thin and wiry, and dressed in a colorless shift that didn't cover the grime and scratches etched into her knees and elbows. She looked as if she'd never had a bath in her whole life.

Her lips were still drawn in a feral manner over her teeth, but she made no further move with the trident. She watched him with a cool, speculative gaze that reminded him of a cat watching a mouse. His muscles tensed with a rush of adrenaline. He put a little more distance between them and gave RinMal a kick to waken him.

"We have a visitor," he said in a low voice, not taking his eyes off the girl.

The PoodleRat jumped to his feet. His fur stood in a ridge of spikes along his backbone.

The girl stared at RinMal and nodded with satisfaction. "I was not wrong. This must be the place. There is magic here. I felt it stretch across the miles I traveled."

Her face grew cold. "What have you done with Jasper? Where is my sister?"

"You're the only girl here," Feltus said hotly. He'd swabbed at his neck, and his fingers came away bloody.

"Just because you broke into my room doesn't mean you get to start making accusations!"

"The pathway was clear. I can't have made a mistake." She raised her chin and looked at them mulishly.

"Sit down," RinMal said. "I'll get us something to eat and drink, and you can tell us who you're looking for." He pushed her gently toward the floor pillows.

She sat cross-legged, keeping one hand on her weapon, as the other clasped the leather pouch she wore around her neck. She turned her sullen eyes on Feltus. Now that she was across the room from him, he felt confident enough to sneer back at her.

RinMal emerged from the closet with three sodas and a bag of ridged potato chips. He hooked his claw under the bottle cap, flicked it off, and held the bottle out to her.

"It's good," he reassured her. "Sweet and bubbly."

She looked at the bottle in his paw with horror, then raised her weapon and scooted backward until she had put some distance between herself and the PoodleRat.

"Crazy," Feltus pronounced with satisfaction and took one of the sodas. "I should call the police and get her hauled out of here." He walked over to the window and suavely opened his own drink by banging it on the edge of the windowsill – a move he had perfected after years of practice.

He noticed that the panes of glass were covered in a fine silt that sparkled in the light. The window was a magnet for dirt, and he could never get it open in order to sweep it out.

"How did you say you got in?" he asked, thinking of the squashed fairy and the noise explosion that had heralded both arrivals.

"I came though the Veil," she said as matter-of-factly as if she'd come through the front door. "We followed the traces left by my sister and they led here. I'm sure we're not mistaken. It was all so clear, I could have found this place with my eyes shut."

"We? There aren't more of you are there?" Feltus asked, sweeping his gaze quickly over all the corners of his room.

She shook her head. "The elders could not make the trip, but they helped guide me."

"So what are we talking about? Interstellar travel? Time exploration? Teleportation?" Feltus asked.

"You speak as if you have mud in your mouth," she said, holding a bag of potato chips under her nose and then tearing it open with her sharp teeth.

"Don't insult me while you're eating my food!" he said. "It was just a simple question."

She picked a chip out of the bag and licked it. Her cat eyes looked at him with such disdain that he felt his face get hot.

"I think she was just saying that she didn't understand the words you used," RinMal pointed out. "It wasn't actually an insult."

"I don't know what it's called," she answered Feltus. "I just do this."

And suddenly she was three feet closer to him. There was no ripple of air, no blurring, no sprinkling of fairy dust. She simply moved as fast as a thought, and then her hand reached out and slapped his cheek. Hard.

"Ow!" cried Feltus.

"Whoa!" exclaimed RinMal. Feltus shot him a dirty look. It bothered him that the PoodleRat was so obviously impressed.

"It's easy," the girl said, preening. "At first I had to concentrate, but now it's just like breathing. All of the young ones can do it."

"Tell us how you think your sister came to this world," RinMal said gently. "Perhaps it will help us to help you find her."

She sat up straighter and brushed the salt from her

fingers. Her dark hair flopped into her eyes and she pushed it back with impatient hands. Her mouth slanted downward at the edges as if she had never smiled.

"This is what my father calls conjecture," she said. "But if we didn't act on things, then nothing would ever get done. He'd leave her out here in the wilderness forever, and the elders would just talk and talk and do nothing." She straightened her back and two deep lines appeared between her eyebrows.

"I come from a dry world," she continued. "It was not always so, but the water was taken from us many years ago, and it is less than a memory now even to my grandparents." She cast a darkling look at the opened soda bottle. "It is anathema to us now."

"What do you mean?" Feltus asked. "You don't need to drink to live?"

She shook her head.

"Who stole the water from you?" RinMal asked.

"We call them the waterlords. They kept us separate, built walls and locking doors so that hundreds of feet of earth lay between their world and ours. After a time we didn't miss the water anymore, and the tales became just that – stories, fairy tales to scare the little ones, cautionary myths that told of cruel punishment to trespassers. I didn't believe any of it until Jasper disappeared seven days ago."

"What do you think happened to her?" RinMal asked.

"*I* think she got captured by the waterlords." She sat up straighter. "I traced her up to one of their secret passageways before I lost her trail. My parents don't want to believe it. She was always too curious for her own good, always sneaking off and spying and looking for adventure. *And* I've heard rumors of an evil magic that allows the waterlords to trap a soul within a glass flask."

"If your sister was imprisoned, then how would she

come to be here?" RinMal asked.

"She could will herself somewhere safe – somewhere she could find help," she replied casting a derisive look at Feltus.

Feltus stiffened. Then he made a noise that sounded like a stifled laugh. RinMal laid a warning paw on his arm.

"I feel like I'm living in a science fiction book," Feltus muttered.

"You have an odd mind," RinMal whispered to Feltus. "You accept some things without question, and yet other things that are obvious to me are incomprehensible to you." The PoodleRat pinched him.

"Oww!" said Feltus rubbing his arm. Everyone was picking on him tonight.

RinMal continued in a low voice. "You've had no trouble accepting port holes, PoodleRats, and the prophecy, not to mention the Kehezzzalubbapipipi – stop me when you've heard enough."

"Yeah, but waterlords and soul stealing! That's just nuts!" Feltus said, trying to put on a façade. Inside, his guts were starting to tie themselves in knots.

"How do you know?" the PoodleRat asked. "Trust that there are things beyond rationalization. You just saw her teleport. Listen to her."

RinMal directed a question at the girl. "How did you find your way here? To this place?"

"The traces of my sister's journey are as plain to me as footsteps," the girl said. Her fingers traced a swirling pattern across the floor. "I see other paths too. They diverge and intersect, but they all originate here." Her fingertip tapped a spot in front of the window.

"Her passing-through looks violet to me," she said as she followed a looping, invisible trail to the middle of the room. "And here, something happened."

Feltus's eyes moved to the spot where she was

standing. It was exactly where his mother had stood waving his shorts around right before the vial shattered. A large area of the wood was stripped of varnish. He wished he could believe she'd just made a lucky guess. An awful certainty was beginning to insinuate itself into his mind and looking at RinMal, he could tell the same thoughts had occurred to him. He decided to take refuge in sarcasm. He didn't know why, but this strange girl irritated him.

"Listen, what should we call you?" RinMal asked the girl.

Feltus snorted impatiently. This was no time for socializing. He wanted to get to the nitty-gritty.

"Mica," she said.

Feltus interrupted. "Okay, Mica. You think" – he managed to inject a lot of patronizing doubt into the simple phrase – "that your sister was imprisoned in a glass tube, and then propelled herself through space until she arrived in my bedroom – is that right?"

Mica stared at him, her face slowly reddening, and suddenly her sharpened fork was pointed right at his chest.

RinMal trod on Feltus's foot and then hurried over to Mica and gently forced her weapon arm down. He shot Feltus an angry glare. "Are you trying to sabotage your life?" he asked. "I thought you wanted to help your mother."

He turned back to the girl.

"One night ago, a vial full of green smoke was broken in this room, right where you are now standing. My friend's mother was completely engulfed and has seemed odd ever since."

"Strange in what way?" Mica asked.

"She just isn't herself," Feltus said shortly, not wanting to discuss his mother with a stranger.

"Normally she's quite reserved. Quiet, well-mannered, conservative," RinMal clarified. "And the morning after the tube broke she became ... unrestrained."

"Wild," Feltus added, starting to feel a little bit better now that it was all out in the open.

"And perhaps just a bit inappropriate," the PoodleRat concluded. "The things that always mattered so much to her don't anymore."

Feltus looked at his friend with affection. He hadn't realized that RinMal knew his mother so well.

"Jasper is very high-spirited. Have you noticed an increased appetite for dried fish? Salt? Sweet things?" Mica asked.

"Yesterday I found her sucking whipped cream out of the canister," Feltus admitted. "But I figured it was just a hormonal thing." He'd heard his father use that phrase with his mother before. It usually made his mother burst into tears or start throwing plates.

RinMal shook his head. "I would say that this new behavior is definitely arcane. It happened so suddenly, and you've never mentioned any weird quirks in the past."

"No, she's always been pretty normal. I mean, she's ... a mother. Obsessively organized ..." Feltus explained.

"You miss her," Mica said.

Feltus cleared his throat quickly. "I just want things to be the same as before."

"I'd like to see this mother," Mica said, standing up.

Feltus stood in front of the door to bar her way. "No way! Not with that pitchfork, you don't," he said firmly. He wasn't going to risk any harm coming to his mother. He could be quite as stubborn as this girl, and he hated the way she talked to him like he was nobody. He'd noticed she was much more civil to RinMal, and that made Feltus inclined to be rude.

RinMal looked from one to the other, observing the set expression on Feltus's face and the unreasonable slant to Mica's mouth.

"Of course you can see her," the PoodleRat said easily to Mica. "But your weapon has to stay here."

"And you have to be quiet. And listen to what I say," Feltus added.

Mica's eyes flashed, but she nodded abruptly.

Feltus led the way out his bedroom door and down the dark hallway, his fingers covering the beam of his flashlight so that only spidery filaments of light shone through. His hand glowed red, and it reminded him of summer camp a couple of years ago when he and his friends had told ghost stories in the tent – which in turn reminded him of Percy. Feltus thought he'd almost rather face a mess of mathematical word problems than the disaster his summer was turning into.

He wondered fleetingly if maybe this was what his life was like now – constant turmoil and disaster at every turn. He just wished it would stop long enough for him to catch his breath. At least Mica was stealthy. He could barely see her behind him – only the gleam of her teeth – and RinMal trod softly on his big furry feet.

His father's study was all the way at the end of the hall. The space under the door showed a sliver of light, which meant his dad was working late again. His father had had the room sound-proofed before they'd moved in, and usually once the door was closed, it stayed shut for hours.

They took a right turn to the intersecting corridor and tiptoed past Eunida's room. It was dark and quiet. She'd pinned a "Do Not Disturb" sign to her door and also a breakfast menu filched from some five-star hotel, with the words waffles, kippers, and hollandaise heavily underlined.

Feltus's mother's door was the second on the right. He eased it open, holding his hand up to halt the others. "Wait," he breathed.

He listened hard. His mother was an indistinct lump

under the covers, but he could hear her soft exhalations over the whirring of an electric ceiling fan. He went closer. The shaded flashlight picked out the worry lines across her forehead, the mauve circles under her eyes, and the paleness of her skin.

*She doesn't get out enough,* he thought. *And she frets too much over stupid things.*

Her hair was braided into dozens of little pigtails, some of which stuck out at right angles from her ears. He raised the light higher. She grumbled and muttered, moving slightly, and her eyelids opened a fraction. It was eerie seeing the slice of emerald green iris and hearing the deep regular rhythms of sleep. He wanted to reach out and slide the lids closed, but feared waking her.

Mica jostled his arm, and the flashlight beam cast crazy dancing shadows on the ceiling. He felt like shoving her back, but she grasped his forearm to steady it and leaned in to study his mother.

"Look, she has eyes like mine," Mica whispered. "And Jasper would do her hair like that when she was bored. It used to drive me crazy, watching her fiddle with all those tiny braids."

"That seems a little circumstantial to me," Feltus muttered, yanking his arm away. He was still mad at the girl for waking him up and pulling a sharp utensil on him. He decided, however, that when he told Percy eventually, the fork would be a knife, six inches long, and sharp enough to bone fish, or – what did that commercial say? – "Slice through this tin can as if it were butter."

"Maybe you two would like to continue this conversation in Feltus's room?" RinMal said, gently drawing Mica toward the door.

"Wait. Let me check one more thing," she said.

She walked back over to Feltus's mother and brushed

her hair aside. Feltus sprang forward, ready to pummel Mica if she tried anything, but her touch was gentle.

Behind his mother's right ear was a small discoloration, a red mark like a sea shell. It had definitely not been there before.

"Jasper," Mica said with a sigh. "You always get yourself into trouble."

RinMal met Feltus's eyes over Mica's bowed head. "Well?" he mouthed silently.

Feltus shrugged, and finally muttered a slightly whiny "Okay."

"Mica, we're all together on this, right?" the Poodle-Rat asked.

She nodded.

"Then let's go back to Feltus's room and get started on fixing it," RinMal said.

Feltus lingered for a moment after they left and watched his mother's eyelids tremble as she dreamed. Then he straightened the covers under her chin and went to join the others. He didn't think he'd be able to relax with an armed girl in his room, but maybe exhaustion would grant him at least a few hours of sleep.

# CHAPTER 15

## Operation Separation

FELTUS JOLTED AWAKE. He'd fallen asleep bolt upright, but at some point during what little had been left of the night, he'd collapsed to one side, pinning his arm underneath him and imprinting the rubber grip of the flashlight onto his cheek.

He remembered watching Mica and her unblinking gaze observing him. She hadn't said much after the discovery of the birthmark, but her mouth had thinned and her eyes had darkened. She'd accepted the blanket RinMal gave to her, but nothing more. And when Feltus had given in to exhaustion, she'd still been looking ahead, obviously deep in her own thoughts. She unnerved him.

He took some pleasure now from noticing that she had drooled a little in her sleep. For some reason, he felt calmer about everything. Yes, his mother was sharing her body with someone else; someone who was not even of this world and was capable of teleportation if nothing else. But now that they knew they could move on, they could work out how to free them both. And the first step, which was suddenly crystal clear, was to talk to Great-Aunt Eunida, and make their uninvited guest known to her.

\* \* \*

"Feltus! Who is this filthy and half-naked person?" Eunida shrilled, tossing one of her moth-eaten shawls at Mica. The girl looked at it, poked it with one dirty toe, and left it heaped on the floor. RinMal closed the bedroom door and placed a chair under the knob to keep anyone else from coming in.

"We have a high opinion of ourselves, don't we?" Eunida said to the girl in a deceptively mild voice.

Mica's chin came up, and Feltus had a pretty good idea that she was readying herself to deliver a blast of insults. He stepped in between the two of them even though he was quite happy that Eunida seemed to find the girl as objectionable as he did.

"Do you think you two can focus for a minute?" he asked them. "We need to concentrate on my mother. We don't have a whole lot of time to sort this out. I need to get back to working on the PoodleRat prophecy – there isn't much time left! – and Mom is liable to implode or do something really inappropriate any minute."

"Mica showed up last night looking for her sister," RinMal filled Eunida in. "She followed a path through the Veil and it led straight to Feltus's room and the spot where the vial broke. The entity we learned about through your spell," and he bowed to Eunida, who seemed to enjoy the attention, "must be Mica's sister."

"Mmm," Eunida said, throwing Mica a look of dislike. Eunida then bent over the cloth-covered birdcage and whispered something too low for others to hear. She straightened up with a groan and a creaking of feminine undergarments.

"One of the mud-bellies, are you?" she asked Mica.

"Yes," Mica replied.

Feltus waited for an explanation, but there was none forthcoming.

"Then you have come a fair distance. Let's put our heads together."

Feltus saw some of the tension leave Mica's shoulders. Feltus realized with a start that he, RinMal, Eunida, and

Winston were her only hope. It made him feel a little sorry for Mica, especially since she was so far from home.

"There must be a key to this," Eunida said. "We know that she is in but how to get her out?" She rounded on Feltus. "What were you jabbering about last night?"

"It was just something we learned about in science."

"Explain it to me, come on. Your science is so different."

"Well," Feltus began. "Bear in mind that it's not one of my strong subjects." He stopped and tried to organize his thoughts.

"Basically," he continued, aware that Mica was looking at him intently and that his face was red, "there's some law that says that objects can't occupy the same space without dislodging space equal to their size ... or something like that."

"Wex Lethoo Radok! Help us if you ever ascend to political power," Eunida muttered. "Such woolly-headedness!"

This seemed a little harsh to Feltus given her tendency toward garbled sentences.

"You're saying that your mother and the girl's sister could be trapped in an unstable state?" his great-aunt continued.

"I think so," Feltus said miserably.

"But that means," RinMal interrupted, "that all we have to do is find the trigger to dislodge them."

"What could that be?" Winston's deep voice came from the depths of his birdcage. Mica jumped and moved away from the bed.

"I don't know. They're not apples," Feltus said.

"Who would know?" Eunida asked, and then turned to Feltus. "What about that friend of yours – the precocious, curly haired blond boy? He always has his disgusting little nose buried in books, doesn't he?"

"He's away at math camp for the next few days, up in the mountains about ninety miles north of here."

"We could get a message to him," Winston said slowly.

"How? There's no phone line and the mail service is only once a week," Feltus pointed out. Feltus had received one postcard from Percy, and he still hadn't gotten around to mailing his friend the chocolate bars and number two pencils he'd requested.

"I have a rocket," RinMal interrupted excitedly. "I've been working on it at night to keep my mind off of what's happening in the Forest. It's just a little one, but I added solar power packs to it, and I'm pretty confident it could go at least two hundred miles. There and back. We could attach a message to it."

"And Winston and I can do some simple address magic. Do you have anything that belonged to the boy, something he's touched, licked?" Eunida asked.

"I have his study notes for next year's natural history class," Feltus said.

"Does he sweat a lot? Slobber? No? Well, I'm sure there'll still be enough DNA to make a locator spell."

"We can summarize the situation and have him send a solution," RinMal said.

"The only thing is that Percy tends to be a little wordy with explanations. I mean, I'm sure he'll give us some kind of answer – he's really smart – but it could be indecipherable to us. I've looked over those biology notes of his five times and I have yet to make it past the 'Botany 101' chapter headings," Feltus explained.

"It's unfortunate that there isn't a phone," RinMal said.

Eunida suddenly clapped her hands together and hopped a little hop. Her skirts flew up above her knees, exposing the usual expanse of stripy kneesocks and a drift of yellowed petticoats. "Winston," she croaked, "what about the vidogram? It's been so long since we've done one."

Winston crawled out of the cage onto the nightstand. His pimpled skin looked freshly oiled, and there was a remnant of wing casing hanging from his lower lip.

"Feltus," he said in a voice as smooth as molten chocolate. "Can your friend get access to a pool of water? It need be no more than a bowl, but the water must be pure and cold."

"I'm sure he could."

"Good." Winston settled his body down, interlacing the long digits on both front legs. Folds of liquid skin spread in a pimply pool.

Mica stared at him aghast, her hand clasping the pouch around her neck, and backed up against the wall. Feltus admitted to himself that he was happy she'd been shocked into silence – she didn't seem capable of saying anything nice to anyone.

"RinMal, we will send a message and instructions using your rocket," Winston continued. "If all goes well, at the appointed hour we will be able to converse with Percy face to face."

"Where are we going to do it?" Feltus asked, feeling a rush of excitement. He hadn't really known Percy for long, but he was already in awe of his friend's brain, and the good thing about Percy was that he seemed game for pretty much anything.

"You'll see soon enough," Eunida said curtly. "We have to get that rocket sent off, hope the blond worm is around to receive it, and wait for his reply before we can start the vidogram."

She pulled a gigantic pocket watch from one of her many pockets and consulted it. Feltus noticed that the hands spun counterclockwise. "I'd say we've got quite a few hours before we can get down to business," Eunida said.

* * *

Squeezing a gigantic toad, a PoodleRat, a fat old lady, and two kids into a medium-sized bathroom at 7:16 p.m.

proved difficult. Feltus found himself jammed between the toilet and the edge of the claw foot bathtub. But that, as it turned out, was the place to be. At exactly 3:32 p.m., RinMal's rocket ship message had blasted off from the fire escape without anyone but a couple of seriously annoyed pigeons noticing. Percy had sent back a reply scratched in his familiar spidery script almost immediately. The time was set, and now it was just a question of waiting around and seeing what kind of magic Winston and Eunida brewed to reunite them all.

There were no colorful fires or rainbow-hued smoke, no incantations or strange flashes of light, no curious odors. Eunida had stuffed her greasy hair into a woolen hat and changed into a pair of sloppy slippers, and at 7:17 p.m. the only thing that happened was that she raised the seat on the toilet and stuck her nose into the bowl. She made a little twist of toilet paper, filled it with a pinch of blue crystals and a few shreds of Percy's biology notes, and tossed it in.

"Oh, man!" Feltus groaned disbelievingly. Mica looked at him with curiosity.

"What's the problem now, Feltus?" Eunida asked, hands on her wide hips.

"Isn't magic supposed to be some noble, glorious thing?" he cried. "Wizards and dragons and cauldrons and wands? Here we are hunched around a toilet!"

And then he shut up because Percy's face suddenly appeared on the shimmering surface of the water.

Feltus leaned forward.

"Hey," said Percy. "Who'd a thunk, huh?"

"What are you talking into?" Feltus inquired.

"Cereal bowl, bottled water. Pretty nifty. I'll want to run some diagnostics later."

"Sure ... Did the note I sent make any sense?" asked Feltus.

"Kind of. You've confused Archimedes with Aristotle, and I'm shaky on the less scientific bits. But you did say that that crazy old relative of yours was involved somehow, right? So I figured there was a heaping helping of nuts mixed in."

"*Ar hehmm*," Eunida said. "Young scallywag!" and she thumped the toilet seat with a toothbrush – his own, Feltus was horrified to see.

"Yeah, my great-aunt is here," Feltus explained, "and a few others."

"Oops," Percy said, looking a little embarrassed.

"Don't worry about it right now. Seriously, she's been called much worse," Feltus replied, ignoring the thump across the back of the head Eunida gave him.

"So do you have any ideas? We're relying on you." He felt Mica's hair brush against his cheek and he pulled her forward. "This is Mica. It's her sister Jasper who's stuck in my mother."

Percy's eyes widened. "Pleased to meet you."

"What's the story?" Mica asked, keeping well clear of the toilet water.

Percy took a deep breath. Feltus could tell he was twirling a pencil, a habit Percy had when he was thinking hard. When Feltus was thinking hard, he stuck his pencils up his nostrils and pretended he was a walrus.

"It's funny that we're communicating through the medium of water, because that's what started this little germ of an idea I've had. You know the expansive quality that water can have, especially in relation to certain forms of matter?" Percy paused.

"What's he going on about?" Eunida said shrilly. She elbowed RinMal, who was keeping well out of Percy's sight, in the ribs. "Too much book learning and not enough non-interactive entertainment, that's his problem. Goes spouting off about some half-baked notion, and thinks he's Nostradamus. Remind him he's in a toilet," Eunida yelled, spraying spittle over everyone in her excitement.

Winston handed her a towel and said sternly, "Give the boy a chance. Sometimes science can solve that which magic cannot, and vice versa, of course. I think his premise is intriguing."

Percy apparently heard the deep tones of the toad's lugubrious voice. "How many people are with you, Feltus?" he asked. "I can only see you and Mica."

"People? Oh, just one or two. Anyway, go on with your idea."

"Okay, well, you mentioned in your note that Mica and her sister are from a dry world. That fact, along with Archimedes' principle, got me wondering if maybe hydration was the key. Like instant onion soup, or dunking a sponge in the sink. Just get your mom to drink a whole bunch of water and that could expand the space inside her and push the sister out."

"That's lunacy!" Eunida shrilled, at the same time that Winston uttered, "So improbable it just might work."

Percy ticked off the points of his argument on one hand: "The osmotic powers of water, the thinness of the cell walls, and the natural law governing the introduction of foreign entities within a host body. It all adds up. I've already started writing a dissertation on it, although, of course, names will be changed and I'll pretend it was all done with hamsters."

"How much water?" Feltus asked.

"I'm not sure. As little as twenty glasses or as much as twenty gallons. It depends on what, no offense meant, the parasitical entity is used to. If its body biology has evolved so that it in fact no longer requires water, then it could be just a few ounces above the recommended eight eight-ounce glasses a day."

Winston looked at Mica. She shrugged. "We don't need any liquid to survive," she said.

"Mom drinks a lot of water," Feltus said thoughtfully. "Sometimes that's all she has for dinner."

"No wonder she over-compensates with all those meetings and groups," Eunida said with a sniff. "She's probably starving for a few donuts and a gallon of full-fat milk. That kind of rigid self-control is never natural."

Feltus faced her. "You be quiet," he said through clenched teeth. "She's always been polite to you!"

Surprisingly, it was Mica who placed a hand on his arm.

"I think your friend's idea is a good one. Let's waste no time," she said and smiled at Feltus. It was just a small smile, but it made him feel better almost immediately.

"Let me know how it turns out," Percy said. "I'll be back home in a couple of days."

Feltus barely had time to say goodbye before Winston reached out from his perch on the bathtub soap dish and flushed the toilet with a thin, bulb-tipped digit. Feltus watched sadly as his friend's face blurred in the swirls and eddies of water.

"Eunida meant no harm, by the way. Sometimes her tongue runs away with her," Winston whispered in Feltus's ear. "She just wishes that it were her spells that had prevailed. Ever since the trouble with her sensors and the barrage of prophecies, she's been a little insecure." The toad plopped down on the floor, oozed over to Eunida's foot, and was scooped up into her arms. They headed for the door.

"Wait!" RinMal said to Eunida and Winston. His voice was hopeful and fearful at the same time. "Can you show me the Grand Gewglab Forest?"

Feltus laid a comforting hand on the PoodleRat's arm. He could feel Mica's warm breath against his neck. It really was too small a room for so many bodies.

Eunida directed a piercing look at RinMal. "Of course," she said. "If you're sure that's what you want. It won't be a true vidogram, however, since there's no known water source there and thus no interaction."

She reached into a small neck-bag and pulled out a tuft of red PoodleRat fur. Feltus wondered if it was the same tuft she'd picked up from outside his room during her first visit. From another bag she measured out a small pinch of the blue powder, then combined the two in another twist of toilet paper. "Return home," she muttered, throwing it in the toilet.

The water in the toilet bowl boiled and spat; when it had settled, a gray, dimly lit scene floated to the surface. Percy's yellow head had bobbed in a sea of blue-green; but the world the toilet was showing now was nothing but gloomy shades of gray and black.

A large group of PoodleRats huddled in a dark passageway. They were crowded and cramped, and their only illumination was a few smoking torches thrust into cracks in the rocky walls. Feltus could see they lay on loose dirt. He heard Mica inhale sharply. His own breath felt as if it were caught in his throat.

There were no mattresses or pillows, no warming fires, none of the comforts he knew the PoodleRats enjoyed. They had gone underground with the basic necessities – some cooking pots, a large heap of what looked like dry leaves, and carefully arranged rows of roughly made weapons, mostly sharpened shovels, mallets, and scythes. The toilet did not hide the upsetting fact that there were far too few weapons. And far too few of the PoodleRats.

"That can't be all that's left?" Feltus whispered, terrified that his slowness in solving the puzzle of the prophecy had resulted in the partial extinction of an entire species. He dug the fingernails of one hand into his palm.

"Some have died since I've been gone," RinMal replied.

"But no great number yet."

The picture moved as if a camera were panning over the motionless bodies. Most of the PoodleRats slept, or stared unseeing with huge blank eyes at the crumbling roof of the cave. Feltus looked for Saldemere. Beside him, he sensed that RinMal was doing the same. They finally caught a glimpse of the venerable old PoodleRat standing guard at the mouth of one of the tunnels that fanned out from the sleeping area.

Feltus exhaled in a long sigh of relief. Saldemere Og's shoulders were slightly bowed, and his proud chest was more concave; but he wore a bright red military jacket and two sharp, shiny swords cross-girded his back. The clothes hung loosely on his emaciated frame.

"Before I left, he began refusing food so that the younger ones could eat," RinMal whispered.

"We'll find the answer," Feltus promised.

"I know you believe that and I believe in you. But I must go. I cannot leave Saldemere to fight alone, and I know now that we must fight. Even if it's the last battle we ever embark on."

Feltus swallowed the lump in his throat. He couldn't speak. He didn't want his friend to leave. But he also knew that there was no way RinMal could stay now, not after what they had just seen. The others stood silent. Eunida swiped vigorously at the tip of her nose with her sleeve.

There was nothing more to say.

With his fingers clasping the carved bone figurine of the PoodleRat in his pocket, Feltus pushed RinMal out the bathroom door. He didn't want to wait and watch Eunida flush the toilet – that seemed almost tragically ironic. RinMal dropped to all fours instantly upon exiting the bathroom. Seeing his friend acting "dog" seemed so demeaning all of a sudden that Feltus had to bite his lip. Together, the group walked slowly to Feltus's room.

Once inside, Feltus went to his closet, grabbed a backpack, and started pulling sweaters and woolen hats down from the shelves and stuffing them into the bag. RinMal sat on the bed and watched him. Eunida, Winston, and Mica huddled in an uncomfortable cluster in the corner by the door.

Then Feltus went through the contents of his chest of drawers, choosing everything and anything that might bring some comfort to the PoodleRats – socks, long underwear, T-shirts. He packed it all in a silent frenzy, knowing it was the only thing keeping him from dissolving into angry tears. RinMal waited quietly.

Feltus stowed the bag by the door, told the PoodleRat in a cracked voice that he'd be right back, and pushed past his great-aunt and the others. Then he ran to the kitchen, where he got a couple plastic bags out of recycling and ducked into the pantry to fill them.

He took cans from the front rows of shelves, cookies and crackers from his father's stores, and bottled water and juices, not bothering with subterfuge for once, not even trying to camouflage the racket he was making. He was like a madman, his breath coming in ragged bursts, and his hands flailing over the shelves, knocking cans to the floor and making a mess of his mother's orderly lines. By the time he was done he could barely lift the bags, but he managed to carry them to the dining room, where he stowed them under the table. Then he went back to RinMal.

"I left some supplies for you to take," he said in an abrupt tone, not daring to look at his friend.

"Thanks," replied the PoodleRat, who seemed similarly afflicted.

"You'll need them underground," Feltus said stiffly.

"Yes. Do you remember where the tunnel entrance is, in Saldemere's house?" RinMal asked. "So that when you come, it'll be easy to find us."

Feltus nodded, hardly believing that they were having this ridiculous conversation and acting as if nothing was wrong.

"There's still time," he whispered.

"Of course there is," RinMal said stoutly.

"I'll just sit down and do some serious work on the prophecy, and I'll be down to hand over the solution in a day or two. Plenty of time before ... before ..."

The PoodleRat nodded. "I'll see you in a day or two."

Neither of them really believed it. But it made it a little easier to pretend.

RinMal bowed to the others and was gone in the direction of the dining room port hole before Feltus could even form the words "Goodbye."

Eunida and Winston had subsided on the bed, and his great-aunt was stroking the toad as if he were a cat. Her nose was very red and her mouth kept quivering. Mica had crouched down and was sharpening the tines of her trident on the leather strap she wore tied around one wrist. Her dirty hair hung in her face. In the awful silence that followed his friend's departure, Feltus looked around his room The things that normally made life bearable seemed childish and silly – his comic books, his computer games.

Far below him, a life-or-death war was being waged; and his friend, who had never asked anything more than Feltus's help in deciphering the prophecy, had gone to die in it. And Feltus could do nothing!

His angry gaze swept around and fixed on the window, where the Veil was supposedly torn. He threw the prophecy with all his might. It struck beside the frame, chipping off a nickel-sized flake of paint.

He sensed rather than heard Eunida, Winston, and Mica leave the room. After a moment of standing immobile, clenching and unclenching his fingers, he retrieved the small disc and closed his fist around it. He felt the blood thrumming in his ears. He was so angry and it was too hot.

He needed to get some air circulation in the room so that he could clear his head.

His eyes went to the window. Surely he could get it open. He grabbed a screwdriver from his desk, slid it under the frame against the sill and waggled it back and forth. He applied pressure downward, using the screwdriver as a wedge, but the window still didn't budge. It had suddenly become really important to him that he get it open. He pulled and pushed and shoved until his head felt fuzzy and his knees started to buckle.

And when he looked at his hands, they were transparent.

He wiggled his fingers. They were sore, so he knew they were still there, but he could see the floor through them. Within an area of roughly two feet by three under and around the glass panes and yellow-painted sill, his hands were as insubstantial as mist.

*The rogue portal!* He backed away hurriedly, then pushed his heavy desk in front of the window to block it. Maybe he couldn't keep everything out, but at least he could avoid falling in.

At that moment, a final small puzzle piece dropped into place in his head. And Feltus Ovalton realized that he believed.

Magic, the paranormal, the supernatural, alien life forms, just plain craziness – however you wanted to think of it, he knew it existed now. It didn't mean he had to like it, but he accepted it; and with that revelation came a new sense of determination. First, he would help his mother by pumping her full of water. Then he would tend to the prophecy.

With a backward glance at the innocent-looking window, he went to find Great-Aunt Eunida and the others. As expected, they had congregated in her bedroom. Mica was in the corner, kneeling on the floor and looking out onto the road. She seemed to be wrapped up in her own thoughts, although whenever a car honked or brakes squealed she ducked down and covered her head.

Eunida and Winston were huddled on the bed playing some kind of strange checkerboard game with counters and tarot cards. They each had a small heap of dead bluebottle flies in front of them, although Winston's pile was slightly bigger.

"Eight of swords!" Eunida yelled as Feltus walked in and slammed her card down so hard that all the counters bounced. She then proceeded to dance a little jig around the bed.

"That's the seven of swords, Eunida," Winston pointed out drily. "Do I need to remind you that I can count and that your creative rule-bending doesn't work with me? I'm no rabbit, you know."

"It's just a game," Eunida replied sulkily, popping a fly into her mouth. She caught sight of Feltus and her face brightened.

A surge of anger washed over Feltus. He couldn't believe that with everything going on, Eunida and Winston were playing games and having fun.

"I just came to tell you that I'm going to start the experiment. With my mother, I mean."

Mica turned around. "Now? Thank goodness. I'm going crazy just sitting here."

"Yes, now," he replied irritably. "The sooner the better, as far as I'm concerned."

*Am I the only one with any motivation here?* he wondered.

Mica bounded up and joined him by the door. "What can I do?"

"Nothing yet," he said grudgingly. "I'll start giving her water and we'll see what happens. Hopefully, it'll all be over soon."

He closed the door carefully and went to find his mother. He made a detour to the kitchen on the off chance she was there; she wasn't, but he took the opportunity to pick up a gallon jug of springwater.

It was not a hard feat to track her down. As was usual lately, she was sprawled on the couch, her feet slung over the arm, and bowls of snacks nearby, watching the big-screen TV with the fans going full blast. Feltus glanced at the monitor and cringed – it was a reality show about lapsed nuns and a bobsled race through giant ant farms. She looked up through glazed eyes, popped another Day-Glo orange corn twist into her mouth and said, "Hey, how's it going, F-dude?" She seemed to be deteriorating.

He sat down casually on the edge of the couch next to her socked feet. "I brought you some water," he said, offering her the full glass he held in his hand.

Her mouth turned down in an overly dramatic way. "No more soda? Oh well, hand 'er over."

Feltus held his breath as she tilted the glass and drank, then wiped orange crumbs and moisture from her mouth onto the sleeve of her pink velour tracksuit top. Her hair, freed from all the tiny braids, stuck out in a fluffy halo around her face. She looked rather like a dandelion puff, and her face was very pale and delicate in the middle of all that hair.

"I'll get you some more," Feltus said, getting up and going to the table where he'd left the jug. He brought it back to the couch, filled her glass and set it down on the ground close at hand. "You look ... dry."

She waved a negligent hand and scooped up another handful of the cheese snacks. He watched anxiously as she drank the second glass.

"I must be thirstier than I thought," she said. "In fact, I can't remember the last time I drank water this cool and refreshing." Her eyes looked puzzled and a tiny line appeared between her brows. Then she looked at him and her face cleared.

"Come and sit by me, Feltus." She patted the sofa cushion and turned down the volume of the TV with the remote. "I feel like I haven't seen you for a while. How are you?"

"Me?" He was astounded by the question. "Um, I'm fine, I guess. I miss, I miss ..." She waited for him to continue. "I miss Percy," he said finally.

"You need someone your own age. Someone who understands," she said. "But I'll always try to understand too, Feltus. I promise." She grinned at him. Her eyes sparkled like the sun on bright greeny-blue water.

"Okay," he said, hardly trusting his voice. "I'll remember that." *But will you?* he thought.

He filled her glass again, and again she drank it down as if she were dying of thirst. She was so intent on drinking that she didn't hear the *pssst* that came from the hall. Feltus went to see what was going on.

By the doorway, six pairs of eyes met his. Eunida raised her wizened brown thumbs in victory, Mica gnawed on her knuckles, and Winston tried to camouflage himself as a large brown puddle that had somehow ended up on the floor.

"Mom," Feltus said, improvising rapidly, "I'm just going to go make my bed. Keep drinking your water and I'll be right back." He refilled her glass to the brim, left the jug next to her and herded Winston, Mica, and Eunida into his bedroom. Eunida and Winston were already acting as if Percy's plan had worked perfectly. Eunida pulled a celebratory jar of banana peppers and a wedge of gorgonzola from a pocket, and settled down on Feltus's bed with Winston.

Feltus approached Mica shyly. She was standing next to the window looking at the whizzing cars on the street below. "This is a strange and noisy place," she said. "I've never felt so alien before."

"Welcome to my life," Feltus said jokingly, before noticing that her face was grim. "I think you were very brave to come here at all. I couldn't have done it."

"I love my sister."

"I love my ... chocolate," he said aloud, but the thought that echoed in his mind was I miss my mother.

Mica nodded as if she'd heard him. "Me too. So now we just wait and see?" she asked, her gaze clear.

Feltus shrugged. There was nothing else to say, just time to kill.

The hours dragged on. Feltus flipped through the pages of his biology book. He vaguely remembered something that had happened right before final exams. Percy had tried to tutor him using a series of peanut butter sandwiches, a serrated knife, and a box of raisins. All Feltus recalled was that the raisins represented chromosomes, and chromosomes were why his eyes were hazel and his father's were brown. How Percy arrived at this conclusion Feltus still could not say, but afterward Feltus had eaten all the sandwiches.

He zoomed in on an entry in the book that he'd highlighted in yellow pen: mitosis – that was it – cell division! He knew that Jasper and his mother hadn't merged fully – they were more like two bodies trapped in one sweater – but he'd wanted to look again at the illustrations of the complete separation that followed mitosis. It calmed him. Otherwise he'd spend too much time imagining his mother with two heads like those crazy waitresses at the Magical Ewe ... and Jasper with none; or a three-armed Mom; or a mono-pod Mom hopping along like some giant jack-in-the-box; and how would he explain that at the parents' night at school? The best thing was to believe that both his mother and Jasper wanted to be their whole selves again, no matter what the two of them had shared during their time together – despite the fact that Jasper was obviously having a profound effect on his mother.

He glanced around the room. Mica was throwing her weapon up in the air and catching it in all kinds of dexterous ways – behind her back, under one of her legs, in mid-spin like some kind of ninja cheerleader. Eunida and Winston had gone on another pantry raid and stocked up on seaweed, peach liqueur, dinner rolls, and octopus in tomato sauce, which they were eating messily on his bed.

Feltus couldn't relax. Every time he sneaked down the hall, his mother, apparently mesmerized by the raucous scenes on the television screen, had a glass in her hand. And he thought, though he couldn't be sure, that the level of water in the jug had gone down considerably. *But what if Percy is wrong – and worse, how could he possibly be right?* The thought kept rattling around Feltus's brain.

It was ludicrous. The whole thing was absolutely, totally impossible, and yet ... over there was a shriveled old soothsayer conversing with a humongous toad; and there in the corner was a being from another world who could move around with the power of thought; and a PoodleRat had just departed.

Feltus chewed his fingernails and tried to think of something else. But he couldn't. The one good thing was that there was no immediate room in his brain for worrying about RinMal. *First this, then that,* he decided.

He rose from his chair to go check on his mother again. He'd barely made it to the hallway when he heard the rattle of keys in the lock and the heavy front door opening. Every nerve ending sizzled as he peeked around his bedroom door and saw his father standing in the doorway. His heart sank. *Dad! What is he doing home so early?*

Feltus's father never paid attention to much, but Feltus was willing to bet he'd notice there was still something seriously strange going on with Feltus's mother. Even if he failed to detect the remnants of her junk food binge, he couldn't miss the pink velour tracksuit/leather miniskirt/ski boot combo she was sporting today. And if his father picked another fight with her regarding her appearance and behavior, as he most certainly would, the plan would be in jeopardy. Feltus knew there would be no way for them to conclude their experiment under his father's critical and penetrating eye.

# CHAPTER 16

## Madhouse, Monkhouse

FELTUS WATCHED FROM his room as his father closed the front door. To make matters worse, his father was not alone. "Let me take your coat, Mr. Monkhouse," Feltus's father said to the young man who was following behind him. He stepped aside with a small bow, helped Mr. Monkhouse off with his garment, hung it carefully on a wooden hanger, and placed his fine silk umbrella carefully in the rack. Mr. Monkhouse stood stiffly with a sour look on his face. He had pinched, sallow features, bulbous pale blue eyes, and thinning blond hair, which was carefully slicked back over a very round head. "Do you have cats?" he inquired in a nasal voice. "I can't abide cats."

"No, no. Absolutely not," Feltus's father replied.

Mr. Monkhouse sniffed disbelievingly. "It smells damp in here."

"Err, well I'm sure you're right, and I'm sorry."

Feltus judged the distance between the coatrack and the sitting room door. He steeled himself mentally, made an attempt to swallow the huge lump in his throat, and walked out into the open.

"Dad, hi, hey, I have something I need to talk to you about."

His father frowned. "Can't it wait, Feltus? Mr. Monkhouse and I have some serious matters to discuss."

"Umm," Feltus scrambled. "It's pretty important."

"All right then," his father said impatiently, then

turned to the unsmiling man next to him. "Kids. With them everything is always such an impending disaster. Can I fix you a drink while you're waiting? I'll show you to the living room. The view is spectacular. You can see clear across to the financial district – you could count the buildings you own, ha, ha."

Mr. Monkhouse didn't crack a smile. His anemic gaze trickled over Feltus from head to toe. "I attended military boarding school," he said. "From the age of six."

"Excellent!" Feltus's father said, clapping his hands together. "I'll look into it immediately."

"Not the living room," Feltus said desperately to his father. "I had an accident in there."

"What kind of accident?" his father murmured, steering him toward the wall with two fingers firmly pinching his elbow.

"I spilled my juice, and, um, a box of cereal. The sugary kind."

His father looked at him in silence. "Okay, we'll go to the kitchen while you clean up. Say ten minutes?"

Feltus nodded.

"And Feltus," his father whispered, "if your great-aunt is hovering around, make sure she isn't wearing a lampshade or eating oysters out of the can with a straw. And tell your mother I need her here immediately – and looking her best."

He turned back to his guest, a smile pasted on his lips again. "Mr. Monkhouse, I have a lovely Burgundy we can sample before we get down to brass tacks. Right this way."

Feltus's father led his client in the direction of the kitchen and Feltus bolted to the sitting room.

His mother was hanging over the edge of the sofa, her hair sweeping the floor. The nuns had concluded their battle, and now she was mesmerized by hordes of men in tiny red bathing suits attempting to complete an obstacle course.

Feltus shuddered.

"Mom," he said loudly. "Dad's home – he brought a client with him."

His mother grunted and tried to shrug her shoulders while upside down.

"Mom, *seriously*, we need to get you spruced up and vertical," he pleaded.

She twisted her upper body, let her legs collapse, and sat up. For the first time in a long time, she seemed to look at him. *Really* look at him.

"*Please*," he said.

"What do you want me to do?" she asked.

"I think you need to change your clothes," he said. "Maybe put on a dress."

He helped her to her feet. She was being oddly obedient. She stood without speaking while he straightened cushions, picked up empty chip bags and cans and stuffed them behind the potted plant, and turned the television off.

"Let's go," he said, feeling oddly like the parent in charge.

She followed him to her bedroom. He opened the door, told her to pick something flowery, and then shut her in the room. Then he squatted down with his back against the wall in the hallway and waited until his mother summoned him.

When she called out to him fifteen minutes later, he opened the door and saw her standing in front of the mirror, dressed in a simple, summery gown with a ruffled hem and spatters of blue flowers on a cream background. She'd pulled her hair back and let little wisps frame her face and curl against her neck. She would have looked like an ad in a magazine if it weren't for the combat boots and polka dot tights. *Where did she get those?* he wondered.

"Okay?" she asked.

He nodded.

"Let's do it then," she said, before stomping out.

As they passed his bedroom, they caught sight of Mica and Eunida, who were peeking through the door. His mother stopped and made a deep curtsy.

"Was it your father?" Eunida asked in a theatrical whisper, as she checked out his mother's ensemble. "I'm guessing by the fashion statement that she's not cured yet," she observed to Feltus.

He shook his head wearily.

"Who's the girl, Feltus?" his mother asked, poking him in the ribs.

"Just a friend," he muttered.

She raised her eyebrows, then winked.

"Come on then, all of you," she shouted in high good humor. Eunida and Mica fell into line behind her. Feltus followed them, feeling as if he were having a dream in which he was trying to run naked in molasses. Everything was happening in excruciatingly slow motion. Even so, he was the first to enter the sitting room, the others being distracted by the sight of Feltus's mother turning cartwheels down the length of the hall.

The tension was almost palpable. Feltus's dad hovered, picking up and putting down trays of stone-ground crackers, brie, and shellfish in truffle oil, which Mr. Monkhouse waved aside with an impatient gesture.

"My palate is very sensitive," Mr. Monkhouse said finally. Feltus's father removed the platters and stood shifting his weight from one foot to the other uncomfortably.

Sheaves of paper, carefully color-coded and sorted in different shades of file folders, were stacked on the nearest side table, but Feltus could tell that no one had so much as glanced at them. Mr. Monkhouse stared grimly at the city skyline through the large picture window, the rigidity of his spine betraying his disapproval. Feltus's father's shoulders were bowed, and his forehead sweaty.

Feltus's mother swept in, trailing Mica and Eunida. Winston, who was mostly unnoticeable except for the tip of his brown snout, was stuffed into an oversized handbag that dangled from Eunida's arm.

"Thirteen flips in a row. That's a personal best!" Feltus's mother announced in a ringing voice.

His father ran trembling fingers through his hair and tried to smile. Feltus watched as his gaze passed over the group.

First he noticed Mica and he frowned in puzzlement. Fortunately his attention was immediately distracted as he caught sight of Eunida. His frown deepened until his face was positively stormy. Feltus, who was perched on the edge of the dining room table, tried to gauge exactly how disastrous the evening was going to be.

Into the middle of this tense situation, his mother advanced with her hands outstretched. Mr. Monkhouse leapt to his feet.

"Mr. Bathouse," she said in her musical voice, "we're so pleased to have you in our home."

Feltus wondered whether she would continue to speak using the royal "We." Perhaps it was a side-effect of sharing her body with someone else.

"'Monkhouse,' darling. 'Mr. Monkhouse,'" his father corrected with a tight smile. "The firm's biggest financial client."

"Thank you, LeRoi, I know what my ranking is," Mr. Monkhouse said in a clipped voice. "Your home is very cozy, Mrs. LeRoi."

She arched her eyebrows at him. "Your bank is very rich, Mr. Bathouse. Would you care for an appetizer?"

She picked up a tray, balanced it on her forefinger, and spun it like a basketball player spinning a ball before offering it to him. He selected a cracker and a wedge of blue-veined, smelly cheese, and stood looking at her in a bemused fashion. She put the tray down; Eunida descended upon it like a vulture, stuffing a greasy handful of fish into her bag.

"Drink, Mr. Monkhouse?" Feltus's mother offered, playing with the soda siphon from the drinks trolley. She directed a spray of water past the tip of Feltus's father's nose, then threw back her head and laughed.

Mr. Monkhouse's mouth twisted and Feltus realized with amazement that he was trying to smile.

"Call me Montague," Mr. Monkhouse said. "And I'll have a martini."

"I'm Karen," she said, extending a hand. He shook it heartily.

Feltus's mother crushed ice, juggled olives, squeezed limes, and spritzed soda like a bartender in a top hotel. Her hair had escaped from its bun, and her collar bone shone with a faint sheen of sweat.

Mr. Monkhouse watched with unmistakable admiration, oblivious to everyone else in the room but Feltus's mother. However, the smacking noises Eunida was making over by the hors d'ouevres did capture his attention for a brief moment. His eyes moved from the pretty picture his mother presented to Mica who, completely enthralled, was hunched over the television, running her hands over the blank screen. Enough electricity remained to raise the fine hairs on her head.

"My friends," Feltus's mother said by way of explanation with a sweeping motion that encompassed the room and possibly also the world outside the window.

"My wife collects, err, strays," his father explained, watching as she sashayed around the room. He had loosened his tie and his expression seemed a bit less frozen.

His mother was jocular, almost giddy. It was awful, but

Feltus could barely contain the laugh that bubbled up inside and threatened to burst loose.

"Delirium. Probably induced by the separation of both entities. Jasper is struggling to free herself," Winston whispered from the depths of the handbag, which Eunida had left casually on the coffee table while she selected another plateful of nibbles.

Feltus watched his mother as she tossed an olive into the air, caught it in her mouth, and collapsed with a giggle into the nearest chair.

"It won't last," Winston said reassuringly.

"Good. I'm not sure I like it anyway," Feltus admitted quietly, speaking into the handbag. "It would be nice if she could be a little happy, but this is too weird – one minute she's depressed, and the next she's just seconds away from swinging on the chandelier."

She was definitely the opposite of miserable now. She seemed filled with energy. As he watched, she yelled "Peanuts!" unfolded herself from the winged armchair, and skipped out of the room.

"Feltus." His father beckoned him to the window where he stood cracking his knuckles. He spoke under his breath. "I have a lot riding on this meeting. Can you talk to your mother, tell her to tone it down?"

"Why don't you tell her? She doesn't listen to me."

His father sighed. "I guess we're in the same sinking boat."

Feltus hesitated. "If you're worried about your client, I think he's having a good time."

His father straightened up. "You're right," he said slowly. Mr. Monkhouse was leaning casually against the TV console, his drink half gone and a trail of crumbs down the front of his pressed cotton shirt. A small smirk danced across his mouth.

Feltus's mother came back in laden with cheese puffs, roasted peanuts in the shell, and potato chips. She arranged the bowls on the coffee table and launched herself again into the nearest armchair. The last pin had fallen from her hair, and the locks fell in loose curls over her shoulders. Feltus's father eyed her with an expression halfway between exasperation and amusement. His shirt cuffs were unbuttoned and he'd rolled the sleeves up.

"So, Monty, how's business?" she asked. She munched loudly on the salted peanuts, throwing the empty shells over her shoulder one by one. Mr. Monkhouse leaned forward. It was as if she'd hooked him on an invisible line.

"Good. Couldn't be better," he answered. "We have some new developments in the works."

"Thrilling! Absolutely! Your plans include aligning yourself with my husband's firm, I hope?" She licked salt from her fingers, and Mr. Monkhouse cleared his throat and nodded.

"Get in there, Dad. She's reeling him in," Feltus said and gave his father a little push.

"Mr. Monkhouse," Feltus's father said with new assurance, taking a fountain pen from the breast pocket of his suit. "If you're ready to sign the authorization for the Midas Project, I have the papers right here."

Mr. Monkhouse penned his name with a flourish, barely looking at the pages. His attention was glued on Feltus's mother, who was making origami birds from paper lace doilies.

"And if you're interested in the downtown development deal, we could grab a cab to the office and I could show you the numbers. I think you'll be impressed," Feltus's father continued.

"Sure, sure," Monkhouse replied, his words only slightly slurred. "Another martini and I'll be good to go."

"Shoor, shoor," Feltus's mother said, mimicking Mr.

Monkhouse's precise tones almost exactly, as she sent a paper airplane whizzing against his starched white shirt-front. He didn't appear to mind and they both erupted in peals of laughter.

Mr. Monkhouse seemed only a bit worse for wear, although he did lean rather heavily on the mantelpiece after his third martini; and he insisted on taking the entire cut-glass bowl of cheese popcorn with him, for some long-winded reason that had made absolutely no sense to Feltus. His father was so thrilled about getting the contracts signed that he threw the bowl and its contents into a carrier bag and gave it to Mr. Monkhouse. As he said his goodbyes, Monkhouse clutched the bag to his chest as if it were a treasure. Feltus watched in disgust as he pressed a few wet kisses on his mother's outstretched hand before stumbling his way out the front door. Feltus's father followed closely behind, carrying their coats, the umbrella, and his attaché case. With a sigh of relief, Feltus double-bolted the front door and, steeling himself, returned to the sitting room.

His mother clapped her hands in glee. "More! More! More!" she yelled. "More fish, more salt, more martini!" Her skirts flared as she pirouetted down the hall toward the kitchen. Feltus followed closely behind her, avoiding her flailing arms, and when the opportunity arose, he pushed her through the doorway of her own bedroom. She fell on the bed, pouting slightly.

"So mean," she muttered. "You need to relax."

"I need to relax? Well, why don't you help me then? Maybe if I didn't have to worry about everyone in this apart-ment I could relax!"

"Okay. What do you need?" she said playfully. "More allowance?"

"First, I want you to drink some water. All those chips

have probably dehydrated you." He thrust the jug at her.

Automatically she drank. "Salt cod would go really well with all this water," she mentioned hopefully.

"You can have fish later," he said, pushing the jug back at her.

Eunida had come into the room and stood behind him, clutching her handbag with Winston safely ensconced inside in one hand, and a potato chip sandwich with mayonnaise in the other. He knew it was mayonnaise because she sported a thick, greasy white mustache. Mica hovered in the hallway, twisting her fingers together. She was full of nervous energy.

"How do we know when the separation will happen, if it happens?" he whispered to his great-aunt.

"How much water has she had?"

"Almost two gallons."

"Should be any minute, then."

"You think?"

"Well, either that or a few hours. What does it matter really?"

"It matters," Feltus said tightly, "because I need to get back to the prophecy before a large number of my friends are killed, and I can't do that if I'm worrying about my mother hitching a ride to Alaska, or joining a motorcycle gang, or moving to Los Angeles to lead a rock band."

"Those aren't necessarily bad things," Eunida pointed out.

Feltus buried his face in his hands. Did no one understand how he felt? There were certain things in his life that had to stay in one place, so that when things were out of control, like now, and he felt as if he were spinning around at a dizzying speed, he could still count on the fact that his shoes would never be polished enough for his mother, that his room would never be clean enough, and that she would always find fault with his hairstyle.

"Feltus Ovalton!"

The shriek brought him hurriedly to his feet. Mica crowded through the door. His mother stood before the bedroom mirror, pointing a finger at her reflection.

Eunida dropped her bag with a thud. Feltus heard a squelch and a muffled oath from Winston.

His mother's mouth was an *o* of astonishment. "What did you put in that water?"

"Nothing!" Feltus sputtered. "It's just water!"

She turned to face him and he noticed that her hands were trembling. "Look," she said, breathing in short gasps.

He looked. At first he thought there was something wrong with his eyes. There was a faint halo around each of her fingers – a doubling, like when a camera moves slightly while the picture is being taken. And it wasn't just her fingers, it was all of her. Every part of her was reproduced, almost like a shadow, but so faint that it almost seemed like a trick of the light.

He rubbed his eyes and looked again. It was the same, but worse. The twinned part of her was growing – she appeared to be one-and-a-half times her normal size now.

His first instinct was to back out of the room, but Eunida pushed against his shoulders, halting him. Gathering his courage, he stepped toward his mother, grabbed one of her oddly thickened hands, led her forward to the ottoman at the foot of her bed and made her sit down. Eunida, Winston, and Mica watched with wide eyes. Mica had twisted a few dark strands of hair around her fingers and she chewed nervously on the ends. Feltus knew how she felt. He would have been biting his fingernails, but one hand was held captive by his mother and the other was trying to keep her from falling on the floor.

He felt dizzy, like the time he'd had a fever for a couple

weeks and even the whiteness of his walls had become painful to look at.

He patted her fingers feebly without focusing on them. They felt the same as he remembered, but there seemed to be more of them. It was ghastly. Holding her hand was like holding onto a giant fleshy, leggy insect. He concentrated on the blue flowers of her dress instead. She'd stopped whimpering, but all twenty of her fingers were latched on to his.

"It's miraculous," Winston breathed from his position in the bag on the floor. "Not exactly like birth, but something phenomenal all the same."

"It's terrible," Feltus replied. "We did egg hatching in biology and that was pretty horrid as well; all slimy and goopy."

"There's no mess with this, it's just a slow and gentle separation of two souls joined by accident," Winston said.

"Well, I wish they'd hurry up." Feltus closed his eyes against the sickening sight.

"I think, although I may be wrong, that the division is almost complete. They seem a little groggy," Eunida said.

Feltus opened one eye, just in time to catch his mother as she slumped sideways. Eunida lumbered to her feet and grabbed hold of the slender brown-haired girl who was falling off the other side of the ottoman. Mica stood motionless by the door, turning the hasp of her trident over and over in her hands. She seemed incapable of speaking.

"Did they both pass out?" Feltus asked his great-aunt.

"No, mine's fluttering her eyelids," Eunida observed.

"Mom's breathing, but she's so still. Should we throw water on them?"

"And risk your mother's wrath? No, let me get a washcloth from the bathroom and we'll sponge their faces."

Eunida propped the girl up so that she leaned against

Feltus's shoulder. Her hair tickled his ear. There was a small red birthmark on her neck.

At last Mica made a curious sound deep in her throat and teleported ten feet forward until she was standing directly in front of Feltus.

"It worked?" she whispered. "Is she ... ?"

Her eyes went to the drooping figure of the brown-haired girl. She came closer slowly. Her fingers were clenched, the knuckles white, and her mouth was a thin line. A tear rolled slowly down one of her white cheeks and she angrily brushed it away.

"No, no," Feltus said, "she's okay. They're both okay. Percy's crazy plan worked." He felt his mouth twist, but there was no way he was going to cry in front of a girl. He concentrated on Hercules, that manly hero of no visible emotion, and got a grip.

Jasper opened a pair of eyes that were as green as Mica's. She blinked a few times and then stretched like a cat. When she caught sight of her sister, her mouth spread into a huge grin and she threw her arms open wide. "Small one, I am so glad to see you!"

Mica punched her on the shoulder, then relaxed against her in one quick motion, letting her older sister stroke her hair, pinch her cheeks, and wipe the dirt from her forehead with a moistened finger.

Mica must have sensed Feltus watching her, because she looked up. He was surprised by the warmth of her expression now, and he grinned back at her like a fool for a moment before he collected himself and reverted to his customary scowl.

Eunida returned with damp cloths and handed one to Feltus. He pressed it against his mother's forehead, against the purple hollows above her cheekbones, against her eye sockets. She stirred. Then she opened her eyes, and they were as blue as the ocean and as calm as a lake. Her vision shifted into focus and she smiled at Feltus.

"Have I been asleep?" she asked. "I feel so rested." Her hand reached out and pushed the hair back over his fore-head, then rested for a moment against his face. "Are you okay? You look like you've been worrying."

"I'm fine," he said gruffly.

Feltus was thankful that the mushy stuff didn't last long, because public affection and silly nicknames always embarrassed him. It was enough that his mother was herself again and that everything was back to being as close to normal as his life ever got.

She had already seated herself in front of her dressing table and was combing out her hair, pinning it back until not a stray wisp could escape. For some reason she seemed unaware of any other people around her, including, he was glad to see, Eunida, Mica, and Jasper, who were being remarkably slow about exiting. "Go," he said to them in a savage whisper, and waved them out of the room. Feltus wondered if his mother were oblivious because of the part of her brain that refused to accept anything out of the ordinary. After all, he'd had no trouble convincing her that RinMal was a dog.

Before he left his mother, he gave her one last glance as if to convince himself that she were really there. She paused in the act of applying her face cream, caught his eye in the mirror, and winked. He backed out of the room and closed the door quietly.

When he walked into his own room, feeling exhausted but quite pleased with himself, he found no one there but Eunida and Winston who were inspecting the area around the window. The desk had been moved a few feet away and was no longer blocking it.

Winston was hopping back and forth in front of the

window, shouting numbers at Eunida. "Twenty-six-and-a-half inches by roughly thirty-two, I'd say, but of course I can't get close enough to be more exact. It seems like more of a hole than a tear. "

"Where are Mica and Jasper?" Feltus asked. "They're not raiding the refrigerator, are they?"

"They've gone."

"What?" he said, taken aback. He'd been dreading the goodbye, but he couldn't believe they'd just go without saying anything.

"Mica left you this," Eunida said, throwing something metallic in his direction.

The trident flew through the air and embedded itself in the wall by his head. He only narrowly avoided being skewered.

"Hey, watch it!" he yelled.

"Beautifully weighted and obviously very sharp," Winston observed.

"She must have liked you after all," Eunida said in a deceptively mild tone.

Feltus flushed, his ears going pink. He turned around and yanked the weapon out of the plaster. It left four very deep holes in the wall. He tossed it up in the air, watched it spin, then caught it by the handle. It *was* a pretty cool gift.

"Did they leave by the portal?" he asked Eunida.

"Yes." She pointed with a crooked finger and muttered a couple of inarticulate words under her breath. For a few seconds, Feltus could see the swirling patterns of two pairs of feet in blue-tinged sand on the floor. They led up to the window and then disappeared.

Eunida, Winston, and Feltus all looked at the yellow-painted sill, the dirty panes of glass.

"If there's a rogue portal in my bedroom," Feltus said

with difficulty – he still had a hard time dealing with all of this – "does that mean that I put it there? With the unlocking spell?"

"I think we must accept that that is probably true," said Winston.

"And a rogue portal would make small rips and holes all along the Veil like you told me," Feltus said. He faced Eunida who just stared back at him with her shrewd, bright eyes. "Ruptures that let so many voices and messages in that your dampeners were overloaded ... the rogue portal that drew Jasper here in her vial, which resulted in my mother being invaded. And," his throat felt uncomfortably tight, "the rogue portal that made the tearing in the Veil around the Grand Gewglab Forest that let the Kehezzzalubbapipipi cross over."

He repeated the last bit in a whisper. "I let the Kehezzzalubbapipipi in."

He sank down against the wall, staring at the sharp points of the trident in his hand and rubbing his thumb against the smooth bone handle.

"You can't be too hard on yourself. You didn't know what you were doing," Eunida said encouragingly.

"No, I didn't. But it doesn't matter. It's still my mess."

"And you've managed to solve two of the problems. You helped your mother and Eunida," Winston added.

Feltus looked doubtfully at his great-aunt, who was gnawing on a large, meaty bone she'd pulled out of her handbag. *At least it's cooked.*

"Soon the Patrol will have fixed the largest tears and we'll be seeing things settle down," Eunida said through a mouthful.

"Have they been in touch?" Feltus asked. "Did they say anything about the PoodleRats?"

"They sent a short note via moth, so there wasn't room

for a lot of information," Eunida mumbled as she looked at the bone. "Moths have such small wings."

"They're still not doing anything about it, are they?" Feltus demanded.

Winston hopped over. He was very ungainly on the unpolished wood floor. Feltus stared at him with angry eyes.

"I know it seems unfair to you," the toad said. "But the Patrol must think of the Veil first and foremost, or else mass transmigrations will occur and all balance will be lost."

"Well, what about Dare Al Luce?" Feltus asked, suddenly remembering that a member of the Patrol was relatively close by. "He's still at the Magical Ewe doing good deeds, right? Why don't we go force him to help? I can show him the prophecy – explain that the PoodleRats only have a few more days."

"You can't force a member of the Patrol to do something. Even though Dare Al Luce is doing penance, he chooses when and if he'll extend aid," Winston said. "Don't confuse goodness with power."

"I had to do some pretty creative wheeling and dealing to get such precise directions to the Magical Ewe," Eunida added. "In fact, although I wouldn't exactly call it ..."

"Blackmail?" Winston interrupted, with a quizzical look. "Bribery?"

"Oh, be quiet," she told him. "I may have promised Dare Al Luce a little help. You know, so he can go back home."

"But there's no problem getting back there?" Feltus asked.

"No," Eunida admitted.

"So, why don't you call in another favor so I can ask him for help?" Feltus begged.

"You know, that's not a bad idea," Eunida answered thoughtfully. "I think I still have some leverage."

"Can you set it up soon? We can meet him at the Magical Ewe again," Feltus said, jumping to his feet.

"I'll get a message to him and we'll see about tomorrow," she said. "I think that you should go alone though, Feltus. Dare Al Luce seems to be intrigued by helpless creatures. After all, he did answer your call from the school. And I can't stand all those weirdos that hang out at the Ewe. "Yes," she said, ignoring his protestations and wiping her greasy fingers on his bedspread. "I think that would be best."

# CHAPTER 17

## Magical Me, Magical Ewe

FELTUS ARGUED exhaustively that he couldn't go by himself: "I hardly know Dare Al Luce – I'm just a kid – I'll get lost!" But Eunida proved to be very stubborn.

"I just have a feeling about this and you'll have to trust me," Eunida said, before locking herself in her bathroom with Winston, a carton of eggs, and a small blowtorch his mother used for crème brûlée, to make the spell that would allow her to contact Dare Al Luce.

"I'll let you know what he says," she reiterated and then closed the door in his face.

Apparently, the magic worked because after exactly seventeen-and-a-half minutes – Feltus knew this because he'd camped out in front of the door with a stopwatch and a chocolate bar – Eunida emerged with a triumphant grin.

"No one can say that I am not quite convincing in my own way," she crowed.

From her shoulder, where he sat in a harness that was strapped across her back, Winston rolled his eyes.

"She has no shame," the toad said to Feltus. "I actually felt quite sorry for the poor fellow. When she gets going, she's like a steamroller. He didn't have a chance."

"So he'll see me?" Feltus said excitedly. His hand went to his pocket and he gripped the prophecy.

"Tomorrow."

Feltus threw his arms around his great-aunt and hugged her, squishing the unfortunate Winston in the process. Neither of them smelled very pleasant up close, but for once Feltus didn't care. Things were moving along.

Before he went back to his own room, he dropped a garbage bag filled with canned goods down the dining room port hole, crossing his fingers and hoping he didn't brain anyone at the other end. He also left a bag of cheese popcorn, three packages of assorted cookies, and his second-best penknife under the kitchen sink. But if everything went according to plan, the PoodleRats wouldn't be needing emergency supplies for too much longer.

Lastly, he stopped outside his mother's door and listened hard for a few minutes. He heard nothing – not the whirring of the air conditioner, or any explosively loud music. She must have been asleep. And that made him feel ridiculously happy.

He fell asleep that night holding the prophecy in one hand.

* * *

Feltus left early the next morning, as soon as the sun had cleared the rooftops, but before the daily broil began, and even before his mother had come down for breakfast. He'd heard her singing behind her bathroom door and he lingered for a moment, listening to the sweet, out-of-tune lilt of her voice. The only shadow on the day was that the supplies he'd left under the kitchen sink were still there.

He took the stairs down to the bottom of the building, grabbing onto the banister to swing down the last five or six steps. Once he was outside on the sidewalk, he stopped and looked to his right and left.

From what he remembered, there had been no precise path that his great-aunt had taken when they'd made the first journey to the Magical Ewe. First she'd merely circled the block, so that's what he did too.

Then there'd been a pigeon, some broken glass, and an irate cab driver, but he was uncertain as to the order in which they'd appeared. He contented himself with a pause at a tree, another short stop in front of a garbage can, and a third pause in the middle of the road where, in fact, he barely missed getting creamed by a taxi.

Feltus suddenly remembered the dog and Eunida's gleam of satisfaction when she'd spotted it. The dog seemed to be the hinge of the whole operation.

He leaned against a scaly horse chestnut tree and waited for the canine to show itself. Warm air gusted from the grates in the sidewalk and Feltus began to perspire quite heavily. He was regretting wearing a windbreaker, when he caught sight of movement down the street. It was a small Jack Russell terrier, brown and white, and intent upon its business, which seemed to be sniffing garbage, eating garbage, and occasionally coughing as if a chicken bone had caught in its throat.

Feltus followed it at a distance until it ducked down a dark side street and promptly disappeared. He turned the corner and the air was about twenty degrees cooler. He saw the same boarded-up windows he remembered from before, the same windblown newspapers flapping around the mailboxes, and he felt the familiar crunch of broken glass under his feet. The carpet of dead leaves seemed thicker, but the chalk outline of the hopscotch game was no more faded than last time. It was apparent if you only knew where to look. Finding it turned out to be the easy part. The difficulty arose when he suddenly realized that he was petrified of what might happen when he tried to go through the Veil alone.

Maybe he didn't have enough magic. Maybe the Veil would recognize that he was just a boy. Maybe he should have brought something of Eunida's along with him – a scarf, or something else impregnated with her smell.

He dawdled by the number one square then finally poked his foot in and felt the coldness and vertigo he associated with the Veil. But he took a deep breath and launched himself up.

Once he'd made the first hop, the skip and the jump came naturally and too fast for him to have doubts. As he moved through the Veil, he shut his eyes tightly, unable to bear the sight of that long drop through nothingness. He gripped the prophecy and pinched the flesh on his forearm with the other hand, so that he could be certain that his body was still there. The sensation of free-falling went on and on, until he landed quite abruptly, and gravity, a real force once again, forced him painfully to his knees.

He found himself on the sidewalk directly opposite the Magical Ewe. Nothing looked much different. The sad, grimy window display was the same. The winged sheep had acquired yet another coat of dust, an orb weaver spider had moved into the plastic jack-o'-lantern, and dead flies and iridescent beetles hung from silken threads like Christmas ornaments. The curtain of chimes still hung in front of the door and he ran headfirst into them once again. The dozen or so customers in the café greeted his arrival with an awful silence. The hush seemed interminable, and he was wondering once again if one could die of shame, when two loud voices broke the peace.

"It's the boy. Eunida's kid!" announced Bobbie.

"The wee, simple child," Sue added, advancing on him with open arms and a pursed wet mouth that reminded him of a sea anemone.

There was nowhere to go but back into the curtain of bells, so Feltus stood still and closed his eyes until it was over. Then Bobbie and Sue took him companionably by the arm and led him forward.

"Breakfast? Lunch? Dinner? All three? You must be ravenous. How's the old lady? We absolutely adore her –

such a gourmand," they said in unison. "And we've missed you! Your meal will have to be something really special. Anchovy petit fours. Partridges in pastry with a nice raspberry coulis. Fowl in lard. Tripe a la mode." Both of them beamed at him.

"Is Dare Al Luce here?" Feltus asked, trying not to stutter. "I'm supposed to meet him."

"If a meeting has been arranged, he will appear," Bobbie said sternly. "You can't rush these things."

"That's right," said Sue. "Plenty of time to have something to eat."

The twins steered Feltus toward an empty table in the middle of the room, pressed him firmly into a chair, and then continued on to the kitchen. He looked around nervously. *I can't believe I'm here again.*

The customers were all new from the last time, and some of them seemed unsafe, or at the very least, contagious. The three tables to his immediate left were occupied by a colony of jellyfish that were ghostly, quivering, and pseudopodium by the looks of it. They clung to the backs of chairs, both over and under the tables, and occasionally fell onto the floor with a loud, wet flop.

To his right, a leopard-spotted man clad in a three-piece suit finished off the last of a bloody haunch of antelope; and directly in front of him was a purple miasma illuminated by winking golden lights. It moved as softly as a cloud before alighting on a platter of vivid green sprouts and laying a glutinous mass of black-speckled eggs.

Feltus slouched down in his chair trying to look neither right nor left nor straight ahead, but at the same time attempting to locate Dare Al Luce. He stretched his neck up as far as it would go, struggling to peer over the heads of the clientele. But the jellyfish were piling on top of one another and had made an opaque wall of goo, and the leopard man had opened a large newspaper that covered his face and most of the room behind him. Feltus had just climbed onto his chair for a better look around when he heard a tinkling flurry of pure notes, like those of a piano or harp. At the same moment, the purple miasma dispersed.

Then Feltus saw Dare Al Luce, sitting at the same table as before, contemplating another silver teapot and elegant cup. He looked over at Feltus.

Feltus jumped down from his chair and bowed deeply. Dare Al Luce beckoned him with one delicate finger, and Feltus let his feet carry him forward. It was lucky his brain had somehow gone on auto-pilot, because he wasn't actually sure he remembered how to walk.

His mouth had gone bone-dry. Dare Al Luce had agreed to this meeting, but Feltus was suddenly nervous about asking anything of him. All the carefully worded arguments he'd worked up last night before falling asleep had evaporated. The heartbreaking appeal he'd practiced was gone. He'd forgotten how impressive Dare Al Luce was, how beautiful.

He remembered what Eunida had told him the first time they'd come to the Magical Ewe: *Think of him as a snail.* He still didn't know what she'd meant by that, but looking at Dare Al Luce's marble white hands and platinum locks of hair, he couldn't imagine anything less snail-like.

He probably would have stayed frozen and mute forever under Dare Al Luce's piercing and slightly bemused gaze, if his hand had not sneaked nervously into his pocket and felt the familiar shape of the prophecy. He was instantly reminded of the importance of his journey.

*Just get on with it and ask him*, Feltus said to himself.

Dare Al Luce's beautifully molded lips curved into a faint smile. He shifted fluidly in his chair, and Feltus looked down and noticed that the plaster cast on his leg was gone.

Dare Al Luce poured steaming water into his cup then added a stream of sugar. A delicately scented vapor rose from the cup, and Feltus was reminded of his mother's jasmine perfume.

"Ask me what?" Dare Al Luce said.

"Your ... your leg is better ..." Feltus said, stumbling over his words. It was shocking to realize that Dare Al Luce could read his thoughts. He'd have to be careful about what went through his mind.

"We heal quickly."

"I have something to tell you," Feltus said.

There was a long pause. "Very well," Dare Al Luce replied. "Speak your mind." He fluttered his fingers.

Feltus took a deep breath. He felt the chaotic jumble of his thoughts loosen suddenly, and the words came in a rush. "I found out there was a hole in the Veil, an approved one, I mean, a port hole under my dining room table, and it led the PoodleRats to me, and they were in need of help because they've been invaded by a horrible enemy, and because of the prophecy they thought it was me that could help them because of my last name being LeRoi – it means 'the king' in French, but of course I can't ..." He inhaled and went on. He sensed that if he didn't get it all out, he'd freeze up.

"Although more than anything in the world, I'd like to help. And I thought it must have something to do with why you're here. I mean, looking for the rupture in the Veil that caused all those tears, and everything – because that must be how they got in, the Kehezzzalubbapipipi. And also why my great-aunt had all of those confused frequencies, you know?" he said frantically, directing a questioning look at Dare Al Luce. Dare Al Luce nodded sternly, but also seemed to have a smile tickling his mouth. "It's why she was losing her mind, being inundated with all those crazy prophecies, and why Jasper, who came from another world, got mixed in with my mother.

"So I thought I'd come tell you that the rupture is in my bedroom and I made it happen with a spell, but by accident of course." He paused and checked Dare Al Luce's expression, which was still stern but not scary at all.

"*Please* come and fix the breach, so things can go back to normal."

Feltus took another deep breath and tried to gauge how he was doing. He felt sweat trickling down his back and resisted the temptation to wipe his moist forehead on his sleeve.

Dare Al Luce had leaned back in his chair, but his eyes never wavered from Feltus's face. He handed Feltus his napkin.

"And?" Dare Al Luce asked in his musical voice. "Or is it 'but?'"

Feltus swabbed his neck with the napkin and looked around the café. It seemed to have gone silent again, but maybe that was just because everyone and everything in it was eating. No one was paying any attention to him at all.

He cleared his throat and gripped the prophecy more tightly. "And I thought maybe you could do me a favor like you did for Great-Aunt Eunida."

Dare Al Luce's marble brow wrinkled just a little. He laced his narrow, tapered fingers together. "It is true that I am looking for a rupture in the Veil, and it is true that a large enough one would cause tiny tears throughout the length and breadth of the Veil."

"The Kehezzzalubbapipipi are only as big as mice, but they can knit themselves together and make something huge and absolutely disgusting," Feltus said with a shudder. "And mice can get through the tiniest crack in a wall."

Dare Al Luce nodded. "I am glad to have the information, but I am still unclear as to what else you want from me?"

"I want you to save the PoodleRats, of course. Can't you sweep in and pour fire from the sky or conjure up a mighty wind and blow the Kehezzzalubbapipipi back to where they belong?" He scrabbled for the prophecy in his pocket and slapped it down on the table. "Look," he said. "It says 'a king.' That's far more likely to be you than me. And 'spear' – I can't even handle a pencil properly."

"I can promise you that the prophecy does not refer to me," Dare Al Luce said. "My only concern is with mending the Veil. I cannot interfere with anything more specific."

"But that's just ... just ... stupid! Why do you have all this power if you won't *use* it?"

"I have misstepped once already. I was severely reprimanded and I'm still serving out my punishment. I cannot challenge the authority of the Patrol again. There are rules that govern all of us who serve."

"What did you do?" Feltus asked, terrified that he'd dared to ask the question.

"I did not take my duty seriously," Dare Al Luce answered. "But now I do."

"But the PoodleRats will *die*!" Feltus said.

Dare Al Luce shrugged, and his gold-clad shoulders ruffled like the feathers of some exotic bird. "It is but a different journey through the Veil."

Feltus stared angrily down at the prophecy, tightening his grip on it until his knuckles whitened. He felt as if the words were imprinted on his brain.

Just then, Bobbie and Sue plunked a plate down in front of him. It looked like phlegm covered in multicolored sugar sprinkles. He tried to manage a polite smile, but his mouth wouldn't turn up at the corners.

"We thought you'd enjoy tripe in a nice sweet omelet instead," Bobbie said.

"And how about a drink?" Sue asked. "We have a

lovely banana-liver smoothie today, or if you're feeling adventurous, organic algae lemonade."

Feltus tried to think of a safe beverage he could order instead.

"What about tea?" Dare Al Luce recommended, noticing Feltus's distaste.

Bobbie and Sue recited the tea list in a bored tone. "Wintergreen mint, Catmint, Peppermint, Spearmint, and Earl Grey."

*Wintergreen mint, catmint, peppermint, spearmint,* echoed Dare Al Luce's voice in Feltus's head.

"Winter, cat, pepper, spear," Feltus repeated in a dazed voice. His hands gripped the sides of the table. *I know those words.* He had repeated them over and over again until they'd become just a jumble of letters. He knew the words better than he had known any poem he'd ever been forced to memorize, or any scientific formula that had been shoved down his throat by an exasperated teacher.

"They're all kinds of mints? What could mints have to do with the Kehezzzalubbapipipi?"

He looked down at the prophecy and recited it out loud, emphasizing the word 'mint':

> *When summer's bounty*
> *Is turned to dust, and*
> *The ravenous flood runs wild*
> *On sharpened claws*
>
> *And all hope is lost,*
> *Then shall wintergreen mint come again,*
> *And the catmint that lurks amongst the peppermint pots,*
> *When at last in the red dawn of the very last day,*
> *Like a spearmint in the hands of a king*
> *Will rise again the Folk of Gewglab Forest*

"But that seems stupid," he said finally. "I mean, if I'm 'the king' after all, it's saying I should attack the Kehezzzalubbapipipi with a breath freshener."

He turned the disc over, almost hoping that a further explanation might have miraculously appeared since the last time he'd studied it. "It can't be something so ... so ..." he searched for the word, "... mundane. I must not be getting the full meaning."

"Perhaps the author lacked talent for clever phrases," Dare Al Luce suggested. "Why don't you go home. I'm certain you'll figure it out there, where you can give it your full concentration," he continued idly. His eyes seemed illuminated by blue fire, and Feltus found himself on his feet without knowing quite how he got there.

"I have to go," he sputtered. "Right now. I have to get home."

"I think you should," Dare Al Luce agreed.

"Thank you."

Dare Al Luce nodded.

Feltus looked down at the omelet quivering on the plate. He swallowed hard. There was no way he was going to sample it, even if it meant hurting Bobbie and Sue's feelings.

"I'll eat this next time," he yelled. He waved vigorously at Bobbie and Sue who were folding takeout menus behind the counter, and left, successfully escaping the gauntlet of their wet mouths.

He sprinted for the turnstile at the back of the café, knocking over a few empty boxes as he ran, and was overcome almost immediately with that awful sensation of vertigo as he tripped and fell through the Veil. He still closed his eyes during the dizzying trip; but, perhaps because it was becoming familiar to him, the journey seemed shorter this time.

* * *

He didn't stop running when he found himself back on the dark, cold side street where he'd first entered the Veil; and when he got to his apartment building and found that the elevator was engaged on the top floor, he took the stairs – two at a time – all the way up to his apartment.

He burst through the front door like a whirlwind, for once not bothering to be quiet, remove his shoes, and hang up his jacket. He bolted down the hallway to Eunida's room. He finally had some kind of key to the prophecy and surely she could help him put it all together; or Winston could, if it required some powerful magic that needed to be done. He felt light-headed and excited and a little bit sick with the thrill of being so close after all this time.

He pounded on the guest room door and then pushed it open. His great-aunt was not there, and Winston's cage was empty, his blanket neatly folded.

He couldn't find Eunida in the living room, nor was she in the kitchen when he burst in and scared Rose into dropping the potato she was peeling. He skidded to a halt, gasping for breath and feeling the sweat drip down his back.

Rose looked up at him with tender amusement. "Looking for something?"

"Eunida!" he blurted out.

"She said she had some business somewhere in town. Must have been important because she wouldn't even sit down and enjoy the cinnamon buns I made especially for her. I didn't quite catch what she said, but it may have had something to do with a bridal shop, although why she would be going to one of those is a mystery."

"No! No! *No!*" Feltus shouted. He leaned against the wall and slid down until he was sitting on the floor, his enthusiasm deflating like a pricked balloon.

"I'm sure it's not as bad as all that," Rose said. "Come on, you can help me finish off this feng shui list your mother left for me. Eat up some of those buns – they'll be stale by tomorrow."

"Where is she?" Feltus asked.

"Floribunda business," Rose answered. "Apparently the committee was really impressed with the simple direct-ness of her speech after so much fluff and snobbery the other night. They voted her in."

"Wow, that must have upset the Herrings."

"Majority rules." Rose answered. "Isn't democracy a wonderful thing?"

She glanced down at the closely-written page of instructions his mother had left for her. It looked as if his mother were fully recovered and back in fussy organiza-tional mode. Feltus supposed that she'd be barging into his room again soon and telling him to pick up his books and put away his laundry.

That thought reminded him of RinMal. He felt the despair well up. He was *so close*. But where was Eunida? The longer he sat there, the more certain he felt that he was no longer on the right track. It seemed too ludicrous to be true.

"Alphabetize and replenish the spice shelf, making sure that any reddish seasonings are grouped together near the rock salt," Rose said, reading aloud from his mother's instructions. "Okay," she said, as she rolled her sleeves up and smoothed the bright blue kerchief she wore on her head.

"Know anything about feng shui, Feltus?"

Feltus, distracted and upset, shrugged.

"Me neither, but I think it has something to do with changing energy flows or opening them up if they're obstructed. Pretty far out for your mother, don't you think?"

"I guess so," he muttered, thinking his mother had done crazier things than that recently.

He poured himself a glass of orange juice, grabbed a cinnamon bun, and moved over to the counter by Rose's side. He watched her capable hands with their short, square nails arrange packets of dried spices and ready the jars. A number of jars were made of blue glass with cork stoppers. Each one was labeled with a metal plate on which the name of the spice was written in tiny, fine handwriting.

Bulk herbs were kept in blue and white china jars with hairline cracks all over their glazed surfaces. Feltus knew that they had belonged to a great-great-grandfather who was a pharmacist, and they had once housed exciting things like belladonna, wormwood, and aconite.

"Did you see what your great-aunt brought me?" Rose asked, holding out a twist of paper filled with dried yellow wisps. "Saffron – hard to get. And this is bergamot, very good for flavoring teas." Her eyes grew dreamy. "You know, herbs and spices bring the far-away places home."

Feltus thought about how the smell of Dare Al Luce's tea had reminded him of his mother's perfume and more unpleasantly, how Eunida's scent often reminded him of low tide at the beach.

Rose folded the papers back around the herbs and carefully tucked them into separate opaque glass jars.

"*Tch*, this doesn't belong here," Rose said. She pulled out a large, round bottle from among the vials of lemon, anise, and orange essence. The label said "Peppermint Oil" and there was a small picture of a mouse on it.

Feltus looked at it with interest.

"What does peppermint oil do?" he asked.

"Your mother bought it to keep the mice out of the pantry. She didn't like the squeak squeaks when they got caught in the glue traps. So instead, I brush a little oil around the food shelves and the mice stay far away. They hate the smell. Can't abide any mint."

He felt a sudden rush of excitement. "You mean mint repels mice? Does it work on all rodents?"

"Sure. At home I grow a little spearmint around the back door where I keep the garbage cans, and the mice and rats keep clear. And catmint works too, although then you get every cat in the neighborhood rolling around in it and acting wacky."

As Rose said something about putting the peppermint oil away under the sink with the ant bait and flypaper, Feltus grabbed the bottle from the counter, ignoring her surprised look, and ran to his bedroom. Inside, he sat down on the edge of his bed and kept very still for a moment.

He was right. The prophecy was full of symbolism and hidden meanings, but once the 'mint' key was figured out, the lines actually meant what they said, crazy as it seemed. That two-hundred-year-old PoodleRat Horrofallalice was a sly old dog. The Kehezzzalubbapipipi were mouse-like. Saldemere Og had referred to them from the beginning as rodents. And Feltus was the king referred to – he had to be. It seemed crazy, but it all made a weird kind of sense now.

He changed hurriedly into an old pair of jeans and a threadbare T-shirt that was still his favorite, even though his mother wouldn't let him wear it and had thrown it away a few times, and a light jacket. He then shoved Mica's trident – which he carefully wrapped in a sock – the flashlight helmet, the peppermint oil, a bottle of water, a package of mint chocolate chip cookies he'd filched a few nights before, and some candy bars into a backpack.

Thinking furiously, he also grabbed his father's extra-strength mint toothpaste out of his parents' bathroom, and then ran back to his own bedroom, where he spent several minutes rooting around in all the pockets of his shorts for the spearmint gum he knew he'd picked up at the corner store. The moment he found it, he shoved his arms into the back-pack straps and sped to the dining room, taking the last ten steps to the table so fast that he ended up sliding headfirst into the port hole like a baseball player making a home run.

It was curiously exhilarating to rocket down the shaft with the wind blowing his hair back and his arms pressed tightly to his sides so he could get a little extra speed on the sharply-angled turns. After some time, the incline of the shaft straightened out and he slowed down.

He lay on his belly for a minute and tried to catch his breath. As the thrill ebbed away, it was replaced by anxiety. It should have been the middle of the day in Gewglab Forest, bright and sunny like the world he'd just left; but instead he exited the darkness of the tunnel and found himself in more darkness.

It took a moment for his eyes to adjust. In the distance was the red blinking light that he remembered topped the roof of Saldemere's house. But other than that, it was difficult to get his bearings.

A gray gloom shrouded everything, and although Feltus knew that the path began only a few paces in front of him and that those wonderful ornate beehive houses bordered the road, not being able to see them made him feel disoriented and unsure about where to place his feet.

He felt a cold prickle of fear inch down his back. It was so quiet – everything was muffled as if a heavy black cloth hung over it all, and the air seemed oppressive, like a thunderstorm was imminent.

He suddenly remembered the flashlight helmet. He dug it out of his pack and flicked it on. The broad beam illuminated everything in front of him, and he clearly saw the reason for his instinctive reluctance to walk any farther into the Grand Gewglab Forest.

The houses were gone – completely razed to the ground. The fences had been obliterated too, as well as the clever windmills and bird baths and growing frames for string beans. Metal, wood, plastic, rubber – all had been consumed. Feltus dug into his bag again and pulled out the trident. He felt better with a weapon in his hand, though he hoped he wouldn't have to use it.

He raised his head again and the light picked out the path ahead. It was stripped of paving stones and glass mosaic – it was nothing but packed dirt now. Earth must be the only thing the Kehezzzalubbapipipi did not eat.

The red beacon light blinked on and off in the distance. It was perched atop a thin steel girder that adorned the bare framework of what had once been Saldemere's proud home. Feltus guessed that the Kehezzzalubbapipipi hadn't bothered with the light because it was some forty feet off the ground, which was higher than their combined height.

He moved quietly toward it.

The feeling of terror was almost unbearable now, causing him to hear steps behind him, breathing by his ear, voices and shrill noises in the wind. It took all his will not to break and run, but he knew that if he did, he would not be able to stop. Then he might find himself lost forever in that wide expanse of desert beyond the town. And somewhere out there was the tear in the Veil that had let the Kehezzzalubbapipipi in. Who knew what else might get through there?

He was too afraid to call out – afraid to risk being heard by ears other than those of the PoodleRats. He imagined that the Kehezzzalubbapipipi must be ravenous, and he had no intention of becoming their next meal.

He padded along the dirt path, placing his feet carefully but feeling very exposed in the middle of all the rubble. He would have felt completely hopeless if it weren't for the memory of what the toilet scrying bowl had shown him. A couple days ago, Saldemere and the others had been alive. Feltus and RinMal had seen them. The PoodleRats had been preparing to fight.

Feltus climbed through the empty, rusted frame of one

of Saldemere's windows. The edges were roughened from the gnawing of thousands of sharp little teeth, and he felt the leg of his jeans behind his knee snag and tear. Amidst the shards of broken glass, a metal ring shone dully. He knelt and saw that the ring was attached to a square of the floorboards. He grasped it with both hands and pulled, and with a creaking groan, the hatch opened.

He remembered Saldemere showing him the entry into the subterranean passages from the house's hallway. He recalled that RinMal had reminded him of this too, as if the PoodleRat had really believed, even then, that Feltus would find a way to save them. That he would come.

He pointed his flashlight at a rickety ladder attached to the side of the tunnel. The unpleasant smell of stale air wafted up to him from the small, dark passageway. He felt the fear rise up in him again.

*What if I'm alone here?*

He pushed the thought from his mind, and clung to the hope that the PoodleRats were safe underground, preparing themselves for battle, and that RinMal had convinced them to wait for him.

But with each passing second in this silent and dead world, it seemed less and less likely.

# CHAPTER 18

## In Which the Kehezzzalubbapipipi Play a Prominent Role

HALFWAY DOWN THE ladder a rung gave way, and Feltus plunged twenty feet before he hit the ground face first. Fortunately, the floor was made up of relatively soft, sandy earth with a few pebbles, and after he had removed the small stones embedded in his cheek and dusted himself off, he felt capable of continuing. Unfortunately, the fall seemed to have damaged the flashlight helmet and he had to thwack it a few times to get it going again. He fastened it back onto his head and looked around for the weapon that had been knocked from his grasp. He found it and curled his fingers around the bone handle.

The light picked out a narrow, meandering tunnel barely taller than he was. It was earthen and reinforced with welded copper piping. Roots tickled the top of his head and he could smell decayed leaves and other organic matter. It reminded him that Gewglab Forest had once been a place where natural things grew and thrived. It was the desert above his head and the creatures that had made it that were unnatural.

Feltus carefully made his way deeper into the tunnel system. He didn't see the side passage, nor did he see the long pole that hooked his legs out from under him. The pointy end of the same pole was then placed against the back of his neck, just under the flashlight helmet that had ceased to work. He spat dirt out of his mouth and tried to blink it out of his eyes. One arm was twisted under him and he'd lost the trident once again. He was still half blind when a wiry arm pulled him to his feet.

"Feltus!" RinMal said in an excited whisper. "I'm sorry! I've been on guard duty ever since I got back and I'm a little nervous – I've been jumping at shadows. I didn't recognize you with your head covered."

Feltus tried to clear grit from his mouth. "You must be keyed up if you thought I was the enemy," he said and then found himself grinning at the PoodleRat.

"You dropped this," RinMal said, handing over Mica's trident. "She's gone then? Percy's method worked?"

Feltus nodded. "And my mom is back to her nutty ways," he said with just a bit of irritation in his voice.

The PoodleRat smiled as if he understood.

Feltus pulled the backpack off his shoulders and hugged it to his chest. "I finally solved the prophecy!" It sounded so great to finally say it that he said it again in a loud voice. "And I have your secret weapon right here."

"I knew you would figure it out! You're just in time. Saldemere Og is rallying the PoodleRats for a battle. Let's go!"

Feltus followed RinMal deeper underground. Twenty yards ahead, the tunnel opened up into a large, circular room. Rough wooden benches surrounded a raised center platform. As Feltus entered, a throng of seated PoodleRats, sadly unkempt and thin, turned their ink black eyes on him. It was shocking. The careful maintenance of their luxurious coats and the attention they had once paid to beauty in every detail of their lives had vanished.

"We cannot possibly fail now that our young king has come," boomed an overly cheery voice. Saldemere Og appeared from the shadows. "The prophecy holds true." He walked across the platform slowly, as if it pained him, but his back was held straight and his head high. Feltus recognized the red uniform with gold braid and buttons. Saldemere had exchanged his swords for a rapier and a rusty revolver that looked positively medieval. A lethal, curved dagger hung at his side, and he fastened a pair of feathered gauntlets at the wrist as he approached.

Feltus could barely contain himself. "I found the key to the prophecy!" he burst out.

He quickly outlined his discovery and brought forth the flask of peppermint oil, the toothpaste, and the gum. A loud murmuring rose from the PoodleRats as the news spread. They seemed energized, and the empty, hopeless look in their eyes was replaced with a spark of fire.

"We must go see Professor Krankle!" Saldemere proclaimed and flourished his blade. Feltus and RinMal followed him, followed by the revitalized PoodleRat army.

The professor had set up temporary digs in a cramped and suffocating pit. The smoke belching from various pots and urns made breathing almost impossible, and Feltus was sure that the continual inhalation of toxic substances had affected the PoodleRat.

The professor removed the stopper from the bottle of peppermint oil and held it under his nose. "Hmmm. Tincture of peppermint essence in a linseed base." He sniffed again, "Bottled one-and-a-half years ago if I'm not mistaken." His good eye watered copiously. He dabbed a little of the toothpaste on his tongue and grunted, "We can smear this on the fighters' helmets for added protection."

"And the gum can be chewed up and then stuck to pretty much anything," Feltus explained.

"It should not be hard to reproduce more of this formula. I can have sufficient quantities ready in three hours. I'm thinking simple packs with spray nozzles and dousing wands for the fighters," the professor said, "and perhaps, if I can borrow a few strong backs, a catapult or two for the rear line. I can mix the oil with dry earth and hay and make mint cakes that will disintegrate on contact. Whatever's left over can be eaten for dinner."

"Three hours – will that be enough time before the Kehezzzalubbapipipi return?" Feltus asked, a little frantic. The professor's fur was badly scorched – his tail was almost non-existent now, and he walked with a pronounced limp. Feltus wasn't even sure he could handle a screwdriver, let alone a heavy weapon. After all his hard work, everything came down to this raggedy, crazy, disreputable PoodleRat. However, he sighed and admitted to himself the one thing he had learned from dealing with Eunida and Winston – don't judge by appearance.

"Indubitably-blee-blee," said Krankle with a wild glint in his eye.

Feltus nodded reluctantly and handed over the gum. Krankle clasped it in his grimy, blackened paws.

"Dawn is still a handful of hours away, dear boy. We will be ready for them," Saldemere promised. "The prospect of a fair battle, now that we have the means for fighting back, will hearten us."

The Professor retreated into the gloom with his workers, and Feltus, RinMal, and Saldemere were left with nothing to do but wait.

They returned to the main gathering room where RinMal built up a roaring blaze in the fire-pit. They shared five chocolate bars between one hundred PoodleRats – barely enough for a lick apiece.

Feltus tried not to think about the battle ahead, but his stomach was empty, his face was sore from the fall, and his fears were rampant despite RinMal's contagious optimism. The atmosphere was now unmistakably war-like. Saldemere Og had teams of PoodleRats sharpening and polishing crude weaponry, and others sorted dwindling rations into food packs for the battle.

It occurred to Feltus that he had voluntarily put himself

in danger.

"I'll be supervising the water rations, filling canteens, that sort of thing, right?" he asked Saldemere Og.

"Such nobility, such humility in one so young," Saldemere said as he reached up and placed a warm paw on Feltus's shoulder. RinMal, who was filing the edge of a spoon into a point, looked up at Feltus and grinned. "Of course, you'll be by my side – right in the thick of it. It will be epic!" the old PoodleRat promised.

Feltus was horrified, but he had no one to blame but himself. He should have admitted how terrified he'd been the first time he'd faced the enemy, instead of letting them believe he was as brave as they were. If he had spoken up then, perhaps he'd have been able to sit the battle out on the sidelines, wiping sweaty brows and preparing thermoses. He attempted a humble smile, but his lips felt as if they would crack with the effort. He decided that, in order not to be exposed as the coward he knew he was, he would avoid actual battle as much as possible. With that thought, he started chewing his nails down to the skin.

As the long night wore on, interrupted only by the faint sounds of frenzied sawing and hammering and the ear-splitting squeal of metal on metal, Saldemere Og reminisced in a gently rambling way about his brother, the founding of the town, the glory of the surrounding forests, and the creation of countless beautiful things.

"For I have lived many, many years, my boy. Nearly three hundred as you would count them."

"Tell me about the battle when you first faced the enemy," Feltus asked, thinking he might be able to pick up some pointers.

"*Ahhh* ... The Battle of Nantly Dun. It was horrible and glorious all at the same time. We met the Kehezzzalubbapipipi at the iron gates of the city. Of course, those are long gone now; we melted down the gates for pikes and mallets some time ago.

"The sun was bloody, and as it died, the waning light bathed us in a red glow. From out of the west they came with the night, and we stood against them for as long as we could. But we were ill-prepared, and they were too many. I am ashamed to say that when my brother fell, the other survivors and I lost heart. We slunk back to our homes, tails between our legs.

"They cut us down like so many stalks of wheat. We could not stand against them. Each time it grows harder."

*So if I run, I'll probably survive*, Feltus thought to himself. He wished he could get caught up in the rising excitement the PoodleRats were apparently feeling, but all he felt was a nausea that had started in his belly and was working its way up his throat.

"And now? What gives you hope?" Feltus asked, praying he'd hear something that would boost his own confidence.

"The prophecy and you, dear boy. We pin our faith on a biscuit and an Overlander."

"Oh," said Feltus, feeling inadequate.

As the fire died to a few glowing embers in a bed of ashes, Feltus was suddenly overcome with exhaustion. He stretched out on the sandy ground, pillowing his head on his arm, and was lulled by the rhythm of Saldemere's speech. He must have fallen asleep for a few minutes because when he opened his eyes, the cavern was buzzing with excitement and activity. He tried to work the cramp out of his neck with numb fingers. The fire had gone out, and he was cold and hungry. He rubbed the sleep from his eyes and felt sand crusting his eyelashes. He wanted a hot meal and a tall, cold glass of milk. Instead, he got a stale cracker and a sip of dusty water.

Krankle, missing a few new swathes of fur from his

forearms and stinking of sulfur, pushed a wheelbarrow filled with hoses. The metallic inner workings of dismantled vacuum cleaners were wheeled in next, just as Feltus was occupied with trying to talk a yellow PoodleRat out of his food ration.

As the last of the equipment arrived, the professor blew three short blasts on a conch shell, instantly getting everyone's attention, so Feltus had to make do with his small cracker even though his stomach was cramping with hunger. It was about as far from one of his heroic tales as things could get. At least Hercules never had to go hungry.

Feltus cast a black look at the professor, who was hopping in place from sheer excitement. Krankle had strapped a metal canister that looked like a fire extinguisher to his back. A hose capped with a flexible nozzle protruded from one end of it.

"Behold, the Vaporizer," Krankle said.

He pointed the business end of the nozzle at Feltus who backed away then made a grand sweep over the crowd of silent PoodleRats. Saldemere placed a warning paw on the Professor's arm.

"It looks wonderful," Saldemere said encouragingly. "What does it do?"

Krankle examined the large timepiece he wore around his neck. "In exactly twenty-four minutes you will see for yourself."

"*Twenty-four minutes!*" Feltus shouted in terror.

"Twenty-four minutes!" The cry was taken up and repeated, and the cavern reverberated with the sound of a hundred inspired PoodleRat voices. Feltus huddled in the corner and tried to remember why he had come. Everything was suddenly happening so fast that he barely had time to tighten the laces of his sneakers before RinMal pulled him toward the racks of recycled armor and altered kitchen utensils, none of which was any sharper than the weapon he'd brought from home. He wrapped the trident carefully in its sock sheath and slipped it into his back pocket, then watched to see what RinMal did. The PoodleRat lifted the flattened aluminum vest over his head and tied the side laces so that his chest and back were protected. Feltus copied him, although his own armor only came down about halfway over his stomach and shoulders, and was almost unbearably tight across his chest.

"I'm going to war disguised as a soda can," Feltus joked nervously, but it wasn't really that funny. He remembered that the Kehezzzalubbapipipi had consumed all of the aluminum wind-chimes hanging in the PoodleRats' gardens.

After his own preparations were made, Feltus watched as Saldemere anointed each PoodleRat with a salve so infused with mint that the warriors had to wear special goggles to protect their eyes. They were going into battle attired in protective pads and helmets, with canisters of extra-strength liquid mentholatum strapped to their backs and pressure-sensitive spray guns clasped in sweaty paws. RinMal tossed Feltus a pair of plastic aviator goggles.

They marched down the dusty corridors in single file. Feltus walked along unwillingly, then climbed the long ladders to what had been the PoodleRats' homes. Saldemere led the way, but even he faltered at the sight of the devastation once they got to the town. But Saldemere recovered quickly; he positioned himself on a mound of twisted metal and broken pottery where everyone could see him, and started barking orders.

Some PoodleRats manned the simple catapults, which had been hastily constructed from salvaged wood and metal remnants and hauled up from the depths of the subterranean tunnels. The catapults were aligned behind the front troops and primed to hurl powdered mint into the midst of the

Kehezzzalubbapipipi. Others heaped bags of leaves and rocks, and readied themselves behind this simple barricade to repair and refill the weaponry and encourage their companions.

In the middle of this hubbub, Feltus, feeling useless, hopped from one foot to the other, passed pieces of chewing gum around, and braced himself. He wished he'd had time to visit the bathroom.

Then a horn sounded.

"They've been sighted," Saldemere Og yelled, and the news was relayed down the line.

After the initial alarm, they waited in silence. In his head, Feltus ran through a list of possible excuses for why he couldn't fight and came up with nothing better than short-sightedness. Even if he'd tried to run, he couldn't get away. The PoodleRats stood pressed together in one solid formation, and he was wedged between Saldemere and one of the brawny young PoodleRats who'd appeared under his dining room table all those months ago – Fosden, he thought his name was.

RinMal was positioned farther down the line, heading up what Saldemere Og had called "the left flank." Feltus attempted to wave to his friend, but could barely move his arms. He tried to scratch an itchy rib, but he couldn't reach under his vest. His armor was heavy and uncomfortable, and it chafed under his armpits. It was definitely fitted for a smaller torso than his. He shifted uncomfortably, and heard the sloshing of the water bottle in his backpack. He was instantly thirsty.

Toward the east, the rising sun stained everything red. RinMal's young eyes picked out a gathering dust cloud, and the information was passed along the ranks and back to the equippers. An excited murmur swelled as the cloud became a dark shadow upon the sand and a thrumming drone rose through the air. They steeled their backs against the onslaught.

Suddenly the ground opened up before them, and it seemed as if the sun were blacked out. The crawling multitude rose up in a wave five feet high and thirty feet wide.

They came on tiny, razor-clawed feet. They came with sanguine eyes and empty stomachs. They were like a mighty wind that rocked the lines of stalwart defenders. And the PoodleRats bent before the onslaught – but they did not break.

The horrible mass of the Kehezzzalubbapipipi retreated a little and readied itself to come again. Feltus could see wriggling worm-like tails within a tightly woven carpet of small, black-furred bodies, and his stomach turned over.

"Fire!" yelled Saldemere. The catapults were put into action. A fine dust fell upon the enemy and the dark swathe of creatures sagged a little.

Holes appeared here and there in the enemy ranks, but the Kehezzzalubbapipipi slowly gathered themselves and came on again through the mist of mint.

Saldemere Og and his brave companions, the Poodle-Rats of the High Court, advanced and met the enemy head on. Although his hands shook, his knees quaked, and his goggles impeded his vision, Feltus marched with them, hip-to-shoulder with Fosden. If he'd had time to stop and think about what he was doing there, he wouldn't have been able to come up with a single reason. But there was no time to think. His heart leapt into his throat where it twitched and jumped like a frog, and still he moved forward despite himself, one small step at a time, with the others.

Suddenly, Feltus realized that he couldn't access his weapon. The armor was so tight that bending his arm behind to reach into his back pocket was impossible.

With a lot of squirming and maneuvering, he finally managed to untie one side of his chest plate and free an arm. He gripped the trident, unwrapping it from its sock scabbard. The weight was comfortable in his hand but it didn't seem like enough. He needed something more – anything really, a screwdriver, a paperclip, a door key. He pulled his backpack free and rummaged around in it. His questing fingers found a lone piece of gum, a plastic bottle, a quarter, and the mint chocolate chip cookies he'd brought for the anticipated victory celebration.

*Mint chocolate chip!*

The blackness surged and bulged and reared above them. It rose above Saldemere Og, who was resplendent in his scarlet tunic and gold brocade, rapier at the ready. It gathered itself, concentrating all its power and strength, and prepared to deal a mortal blow.

Feltus threw the gum, the quarter, and the bottle of water, but they had no effect. Then he fumbled with cookie package, ripping at it until it tore.

A thousand mouths opened; tens of thousands of razor-sharp teeth gleamed within. Out of the corner of his eye, Feltus saw RinMal move forward to shield Saldemere Og.

The outer edges of the Kehezzzalubbapipipi spread like a cobra's mantle, and as quick as a flash, the mass darted forward and back again, each individual mouse striking like a snake. Together they delivered a thousand bites at a time. Feltus sensed, rather than felt, the blow that struck him.

The PoodleRats held firm, although Feltus saw RinMal stagger and almost fall to his knees. "RinMal!" he yelled, trying to fight his way to his friend. But he lost sight of him in the crush.

The row of PoodleRats stood solidly, silently awaiting Saldemere's command.

The Kehezzzalubbapipipi changed shape again, morphing into a thirty-foot tall hammer. It reared up directly above them. *This is it*, Feltus thought to himself. His mouth dropped open. Those teeth would fall on them and bite and rend and chew, and they'd be crushed under the weight of all those bodies.

All around him the PoodleRats were shouting their battle cries; Feltus heard himself yelling "RinMal, RinMal!" Feltus raised his arm up, clutching the cookies, and threw them with all his might into the middle of that mat of squirming fur.

Where the cookies landed, the Kehezzzalubbapipipi fell away. As holes opened up, the tower of Kehezzzalubbapipipi began to sway, and tiers of wriggling animals came crashing down.

"For Koncriticon Lar!" Saldemere sang. One of the PoodleRats aimed the nozzle of his vaporizer and fired. Others followed suit, and soon the air was filled with droplets that burned the nose, stung the eyes, and singed the lungs, despite the face-masks. Where the drops fell, they seared the Kehezzzalubbapipipi and expunged them from the earth. Feltus felt a great joy rise up in his heart as their foe fell to the ground, writhing and pulsing and finally dissolving into small black puddles that were sucked into the dry earth. A moment later he felt sick. All the adrenaline he'd felt pumping through his body during the fight had disappeared and he was left with an overwhelming feeling of exhaustion and disgust. The Kehezzzalubbapipipi had been devoid of emotion and pity, and he was glad they were gone but he realized he didn't have the stomach for war and killing. He was no Hercules.

Feltus slipped the trident back into his pocket and let his breath out in a great whooping rush. He pulled his dented armor off, threw it to the ground, and could find nothing but a small v-shaped cut above his heart and a bruise on his ribs that had probably come from his fall down the ladder. The cut had bled a little and stained his T-shirt, but he wasn't badly hurt.

He scanned the battlefield, hardly believing that it was

all over. He looked for RinMal wanting to share the victory with him. PoodleRats milled about, yelling and hugging one another. It was impossible to pick out the russet brown of RinMal's fur from among all the armored PoodleRats. He gave up for the moment and surveyed his immediate surroundings. Drops of a thick tar-like substance were all that remained of the Kehezzzalubbapipipi. He stamped on one droplet, obliterating it. All around him the PoodleRats were doing the same thing – stamping on the last vestiges of the Kehezzzalubbapipipi. They began casting aside their weapons, throwing off their armor, goggles, and visors, and jumping up and down like madmen while the sun rose higher in the sky and drove away the last of the shadows. *Where is RinMal?*

"Feltus, my boy," Saldemere Og said in a voice strained and hoarse from shouting. "The prophecy was true indeed!"

Saldemere's uniform was streaked with grime and sweat. He'd sustained a deep scratch across his forehead, and his monocle, shattered, hung from its black ribbon

The other PoodleRats drew nearer to them. Some nursed gouges, slashes, and bites, and everyone's eyes were reddened and raw from the pungency of the mint salve. Feltus searched the assembled crowd for his friend. Now that the horror was over, he wanted him by his side.

"Feltus," Saldemere continued, "without you to unravel the meaning of the prophecy, we would surely have been lost." He pulled Feltus into a firm embrace. It was nice but uncomfortable since Feltus had to squat down to PoodleRat height. The PoodleRats cheered.

From the safety of that furry hug, Feltus looked again for RinMal. After a moment, he saw him. He disengaged himself from Saldemere's hug and stood up slowly, not believing what he was seeing. RinMal was alone, away from the crowd. The sun shone on his russet fur. He was bent over awkwardly, his fingers clasping his stomach. Feltus watched in shock as bright red blood seeped from between RinMal's fingers.

Then Feltus's knees buckled and he dropped to the ground.

\* \* \*

"RinMal," Feltus whispered. And then Feltus was up and running in a mad headlong dash. On his way, he tripped over a chunk of mortar, twisting his ankle painfully, but he didn't slow down until he'd reached his friend, who was now kneeling on the rubble, holding his abdomen with bloody paws.

Feltus sank to the dust beside him. RinMal's chest plate was badly dented, and Feltus could see serrated metal edges where the Kehezzzalubbapipipi's teeth had torn through. The blood dripped steadily, and Feltus looked at it in horror. "RinMal ... I'm so sorry," he said.

"Sorry? Don't be sorry. You saved us."

"Is it very bad?" Feltus asked in a broken whisper. The blood was so vivid, so scarlet.

"No," RinMal answered through clenched teeth.

Feltus placed his hand over the PoodleRat's paws. "You're coming home with me. There's no way you'll heal quickly in a wasteland like this."

"If Saldemere can spare me, I'll come," RinMal promised.

"Move out of the way, boy," said a gruff voice. Professor Krankle stood above them, his chest heaving and his good eye jittering about. He held a wrench in a menacing manner.

Feltus moved so that his body was between RinMal and the scientist. "You're not using that on him," he stammered. At that moment he would have protected RinMal against a thousand Kehezzzalubbapipipi.

"It's okay," RinMal said.

"I'm not going to let anyone hurt you! Especially not some crazed pseudo scientist!" Feltus blurted out.

"Have to bend the metal out of the way. It's putting too much pressure on the wound," Krankle explained in a raspy voice.

"Oh," Feltus said meekly.

Feltus hesitated, then reluctantly stepped away so the professor could get to work. Feltus had to admit that Krankle had quite a gentle touch with a wrench. Krankle peeled the metal back as if he were opening a sardine can. Feltus observed a couple of winces and one groan from RinMal, but it was over quite quickly. The wound when exposed was significant. It was long and jagged, but not as deep as was feared – an incisor cut from the strike aimed at Saldemere Og. The bleeding had slowed to a trickle.

"Excellent coagulation," Professor Krankle muttered. "We'll seal you up and everything should be fine."

"I feel better already," RinMal gasped, although his face was still pale and his breathing was shallow.

Feltus stripped off his jacket, removed his raggedy T-shirt and started to rip it into long strips. The worn material tore easily. "It's mostly clean except for some nervous sweat," Feltus said. He handed the makeshift bandages to Krankle and watched closely as the scientist carefully wrapped RinMal's belly, tying the ends in a neat bow at the back. Fosden and Maurph stepped forward to link paws and carry RinMal back to what remained of the town square.

Miraculously, most of Krankle's laboratory seemed to be intact, at least the part under the ground. Feltus and everyone else waited while the professor disappeared down the dusty, noxious hole in the floor, and after what seemed to be an interminable silence punctuated by swearing and odd phrases – "darn hose, darn elliptic humidifier, darn omnipotent salad spinner" – Krankle reappeared triumphantly holding a half-used tube of instant glue. Feltus, having a slight phobia of needles, was glad to see that rather than stitch the wound, Krankle proposed to glue the edges closed, a method that seemed simple and ingenious to him. Once he was finished and RinMal had relaxed the grip he'd had on Feltus's hand while his bandages were being rewound, they were ready to go. RinMal was able to walk with a little support from Feltus and Saldemere Og. Followed by every last PoodleRat, they made their way slowly down the main road toward the port hole that led to Feltus's dining room table.

Saldemere stopped and picked up a vivid chip of blue glass lying in the dust and turned it over in his paw. "With the memory of what once was, we will be able to retrace our steps," Saldemere said before he slipped the shard into the pocket of his uniform. "Rebuild, my boy, rebuild."

Feltus didn't like goodbyes. They made him nervous. He thought back to that last day in the suburbs, outside the worn brick of his old house. He'd barely looked at Fuzzy when his friend had shown up just as the final pieces of furniture were being taken from the house. He'd been made uncomfortable by the silent faces of the neighborhood kids, all of whom he'd known since kindergarten, who stood around watching the movers pack the truck. But since then, he'd wished many times that he'd said something meaningful, or anything at all.

As he thought back on that day, he realized something: goodbyes were hard because you never knew if it would be forever. But it was for precisely that reason that you should always say goodbye, or at least say *something*. Because then, you'd always have that to hold onto. And this time, he knew he had RinMal too. Because RinMal wasn't going to be leaving him anytime soon.

Shaking hands with all the PoodleRats took a long time, and halfway through his hand felt bruised and limp.

"Your bravery and strength will be sung of forever, Feltus Ovalton LeRoi," Saldemere Og proclaimed. "Your name will shine like a testament to honor, perseverance, and strong will, and we will write poems and histories in which you will be praised."

Feltus wondered how they'd get a heroic tale or an epic poem from the life of someone who'd muddled his way through everything and then done nothing more than throw a bag of cookies in the air. It struck him as funny that he was revered in this world and mostly ridiculed in his own. *I guess it's all a matter of perspective.*

"Listen," he said, "I'd be honored if you wrote songs about me – "

He paused. He was going to tell them that he didn't deserve praise – that he'd procrastinated when he was supposed to be working on the prophecy, that he'd resented the burden of being their predicted hero, that if his legs had worked he'd have run away, and that he'd been so scared during the battle that he'd just wildly thrown the contents of his bag. But they were all looking at him with such warmth ... and he found himself shutting his mouth on his words.

They all looked at him expectantly. RinMal kicked him.

"I'd be honored, that's all," Feltus finished lamely. Saldemere's paw thudded across his back, and Feltus looked into the PoodleRat's face. He was shocked to see that although the lines of worry had eased, Saldemere had tears in his eyes. Saldemere noticed his concern and smiled.

"It's the mint salve, dear boy. It's everywhere. Awfully powerful stuff," the old PoodleRat said as he wiped his nose with an embroidered handkerchief. "We will be okay."

Feltus stuck out his hand automatically, ready for whoever was next in line.

Professor Krankle, his eye red and raw, limped toward him, looking at Feltus's hand as if it were a particularly malignant spider. Feltus let it drop by his side. During the uncomfortable silence that followed, Feltus racked his brain for something to say. Eventually the professor spoke.

"*Harumphh.* You did a good job," he croaked, staring at the ground and fiddling with his claw hammer. His coveralls were stiff with grease and ground-in dirt, but he smelled as fresh as a breath mint. After a moment, he held out a greasy ratchet tied with a wire bow. Feltus stared down at the offering in amazement. "Thanks," he replied awkwardly, accepting the gift. "You too."

With a curt nod, the professor hobbled off.

RinMal, as pale as a PoodleRat could ever be from Krankle's ministrations, nudged him. "Krankle doesn't like or trust foreigners. You should be pleased."

"I am, I guess, and I'm sorry I called him names," Feltus whispered. "But I really just want to go home now. I'm glad you're coming with me. If you weren't – you know – if you weren't okay ... I'd be a mess right now."

RinMal smiled at him. "I'm glad you're all right too."

The line of PoodleRats waiting to shake his hand had finally thinned out, and Feltus noticed that some of them had brought lengths of thick rope woven from grasses, twine remnants, and plastic string which they were knotting together into a large circular net.

Feltus looked at the complex hammock that was supposed to haul them safely all the way up the port hole. It seemed like a ridiculous amount of distance for his wounded friend to travel. Back in the apartment he'd actually thought about bringing the climbing gear Krankle had fabricated for him, as much as he dreaded ever having to make that climb again, but in the end he left it, having no room in his backpack. He was glad he hadn't brought it because there was no way he could have scaled the heights carrying RinMal with him. As it was, ten strong, young PoodleRats stood at the ready and Feltus had to admit that they looked capable. One of them had already climbed up at a fast speed to attach the pulley at the top.

"Will you be safe going up in that? It won't hurt you, will it?" Feltus asked RinMal. He wasn't used to his friend looking so weak and unsteady on his feet, and he didn't like it.

"I'll be fine," RinMal reassured him. "They've hauled hundred-pound bags of discarded rubber down the port holes before."

"That was 'down' not 'up' with the force of gravity to help them," Feltus pointed out. "Plus I weigh a bit more than you, and Saldemere insisted on giving me a flour sack full of beans."

"They'll manage," RinMal said.

"Once we get up there, you won't have to do anything but rest and get strong again, I promise."

"Ok, I'm ready," the PoodleRat announced.

They both carefully stepped into the middle of the hammock. The edges were drawn together and then the whole bundle was raised up until they were dangling a few feet above the ground. The rope was scratchy and rough and Feltus tried to position himself so that RinMal stayed in the middle, buffered by the beans, where he was somewhat protected. Through the web, Feltus could see Saldemere standing proudly. The old PoodleRat had managed to salvage an admiral's hat from somewhere, and he'd polished the dirt from the brass buttons of his military jacket until they shone. He saluted them with his sword, and Feltus promised himself he'd return some day. The only good thing about leaving precipitously was that the PoodleRats hadn't had time to come up with any more embarrassing songs about him.

The ride up was remarkably smooth, except for a little bumping when they negotiated a tight turn. RinMal babbled on excitedly about all the things he was looking forward to seeing and doing, and Feltus pretended not to notice when his friend had to clutch his abdomen before he could continue talking.

When they eventually reached the top of the port hole and pulled themselves out into Feltus's apartment, RinMal was looking pale again and his breathing was coming fast. Feltus checked the room for people, stowed Saldemere's gift behind the handy potted plant, and then, ignoring all his protestations, carried the small PoodleRat to his room.

"It's not dignified," RinMal said. "And I'm a blooded warrior now."

"You're wounded and you weigh about half as much as Lafayette," Feltus said. "And after all I've done for you, the least you can do in return is let me help you."

Feltus propped his friend up on the bed surrounded with cushions. He threw him a blanket, and then rummaged in the closet for something to eat.

"Let's hope this is the end of all the excitement," he said as he tossed aside some dirty socks. "The Patrol should be fixing all the tears in the Veil soon, and I told Dare Al Luce all about the one in this room. I figure it'll be pretty high up on their list."

"Did you tell him about your spell too?"

"Yeah, and I'm kind of wishing I hadn't now. But I thought that if I admitted it and told him where problems with the Veil started, that he'd help you when I asked him."

"And did he? Is that how you solved the prophecy?"

Feltus thought about this for a minute. "You know ... I thought he was totally unhelpful. He wouldn't give me any straight answers, and he kept talking about how he couldn't challenge the Patrol. But now I'm wondering if he helped me after all." He shrugged. "I don't know. At this point, thinking about all this magic-otherwordly-Veil stuff just makes me feel tired and hungry," Feltus said.

He tossed RinMal a bag of potato chips and a caramel pecan cluster and went back to rooting around in the closet for something to drink.

The bedroom door suddenly swung open.

"Knock, knock," said a gruff voice.

Feltus straightened up hurriedly, holding two bottles of warm soda in his hands. *What now?* he wondered distractedly.

# CHAPTER 19

## Dare Al Luce Explains a Few Things

GREAT-AUNT EUNIDA barged in. Winston was bobbing in his harness across her back, and she held an open can of something that was leaking red juice onto the floor. She'd knotted her greasy hanks of hair into a rat's nest over her left ear and sported a colorful violet plaid raincoat and a big smile.

Feltus suddenly remembered that he was mad at her.

"Where were you yesterday?" he yelled. "I needed you to help with the prophecy and you weren't here!"

She looked from him to RinMal who had fallen asleep under the blanket, a potato chip halfway to his mouth. "Looks like everything turned out all right. In fact," she continued briskly, "I knew it would."

"That's a fat lot of good now! I needed you *before* the battle. Maybe if you'd been around, RinMal wouldn't have been hurt," he whispered bitterly.

She looked at him with a baleful stare.

"You know what, Feltus? Just because I can see the future doesn't mean I can arrange it. Most of the time, my gift is a burden – especially when it shows me things that impact those near to me, because I am almost never able to stop the bad things from happening. I tried to prepare you as best as I could, and like I already said, it all turned out fine. Right?"

He nodded grudgingly.

"Okay then. Let's move on," she said.

She was eating beets straight from the can, and her

fingers and mouth were stained a bright pink. She smiled at him widely. "Feltus, your parents are safely settled for the night."

"Together? At the same time?" Feltus asked. Obviously they shared a bedroom, but their schedules never seemed to coincide, and more frequently than not, his father slept on the couch at his office.

"Sure," she nodded. "They've been canoodling a lot recently. Disgusting behavior."

"What's canoodling?" He wasn't sure he wanted to know the answer.

"Carrying on like children, whispering with their heads together. Your father in particular has been quite unlike himself. After the Monkhouse deal went through – and I understand it's the biggest deal the firm has ever had – he started coming home earlier, and two or three times he's even brought your mother flowers."

"Did either of them say anything," Feltus asked, "about the ... the other stuff that's been going on? About me?"

"Not a word, dear, not a word. Although I overheard your mother talking about a family outing of some kind, and I do believe I heard your father laugh once or twice! Now *that* was a surprise. I wouldn't necessarily expect either of them to remember exact details. For most people, it's more convenient to forget strange events and pretend nothing untoward has happened," she explained.

"You said a family outing?" Feltus asked in disbelief. "Are you sure? With me?" His voice squeaked a little. "We haven't done anything fun together for a really long time." He pondered this new development and then the source. Eunida had probably gotten it wrong and he didn't want to be disappointed.

"So where were you yesterday?" he asked, not willing to drop it completely.

"Out and about – reconnaissance," she answered. "Frightfully important stuff. The gloves must come off, my dear," she continued in a serious voice, as she sat down on the bed, careful not to disturb RinMal. "You've been kept awfully busy, Feltus, and you've done very well on the whole, although we could have done without your mother's involvement. Always best to keep the parents out of it. But now it is time for us to do all we can to try and return things to the way they were."

"What do you mean? It's over, isn't it? The Patrol is fixing the holes in the Veil and that'll take care of any more transmigration."

"It's not as easy as that," Winston said, hopping out of his harness and making himself comfortable on a pile of RinMal's floor cushions. "Everything that has occurred has had an impact already."

"It's like putting the proverbial genie back in the bottle," Eunida explained. "It seems simple, until you're faced with an angry, green-skinned fellow who's yelling about unfair incarceration and absolutely refusing to go in." She unsuccessfully chased the last of the slippery beets around the can with a crooked finger. "And then you have to use your last wish to get him back in."

Feltus stared at her. His head was a jumble of thoughts. "So what's the problem exactly?" he asked with more bravado that he felt. *What if I'm in serious trouble with the Patrol? What kind of punishment would they dole out? There was that guy in the myths who had his liver eaten every night by a vulture ... I don't think I'd like that.*

"There are two issues here," Eunida replied. "We must look at the bigger picture – ask ourselves why such things should suddenly happen to a grubby, mean little boy like yourself, Feltus. I know you did the unlocking spell, but lots of people speak spells and mess around with magic and nothing happens – nothing changes.

"So the question is, was it solely the spell? Was it you? Was it the apartment – particularly, was it because various folds of the Veil intersect here in this room?

"And we did ask ourselves these questions. 'We' meaning Dare Al Luce, Winston, and myself."

She slipped off the bed and moved toward Feltus in a purposeful way, and he backed up until he stood inside his closet with nowhere to go.

"What do you want? What are you going to do?" he said fearfully, wondering whether the genie story had been a thinly veiled warning. He'd raised his voice without meaning to and RinMal had roused, looked around, blinking a little in groggy surprise, and then sat up with his usual curious expression.

"Call him," she said.

"What?"

"Ask Dare Al Luce to come here."

"I can't make him come here. I couldn't even get him to help the PoodleRats. He already told me that his only concern is the Veil."

"I think that if you ask him for help, he will come, like he did before ... and this is about the Veil."

"Okay ...," Feltus replied, feeling stupid. "What do I do?"

"Just voice a plea," Winston said. "That seems to work pretty well for you."

Eunida's eyes were on Feltus, as were RinMal's.

*Umm*, he thought to himself. *Dare Al Luce ... calling Dare Al Luce ... please come here ... This is so dumb ... I could go for a bowl of ice cream ... chocolate hazelnut ... Why are they all staring at me?*

There was a low hum, like the buzzing of a thousand bees, and then a golden light began to flush the walls of

Feltus's room. The light pulsed and became even more radiant, until it was impossible to look directly at it. Finally, when its light seemed to equal the sun's, there was a small flare and Dare Al Luce appeared.

He seemed incredibly tall to Feltus, as if the room was not large enough to hold him. Feltus made a little bow and wished he'd had time to make the bed, or at least pick up the clothes on the floor.

"Your Excellence," breathed Eunida.

Dare Al Luce looked at her with his impenetrable eyes. "Have you tried to seal the breach?"

"No. But as you and I discussed, my skills are rather limited. I'm only completely competent with prophesying, exorcism, blessings, and some light housekeeping," she explained.

"Very light," Feltus muttered.

"And you, Winston?" Dare Al Luce asked the toad, with an inclination of his head.

"This is more than a rupture. It is a portal – a rogue portal. I haven't the magic," Winston replied.

"It is much easier to tear something apart than to put it back together," Dare Al Luce admitted, walking around the perimeters of the room.

Feltus shoved a pair of dirty underwear under his dresser, then moved over to the bed where RinMal sat and squeezed in. Dare Al Luce stopped before the window. He peered at the fairy blot on the wall, then ran a gilded finger down the sill, leaving a trail in the dust. A slight frown marred the perfection of his face as he inspected the tip of the digit.

"I forget how dirty this world is," he said and wiped it on the curtain. He turned around suddenly to face Feltus, his back stiff with disapproval. "Watch," he said, then turned to the window and trailed his hand through the air. Where it passed, Feltus thought he could see the undulating folds of some wispy cloth outlined against the wall. In the middle was a gaping hole.

The image didn't last long, and soon he was looking at his pictures and posters again.

"Can you close the rupture?" Eunida asked abruptly, looking at Dare Al Luce's pale, stony visage.

"I have done all I can do – this is no simple tear. I fear it may be too late."

"Too late for what?" asked Feltus.

Without seeming to move, Dare Al Luce was suddenly directly in front of him. His long hands cupped Feltus's face and turned his chin up to the light. Feltus sensed that RinMal's hackles had gone up, and he spared a thought for his friend's courage and loyalty. "I mean that the fabric has been torn beyond fixing," Dare Al Luce said. "This is now a portal allowing for travel between worlds. And you have been breathing the air of other worlds ever since you made your unlocking spell. Let's just say that there is something in you that speaks to the other worlds, those beyond the Veil. That you are attracted to them and they are attracted to you."

He looked at Eunida. "He shares your bloodline, no?" Eunida nodded, and he turned back to Feltus. "When you made your magic, Feltus, there was enough pure will to make it potent. You were looking for adventure? A change in your life? Well, now you have it. I will log this as a new portal and we will monitor it, but that is as far as our jurisdiction allows."

"Wait a minute," Feltus cried desperately. "Are you saying that I have to live with a mystical hole in my bedroom?" His voice dropped to a whisper. "There's no telling what might come out of it!"

"Right," Dare Al Luce said. "But it seems like an apt punishment, as you are the one who opened it. You should block it off, by the way, so no one falls in by accident."

"I had the desk in front of it," Feltus muttered grumpily.

Eunida seemed really excited. Her cheeks were flushed and she couldn't stop skipping around the window. Feltus rounded on her. "You should have warned me! You said I had no power!"

"I said you might have a small amount. How could I know it might be magnified near the Veil?" she replied blithely. "Besides, this was all done before I even got here."

"I daresay that things will settle down now, Feltus," Winston interrupted, with a frown at Eunida. "This one area of the Veil has been a hotbed of action, but that is hardly natural. We must remember that the relative normalcy of your life and your parents' lives will even out the balance and that most, if not all, of the smaller tears will be mended soon."

"But doesn't that mean that if there's anything out there looking for an escape route, this would be it?" Feltus said.

"Only a few folds of the Veil intersect at this particular juncture," Winston explained.

"Yes, not more than ten or so," Eunida added, jumping in place. She could not seem to keep both feet on the ground, and her hair had come undone from all the bouncing about. It hung in front of her eyes in greasy clumps.

This was not as much of a comfort as Feltus had hoped for. He looked to RinMal for support, but the PoodleRat had all his attention fixed on the window. There was a curious gleam in his wide, black eyes, and Feltus saw a tremor shiver down his spine. He looked like a dog eyeing a bone. "Just imagine how many worlds there are out there," RinMal breathed. Feltus glared at him and then at his great-aunt. *Great*, he thought to himself. *I must be the only one here without a sense of adventure!*

Dare Al Luce tapped a slender foot impatiently.

"I believe I've answered your questions?" he asked Eunida.

"Oh yes, yes!" she answered. "Not quite what we expected, but you've been most informative."

"Now there is merely the question of the endorsement." He raised finely drawn eyebrows.

Eunida rummaged in her pockets, drawing out first a sadly crumpled bat – "Oh there you are, Nugent!" – a small, red leather bag that jingled as if it were full of coins – "So mean to cheat a rabbit, but the opportunity was present!" – and then, finally, a long scroll of paper, bound with a red satin ribbon. She handed it over.

"It's all there?" Dare Al Luce asked.

"Everything you need to go home. Testimonials, first-person accounts, an epic poem about your prowess, and, of course, a manuscript letter signed by the Girl Scouts association avowing your goodness and helpfulness. I might have fudged that last one, but I'm sure no one will look at it closely." She smiled sweetly.

For the first time, Feltus thought Dare Al Luce looked content. He nodded his head to each of them, and then, in a shower of light that blinded Feltus temporarily, he threw back the folds of his robes and unfurled his wings, which stretched from one wall to the other in a glorious expanse of golden feathers. The air was heavy with a spicy scent.

He could barely squeeze past the bookshelf that held a hideous mushroom lamp carefully chosen by Feltus's mother. Feltus eyed it worriedly, and indeed, a careless flutter sent it rocking wildly on its pedestal.

"If you break that, my mother will be furious!" he yelled. Dare Al Luce looked at him for a brief moment, then drew his wings together and vanished.

Thirty seconds after he had gone, the lamp tipped over and broke.

"Put a lock on the door and she'll never know," Eunida suggested.

"Oh, you're a big help," Feltus replied. "Help me push the desk back in front of the window before someone has an accident." He shot her a meaningful look.

Once the desk was back in place, Eunida perched on the edge. "You seem tense, Feltus," she commented. She was swinging her stripy-stockinged feet back and forth. "Don't you realize that this is quite possibly the most exciting day of your life?"

"It's true," RinMal chirped. "You'll never be bored again. There may never be another incident, but you'll always wonder about what could happen at any minute."

"And that's supposed to be a good thing?" Feltus asked bitterly. "I don't even handle surprise quizzes well. How am I supposed to get any sleep? How can I ever relax if I'm living in dread of some giant, talking wombat falling into my bedroom?"

"What are the odds?" Eunida asked with a little bounce. All the excitement seemed to have shorn years off her age. Looking at her, Feltus wouldn't have guessed that she was much more than a hundred and fifty years old. And she was getting on his nerves.

"Eunida, calm down," Winston said. "Give the boy time to absorb it all."

Feltus paced back and forth, but it was no good. He couldn't relax. He took a deep breath. The air was heavy with a familiar scent. He sniffed and then looked at his great-aunt suspiciously. "Who keeps burning the toast?"

Her nose quivered; she inhaled. "*Ahhh*," she said. "The air of other worlds has permeated the ether."

"Well, it stinks!"

He looked around his comfortable, messy room, his gaze shying away from the window with its gleaming yellow paint ("Butter and Eggs," chosen by his mother, of course). It didn't look like a doorway into strange and savage lands.

"Ironic, isn't it," RinMal said softly, coming to stand by his side. "A portal in a window that doesn't open."

"I think I've had enough irony to last awhile," Feltus replied.

"But just think of the potential for adventures, the excitement!" RinMal exclaimed, miming the jab and thrust of a rapier. "Most people would love to be in your shoes!"

"I daresay most days will be exceedingly dull," Winston added.

Feltus sat down in his armchair and flung his legs over the side. He kicked at the smooth leather. He supposed it wasn't that awful, really – the dull sameness of school during the week and thrilling exploits the rest of the time. And it seemed like it might be bringing his parents back together.

Now if he could only get them to notice him. He began to frame it as a wish, but stopped, afraid of what might happen.

"Oh, all right then," he said with a sigh. "I guess this is kind of what I wished would happen when I first made the spell. I just thought I'd have more choice in the matter."

"You have no choice," RinMal pointed out. "But I'll be here to help."

"And Winston and I will be here as well. We can be the Intrepid Foursome or the Brave Band of Thrill-Seekers or the Association of Adventurers!" Eunida's face was a vibrant shade of pink, and it was obvious that only a small degree of control kept her from prancing around the bedroom or, Feltus cringed, jumping on his bed like a madwoman.

He needed some air. Some good old plain, city air stinking of ripe garbage and gasoline, not smelling of burnt toast and spice, or the atmosphere of other worlds.

"I need a break," he said and walked out the door, leaving his great-aunt to her toad and RinMal. *Let them dance around and act like happy fools. I don't even want to think about the portal right now.*

In the hallway, he heard the low murmur of voices coming from his mother's bedroom, and he stood by the closed door for a minute, just happy that his parents had something to say to each other.

He went outside and spent half an hour sitting on the marble steps of the apartment building, listening to the warble of drowsy pigeons and the drone of traffic, smelling exhaust from a thousand cars, and watching newspapers and plastic bags catch and fly in the air currents whipped up by passing traffic. He tossed pebbles against the curb, and thought of nothing in particular.

It did a lot to clear his head. By the time he had trudged up three flights of stairs and gone back to his room where his three friends waited expectantly, he'd decided to make the best of it.

* * *

The next day began uneventfully, although Feltus could not help but check the portal every five seconds. He knew he'd never again feel comfortable getting dressed with his back to it.

He and RinMal had stayed up late, and the PoodleRat had spun such wonderful stories of adventure and possibility that Feltus had started to feel excited despite himself. Wasn't this what he had wished for when he made the spell? And even though it hadn't played out exactly the way he'd hoped, the end result was pretty close. He'd made some friends, definitely had some excitement, and lived through experiences that he could only just now believe and couldn't talk about with anyone besides RinMal. And maybe he'd kind of started to think of the apartment as home.

All of this was going through his mind as he lounged in the park with his family that afternoon, enjoying a day that was sunny but not too hot. *Things are pretty good, actually*, Feltus thought as he helped himself to another piece of Rose's fried chicken. He handed one to Percy, who had just returned home from math camp. RinMal lay tail to nose at his side. It was not a normal position for him, but he was acting "dog" for the benefit of the parents and other inferior mortals in the vicinity.

Feltus had carried him most of the way to the park because the PoodleRat was still weak, although his bandages had come off and his fur was beginning to grow back. Like most PoodleRats, RinMal was quite vain about his appearance, and Feltus had caught him that very morning in front of the mirror trying to comb some of his fur over to cover the bald patch.

RinMal liked to be propped up on Feltus's shoulder anyway, and he was light enough that it was no problem to carry him around. On the way to the park, RinMal had pointed out places of interest in a loud whisper, until Feltus finally begged him to shut up.

His mother had looked at RinMal suspiciously until Feltus, suddenly inspired, confided that he was working on his ventriloquism act with his pet dog. He hadn't exactly explained RinMal to Percy yet either. Just mentioned that his dog was really smart and more like one of the family. It was still hard for him to talk about magical things, and his mother, although she was quite relaxed these days, still possessed accute hearing and an irritating curiosity about his private affairs. There'd be time to tell Percy everything later when the parents weren't around.

Feltus's mother sighed and turned over on her blanket. Her cheeks were rosy and a spatter of freckles had appeared on the bridge of her nose. She was sleeping a lot these days. Her knitting – she'd taken to making humongous woolly socks even though it was the middle of summer – was pushed into a motley heap on one side of her; and Lafayette, swaddled in a polka dot vest that made him look like a trussed chicken, drooled and snored on the other. His dad appeared to be napping. The sports section of the newspaper was draped over his face. It was the first time Feltus had ever seen his father without the financial reports nearby.

Feltus heard loud yells from the playing fields over by the jungle gym and sat up. Percy, lying near him, raised his head too. It sounded like a major argument had started up again. Great-Aunt Eunida was engaged in a rough-and-tumble game of Frisbee with some kids, and Feltus had already had to go over there once to talk her out of a fight. She swung Winston, who was confined in a bowling bag she had slung over her shoulder, around like a chain mace when she got excited, and one of the boys had taken exception to being bonked on the head just because he'd intercepted the Frisbee from her.

After that, the kids had delegated her to the position of goalie, and she finally seemed to be behaving, since the position gave her ample opportunity to think up mocking rhymes and make insulting hand gestures. In addition, she'd been welcomed in the role of goalie because she'd rucked her skirts up around her waist and her skinny, spindly legs clad in their colorful stripy stockings were like a beacon. A long purple and orange scarf knitted by his mother was wrapped around her neck and threatened to trip her at any minute.

Feltus was just wondering if he should try to explain her to Percy, when the blond boy said, "She reminds me of my grandmother."

"Really? Is that good?"

"Grandma was great. She'd wear her nightgown on the

street. Talk out the side of her mouth like a cartoon character. Carry a baton. And eat fish and stinky cheese for breakfast. She ended up going away for a long time and when she came back, she was different. Not as much fun. Sleepy."

"That's sad," Feltus's father said, pushing the paper aside and opening one eye lazily. Feltus had thought he was asleep. He checked out his father's unfamiliar appearance – faded jeans, light western shirt rolled up at the cuffs, disheveled hair, and the skin on his neck already burned red – and tried to remember the last time he'd seen him out of his customary suit and tie. "It sounds like she lost what identified her, what made her happy," his father continued. "Like she was swallowed up by societal expectations of behavior."

He propped his head up and stretched. "Feltus, hand me a piece of that chocolate cake, please," he said. "And carve out a couple of hunks for yourselves. It's Rose's best. I should know – I licked the bowl."

Feltus wonderingly handed him a gooey slab. He and his father were actually having an exchange of sorts.

"Hey Dad, can Percy stay for dinner?"

"Sure."

"Can we have hamburgers?"

"That can probably be arranged. For now, eat your cake. And then later we can toss the ball around. Burn off some of these calories."

*Who is this strange man impersonating my father? And how long will it last?* He shrugged his shoulders. With a rogue portal in his bedroom, he'd have to get used to things changing radically on a day-to-day basis. He'd take his father's metamorphosis at face value and try to get as many ball games, movies, and soccer matches out of it as he could while it lasted.

He sneaked a piece of cake to RinMal. The drowsing PoodleRat yawned and licked a dollop of frosting from his paw. "Make hay while the sun shines," he said to Feltus.

*Whatever that means*, Feltus thought. *It's probably some strange harvest analogy – the PoodleRats are big into gardening.* Feltus lay back down and felt the comforting weight of RinMal against his shoulder. The summer stretched ahead and he *could* spend it worrying about when his parents might change back into self-absorbed robots, or worrying about what might appear suddenly out of the portal or how many beatings from Rusty he'd have to endure in the coming year, or he could decide that there was a limit to how much he could control in his own life.

He decided just to enjoy things for a while.

## THE END

\* \* \*